Advanced Praise for *An Apology Gone Horribly Wrong*

━━━━━

Wow, William Hammes has quite the gift of storytelling, from Johnny Carson to gang bangers. My favorite was the hospital scene with the sick kids. Amazing!

- Pam Fillmore

An Apology Gone Horribly Wrong was very well written and I could vividly imagine every scenario. This book compelled me to come back every night because I just wanted to know what was going to happen next. It will make you laugh and cry weaves its story into your heart.

- Bobby Rulon

A fast-paced and entertaining read set in the place I spent my teenage years - Malibu. I highly recommend you grab a copy!

-Toni Trott

I love William's storytelling, the humor, and the gotcha moments! This easily could be a script for a movie! I am thrilled beginning to end. Bring it on!

- Virginia Emery

I highly recommend *An Apology Gone Horribly Wrong*. The characters are expertly interwoven in an engaging, intriguing, and entertaining story. The dialogue is witty and the plot is especially relevant to today's culture.

- Robert Allen

It wasn't long enough! I want to read it again.

- Bonnie Bayer

An Apology Gone Horribly Wrong will keep the reader captivated & reluctant to put it down.

- Judy Perez

I loved how *An Apology Gone Horribly Wrong* kept my attention with twists and turns, and how eager I was to read more. Not only would I buy it, I had my husband track William Hammes down to have him sign my copy of the book! That's how much I enjoyed reading this book.

- Donna McConathy

I didn't want to put it down and really enjoyed that locations included are all very familiar to me.

- Donald Sayles

An Apology Gone Horribly Wrong was a page turner...very unpredictable. I would recommend it.

- Linda Sayles

An Apology Gone Horribly Wrong

An
APOLOGY

Gone Horribly Wrong

A NOVEL

William Hammes

NEW YORK

LONDON • NASHVILLE • MELBOURNE • VANCOUVER

An Apology Gone Horribly Wrong

A Novel

This story is adapted from *Five Yellow Roses*, a screenplay I wrote thirty years ago. This is a work of fiction, and aside from Johnny Carson, any names mentioned related to *The Tonight Show* described in this book are purely coincidental. Neptune's Net restaurant in Malibu, The Old Place restaurant in Agoura Hills, and the First African Methodist Episcopal Church of Los Angeles, are still in operation, and I highly recommend all three.

Published in New York, New York, by Morgan James Publishing. Morgan James is a trademark of Morgan James, LLC. www.MorganJamesPublishing.com

ISBN 9781642790788 paperback
ISBN 9781642790795 eBook
Library of Congress Control Number: 2018943135

Cover Design by:
Rachel Lopez
www.r2cdesign.com

Interior Design by:
Chris Treccani
www.3dogcreative.net

Morgan James is a proud partner of Habitat for Humanity Peninsula and Greater Williamsburg. Partners in building since 2006.

Get involved today! Visit
MorganJamesPublishing.com/giving-back

Table of Contents

Prologue

The small soundstage has two chairs placed in front of a black curtain, with a third facing the two. On the curtain is a logo for *Entertainment Tonight*. Cameras and sound equipment are at the ready. Seated in the chair on the left is a distinguished looking Caucasian man in his mid-sixties.

A young intern wearing a headset approaches him. "Good afternoon, Mr. Milton.

We are just about set. Are you doing okay? Would you like another bottle of water?"

The man shakes his head no.

"Okay, then. Miss León is finally here and is just finishing in makeup. Oh, here comes Miss Michaels; she will be taking it from here."

Sam gives her a nervous nod.

"Hi, I'm Jessica Michaels," the anchorwoman says, walking in and taking Sam's hand. "I will be doing the interview today. Oh, but why are you so nervous? You must have done this many times before."

"Many times? Yes. Gotten used to it? No."

"But I thought you were a preacher."

"Miss Michaels, there is a big difference between God speaking through me and me speaking through me. Besides, I am just the associate pastor, one of four, so preaching is a rarity."

"Oh, please call me Jessica, and if you don't mind me asking, how does a shy white man become an associate pastor of an all-black church?"

"Well, as for my shyness, Miss Chantell León kicked that out of me, as you are about to hear. Prior to meeting her, I had always been shy around pretty girls. It became amplified tenfold with my PTSD that I acquired from being involved in an industrial accident. It's a strange thing. I could walk up to a microphone and speak to a thousand people and be only slightly nervous. But, if I have to

ix

introduce myself to some pretty woman, I completely freeze up. That's why my lovely wife has never had to worry about me straying. What woman would want an affair with someone who acts shell-shocked at a simple introduction?

"As far as me pastoring an all-black church, someone invited me to this church once, and I loved the music and the preaching so much that I kept coming back. I would always sit up front and sing loudly. Well, what do you do when you have a white guy with no voice and no rhythm in the front row of a black church? You have him preach. It's been said I sound a lot better speaking from the pulpit than I do singing in front of it." When Sam Milton sees Jessica and the crew break out in laughter, he calms down.

The intern puts her left hand to her headset and says to Sam and the crew, "Miss León is coming out now." Sam and Jessica look to the right and see a beautiful black woman walk in. Though she never quite got her figure back after her fourth child, her beautiful face and skin make her look ten years younger than fifty-five, the age on her driver's license.

"Good afternoon, Miss León," Jessica greets her guest.

Chantell answers in a strong, clear voice, "It's good to see you again, Jessica."

Since Sam is still getting the final touches from a makeup artist, the only acknowledgment he gets from Chantell is a quick squeeze of his hand.

Jessica quickly asks Chantell, "Is it okay to use your maiden name?"

"Actually, I would prefer using my married name—" Chantell quickly glances at Sam and then changes her mind. "Chantell León will actually be fine."

Jessica sees Sam look away and acknowledges the brief exchange. "I guess it's been awhile since you two have seen each other. Have you had a chance to catch up?"

Sam responds with, "We had dinner together last night."

"Oh good. I guess the next thing I should be asking is how is Dwain doing."

Chantell lights up. "He's doing very well, thank you. Bless you for asking."

"I would presume being out of the country for the past three months makes things difficult for you, Miss León."

An attendant is now touching up Chantell's face and has her looking away. Chantell manages to answer, "Yes, being on tour for three months can make it very difficult to keep connected with anyone, including my husband."

"Well, I know each of you has a lot going on, so let's get to it. As you know, we are doing a follow-up to your story from thirty years ago."

Sam looks skeptical. "Jessica, my dear, that means either you are thirty years late getting the story, or it is a very slow news day."

As Jessica laughs, Chantell answers, "Sam, you have to admit, we were the biggest news story thirty years ago, and we are still making news with our joint foundation. I know you have never been comfortable talking on camera, so just imagine you are telling one of your famous stories to the kids at Children's Hospital."

Sam reaches over and takes Chantell's hand and kisses it. "You know, Chantell, for thirty years now, you have been the most compassionate person I know."

Chantell smiles softly and says, "That isn't what you were saying about me thirty years ago."

"Neither was the rest of the world—especially when I proposed to you."

Still holding Sam's hand, Chantell looks down and says, "I kind of shredded you that night, didn't I?"

"Kind of! Oh yes, you did—and on national TV, no less, with Johnny Carson standing next to us."

"But I had a very good reason for doing it, didn't I?"

Sam looks at the floor. "I suppose, but I was never the same after that."

Chantell looks at Sam and says, "And that was exactly my intent. I was just making a slight surgical adjustment to your personality."

"Yes, but did you have to use a sledgehammer?"

"Are you complaining about how things turned out? You were the shyest person on the planet. What I did, at the very least, allowed you to get married, didn't it?"

Chantell and Jessica watch Sam shrug.

Chantell answers his gesture with, "Yes, it did, Sam. I know it did. I was there, remember?"

Sam, still holding Chantell's hand, squeezes it hard, and while looking at her, he tells Jessica, "I had it all set up so she could apologize to me after I tried to apologize to her. But, you should have seen what this lady put me through that night!"

Jessica smiles and answers, "Oh, but I have! It was all filmed on tape thirty years ago."

"Yes. The events were filmed that night, but did you know that she almost got me killed three times prior to that?"

"Really, three times?"

"Oh yes. First, I came way too close to committing suicide; then, I was in a coma for three weeks after getting my head bashed in. And, as if that wasn't enough, I got shot—all for trying to apologize to her!"

Jessica smiles. "That's why we are here, Mr. Milton, to revisit that night and what led up to it. And, Mr. Milton, it will all be from your perspective."

Sam looks at Jessica with surprise. "Really?" Sam then looks at Chantell with a mischievous grin and says, "Finally, the world gets to see the other side of Chantell León."

A reserved Chantell looks back at Sam. "Careful, Mr. Milton. Remember what I did to you thirty years ago." Sam's smile only intensifies.

1

Dreaming

A red stiletto stabs the spotlight and is planted dead center as the orchestra's brass sounds its arrival. The shoe's splendor is only surpassed by the body that follows it. She is a tall, black beauty with long, shimmering raven hair. She's dressed in a vivid crimson-red gown, slit up the thigh and cut low in the back.

Once fully in the spotlight, she turns sharply to the left. With her body in profile, she slowly brings a microphone to her lips. She dives into a powerful number reminiscent of the forties but with a strong contemporary twist; her movements combine the best elements of both eras. Possessing unparalleled confidence and conviction, this scene will no doubt be repeated on every dance floor for years to come. Her voice radiates with such power and clarity, it makes her pedigree of both stage and opera clearly evident.

After a couple of minutes, the focus changes from her to the man who has appeared behind her. Though his skin has a rich tan, it makes a sharp contrast to his counterpart's; his pale blue eyes and chestnut hair likewise stand out. He steps forward, puts his arm around her waist, and takes her right hand in his, leaning her back until her hair is touching the floor. With one quick jerk, she is upright again as the two tango across the stage.

They make a sharp turn, and the tango blends into a rumba. The music soars to a climax, with him holding her up by one leg, her knee even with his face. She raises the other leg up and out to give a sense of balance to their turn. She stretches out her hand as if reaching for a forbidden fruit. Grasping it, she takes a bite as she is swung around to take a seat on his bent knee.

The hand bearing the imaginary fruit offers a bite to him. Their dance ends as they stare off in opposite directions. Just as the music completely fades, the entire brass section sounds one sharp note. At the same time, a spotlight hits both of their faces, causing each to look up as if they just got caught.

As the two hold their final position, the sensuous dream evolves, with the focus slowly closing in on him until only his profile is seen. The brass section fades out, allowing traffic noises to fade in. The background slowly brightens, revealing the backseat of a convertible with a long line of cars behind it. All drivers are impatiently waiting on the Pacific Coast Highway as a scene for a movie is filmed on location. The man in the dance scene also evolves into the driver of the convertible. As he does, he becomes less muscular and far less debonair.

The announcer on his car stereo says louder than necessary, "That's 'The Forbidden Fruit of Love,' the latest from Chantell, with a little help from her beau, Slash. Oh, how I envy that man!"

The annoying voice brings a thirtysomething male driver back to reality. He is shocked to see he has been staring out his window at a security guard standing next to several portable dressing rooms used for the filming.

To save face, the driver shouts out his window to the guard, "Say, what's the movie?"

He gets no response.

He continues his questioning, unabated. "Then asking who the stars are is totally out of the question? I see. Well, how about something more generic? How long are they going to be filming here?"

He still gets nothing.

"You know your fly is open, right?"

The guard doesn't even flinch.

Still determined to get a reaction, he ponders a moment, then asks, "I take it by all of the camera equipment facing east that they are trying to get a background sunrise for two silhouettes? Let's say Farrah Fawcett kissing Lee Majors? No? How about Farrah Fawcett and Jacklyn Smith?"

The guard keeps his deadpan face.

"Still no? So what if they were wearing sexy kimonos? . . . How about sumo-wrestler diapers?"

Still, he only has a blank stare.

"You are good. At a stare-down contest in Vegas, I am placing all of my black chips on you!"

The young man looks ahead and sees that the police car holding back traffic has shut off his lights and pulled over, finally allowing traffic to pass. "Gosh, this has been such fun. Same time tomorrow?"

Still no movement.

"Your fly is really down, by the way."

He revs the V8 of his vintage Barracuda and pops the clutch to chirp the tires, but instead it stalls the engine. Embarrassed, he quickly restarts and pulls forward as the guard watches him and finally breaks into a smile. The driver quickly points back and yells, "Got ya!" The guard's eyes and smile instantly go back to deadpan.

When the guard feels the red Barracuda is far enough down the road, he checks his fly. Embarrassed, he quickly turns to face the wall as he pulls it up.

The '68 Barracuda driver pulls off the PCH and onto a narrow residential street on the west side of Point Dume. The farther he drives, he notices the smaller homes become estates. He pulls into one of the largest and stops in front of a wrought-iron security gate that has a plaque engraved with the name Langston. He leans over and pushes the intercom. A moment later a voice answers, "May I help you?"

"Come on, Ida, I know you can see me. This is Sam Milton!"

"The only Sam Milton I know drives an old, beat-up pickup truck from the '50s, not a kid's toy from the '60s. This is 1986, so if you're gonna drive a real car, get a Mercedes."

"Mercedes! Now you did it. I was going to take you to lunch at Geoffrey's, but now all you're going to get is a burrito off the lunch truck."

"You take me to Geoffrey's? My two-hundred-pound fat butt you would! Anyway, the electricians are working on the gate controls again, so I'm going to have to come all the way down and open it up for you."

"Aw, I feel so bad for you. But hey, you will be building up an appetite for our date at the lunch truck." Sam laughs as Ida responds with laughing profanity.

He looks in the mirror to see the famous face of one of the neighbors jogging up to the car. "Hey, Mr. Carson, how's it hanging?"

Out of breath, Mr. Carson leans on the passenger door. "When are you going to start calling me Johnny? We play tennis every week, for God's sake."

"When I win a match."

"Well, if you stop spotting me three games, you might have a chance. Say, I'm glad I caught you. I have to cancel on Friday. Freddy's got some real hot guest lined up for that night, and it's going to take a lot of coordination to be able to pull this one off."

"Let's make it next week then."

"Sounds good," Johnny says, tapping the car door before jogging off.

"Well, at least I don't have to wake up so early," Sam says to himself. But, when he looks in his rearview mirror at Johnny's tennis courts, he adds, "But then, how many dumb-luck carpenters can say they play on those courts and with the 'man' himself?"

The large gate cracks open, and a black hand appears on the edge of the gate as the full-figured Ida manually opens it. When Sam hears a thud, he knows the gate is fully opened. He jumps out and runs around to the other side. In the worst British accent he can muster, he says, "Since thou fair maiden openeth the castle gates for thy humble servant, may I openeth the carriage for her fair princess?"

Without missing a beat, Ida runs over to the driver's side and jumps behind the wheel. "Screw the riding, dearie. I be doin' the driving," she says as she stomps on the gas.

Sam jumps in the passenger's side before the door slams shut, and it only takes seconds to hit sixty-three miles per hour on the speedometer. Ida screeches to a stop at the front door, forcing Sam to push himself back from the dashboard. "That oughta get the missis up. Man, that felt good!" Ida says, laughing.

"Aren't you ever worried about getting fired, Ida?"

"No way, baby. I'm trying to. Say, where you goin' next?"

"Over to the Bernsteins' for a few weeks. They've asked for new cabinets."

"Good. Find out if they need a housekeeper. I'm gonna follow you around, 'cause you're the best thing to happen to the Langston household in years. With you going away, I will slit my wrists if I have to hear one more story about the missis's cat. By the way, she's changing her mind on the kitchen color again."

"Good lord! That makes the sixth time! What's her problem?"

Ida turns to Sam to ask, "Haven't you figured it out yet?" Sam gives her a quizzical look that she answers with a laugh. "You don't get out much, do you?"

"Well, considering Linda and I are kinda on the outs again, you're the closest thing to a girlfriend I have right now. So, I would say the answer is no."

"As good looking as you are, I doubt if my husband would care for you hanging around the house. Listen, dearie, you're the only other person who has a personality in the missis's life—next to me, of course."

Sam answers, "I'm beginning to feel like the painter on *Murphy Brown*. How am I going to get away from her? If she keeps changing her mind about projects, I'll never get to leave."

"Get yourself married."

"Well, if Linda doesn't soften up again, that's not going to happen. Besides, I couldn't afford a wedding anyway."

"Missis Langston will throw the wedding for ya," Ida chuckles.

"Great, now all I have to do is find someone. Hey, you got any eligible ladies in your neighborhood?"

"Ha! You date a black girl?" Ida scoffs. "That'll be the day. A black chick would eat your butt up. Besides, you wouldn't last ten minutes in my neighborhood."

"Hey, I've been to your house. Your neighborhood isn't that bad."

"Yeah, this car you drive saved your sorry butt. Anyone drivin' wheels like this gets respect anywhere you go. But don't push it. Anyway, bring your paint samples so we can get you out of here before she invites you to tea."

The next morning on his drive to work, Sam again finds himself stopped in traffic as the on-location shooting continues. He and the movie-set guard face off again in an unspoken staring competition. Without breaking eye contact, Sam states, "It's amazing we are together in the same spot as yesterday, isn't it? It's almost like destiny. You know, like some huge, cosmic force is drawing us here for some unseen cataclysmic event. Don't you feel it?"

Without even blinking, the big guard answers bluntly, "No."

"What do you know? The statue speaks! Well, maybe instead of sensing a cosmic force, I am sensing the breakfast burrito I had this morning."

A horn signaling the end of shooting blows, the road sign is flipped, and traffic moves. Sam gives the guard a two-finger salute. Sam's surprised when the guard touches the brim of his hat. "Wow, friends at last! I'm so touched."

Not more than five seconds after Sam drives off, the guard tips his hat to the girl of Sam's dreams, saying, "Good morning to you, Miss Chantell."

"Good morning, Joey. Do you know that man in the red Barracuda?"

"Only in passing, ma'am. I see you know your vintage muscle cars."

"Joey, have you forgotten what I do for a hobby? I've gone up against that model many times and haven't lost to one yet."

"Yes, ma'am."

Miss León squints at her friend and asks, "Joey, do you ever smile?"

"Yes, ma'am, every Thanksgiving and Christmas—and when I win at poker."

Chantell laughs. "Then I hope to see you win a game of poker. I bet you're cute."

"Yes, ma'am. Good luck with your close-ups tomorrow."

Standing on the top step to the portable dressing room, she turns back and smiles. "Thanks, Joey! I wish I wasn't so nervous."

"You'll do just fine. Don't take it so seriously, and have a good time."

"Thanks, Joey. I really appreciate it. Sometimes I forget this is supposed to be fun," she calls back, opening the door to head inside.

The director's assistant stops her. "Don't make any plans for the weekend. Benny's got it filled, and what Benny hasn't spoken for, Carol has." The assistant then walks on without waiting for any acknowledgment.

Chantell turns to look at herself in the mirror. "Great. I'm working past nine tonight. I have close-ups tomorrow, and the crew from *Entertainment Tonight* will follow me around all day, ending with a spot on *The Tonight Show*. Now, my only free weekend is booked up, too! Dwain is going to be pissed!"

She taps her forehead on her dressing-room mirror but quickly stands up straight again as she remembers out loud, "I can't even bang my own head against the wall without damaging someone else's work." Looking in the mirror again, she notices the cross around her neck. She fondles it while saying, "I remember when life was so simple and easy. The most exciting thing for me back then was having a solo in the church choir. Now, I have record contracts, concerts, music videos, and movies. I can't even stop to take a breath, and Joey tells me to enjoy myself. Boy, would I like to trade places with him for a few days, doing nothing more than talking to people."

Out of her dressing room, she steps through another door, and pandemonium kicks in. She is quickly taken by the arm, led to a chair, and set upon by one lady doing her hair, another working on her face, another fixing her nails, and still another making changes to her outfit.

All of this is happening as a tall blonde in her late forties, desperately trying to look like she's in her early thirties, is giving Chantell her programming for the day: "First thing, Benny wants to retake the car scene. It seems the background wasn't clear enough, even for special effects to take out. That should take us up to ten thirty. Then you have a dress rehearsal for scene forty-five, which should take us to lunch from twelve thirty to a quarter past one."

Chantell cuts in, "Good, that gives me a chance to get to the store so I can pick up some cat food for Tia."

Carol counters with, "Can't I send a gofer for it? Someone from *ET* wants to talk to us about the schedule for tomorrow."

Chantell frowns. "Can't it wait till after lunch? I haven't had a minute to myself in three days!"

"Oh, all right. I will see what I can do. Just be back at one fifteen."

"Thanks, Carol. I owe you one."

"You owe me a lot more than one! Anyway, *ET* will be here at one fifteen. There's a meeting with Benny at two, followed by wardrobe at two thirty and makeup at three. All of this is for scene forty-five, to be shot at three thirty-five p.m. We should be finished at nine thirty tonight. Oh, and don't forget about your close-ups tomorrow, so get some sleep!"

"Can you schedule me in for a pee break at 4:07 p.m.?" Chantell jokes.

"Make it 4:04 p.m. You know how Benny hates to be kept waiting." Carol looks at the hairdresser. "Her hair is to look *slightly* windblown! She looks like she just stepped out of Hurricane Camille!"

Frustrated, the hairdresser jerks Chantell's head back, which leaves a streak of red down Chantell's chin.

The angry woman who had been applying lip gloss turns and glares at Carol, who responds with a blunt, "Just fix it!"

Chantell looks in the mirror and giggles. There's a knock on the door as a voice warns, "Benny wants everyone on the set in ten minutes."

"Can everyone please give me a few minutes alone?" Chantell asks. "I need to get rid of a few butterflies before I go out."

"Sure, no problem. Everyone, clear out," Carol barks and turns for the door. She stops and turns back. "By the way, I booked a flight for eight twenty Saturday night."

Chantell looks blankly and asks, "What for?"

"I take it you forgot about Reverend Marcus from Saint Anthony's in Atlanta? You promised to sing at the dedication of his new church on Sunday."

"Oh, I forgot all about it, and this is the only free weekend I have for the next four weeks!"

"Well, it isn't quite as free as you thought; besides, you promised. See you on the set." Carol walks out the door.

When Chantell is by herself, she shakes her head and yells silently, "Aw shi—" but catches herself before she speaks the last letter. She looks up and says, "Okay, you were right. I should have thought through it more when I prayed to be a successful singer and actor."

───

Across town, Sam peruses a set of blueprints for the mansion he is standing in. The sound of hammers and power saws can be heard as two men enter the room. The shorter of the two walks up to him and asks, "May I help you with something?"

"Oh, excuse me," Sam answers. "I just like to look at plans whenever I get the chance. But, I noticed something over here that you might want to take a look at." Sam points to the blueprints. "The plans are calling for this exterior section over here to be a number-four sheer wall, which requires two layers of plywood on both sides. You only have one layer on each, and the lathers are starting to cover the exterior. The first big wind, and your two-story house could end up a one story."

The man looks at Sam with contempt and asks with extreme bluntness, "And just who the hell are you?"

"Oh, I'm sorry. I am Sam Milton. I'm here to measure for the cabinets in this room."

"Well, Mr. Sam Milton," the man says, refusing Sam's hand, "my name is Jay Huff, the foreman of the project. Over there, looking at the wall in question, is Andrew Foster, the project engineer. Now between us, we have over sixty years in construction. So, why don't you let us do our jobs and you build some cabinets. Okay?"

Sam looks embarrassed but tries to say, "I just thought that—"

Jay is about to explode when he hears the engineer say, "He's right, Jay. This is a number-four wall, and you have it marked on the floor as a number two."

Andrew then turns to Sam. "Thanks, Sam. Say, how've you been anyway?"

"Better," Sam says. "It's still not easy, but I'm making it." Sam, still looking embarrassed, picks up his own set of plans and heads to the other room.

"You know that guy?" Jay snorts

The engineer answers, "Yes, and I'm surprised you don't. That's Sam Milton. Ten years ago, he was the only game in Malibu."

"Well, if he was such a hotshot builder, why is he just doing cabinets?"

Andrew answers, "Do you know the Sheets' house down the street?"

"That wild, twisted concrete one with the cantilevered swimming pool? He did that one?" Jay asks quizzically.

"He and his partner, Ben Bradshaw, built it. After that one, they were building the Schwinger residence. Sam missed replacing part of the scaffolding after a delivery, and it collapsed, killing his partner. There were no negligence charges filed, but it sure screwed Sam up good. Ben and his wife had a four-year-old son fighting leukemia, and when the boy passed away, she blamed Sam for both deaths. He spent three years in a mental hospital. Everyone was expecting him to get out of construction all together. Word has it that while in the funny farm, he started working in the woodshop as part of his therapy. I guess he took a liking to it; when he got out, he sold his business and bought a cabinet shop. As luck would have it, he got Johnny Carson as his first client. He's now more famous for his furniture and cabinets than his houses."

"He's that good?" Jay asks.

"Enough to save you about ten thousand dollars in rebuilding costs. And speaking of that, let's talk about this number-four sheer wall."

━━━━━━━

Sam walks into the kitchen and says to the guy hanging the drywall, "Hey, Rick, when do you think I can have the kitchen? I need to start making templates."

"Should be finished sometime tomorrow. When are you bringing the bathroom cabinets?"

"I would have brought them today, but my truck took a dump. I think it's the starter again."

Rick scoffs. "Say, when are you going to junk that old thing and get you a real truck?"

Sam chuckles as he says, "Why? It's only got four hundred thousand miles on it. It's just getting broken in."

"It sounds like you're restoring it, piece by broken piece," Rick says jokingly. "Speaking of restoring things, I take it you're driving the Barracuda? How's she running?"

"Great! It's a nice change of pace from the truck."

"How long did it take you to restore it?"

"Every weekend for three years. It was part of my outpatient therapy. I just took second place in a car show last week."

"Not bad." Rick continues, "Have you met our new foreman yet?"

"Just a minute ago. A real sweetheart, isn't he?"

"He's got an ego bigger than God's and is more demanding."

"Not anymore," Sam gloats. "Say, do you need anything from the hardware store? I need to get some air."

"Just some knife blades."

"I'll be back in thirty minutes. If his lordship should ask for me, tell him I ran off with his wife."

"Obviously, you haven't met his wife! Ugly woman—I mean she's *ugly*! But I will let him know you have a thing for her."

Sam leaves, scratching the back of his head with just his middle finger.

2

Chance Meeting

―――――

A slight wind is blowing a young woman's long blond hair back over her left shoulder as she walks across the parking lot. Her dark-bronze skin is set off by the white of her French-cut bathing suit. Sam marvels at the fact she is looking so incredibly sexy yet probably is not even aware of it. He imagines she has dark-blue eyes as he watches her pass in front of his car. Just as if cupid himself arranged it, she glances back for just a second, but it's long enough for him to see that her eyes aren't blue at all but the most vivid green he has ever seen. She gives a glint of a smile when she sees him.

The words, "Oh my, my, my. Aren't you gorgeous?" form on Sam's lips. His opinion of her is enhanced when he detects a subtle strut in her steps. It brings a question to his mind: *Lord, I have been struggling with this relationship with Linda for too long, so please open the door big and wide, or slam the door shut, so we can both move on.*

Tired of being frustrated from what he is missing, he slowly turns away from looking at the blonde and gives the car some gas. Out of the corner of his eye, he suddenly sees a blue blur approaching him. Turning, he hears squealing brakes, which causes him to slam on his brakes, but it's too late. He runs head-on into the coming car. The bumpers of both cars fail to take the full impact. As if in slow motion, the famous three-pointed star of a Mercedes hood ornament disappears from view as his own hood bends upward. A short blast of a car horn sounds when Sam sees the face of the other driver hit the steering wheel.

In the same instant, Sam has both his seatbelt off and his car door open. He races around while praying out loud, "Oh God, oh God, oh God! Please let her be okay!" When he gets close, he can see it is a young woman, who, fortunately, doesn't look too badly hurt.

He's about to ask if she's okay when he recognizes who she is. He instantly turns and stands a few feet away. Paralyzed with shyness that hasn't plagued him since his early days of high school, he is unable to speak or even look in her direction.

"My God, that's Chantell!" he says to himself as he glances back to see her rubbing the bridge of her nose. "And here I am looking like a complete dork!" He can feel all of the blood rushing to his stomach. He stands helpless, unable to do anything.

As Chantell grasps what has just happened, she looks over the steering wheel at the front of her Mercedes and then quickly looks at her watch. It amplifies her stress tenfold. She exclaims, "I have to be back on the set in fifteen minutes, and just look at this!"

She looks up at Sam standing a few feet away. "Are you going to just stand there, or are you going to do something?" As she continues to look at him in disbelief, a strange thought comes to her, and it causes her to stare at the frozen Sam even more intently. She answers the thought by shaking it off. She then turns to look in the rearview mirror and rubs her nose again. "Oh dear God! My nose is starting to swell, and I'm supposed to be filming this afternoon, and my close-ups are tomorrow! Dear God in heaven, why today? Why did it have to be today?"

Sam, hearing this, becomes more embarrassed by the second. He steadies his nerve, turns to her, and tries to speak. "Can . . . I help . . . you?"

"Oh, I think you have done plenty, thank you! Why weren't you paying attention?" She opens the car door, pushes him aside, and jumps out to look at the front of the car. "Do you think it's still drivable?"

Sam is too slow to answer, so she yells the question again.

Finally, she hears, "Um . . . no water is dripping, so the . . . radiator is not leaking."

"So, that means its drivable, right?" she yells.

"Uh . . . yes, I think it is."

She shakes her head and states bluntly, "Good, then I'm going back to the set."

Sam sifts through his wallet and responds, "Uh . . . here is my driver's license and insurance." She grabs it and throws it onto the passenger seat while turning the car on. Sam asks, "Hey, shouldn't I be taking down your license number?"

Chantell responds curtly, "Everyone around here knows who I am, so I'm going to let my agent deal with it."

Sam sees her put the car in gear and yells, "Hey, the bumpers are—" She peels out backward, yanking Sam's bumper off his car and causing it to bounce on the pavement. He quietly finishes his thought, *locked together.* He looks up to see her back around the corner, screech to a stop, and then floor it, squealing her tires out of the parking lot.

Sam stands speechless. A woman in the crowd asks, "Say, wasn't that Chantell?"

Another says, "It looked like her, but it didn't sound like her. I've never heard her swear before."

"Well, heaven knows she had a right to. What a moron that guy is. He just stood there!"

Sam, still standing in the same place, notices everyone looking at him, mostly with disdain. He eventually walks over and picks up his mangled bumper. Trying to decide what to do with it, he eventually walks up to the car and sticks it in his backseat.

As he gets into the driver's seat, he hears the first words of sympathy as a surfer says, "That sure was a bitchin' car, man."

Another states, "Hey, dude, sue her, man, for leaving the scene of an accident!"

Sam looks around the car and then responds, "What am I supposed to do now? She ran off with my driver's license."

"Dude, go hunt her down! We're witnesses for you. Just call us, man."

Not long afterward, Sam pulls into his driveway, a short rope tying down the bent hood of his car. Also, a puddle is forming under the radiator. Sam just sits for a few minutes before reaching over and turning the engine off. He leans back in the seat again, listening to the hissing radiator as he tries unsuccessfully not to think about anything. Peace evades him as he is overtaken by flashbacks of every embarrassing thing that ever happened to him. He winces in pain with each one.

As he expects, he eventually gets to the worse one. It has Sam trying unsuccessfully to grab the hands of a man falling as the platform he is standing on collapses. He then hears the man's wife screaming at him, "It should have been you who died! You're the one who screwed up. He's dead, and you're not!" Sam must forcefully shake himself out of the trance. Soon, however, the current nightmare comes back, but compared to the last one, this current one is now giving him a morbid comfort.

Eventually, he speaks softly to himself, "I don't get it, I finally have been able to make some headway with women, and even been dating Linda. I've also met movie stars before—even Johnny Carson, for crying out loud. So, what happened back there? How could I act like such an idiot? She needed help, and I just stood there!"

He abruptly stops talking to himself when he sees his neighbor staring. He feels embarrassed all over again. He takes a deep breath and exhales as he opens the car door. He notices a loud squeak that wasn't there before. Shaking his head, he steps over the ever-increasing puddle and heads to the front door.

Another painful thought hits him as he looks down at a kitten that comes to greet him. "Linda! I almost forgot all about her. Well, Little Paws, I might as well read her last letter and really finish off my day." Picking up the kitten, he says to it, "You were supposed to be a surprise for her for moving in with me. Well, I doubt that is going to happen, especially now."

He picks up a letter that's still caught in the mail slot. He takes it and the kitten over to a couch and plops down. He opens it and reads. Though it starts out "Dear Sammy," he reads it as "Dear John."

3

An Apology Gone Horribly Wrong

———

Sam is driving down the PCH the next day. Up ahead, he sees a now all-too-familiar sight: a long line of cars parked along the highway and large trucks holding camera equipment. He finds himself slowing down, thinking, *Should I, or will it just cause more trouble?* Unable to resist, he pulls over and stops a few feet from the same guard he has become so familiar with. Now regretting that he has been antagonizing the man, he is hoping against hope the guard might be kind enough to pass on a word of apology to the leading lady.

Walking up to the guard and glancing at his nametag, he asks, "Excuse me. Mr. Joseph Dobson, is it? Can you tell me if Chantell is filming here today?"

The guard looks over Sam's shoulder and sees the smashed front end of his car. "That was a very nice Barracuda you once had. Is it a '69?"

"Close. It's a '68."

"I take it you must be—and I quote—'that red-faced moron' who ran into her yesterday."

Sam looks away shyly, figuring he deserves the comment.

The guard breaks into a big smile and says, "Don't mind her. She's a very sweet girl who's been under a lot of pressure lately. However, I must say, you sure caused a big ruckus around here yesterday."

"Well, that's why I stopped. My name is Samuel Milton, and I came to apologize to her, if she will let me."

"You are more than welcome to try, but not here. I'm afraid she's in the studio today. You might be able to catch her there."

"Do you know what studio?"

"She's at Universal, and let's see." Joey pauses, looking at his clipboard. "Miss León should be in studio thirty-four; she had an early call time of six thirty this morning and will be there until her guest appearance on *The Tonight Show*. They start shooting at five o'clock. I would suggest waiting just inside the door, and you can catch her on a break.

"Ask for Carol Schawk—she's her personal assistant. Tell Carol what you told me, and give her my name if she asks. Oh, by the way, if you wear jeans and carry a clipboard, you can walk on to any set, and no one will question you. But just in case, tell the guard at the east gate that Joey said it was okay to let you in. He can give you directions to soundstage thirty-four. Just promise you won't do anything stupid."

"I will try my best not to. Thank you very much."

"Oh, one more thing: I hear that she has a fondness for yellow roses. You never know; it might help."

Sam looks back over his shoulder with a little surprise on his face. "Thanks. Thanks a lot." He gets back into his car and drives off, saying to himself, "Who would have guessed old stoneface could be so nice?"

Sam stops his car at the east gate of the studio. A little steam comes up from under the hood as he waits for the guard to come out of his dark glass office. When the guard appears at the door, he first looks at the front of Sam's car and then at Sam before asking, "Who are you here to see?"

"I'm here to see Chantell León."

"Do you have an appointment?"

"No, but Joe Dobson said it would be okay."

The guard looks at Sam and his car again before walking back into his glass box. A minute later, he reappears at the door with a clipboard. "Miss León is in soundstage thirty-four B. That will be four buildings up to the left. Please park your car in the visitor parking outside the main gate."

Sam looks at the size of the buildings and figures that it is over a half mile to soundstage thirty-four. He looks back at the guard and says, "Doesn't that sign say 'visitor parking' farther up the road?"

The guard looks at the smashed front end of the car, which is leaving a puddle. He says, without looking back at Sam, "Not with that leaking all over the place. Park it outside the main gate, sir."

Sam answers, "I see your point. By the way, you wouldn't happen to have a garden hose around, would you?"

"In the planter by the parking lot outside the main gate, sir."

"Yes, well, thank you very much," Sam says as he puts the car in reverse and heads back out the main gate.

Once in the outside lot, he opens the car door with a loud squeak, picks up the dozen yellow roses from the passenger seat, and starts walking. When he passes the guard shack, he looks in and says, "Four buildings up and to the left?"

"Four buildings up and to the left," comes the answer in a monotone. Sam steps over the puddle his car left and continues to walk.

A little out of breath, he finally rounds the third building to see another large building on the other side of an empty parking lot. It has a sign designating "visitor parking." He nods and says to himself, "Of course!"

The front of the building consists of a large blank wall, with the number thirty-four painted on the side. The only thing on the entire front side is a small metal door at the top of six-foot-high concrete stairs fitted with a tacky pipe handrail. *Not a very glamorous entrance for such famous people*, he thinks.

When he heads for the door, a bus full of tourists stops between him and the stairs to the door. The tour guide says into his loudspeaker: "Now, according to my spies, we might see a famous celebrity come out of this door any minute now."

As Sam passes, he sees someone with a video camera sneaking off the bus in hopes of getting a better shot. Someone else on the bus sees Sam, and yells, "Hey, I think he is someone famous!" With that, everyone on the bus takes Sam's picture. Sam, not wanting to disappoint, waves and takes a bow. Then someone else on the bus yells, "I've never seen that guy before." And, just as fast as his fame had come, it goes. Sam shrugs and heads for the door at the top of the stairs.

He hears someone yell, "Hey, there's William Conrad!" They all turn away to snap his picture.

Just as Sam reaches for the doorknob, the steel door suddenly bursts open, hitting Sam across the temple. It pushes him backward against the handrail. Sam, trying to keep from going over the rail, reaches out to grab the edge of the door. He misses the door and instead reaches beyond, accidentally grabbing the neckline of a top worn by the woman coming out of the building. As Sam is thrown halfway over the rail, the blouse is torn completely off the woman. The woman is Chantell!

Terrified, she shrieks as she bends over to try to cover herself with her arms and hands. Her security team, fearing their client has just been attacked, goes after Sam. One flips Sam around and shoves him hard against the handrail, knocking the wind out of him. He then grabs Sam's wrist, twisting his arm around his back. The other security guard starts patting Sam down, while a third puts his jacket around Chantell.

The distinctive sound of cameras can be heard clicking away as the people on the bus get far more for their fifty dollars than they ever dreamed possible. Meanwhile, the whole scene is videotaped by the crew from *Entertainment Tonight*, who were following Chantell in hopes of getting some good footage for the interview they are doing.

With the air knocked out of him and an intense strain on his arm, Sam is unable to say anything or explain anything. From everyone's perspective, it looks like he intentionally reached around the door and accosted Chantell—everyone, that is, except for the man who snuck off the bus. Knowing what valuable footage he has, the tourist immediately takes the film out of his camcorder, replaces it with a new cassette, and starts filming again.

Within minutes, the police are there in force. Sam is cuffed, shoved into the back of a squad car, and rushed away. Several other officers start rounding up the witnesses. Every tourist is interviewed and their cameras confiscated for evidence. If nothing of significance is found, the cameras are to be returned the same day. Film that indicates what happened or severely compromises Chantell's privacy will be retained until review by the district attorney.

Chantell is rushed to a private office and allowed to lie down. A nurse on staff checks her out and gives her a mild sedative. She cancels the *ET* interview, but knowing *The Tonight Show* appearance is several hours away, she plans on keeping it.

One of the investigators comes in holding a picture of Sam that was just taken and asks Chantell if she knows the man who attacked her. Chantell takes one look and gets scared. "He's the weird guy who ran into my car yesterday! I couldn't believe the way he acted. The man never apologized or anything. He just stood there, giving me this weird look. It wasn't natural at all; it was as if something was wrong with him mentally." She thinks a moment and then exclaims, "And he's here today? Oh my God! I think the guy is stalking me!"

A couple of reporters within earshot hear her call him a stalker. They immediately phone it in. Within moments, Sam's actions are broadcast over radio and news channels. The reporters, acquiring photos that were taken from such a distance they weren't deemed as evidence, make sure both Chantell's and Sam's faces are broadcast all over the world. All photos display a terrified Chantell and show Sam to be a demented, would-be rapist.

Sam is sitting in a small room buried deep inside a Los Angeles police station. It has one door and a window that looks into a hallway. Across the table from him is Detective Bradford, who keeps tapping his pencil on a notepad as he speaks. "Well, I must tell you, Mr. Milton, we have nothing to verify your story. In fact, everything is pointing against it. We have a total of fifty-seven witnesses who saw you pull Miss León's top off. Yet, not one said they saw you get hit by the door. Now, try and explain that to me again."

Sam looks disgusted and groans, "How many times do I have to say this?"

"Humor me."

"As I was just starting up the stairs, someone on the bus saw William Conrad, and everyone turned to see him. So, no one was looking at me when the door opened. They didn't turn around until after the door opened and hit me. By that time, I was behind the door, struggling to keep from falling over the handrail. That's when I reached out for the edge of the door."

"And grabbed her top instead," the detective says, still tapping his pencil. "Can you think of anything else that might help support your story—anything at all?"

Sam sits slumped over, his hands clasped around his head and elbows propped on the table. He tries to think. Suddenly, he springs up and shouts, "Roses, yellow roses!"

"Roses? What roses?" the detective asks.

"I was planning on giving Chantell yellow roses when I came to apologize. Now, why would I be carrying a dozen yellow roses if I planned to assault her?"

The detective looks over at Sam, trying to decide if this story is worth pursuing. He eventually leans over and presses the intercom. "Dave, check the photographs from the bus and see if any of them show Mr. Milton here carrying yellow roses, and get me Thompson in the field. Thanks."

Looking back at Sam, he says, "You stay put. I'm going to talk to the guard."

"Guard? You have Joe Dobson here?"

"Yes, Mr. Milton. It seems your stunt got a few people in trouble."

As the detective leaves, Sam puts his head back in his hands and mouths, *Great! That's just great!*

A few minutes later, the detective walks back in. "The guard did say that he suggested the roses, but he didn't see you with any. The guard at the main gate remembers seeing you, but he also doesn't remember seeing you with any roses."

"I'm not surprised. By then, he took a call and had his back to me as I walked by."

The phone buzzes. "Bradford. Yeah, Thompson, I want you and Sanders to go back to soundstage thirty-four and take a look at the area around the door. See if you can find any yellow roses. Yeah, that's right, one dozen yellow roses, and get back to me as soon as you can."

He presses the phone for another line. "Dave, have you found anything yet?"

"No roses, but I did find something interesting. You need to come down here."

"I'll be right down."

The detective leaves Sam alone for over a half an hour, which makes Sam feel really uncomfortable.

Finally, the door opens and Detective Bradford tosses two pictures to Sam. "Do you want to explain this?" The first picture shows Sam standing next to a naked, underaged girl with whipped cream covering her breast. The next picture has the girl's face concealed by a policeman's jacket.

Sam looks petrified, but manages to say, "If you look in my wallet, you will find a card with the State Department's logo on it."

"Yeah, I have it here. What's it about?"

"It's about that picture. Call the number on the back, and they will explain it."

Detective Bradford leaves again but comes back in less than ten minutes. "You have had an interesting life, Mr. Milton. The phone number checks out for that picture, but now explain this one that was taken just today." The photo shows Sam trying to shield his face with his coat collar as he heads for the door.

Sam first looks scared but then smiles as he remembers out loud, "Someone on the bus thought I might be a movie star. I was just playing along with it." The detective is looking at Sam as if he is not the least bit convinced. "Look, the guard at the gate saw me and told me where I was to go. So, why would I try to hide my face at the soundstage?"

The now-irritated detective retorts, "This isn't helping your case one bit."

The phone rings again, and the detective pushes the intercom as the caller reports back: "This is Dave. We checked all over, and no sign of any roses. Sorry, Gerry, looks like we're just fishing in an empty stream."

Detective Bradford looks over at Sam and is about to hang up when he hears, "Wait a minute. We may have found something. Yes, I think we've found what you're looking for. Detective Sanders found a few rose petals near an empty trashcan about twenty feet away . . . and he says they're yellow. Say, I have an idea. Let me go check the steps again."

"Call me back if you find anything more." Turning to Sam, the detective adds, "Let's hope so, Mr. Milton."

Sam slowly runs his fingers though his hair as the phone rings once again. "Yeah, Thompson?"

"Say, we've found what looks like the remains of rose petals. They've been mashed onto the asphalt like they've been stepped on. The area looks like it has been swept up, so it would explain the missing roses. Let me find the janitor and confirm."

A few minutes pass, and again Bradford answers the phone's ring. "Yeah?"

"We have a janitor here who says he found a bunch of roses next to the steps leading up to the door. He didn't start his shift until the incident had passed. He didn't know where they came from, so he threw them away. Will that do for you?"

"Yeah, that's great. Make sure you get his testimony. That will be it for tonight. Good job, guys. Mr. Milton will be very relieved."

The detective turns to Sam and says, "Looks like those roses got you off the hook, at least for now." He picks up a sheet of paper from a file in front of him. "According to this, we have no priors on you, not even a traffic ticket in the past three years. So, I'm cutting you lose, but stay in the area until this mess is cleared up.

"Oh, by the way, this case has received a lot of publicity and has been seen on the five o' clock news. It's all over the country by now. So, a lot of people, including the press, are going to think you're still guilty. I don't have enough to hold you, but this isn't going to prove to fanatic fans or the press that you're innocent—at least in their eyes anyway. So, watch out for yourself! If things get ugly, give me a call, and I will send someone over. Until something shows up to really prove your story, you're still in a big mess. I'm going to let you out a side entrance so the press won't see you leave. I'll have an officer take you to your car."

"Thank you for your help and understanding," Sam says, shaking the detective's hand.

Out in the hall, Sam sees the guard he befriended on the PCH and goes over to talk to him. "I hope I didn't get you into too much trouble today, Joe."

"Well, I'm afraid they fired me. It seems we're not supposed to give out that kind of information."

Sam cringes as he hears the news. "I am so sorry for getting you into this mess. Is there anything I can do?"

"No, I'm okay; everyone needs guards, so I'll find something. Don't you worry about me." After shaking Sam's hand, Joe Dobson leaves, turning back to say, "Don't be too hard on Miss León; she's really a nice kid."

"I will keep that in mind, and good luck to you," Sam answers back. He watches helplessly as this man, whom he now really respects, slowly walks down the hall. Sam winces again as he thinks of the grief he has caused him.

4

From Bad to Catastrophic

In the famous green room, where nervous guests await their turns to go on *The Tonight Show*, is a very comfortable chair with a very uncomfortable Chantell sitting in it. She nervously fidgets—even Johnny Carson's monologue can't calm her down. The only other guest in the room is a short, fat man who can do one hundred fifty exotic bird calls. He's more nervous than Chantell, and his sweaty face shows it. Air Supply, the musical guest, is setting up behind the multicolored curtain that's the backdrop for Johnny's monologue. *The Entertainment Tonight* film crew is packing up to relocate to the front of the audience. There, they plan to capture the audience's perspective and excitement when Chantell is announced.

As the last of the crew steps out, Carol Schawk steps in, looking extremely agitated. "What's wrong?" Chantell asks as her nervousness escalates.

"I shouldn't tell you. You're about to go on."

"Tell me *what*?" Chantell demands.

Carol pauses, knowing she is about to make a big mistake. "The police let that SOB go!"

"What? They let him go? Why?"

"They didn't have enough evidence to hold him."

Chantell loses it. "They didn't have enough evidence? What about him yanking my top off? Wasn't exposing my bare breasts on national TV sufficient evidence? What the hell am I supposed to do now?"

"Unfortunately, it gets worse." Carol grimaces.

"How?"

"He's also been in an insane asylum."

"What? No way!" Chantell says before she slumps back in her chair, trying to comprehend such news.

"It gets even worse—something about him and an incident with a fifteen-year-old girl when he was twenty-two."

"Good Lord, was the girl naked?"

"Not unless you feel whipped cream constitutes a bikini."

"What?"

"It gets even better. It involved the State Department, but the documents have been sealed, so there's no way of finding out anything more."

"Oh great! He's been in an asylum and accused of molesting a fifteen-year-old, and they still let him go? This is insanity! Do you think he had some connections at the State Department?"

Carol just shrugs and says, "To be honest, it doesn't say anything about him molesting the girl."

"Come on! What else would he be doing with a fifteen-year-old girl? I can't believe this! I'm Chantell, the world's most famous singer, and who the hell is he? Obviously, he still rates better than I do if the police won't hold him for the disgrace he's caused me." Bringing herself to tears, she screams, "Who is this guy?"

As Chantell rants, she doesn't notice Johnny is finishing his monologue or hear the show's intern coming to announce, "Two minutes, Miss León."

"I'm scared, Carol! We don't know when that guy is going to show up again. He could be in the audience, for Christ's sake!"

"Security is all over the place, Chantell. You are as safe as you ever could be."

"Yeah? Was I safe coming out of the studio? I want one of my brothers around me at all times from now on. Let him get past one of the Fearsome Threesome." Chantell lets out a choice expletive and says, "I can't believe they let him go!"

Carol yells back at her, "Chantell, I'm the one who swears in this group, not you." Then, she says calmly, "He's got your halo all tied in a knot!"

"What do you mean *tied in a knot*? He yanked the thing off and flushed it down the toilet!"

"Chantell León!" Carol yells. "Pull yourself together!"

Chantell quickly looks through her purse for a tissue and freezes. Shock turns into delight as she discovers something she forgot was in her purse. She looks up at Carol and gives her a devilish grin that chills Carol to the bone.

They then hear, "Ladies and gentlemen, one of the sweetest young people I know has just gone through a horrible experience, and she has been kind enough to come on our show tonight despite the trauma. So now, please give a warm applause for Chantell León!"

Chantell places her hand on the intern's hand to keep him from pulling back the curtain. She looks back at Carol and says, "Well, if the police aren't going to protect me, then I will just let my fans take care of the problem for me."

She turns and nods to the young intern. Though she hasn't had any formal training as an actress, no one would be able to tell how upset she is as she morphs her persona from scared to complete confidence.

The intern pulls the blue edge of the colorful curtain back, and Chantell steps out to thunderous applause. Though she walks with flair, she's not letting anyone see what she is clutching in her hand. She pauses a moment to acknowledge her fans before turning to Johnny. Johnny gives her a hug, whispers something in her ear, and then does something out of character. He takes Chantell's hand and escorts her around the desk to her seat before returning to his.

It takes several minutes for the applause to die down so that Johnny can make his first comments. "My goodness! What incredible applause! I think that is even longer applause than what Don Rickles got last night."

As the audience breaks into laughter, Johnny turns to Ed McMahon and asks, "Hey, Ed, do you remember how long that was?"

"Oh, two, three seconds, maybe?"

Ed's comment gets a louder response, so Johnny says, "That much, was it?" The laughter gets even louder. "And he was the guest host last night!" Johnny smiles as he gets an even louder reaction. He motions with his hands for the audience to calm down.

When they get quiet, Johnny turns to Chantell and says, "All kidding aside, I am very pleased to say what you just received is the longest applause we've ever had." As more affection pours out, Johnny points to the audience to verify how loved his guest really is. Chantell then stands and gives a slight bow before returning the affection with her own applause.

Eventually, everything quiets down, allowing Johnny to say, "My, my, it is so good to have you here tonight. Now, to keep from getting lost in today's events, I want to first talk about what you have been up to. I hear you have had a remarkable summer."

"Well, I just released the second song from my second album. I love that the whole album has a nice forties flavor to it. The album is called *Uptown Hot,* and the song is 'The Forbidden Fruit of Love.' " The audience applauds and she continues, "At the end of May, I finished a fifteen-city tour, and six weeks ago, I started filming my first movie. It's for Universal and is called *The Last African Countess.*" The audience again applauds. "It's just to keep from getting summer boredom—I'm kidding, of course. It's unbelievably fantastic!"

Everyone applauds, charged up by her enthusiasm.

Johnny counters with, "Well, it beats sitting around watching old reruns of *Let's Make A Deal.*"

When things get quiet again, Johnny changes course. "It's been all over the news tonight about what happened to you just a few hours ago. Can you tell us about it?"

A resolute Chantell turns from Johnny to her audience and begins, "Well, yes, it was extremely traumatic. Let me start from the beginning. I was in a minor traffic accident with this . . . this man. It wasn't really bad; we just bent bumpers and hoods. Fortunately, I could still drive my car, but I did bang the bridge of my nose on the steering wheel. I was freaking out because I had my close-ups today. However, this guy . . . he just kept standing there, but the weird thing is, he was looking away. He wouldn't turn around and face me. That freaked me out even more! I was already late getting back to the set, so I got out of the car to look at the damage to see if I could still drive the car. Thinking back, it was probably a very stupid—and maybe even dangerous—thing to do! Anyway, I kept trying to get information out of this man, but all he did was mumble, which *really* made me nervous!"

"So, what did you do?" Johnny asks sympathetically.

"I got back in my car and got out of there as fast as I could!"

"Then what happened—I mean, this afternoon?"

"Fortunately, they canceled the rest of the shoot yesterday, and I went home. I needed to get in bed early because I had to be on set by six thirty this morning. I don't think I got even three hours of sleep last night, and that's after taking a sedative. I think I was upset because I had seen the Theresa Saldana story awhile back. What was the name of the movie?" Chantell inquires.

Johnny answers, "*Victims for Victims*. She starred in it herself, you know."

"That's it. She survived a knife attack by an admiring fan."

"Yes. It was her own true story. Very frightening!"

"Well, it turns out that this man *was* stalking me because this morning he showed up at Universal! He was lurking outside the soundstage door. I don't know how he knew I was the one coming out, but when the door opened, there he was! He had this weird, fiendish look on his face as he reached in, grabbed the top collar of my halter top, and yanked it completely off me. He then turned and tried running down the stairs before security tackled him to the ground."

Johnny places his hand on her arm. "That must have been horrible!"

"Yes, it was terrifying, but also, there were all of these people around taking pictures. Some of them were even able to get pictures of my naked chest. Oh, and the crew from *Entertainment Tonight* was there filming the whole thing."

Johnny looks at the audience. "Well, I guess there will definitely be *entertainment* tonight!" The laughter lightens the heavy tension. Johnny then shakes his head in sympathy before saying, "That must have been such a frightening ordeal for you."

Chantell looks over at Johnny, and he sees her fear slowly transform into anger. She then lightly slaps the edge of his desk and says, "No. That is not the most frightening thing that happened to me today. In fact, something just happened tonight that scares me ten times worse."

Johnny looks shocked and puzzled as he asks, "What could possibly be worse than that?"

Chantell turns and faces the audience again. "Not more than five minutes ago, I found out that this guy was involved in an incident with a naked fifteen-year-old girl when he was twenty-two. I also just found out that he's been in an insane asylum."

"Really?" Johnny asks. "The man who assaulted you has been in a mental institution? I bet you're glad he's locked up again, right?"

"Oh, but Johnny, that's the most interesting aspect. The police just let that lunatic go free! He is out walking the streets right now."

Johnny looks over to his producer, Fred de Cordova. "Is that true, Freddy?" Freddy taps his headphone, waits a moment, and then nods yes.

Johnny marvels, "That doesn't make any sense. Why would they do that?"

Chantell looks back at Johnny to say, "I don't know."

Johnny watches her anger build.

"The incident with the girl involved the State Department, so maybe he has connections," Chantell almost spits the words out as her face becomes contorted with escalating anger.

Johnny holds on to her arm, trying to calm her down.

She continues, unabated. "Whatever the case, the man who assaulted me is walking around free as a bird and could be planning to do it again!" She pulls her arm away, stands, and walks toward the audience. The boom mic follows above her, capturing every nuance of her powerful voice, now expressing full-scale rage. "What is a girl supposed to do when the police protect a lunatic more than his victim?" She is now screaming. "If the police won't do anything, maybe someone else should! Maybe a lot of people should!"

Johnny is trying to get his producer's attention. Everything is getting chaotic. She stuns Johnny and everyone else when she holds up Sam's driver's license. "I am so scared of this guy. His name is Samuel Henry Milton, and he lives at 5820 Palm Street in Camarillo!"

Johnny is giving the cut sign as Ed McMahon runs over to try and get Chantell to stop ranting. Johnny covers his mic and looks to Freddy on his right. "Did that get out?" Freddy nods quickly and holds his hands up in confusion. Johnny recovers himself and speaks tersely into his microphone, "Let's go to a commercial!"

Off mic, Johnny commands, "Someone please get her backstage and calm her down. Freddy, we need to snuff out this fire before we start a riot! Get someone to write me an apology—and quickly!"

When Chantell hears Johnny ordering an apology, she loses it. "An apology? For what? This crazy lunatic assaults me, and when I look for help, you draft an apology?" She throws Sam's license at him. "You are worse than the police department!"

Members of the crew run over and try to coax her backstage. When they get her back into the green room, Carol starts yelling, "Get your hands off that girl!" Several let go and excuse themselves. A man and two women with official blue blazers stay and try to calm Chantell down.

Carol's anger and resolve grows as she comes up to her client and takes her by the arm. She yells to the others, "I said, get your hands off of her!" She breaks Chantell free and starts guiding her to an exit. "I have the limo outside."

Chantell nods and lets her lead. Carol turns back to the three from the show. "Tell Mr. Carson this isn't the last of this!"

When the pandemonium calms down, Johnny notices the driver's license Chantell threw at him. He picks it up and looks at it. He is shocked to see it is the same Sam Milton he plays tennis with. He slips the license into his pocket before going back to calm his audience.

5

The Nightmare Intensifies

A click of a button and the videotape runs backward until it's pressed again. It restarts as the Budweiser commercial comes to an end. Everything switches to a colorful cartoon of a sleeping lion holding a sign that says "Leo," with the theme of The Tonight Show playing. The camera switches back to the show, with Johnny Carson tapping his cigarette box with a pencil. Johnny looks into the camera and speaks into his microphone, "We're back, ladies and gentlemen." He then looks to his left and says, "Thank you, Doc Severinsen and the Tonight Show Orchestra."

As Doc, in his garish yellow-sequined suit, takes a bow, Johnny gives a short chuckle and says, "Well, if anyone wanted to know what a Fourth of July sparkler looks like when it goes bad, there you have it!"

When the laughter dies down, Johnny leans into his microphone to announce, "Ladies and gentlemen, one of the sweetest young people I know has just gone through a horrible experience, and she has been kind enough to come on our show tonight despite the trauma. So now, please give a warm applause for Chantell León!" After a momentary pause, the muted blue edge of the colorful curtain is pulled back, and Chantell steps out dressed in a flowing black gown. She is escorted by Johnny himself to the single seat between the longer blue couch and Johnny's desk.

The evening's programming is attentively watched by a man with clasped hands, holding up a double chin and chubby cheeks. His elbows are perched on top of an opulent desk as he leans forward to study every nuance of the volatile events. When he sees the young singer stand up and start her tirade, the big man leans back in his huge office chair, props his feet on the desk, and rests his still-clasped hands on the bulge of his stomach. He continues to watch intently, right up until Johnny desperately states, "Let's go to a commercial."

That's when Gordon Osborn leans forward to pick up a phone off the desk. "Rich, she did just what I hoped she'd do. See what you can find on this Sam Milton character, and bring that videotape with you. If it is half as good as we've been told, then we're in business." He puts down the phone, places his feet back up on the desk, and clasps his hands behind his head. He smiles and says to himself, "Miss León, you are about to buy me that beach house on Kauai."

—————

Sam sits staring straight ahead, unflinching, in his car seat, with one hand on the steering wheel and one on the shifter. With no music from the radio or a cassette tape, he sits in total silence, absorbed in his own thoughts—so much so that he's unaware of his surroundings. He doesn't notice the business girl standing on the corner trying to seduce his attention. Nor does he notice the two men shouting obscenities to each other at the 7-Eleven convenience store on the opposite corner. He barely notices the young man in the car next to him, yelling through his rolled-down window, "Bummer about your car, man." His only acknowledgment is a quick flex of his wrist on the steering wheel.

The reflection in Sam's eyes turns from red to green. He puts the car in gear and pulls forward, only using a small portion of what his Hemi can give. He stops and starts at other traffic lights, even changing lanes on the freeway; his only detectable movements are subtle glances to the left or right. He drives as if on automatic pilot, his conscious thought focused on the burning memories of the past two days. Every so often, he flinches and hits the steering wheel with his fist as he remembers another painful moment.

Getting off at his exit and traveling the two miles to his neighborhood barely registers. Sam lifts his watch up to the light of a passing lamp post. It's twelve sixteen a.m. He yawns as he notices the glow of several bright lights rising from the house one block over. They are reflecting off the top of a large elm tree that he recognizes as his own. He stops at the stop sign, and just as he is about to make a right turn onto his street, a van speeds by: *Channel 7 Eyewitness News.*

"What the?" Sam turns and follows the van. As he rounds the corner, he puts on the brakes and comes to a sudden stop, seeing several cars and vans parked in front of his house. In his driveway, he can see reporters and cameramen talking to his neighbors. Some are poking around the front of the house, while the rest are just standing around waiting for something to happen.

Sam continues to absorb the spectacle in front of him until one of the reporters looks up and sees him. She points toward his direction and motions for her cameraman. Others pick up on what's going on and follow suit. Sam, sensing the impeding deluge, throws the car in reverse. He speeds down his street in reverse and turns onto a side street. While the car is still going backward, he throws it into first, stomps on the gas, and leaves everyone smelling burning rubber.

For the first time in weeks, he is using the Barracuda to its fullest. He leads everyone on a short goose chase, heading away from his house. When he doesn't see any headlights in his mirrors, he turns a corner, puts it in neutral, and shuts off his lights. He coasts stealthily down to another intersection. He rounds the corner again and makes his way back toward his house. When he gets close, he parks one block over between two trucks so his car can't be easily seen. He jumps out and runs down the alley. Jumping over his own back fence, he runs to the back door and disappears inside.

Sam walks to the front window and stares out through the sheer drapes. He is amazed at all the moving lights and shadows caused by the activity outside his door. He can hear the muffled voices of the reporters as they prepare their last stories for the night. All of this outside light is enough for Sam to walk freely through the house without turning on lights to indicate someone is home.

He makes his way into the bathroom and prepares to take a shower using only the nightlight's beam. Afterward, he makes his way to his bedroom and falls exhausted onto the bed. When he gets himself all situated, he feels the familiar pounce of his cat joining him. The cat soon settles near Sam's head, but instead of throwing him to the end of the bed, which has become the nightly ritual, Sam just lets him stay there, thankful for the nonhostile company. He lies there, petting his cat, listening as, one by one, the news vans leave for the night.

It is the irritating sound of the telephone, as well as the persistent knocking at the front door, that brings Sam back to consciousness. Putting on his bathrobe, he slowly makes his way to the front door. He stops to peek through the window. He sees an attractive reporter and her cameraman standing at the door. He leaves her knocking as he turns and heads for the ringing telephone. "Hello," Sam says.

"Hello, Mr. Samuel Milton?"

"Yes, this is Sam Milton."

"Mr. Milton, this is Gordon Osborn. Have you heard of me?"

"Everyone has heard of you, Mr. Osborn. Between your ambulance-chasing billboards, your signs on every bus in town, and your TV commercials, we can't get your name out of our heads. But, why would such a famous litigation attorney be calling me?"

"Well, you are getting to be pretty famous yourself, and I would like to represent you in your upcoming legal affairs."

Sam looks down at his answering machine and says, "Mr. Osborn, it seems that I have fifty-two other calls on my answering machine. Now, outside of nosey reporters, angry fans of Chantell, and a call from my mother, I would have to expect that several of these calls are from other lawyers. Now, outside of your famous name and high price tag, why should I choose you?"

"A fair question to ask. It would seem that I have something that you might be interested in. It's a videotape of what happened yesterday at Universal, but someone took this video from a different angle than what everyone else saw."

"As I recall, the only people around were those on the tour bus, and none of them saw anything. So, where did this tape of yours come from?"

"Well, you see, Mr. Milton, one man got off the bus just before this all happened. Seems he wanted to get a better shot of whoever was to come out that door, but instead, he got a clear shot of you getting hit by the door."

Sam tilts his head back as if remembering something. "Now that you've brought it to my attention, I do recall someone sneaking off the bus. So, why didn't he just take the tape to the police?"

"I guess he saw the opportunity for greater monetary gain than what the police would give him—i.e., nothing!" Osborn laughs sarcastically.

"I see. So, he contacted you?"

"Well, I am in the right business for it, I suppose, but I would have represented you anyway. However, the tape does make it a lot easier, and it also makes the punitives a lot higher."

"Oh yes, the money. We can't forget about that, now can we? Well, I'm not interested in suing anybody, Mr. Osborn, especially someone with a nice reputation like Chantell."

"Did you happen to catch *The Tonight Show* last night, Mr. Milton?"

"No."

"I didn't think so. Well, I taped it for you. She maligned you, Mr. Milton. She not only called you out by name, but she also provided the world your address. Then she explicitly threatened you with bodily harm by asking her fans to take care of you because the police didn't. In the Old West, that would be considered calling for a lynch mob. Nowadays, I would consider that putting a contract out on you—except she didn't offer any money. At the very least, she should be charged with inciting a riot. All that being said, I would say her little comments are worth about fifty million dollars to you—minus legal fees, of course."

"Oh good. Does that mean I can be on your next TV commercial? I could use a nice Southern drawl and say, 'Mr. Osborn got me fifty million dollars!' No, thank you! I still don't want to sue anybody," Sam replies, sounding perturbed.

"That is fine with me, but take a look outside, Mr. Milton," Gordon says bluntly. "Your house has already been on the morning news, and it is only going to get worse, especially when the studios and her record companies get into the act. Like it or not, Mr. Milton, you are going to need counsel—lots of it—and that is going to cost you far more than you can afford to pay."

"I see your point."

"Good. How about meeting at my office? Let's say two o'clock?"

"How do I get there?"

"I'm surprised you need to ask. Aren't I on every billboard? Haven't you seen my TV commercials? Nonetheless, I am located on the top floor of the Osborn Building in the Wilshire District. It's the tallest one there."

"Of course it is." Sam chuckles.

"See you at two, Mr. Milton," Gordon says, and the phone goes silent.

A short time later, Sam looks out the front window and sees his paper. Not seeing anyone standing nearby, he quickly goes outside to get it. He barely has the paper in hand when he is set upon by reporters who have been waiting in their cars for something like this to happen. He stands up to find himself surrounded.

"Mr. Milton, Donna Dean from *Eyewitness News*. Do you have comments on what has happened?"

"It's all b-b-been an accident," Sam stutters.

"What do you think of Miss León's comments on *The Tonight Show* last night?"

"I'm afraid I didn't see it." He tries to walk back to the house when he hears her ask another question.

"What do you think of Chantell now?"

Turning back to the reporter, he states bluntly, "No comment." He then looks up to see a young girl holding a sign that says, "WE LOVE CHANTELL!" With a painful expression, Sam looks at the sign for a minute and says, "Please, no more questions." He then turns around and bumps hard into the chest of a tall black man who had purposefully stepped right behind him.

The huge, intimidating man looks down at him to ask, "Do you like to assault white women, too, or do you prefer young black women?"

Sam looks up to see the burning hate in the man's eyes. He steps aside and pushes his way through other reporters and bystanders who are more his size. Breaking out of the crowd, he stops and looks up to see the words, "RAPIST,"

"RACIST," and "WHITE TRASH"—along with other descriptive slurs— painted on his house and garage door.

"We want you out of here!" one of his neighbors yells from the back of the crowd.

Sam loses it. He turns back to everyone and yells, "Enough already! This has all been a tragic mistake, but you can't see that! No! On second thought, it's not because you *can't* see it; it's because you don't *want* to see it! All of you think you're so pristinely righteous, but given the opportunity to hate, you jump at the chance. As for you reporters, you're nothing but a bunch of vultures. Soon as someone gets hurt, you're right there, looking for some choice tidbits. When you get your fill, you go out and feed it to the masses and work them up into a frenzy, like a bunch of barracudas. Then here they come, just like you knew they would! So, here you are, egging them on, just so you can feed on them! Just look at my house! Look at it! What are you hoping for now? Bodily injury? Maybe a little blood? A lot of blood? Well, until then, you got your story, so get the hell out of my life!"

Sam turns back to the house, and all of the reporters lunge forward at one time, fighting each other for an interview. Sam walks in the door, slamming it on the most zealous of the reporters. He walks directly to the back door, opens it, passes through, and then slams it behind him. Continuing through the yard, he jumps the fence and stomps down the alley, mumbling to himself.

6

A Regrettable Alliance

Sam stands in front of a large office building in the Wilshire District. All of the glass and marble, along with the elaborate fountains and sculptures, are making him visibly self-conscious. Two men in fine business suits exit the main doors of the Osborn Building as Sam approaches. One of them looks at Sam, then whispers to the other, both chuckling as they pass. Sam immediately turns to look at his reflection in the dark glass but sees nothing particularly out of place, just a single hair sticking up in the back. Not having a comb, he spits on his hand and presses down on the troubled area.

"Why do I feel like everyone can tell I bought this suit at Montgomery Ward?" he says aloud while adjusting his tie. He tucks his shirt in a bit and then checks his fly. "And why do I feel everyone is stari—" He stops and peers into the dark glass, only to see several people looking back at him. They can clearly see every word form on his lips. He abruptly turns away and disappears through the big entry doors. Inside the lobby, Sam heads to the directory and looks for Osborn and Associates. He sees the Osborn firm is located on the twenty-sixth, twenty-seventh, and twenty-eighth floors. He walks over to the information desk. "Excuse me, I have an appointment with Mr. Osborn, and I am not sure what floor he is on."

"His personal office is on the twenty-eighth floor. You may take the express elevator directly to his personal office. It is just to your right."

"Thank you."

"You're welcome. Turn right as you exit the elevator."

When the door closes, the elevator immediately starts without Sam having to press a button. On the way up, he notices the intricate wood carving and inlays. "Well, if I don't get millions from this meeting, maybe I can at least get some work."

The elevator comes to a stop and the door opens, revealing a large and elegantly appointed reception area. The ceilings extend up two stories, thus allowing for two full-grown ficus trees. Sunlight streams through large skylights above them.

Turning right, he hears, "You must be the famous Samuel Milton." The voice is coming from a pretty and smartly dressed young woman sitting at a desk to his side. "I'm sorry, but I saw you on the news last night. You really seem to be having a time of it."

Sam answers with just a shrug.

"Mr. Osborn is expecting you. This way, please." She walks toward an elaborately carved staircase leading up to his office. Reaching the top of the stairs, she pauses at a large, thick glass door, the words "Gordon W. Osborn" engraved deep into it. She knocks and says, "Mr. Milton is here to see you."

Gordon signals for him to enter.

Sam walks into Gordon's office, looks around, and says, "Wow! I thought only insurance companies could afford stuff like this."

Gordon chuckles and says, "Not bad for an ambulance chaser, is it?"

"Somehow, I doubt all of this came from chasing ambulances."

"No, Mr. Milton. The lawyer stuff is mostly a hobby and comprises only one floor of this building. The rest of these offices are dedicated to my investment company."

"Which is under another name, I assume," scoffs Sam.

The heavyset lawyer answers, "Of course, Mr. Milton. Anyway, it is good to see you. Come on in and have a seat," he says, pointing to a chair opposite his desk. "It's good you could come on such short notice. Tell me, is there anyone who doesn't hate you yet?"

"Well, I suppose I'm not looking too good in the public eye at the moment."

"*At the moment?* I'm afraid it's going to last far longer than a moment, Sam."

Sam looks around again and asks, "Why am I here, Mr. Osborn?"

"I think you are underestimating the situation we have here, Sam." Gordon picks up a remote and points it at a large TV behind him. "This is a videotape of the news clips relating to your particular situation over the past few days—even in the past hour or so."

Sam watches, diverting his eyes every so often.

"Yes, Sam, those are protests and rallies. They are actually burning an effigy of you."

Sam watches a few more moments, then motions with his hand for it to be turned off. Gordon obliges with the click of a button. He then gets up, walks around his desk, and sits on its edge. "And that's just in the States. Would you like to see what they think of you in England or maybe France? How about Japan? However, you didn't do so well there—only fifteen seconds on their late news. You did much better in Italy, a full minute and a half—during prime time, no less."

"I get the point! But why has this been so inflammatory? I just accidently—I repeat, *accidentally*, mind you—pulled the top off a black celebrity, and you'd think we're back in the late 1960s, only in reverse."

"I have three reasons for it, Mr. Milton. First, I have to say that when you decided to rip the blouse off a celebrity, you didn't mess around. Next to Margret Thatcher or Nancy Reagan, Chantell León is the most famous and most loved person in the world right now. If anyone touches her, it is front-page news. Second, two recent events, the wrongful police shooting in the Bronx and the police officers acquitted in Miami, have escalated racial tensions. By you attacking the most-loved person of color, you lit the fuse on a huge keg of dynamite. And third, the studios and the producers are playing it up all they can. Nothing gets an Oscar faster than pulling on heartstrings.

"All of this adverse publicity has caused you a lot of damage, which means it may be years before you can recoup what you had just three days ago. So, let's look at what you lost with all of this negative publicity. Your source of income has been devastated, hasn't it?"

Sam nods.

"You can't even walk the streets, so your social life has turned to . . . let's just say, unprocessed fertilizer."

"I don't care for the wording, but it is accurate."

"Has your love life been affected?"

Sam responds with a flick of his wrist.

"Aren't you engaged to Linda McCall?" Gordon asks.

Sam looks up in shock. Gordon responds with, "I do my research. I take it you are not engaged now?" Sam just sits, staring. Gordon frowns. "By your lack of response, my guess is no."

Gordon continues, "Now, what about your overall sanity? Let's see, you had yourself committed to Channel Islands Mental Hospital for a nervous breakdown. Once there, you were placed on a suicide watch. This is not exactly what I would call a good mental health record. And now this. Will you even survive this? Not without some financial support—*that* I can promise you. And, Mr. Milton, if you don't pursue this, you won't have the money you need."

Gordon's oversized body gets uncomfortably close to Sam when he asks, "Mr. Milton, you had better survive this for the sake of Chantell, whom you so admire. I see your eyes are asking, *why?* How do you think Chantell León will feel when she finds out she was wrong about you—after you've committed suicide?"

"You said that you had a videotape that could clear up this mess."

"Yes I do, and it's undisputable. It vindicates you perfectly."

"Can I see it?" Sam turns toward the TV as Gordon starts the tape.

"Now, I must tell you, there have been a few seconds edited out of this copy, which I will explain later. Okay, here you are walking past the tour bus. Notice the yellow roses. Nice touch. I think we can use that."

"I already did," Sam says under his breath.

"What was that?"

Sam waves him off.

"Now, here you are walking up the stairs. The angle isn't the greatest, but it's just enough to see you reach for the door and then—"

At that instant, the screen goes blank for a few moments. It picks back up with Sam behind the door, the roses spread over the ground, and Miss León standing there with her blouse torn off. "And with that, Sam, the rating on this video goes from 'G' to 'X'—or at least 'R' anyway," Gordon says with a smirk. "I hoped she would be more endowed than that." Gordon is about to add something else but stops when he sees Sam's angry glare.

"This blank spot is where our friend edited this copy so we wouldn't get the wrong idea and forget to include him in the final settlement. However, I have seen the original, and it does show you getting hit by the door. It also shows you falling backward and trying to regain your balance. Though it is a little hard to make out at times, it shows us what we need to see. The bottom line is, this proves your case, and it will hold up in court."

"Well, I'm not sure I want to sue anybody. Besides, Chantell is practically an institution in and of herself, with an impeccable reputation, and I don't want to screw that up by taking her through a long and dirty trial just to get a few bucks!"

"So, you think Miss León is a sweet little angel, do you? Did you happen to catch *The Tonight Show* last night?"

"I already told you no," Sam says brusquely.

"So you did. Well, I taped it for you." Gordon switches tapes and backs away from the screen. He pushes on the remote to speed through the intro and monologue. He slows it down for Chantell's introduction and entrance.

As Sam watches the interview, he seems impressed with Chantell's ease in front of the camera. However, his opinion quickly changes. His eyes soon begin to twitch and blink, pain registering on his face as he listens to her view of the events. He rubs his forehead when she talks about how he acted after the accident and becomes visibly uncomfortable while she describes what she saw and how she felt after Sam tore her top off. Gordon pauses it just before Johnny asks, "Chantell, what could possibly be worse than that?"

"How is she looking so far?"

"Like a scared young woman going through a traumatic event."

"Still impressed?"

"Yes, of course I am. I have no problem with any of this."

Gordon releases *pause*, and Johnny asks the fateful question. Sam watches Chantell go into her tirade. The color drains from Sam's face until he is ghostly white. He looks down and away as the interview comes to its explosive climax. During this time, Sam's eyes fill with water, yet no tears fall.

"So, what do you think of her angelic image now, Mr. Milton?" Gordon asks as he puts his face close to his. "She fried you. She ripped you to shreds, Mr. Milton, on national TV in front of several million viewers!"

Sam just sits there, staring at the blank screen.

"Mr. Milton, you intended no malice because what happened at the soundstage was simply an accident. But this," Gordon says, pointing to the screen, "is both deliberate malice and defamation of character! And in case you didn't notice, she literally tried to stir up a mob to go out and stone you! I'm sure her studio and record label are trying very hard to keep her out of jail for the things she said. Because, quite frankly, she should be imprisoned for what she tried to incite! Anyway, Mr. Milton, I would say that her little speech, and all of this publicity, is worth about fifty million to you—or something far less if they can get us to settle out of court, which I am sure they will try to do to avoid the adverse publicity."

"She hurt me, so I hurt her. Is that it?"

"She hurt herself, Mr. Milton! She hurt herself. Besides, you're going to need a good lawyer anyway. You see, her only defense is justification, so they are going to try and prove she was justified in what she said. The only way they can prove that is to make you look bad, really bad! And if you think I'm an SOB of a lawyer, wait until you see what they will throw at you! Before this is over, you will be unable to do business in California again, and you will never get credit again. Not only will they leave you without a pot to pee in, you won't even have pants to pull down to do it!"

"All right, all right! You convinced me," Sam says, waving his hands. He then slams his fist down on the table and looks directly at Gordon. "But don't you do anything until I get back to you!"

Gordon tells Sam as he walks out of the room, "Well, don't take too long. This guy with the videotape won't wait forever."

Sam Milton heads out the door without saying anything.

7

What Else Can Be Taken?

Pulling out of the underground garage, Sam pauses to look back over his shoulder at the lawyer's office, shaking his head in disgust. He heads back onto Wilshire Boulevard toward the 405 Freeway, getting in the right lane to go north back to Camarillo. He sits at the light. A thought comes to him. The light turns green, but instead of turning right, he punches it, showing everyone why he owns a Barracuda. He crosses all four lanes and takes a sharp left, putting him southbound on the 405 and heading toward the 10, which he takes to LA.

Later, Sam looks at a photo in his wallet while sitting in a chair in the doctor's lounge. He studies the picture a few moments longer before slipping it back into his wallet. He leans his head back and waits. After two hours, he asks how long it will be, says thank you, and leaves. He comes back two hours later and waits again for another two hours. Eventually, a woman in her early thirties appears at the door. Leaning against the jamb, she appears to have had a long day. It's the same girl in the picture in Sam's wallet.

"Hi, been here long?" she asks.

"Not too long."

"Liar."

With a voice noticeably tense, he says, "Okay, I did go out and get some dinner, and then I fell asleep, so I actually have no idea how long I've been here."

"That's better. How are you taking all of this?" she asks, trying not to look directly at him.

"Not good. I feel like Job from the Bible. I've had everything taken from me at one time, without really knowing why."

"I take it you read my letter," she says, looking at him from a mirror while trying to hide her emotions.

"I love you," is his only reply.

"No, you don't, and I don't love you. We've been friends too long, and I'm glad we tried to see if we could have something more. I must admit, it would've been nice, but there just isn't enough there, and we both know it. We're just holding each other back, and it's time to go back to the way it was before we lose our friendship altogether."

She walks over to him, picks up his hands, and continues, "I don't ever want to lose that friendship. It's too valuable to me, to us. But, Sammy, I'm at the end of my residency, and you know what the stress is like. I'm struggling to hang on as it is. This mess you're in could take months, even years. Besides, I'm married to my job, and you need someone who is going to give you more time than I could. You will hate my job, and you will make me hate it before too long."

He touches her lips to cut her off. "As much as I hate hearing it, you're right; we would have just postponed the inevitable. You are a wise woman, Doctor McCall. My heart will ache, you know."

"Only until you meet someone. Then it will become very obvious what we didn't have." After a long pause, Linda asks, "Did you stop in and see the kids while you were waiting?" Sam shakes his head no. Linda answers that with, "You know you're still the best volunteer, friend, and advocate they have."

"I know, but I'm too much of a mess and they would pick up on it immediately. Then how would I explain it to them? I think I should wait until this whole thing blows over."

"They will still love you, no matter what they hear, and they will always believe in you," Linda tells him.

"I know. I just have to be by myself for a while. If you need to get in touch, I will be at Rick's while he's gone for the summer."

"That's a good idea. The ranch is so secluded; no one will bother you up there. By the way, I believe Job makes out pretty well at the end."

Sam smiles for the first time as he responds, "That's right. I guess he does, at that."

He walks to the door, then turns to look at Linda. He lifts his hand, says goodbye without his voice, and then disappears out the door. Linda then takes a deep breath, walks to the same door, and watches him walk down the hall, feeling the same ache he does.

———————

Sam walks slowly down the steps of the hospital, pausing slightly on each step. Finally stepping onto the sidewalk, he checks his watch: ten thirty-two p.m. He looks around, hoping for something to distract him from the difficult conversation he just had. He gives up and heads to his car around the block.

He hears a commotion as he approaches a bar directly behind the hospital. He sees it's still called The Red Light Bar, one he frequented years earlier. Stepping through the door, he sees only a couple of people sitting at the bar. The noise is coming from a highly contested pool game in the back. Sam orders himself a beer and sits on a nearby stool to take in the action. A few minutes later, the game ends and the gang comes up to the bar, with some still a little hot from the game.

On the overhead big screen, the clips of past football games are interrupted by a news bulletin.

"Good evening, I am Donna Dean, and this is a *Channel 7 Eyewitness News* break. There have been more developments in the Chantell saga. The famed attorney Gordon Osborn has been hired by Sam Milton, the man accused of the attempted rape of Miss León. Within the past hour, Gordon Osborn has released a statement saying, 'We have a video taken at the time of the incident showing my client to be innocent of all accusations brought against him by Miss Chantell León. Now, due to the deliberate malice intended toward my client, through the inflammatory statements made by Chantell on *The Tonight Show*, and the resulting damage done to my client, both in terms of economic and social status, as well as severe mental anguish caused by the extreme notoriety of the case, it is our intention to bring about a suit against Miss León, the producers of *The*

Tonight Show, along with Iconic Records and Universal. This suit will be for the damages perpetrated against Mr. Milton by all related parties in excess of fifty million dollars, with the exact amount to be determined at a later time. Thank you.' "

The shock on Sam's face is quickly replaced with anger as he continues to watch. The anger is soon replaced with fear as he notices that everyone else in the bar is also watching, including the rowdy types from the pool game. Sam leans more into the shadows as he watches a news anchor interview Chantell.

"For a further look at this developing story, we have Sharon van Owen, who is standing by in Santa Monica with Chantell."

"With me, as you said, is Chantell León. Chantell, can you tell us your thoughts on the suit Gordon Osborn has brought about?"

"Well, Sharon," Chantell says with nervousness in her voice, "right now I am still kind of stunned at this whole thing. I just can't believe this man would try to rape me in public—with all of those witnesses—and then turn around and sue me! Can this really be happening?" Her voice breaks as she turns from the camera to wipe a tear from her face. Turning back to the camera, she continues, "I thought this whole ugly mess was over with, but then I found out the police didn't even hold him. Now, he's out to get me again—this time with a lawsuit! What did I ever do to anyone?" With tears flowing, she breaks away, leaving the reporter to finish the interview with someone else.

Meanwhile, the bar patrons are becoming increasingly more vocal about the telecast. Sam retreats farther into the shadows.

Sharon continues the interview with Chantell's representative. "With me now is Mr. Jacob Tannenbaum, Chantell's attorney. Mr. Tannenbaum, tell me more about this videotape Sam Milton's lawyer claims to have."

"We have not seen any video except those already reviewed, and according to the police, they have no knowledge of any other tape. And personally, I think if there was one, it would have shown up by now. Therefore, I think this mysterious video is fabricated."

"What do you mean?" Sharon asks in response.

"I believe, knowing Gordon Osborn's reputation, that he is just trying to get more publicity—and trampling on Miss León's reputation to do it. This also shows what type of person this Sam Milton really is. He's someone who is in it just for personal gain, and he's willing to hire a man like Osborn to get it."

The reporter turns back to the camera. "Well, that pretty well sums up the feelings from this end. This is Sharon van Owen for Channel 7 Witness News."

Someone at the bar yells out, "Can you believe that Milton character? What a scumbag!"

Another yells, "Yeah, what's his problem anyway? That girl never hurt anyone in her life, and he goes out and does that to her."

This big drunk at the end of the bar slams his empty mug down. "Well, I think something should be done about this, don't you?"

Sam gets nervous and starts looking around for an easy exit.

"So, what should we do?" another one asks, trying to keep things stirred up.

"I don't know. We'll have to find that little rapist," the big drunk says as Sam slowly moves behind him, heading for the door. Suddenly, the man swings around and catches Sam's arm, pulling him up close to his face. "So, what do you think we should do with him?"

Sam stands stunned, unable to move for what seems like an eternity. Then with all of the boldness he can muster, he yells out, "Let's hang him!"

The man continues to look at Sam for an excruciatingly long moment. Then, with a drunken lisp, he yells, "Yeah, that's what we'll do!" He then slaps Sam on the back hard and turns to the others and continues to yell, "And we should string up that jackass lawyer of his, too!" The others scream and yell in support as Sam slowly moves past them and slips out the door.

Sam turns into a gas station and brings the Barracuda to an abrupt stop in front of a payphone. He jumps out, slamming the door with one hand while picking up the receiver with the other. Fumbling through his wallet, he finds a business card and punches in each number. He waits. After two rings, a woman answers, "Osborn residence. May I help you?"

"Yes, I would like to speak to Gordon, please."

"I'm sorry. He's retired for the night. May I have him call you back?"

"Tell him this is Sam Milton, and I want to speak to him *now!*" Sam waits, banging his fist on the glass.

"Yes, Mr. Milton?" Gordon says.

"You arrogant scum-sucking ambulance chaser! What in the hell do you think you're doing? I specifically said not to do anything until I said so! I barely escaped a bar with my life! The whole country is out to get me, thanks to you!"

"Calm down, Sam. I had to play our hand. Someone seeking to destroy the tape offered our friend five times what we offered. And he would've taken it had I not gone public when I did. Besides, all of this publicity is helping our case."

"Well, it isn't going to help me one bit if I'm dead! And, in case you don't get it, my death won't help you either—though I'm sure you could still find a way to make a buck off it. So, from now on, you don't do a thing without my say-so! Get it? Not . . . a . . . thing!"

Gordon Osborn tries to calm him down, but Sam slams the receiver back into its cradle, jumps back into the car, and smokes the tires as he leaves.

Eventually, Sam slows down. As he waits for another light, he taps the steering wheel with this two index fingers. He sees another payphone up ahead. He jumps out and punches in a number.

"*Eyewitness News* desk. Jackeline Drier speaking."

"This is Sam Milton. I would like to speak with Donna Dean."

"Can I ask what this is regarding?"

"What? Do you ever listen to your own newscast? I said this is Sam Milton, the one who pulled the top off Chantell."

After a long pause, Sam hears, "Sam Milton, it is so good to finally hear from you. This is Donna Dean. Can I put you on the air live?"

"What? No!"

"Then how can I help you?"

"We met briefly outside my house the other day. I'm sorry I was so rude."

"Reporters get that all the time, Mr. Milton. What would you like to talk about?"

"This whole thing was an accident—a simple accident and nothing more."

"That is not what the fifty-seven eyewitnesses we interviewed said, Mr. Milton."

"That's because they didn't see it at the right angle. Anyway, the police also came to the conclusion it was an accident, and that's why they released me. Now, however, I wish the police had not released me. Then, I could've been tried and allowed to prove my innocence. Instead, I have already been tried and convicted by the media."

"We talked to the police, Mr. Milton. They simply said they didn't have enough evidence to hold you. They never said you were wrongly accused or that this was all just an accident or misunderstanding."

After another slight pause, Donna speaks again, but Sam cuts her off. "I'm sorry, Donna; I get very nervous speaking. But let me ask you this: If the police didn't have enough evidence to hold me, then why do you have enough evidence to convict me?"

"We are not judges, Mr. Milton. We are reporters, and we report what we see and hear."

"And, of course, you don't sensationalize anything, right?"

"I'm sure you don't want to spend this time arguing, Mr. Milton, so what can I do for you?"

"I would just like to say something. I have no doubt that Chantell León is the sweetest person in the world, but we saw the exact same thing from two different perspectives, and because of it, suddenly the nicest person in the world isn't so nice anymore! And when she isn't being so nice, you give her a microphone and a TV camera. She then rains absolute hell down on an innocent person. She screams, asking who will protect her, and the world picks up clubs and comes looking for me. Let me ask you, who is going to protect me from her? And let me ask you something else, Donna. Would any of this have gotten so much press if I were black and Chantell wasn't pretty and famous?"

"Mr. Milton, you are Caucasian, yet *you* are going to play the race card?"

Straining to think quickly, he responds, "You didn't answer my question, Donna, and you know the answer to my question would be no, but you would never say it because you would be thrown off TV! Biases and prejudice can go in both directions, Donna, and it is just as wrong either way. I . . . I . . . I guess in some way I am privileged to know what it is like to be wrongly convicted, not to be protected because of my race. Maybe I should start teaching high school; this would make a great example for a current affairs class—if I live through it."

"So, let me get this straight, Mr. Milton. You're saying this is all racially motivated, and you're looking for help in fighting back against Chantell?"

Sam physically sinks at hearing her question. "Miss Dean, I just made a horrible mistake talking to you. That's not what I'm saying at all, and I see you only seek to misunderstand me. I'm just saying it was a simple but embarrassing accident, and if it had been played down, it would have gone away with a simple apology. No one would have gotten hurt. But you aren't going to let it go peacefully, Donna. No, you're going to play it up and maybe even sensationalize it to get more people tuning in. You don't care what is true; you just want a hot story. So, go say anything you want, Donna. I don't give a rip anymore."

Sam hangs up as she tries to talk back. He screams out, "Dear God, why did I ever make that call? And why did you let me make that call? Come on already!"

Chantell, along with her mother and her brother Lawrence, are finishing watching a recorded tape of Donna Dean's on-air take of her phone conversation with Samuel Milton: "Well, the only people who are going to stick up for Sam Milton are members of the KKK. This is Donna Dean reporting. Now, back to our regularly scheduled telecast."

Chantell turns the sound off her big screen and yells, "Can you believe what that Sam Milton guy said? He thinks he's the victim of discrimination because he's white! And he's asking the Klan for protection from me? The gall of that man!"

"Calm down, Chantell," her mother says. "This is Donna Dean we're talking about. She is more ruthless than I am on my talk show. She will say *anything* to get a rating. She's maligned you before and more than once—especially when you started dating Dwain."

Chantell smiles for the first time tonight. "Yeah, I can't believe the way you went after her. I thought you actually liked Dwain for a moment."

"I'm not going to let her rip my daughter apart, even if I agree with her that you're acting stupid."

"Mother!"

Angelica looks past her daughter toward the TV and gives a command. "Quick, turn up the sound."

"This is Donna Dean again. As predicted, after reporting Sam Milton was seeking support for his fight against Chantell León, several white supremacist groups are offering protection for Mr. Milton. This includes an offer from the present leader of the KKK, who is offering his personal support. This turn of events has sparked violent protests in several cities, including Baton Rouge, where fourteen protesters were sent to neighboring hospitals. Here in Los Angeles, outside the Laugh Factory on Sunset Boulevard, an argument over the León /Milton controversy turned into an all-out brawl. Police arrested four and have shut down the entire block until things calm down."

Angelica reaches over and turns off the TV. Turning to her daughter, she says, "Okay, Chantell, you have to make a statement before this turns into an all-out riot."

Lawrence scoffs, "I wouldn't call a fist fight on Sunset a riot, Momma."

Suddenly, the front door opens and Chantell's brother Eddie runs in, yelling, "What's going on? The news vans are piling up outside! Malcom is keeping them outside the gate, but they are demanding an interview."

"Good!" Chantell yells. "I would love to tell everyone what I think of this guy. Lawrence, call Dwain. He and I will light a real fire under this thing."

"I am right behind you, Chantell," Lawrence says, picking up the phone.

Angelica interrupts, "Lawrence, you are going to do nothing of the sort!" Chantell is about to protest, but her mother tells her point-blank, "Chantell, I have lived through too many riots, and no kids of mine are going to be responsible for starting one. So, come on, Chantell, you are going to give an interview and plead that things calm down before this escalates."

"But, Momma!"

"Now, Chantell!"

Sam continues to drive the streets of LA, through downtown and the surrounding areas. He drives slowly, slumped in the car seat and deep in thought. His only movement is the slow shifting of his eyes as he looks at one depressing sight after another: police writing tickets; drunks staggering along the sidewalk; a couple walking several feet from each other, obviously in the midst of a fight. All of this creates within Sam an atmosphere of sustained depression that keeps getting thicker and heavier.

He eventually finds himself at Griffith Park, a place that has always given him solace. He turns on the radio, which is set on a news station, and after listening to the sports, weather, traffic, and a commercial for Forest Lawn, he hears the news anchor say, "We now take you live to the scene of news and to our man in the street, Jeff Symon."

"Barry, I'm standing on the fifty-eight hundred block of Palm Street, here in the city of Camarillo. I am in front of the house rented by Samuel Milton. Until a few days ago, this was a quiet and peaceful street. Just moments ago, however, that peace was shattered with the sound of breaking glass. Fans of Chantell León, incensed by the revelation of an impending lawsuit against her and Mr. Milton's plea for support from the KKK, gathered in front of the house. Things escalated and rocks were thrown through the front window. The police moved in and had to use pepper spray to disperse the crowd. Two were injured, and one man was arrested.

"A sad note to add to this already concerning situation—a small gray cat belonging to Mr. Milton was hit by flying glass. A neighbor took the cat to a clinic, where it later succumbed to its injuries. The man who was arrested is being held to see if Mr. Milton wants to press charges.

"So far, things have gotten back to normal, both here on Palm and throughout the rest of Los Angeles, after considerable pleading from Chantell. Mr. Milton was not available for comment."

Sam hits the off button with the force of his pent-up anger, and the radio goes silent. His eyes are glazed as he turns into a pullout that overlooks the city. With the Griffith Observatory in the background, he shuts off the engine and sits staring out at muted lights caused by an overcast sky. Then, looking up into the endless gray, he yells, "What the hell is going on? Are you finished yet? Or is there something else you're going to take from me? What do you want anyway?" He waits a moment, looking up to the heavens as if expecting an answer. None comes. He shakes his head from side to side, starts the car, and drives back down the hill.

8

Ending It

Later heading west on the 101 Freeway, Sam stares straight ahead, his eyes breaking away periodically to check the mirrors. With a glance at the speedometer, he notices he is doing sixty. He glances at his watch as he passes under a street light: a quarter past two. He gives a small sigh and resumes his blank stare off into the distance. He's been driving most of the night, feeling hopeless and adrift. He drives because he doesn't know what else to do.

Sam drops his speed a bit and tightens his grip on the steering wheel as he cringes at the painful events relentlessly passing through his brain. He winces as the anguish mounts, spewing profanities as he hits the steering wheel with his fist. He sits up in the seat to readjust himself, trying in vain to break the cycle of rumination that has owned him the past few days.

As he drives the Barracuda under an overpass, he looks to his left, noticing the large concrete pillars supporting the road above. For a split second, he has a vision of turning the car directly into one of the columns. He shakes the thought from his mind as a speeding car cuts him off, trying to make the off ramp ahead of him.

As the car disappears down the ramp, Sam fights to regain his composure, admonishing himself, "Don't do anything stupid, Sam!" He slows his pace, not fully trusting himself to resist giving into the speed and losing control.

Farther down the road, the wincing continues as the agonizing thoughts and images begin again. As he passes under another overpass and again notices the concrete pillars in the center of the median, he also notices the metal guardrail around the columns, placed there to prevent the kind of accident Sam is considering. He gives a big sigh of relief. "Well, that takes care of that, doesn't it?" he says, wiping sweat from his forehead. He drives on with a more relaxed expression as he speeds the car back up to sixty.

It is not long, however, before his peaceful expression is replaced with one of agony. He shakes his head back and forth, trying to dislodge the bad memory of him desperately trying to grab someone before he falls. Sweat is pouring down his face as he visualizes their hands slipping past each other. Sam screams, "Why him, Lord? It was my fault, not his! His wife was right—it should have been me who died! His whole family, Lord—his whole family died because of me! I can't forgive you for letting that happen! Do you hear me, God? I will never forgive you for that one!" He drops his head down low, taking deep breaths, willing his body to regulate, to rest.

Lifting his head, he pulls down the sun visor as he drives under another streetlight. He looks at the picture clipped on the back of this visor. In the short glimpse of light, Sam sees a happier time, his arm around his Linda. They are both holding rags while standing in front of his polished Barracuda. Passing under another light, Sam reads the note written on the bottom of the photo: "The day I finished restoring my '68 Barracuda." Sam sighs and thinks, *The car is wrecked, my girlfriend left me, and Little Paws is dead! Not to mention, the whole world hates my guts for hurting someone I really like.* Now, Sam's expression changes from depression to that of dread.

He slows the car again and passes under the Malibu Canyon overpass. Far in the distance, a freeway sign can be seen, showing the exits ahead. On the bottom of the sign he reads, "Kanan Dume Road, 3 miles." Suddenly, he has a clear memory of driving under the Kanan overpass two days before. He remembers that the guardrails in the median had been taken down for construction, leaving the concrete pillars unprotected.

The speedometer now shows forty-five miles per hour, but a strange, dissociated stare appears on Sam's face. His eyes begin to twitch rapidly, as if all the agonizing memories are hitting him at once. Absorbed in thought, his foot lets up on the gas pedal as the speed drops under forty. Sam stares down at the front of his crumpled hood and back up again at the picture on the sun visor.

He takes the picture in his hand and holds it up to the steady stream of wind coming over the windshield. He holds it there for a moment and then lets it go. Grabbing the steering wheel tightly, he leans into the seat and then throws his shoulders back and stomps on the gas.

The acceleration pushes him farther into the seat as the car gains speed. The speedometer moves past fifty, then sixty, then seventy, and beyond. It's only seconds before he is passing under the sign saying, "Kanan Dume Road, 2 ¼ miles." He moves the car into the next lane, closer to the median.

The speedometer passes one hundred twenty, but Sam isn't looking. His hands are cold and clammy, and the sweat makes it harder to keep a tight grip on the wheel. His anxiety builds. He moves to put a hand on his pounding chest but quickly puts it back on the wheel. He tries to swallow, but his throat is dry. The powerful V8 engine pushes the car as the slow drip of the radiator becomes a steady stream. The Barracuda is now doing one hundred thirty miles per hour.

"God, don't let me do this! Please, God, don't let me do this," he cries out. He holds the speed steady and waits a moment, as if to see if something might happen. Nothing does. He steps harder on the accelerator and moves over one more lane. The car streaks pass another sign: "Kanan Dume Road, 1 ½ miles." He glances at his speed, one hundred forty-two miles per hour, and quickly calculates he has less than a minute to go as the tack goes well above the red line, making the engine hum like a sewing machine. The temperature gauge rises as he moves one lane closer to the columns.

As the one-mile marker approaches, Sam notices that everything seems to be moving more slowly than he thinks it should. The sign passes overhead, and everything gets strangely quiet. A deep sense of peace comes over him, as if he is doing the right thing. The fear passes as he moves to the lane nearest the center median. With his foot locked hard on the accelerator, he can see, far off in the distance, the lights on the overpass of Kanan Dume Road and the construction lights below.

The strange calm surrounding Sam continues to intensify to the point that he is oblivious to what is happening around him. He just stares at the approaching overpass and the supporting columns that await him. Then, he hears an audible voice, which sounds much like his own: "What will Linda tell the kids in the cancer ward?"

Sam, not worrying about where the voice came from, slowly repeats the words to himself, his melancholy expression changing suddenly to that of shock. "The kids! What will the kids think when they hear the news? I could never put them through that!"

He takes his foot off the gas as the speedometer reads one hundred sixty-five miles per hour. He grabs the steering wheel tightly as the reality of his speed finally hits him. A vibration comes from the engine. Sam looks at the gauges and realizes the temperature gauge has gone off the scale.

The vibration worsens as a pushrod breaks free from the engine block and shoots through the hood like a rifle shot, followed by two more in quick succession. The engine then explodes, causing the left cylinder head to slam against the fire wall, severing the hydraulic lines and cracking the engine mount. The head finally wedges itself in the steering linkage, forcing the car to turn sharply to the left. The Barracuda slams up against the concrete K-rail.

Sam tries to lean to the right to avoid the sparks coming from the mirror as it rubs against the concrete. The mirror breaks free and shoots by Sam, grazing him on the temple.

The force of the impact against the guardrail causes the cracked engine mount to break, allowing the engine to thrash back and forth wildly until it breaks free all together, dropping down to the road and taking the transmission with it. Sam has his hand on the shift lever as it suddenly rips from his hand and disappears through the floor. The engine and the transmission hit the road and are forced back under the car, ripping out the passenger floor and center console as they continue back, eventually colliding with the rear end. The force shoots the backend of the car upwards as the entire drive train is torn from the body and scattered in pieces across the freeway.

With no brakes and no steering, Sam stares straight ahead, helpless. It is obvious he will hit the pillars before he is able to stop. He is about to close his eyes and succumb to the inevitable when up ahead he sees several yellow safety barrels placed in front of the concrete columns to absorb the impact of an accident. He braces himself as the front of the car hits the first barrel. Both barrel and the water within shoot straight up into the air as the car careens into the remaining barrels. A wall of water overtakes the car as the final inertia is absorbed, bringing the car to a complete stop. One of the barrels lands on the road above, bouncing and rolling as water rains down on Sam. He looks up to see that the car has stopped just inches from the concrete columns.

Sam looks around and checks himself out to see if he is still in one piece. His only injury is the blood running down his cheek from where the mirror hit him. He reaches into the glovebox for a Kleenex and slowly pulls himself out of the seat. Stepping over the missing console and floor, he jumps over the passenger door and collapses when he hits the concrete. As he tries to stand, he can feel that his legs are weak and visibly shaking.

Walking a few feet, Sam slowly regains his composure. He turns to see a car stopping on the other side of the median. The people exit their car and look around for a way to get across the K-rail. Sam sees the flashing red lights of a police car approaching. He staggers across the freeway and disappears out of sight.

The police car stops, and two officers get out. One runs over to the car as the other shines his flashlight over the carnage—first on what's left of the car itself, then on the yellow barrels scattered over the road. He then traces the red streak on the guardrail back down the freeway littered with Barracuda parts.

"Hey, sarge, we can't find a body anywhere, and half of the inside of the car is gone. Do you think the driver might have fallen through the floor?"

"Looks like it."

"Should I call for the ambulance?"

"Better make it the coroner," says the sergeant as he walks back down the freeway, expecting to find the worst.

The door to a modestly elegant condo opens wide and in prances Carol, Chantell's personal assistant. She looks around to find Chantell sitting on the patio, petting her cat. Walking onto the patio, Carol throws the morning paper she had been carrying on the table and leans on the patio's railing. "Isn't it a wonderful day today?" she croons, turning to face Chantell. Carol asks her, "Did you read the paper this morning?"

Without looking up, Chantell answers, "I heard about it."

"It kind of looks like our little problem is over with, doesn't it?"

Chantell continues to pet her cat, without looking up.

Frustrated with Chantell's lack of response, Carol demands, "What's with you? I figured you would be relieved about the whole thing."

"Did they ever find him? His body, I mean."

"No, they never did. But, even if the guy is still alive, an attempted suicide shows he's guilty about something. How much do you want to bet we never hear from him again?"

Still not looking up, Chantell says softly, "They killed his cat."

"Hey, you have some really devoted fans. They're a little overzealous, mind you, but I am sure they never meant to hurt anyone. Is that what has you so upset?"

Chantell sighs. "I don't know. Knowing you had a part in someone's death just sort of changes your perspective on things, that's all."

"Look girl, you didn't kill him. He was just a jerk who killed himself, and that's all I want to hear about it."

"What if they find out he really was hit by the soundstage door? What if it was all an accident? I will have ruined this man's life—and that's if he is still alive. My God, Carol, what if I killed him! How do you expect me to feel then?"

"For God's sake, Chantell. We have no proof it was an accident or that this man is some innocent victim. He hired Gordon Osborn! Even if they do have a tape of the incident, which I doubt, I guarantee you it will be blurry or cut and pieced together. They have no evidence, nothing to make us believe Mr. Milton deserves our pity! No one will believe Gordon and his tape anyway.

"Besides, let's say he was hit by the door. It was still an accident. You and sixty-five others saw the exact same thing. No one could possibly blame you for anything you did or said in interpreting the event as aggression."

"What about the guy's mother? Do you think she will say it's all just a misunderstanding? Do you think she will hold me faultless in her son's death?"

"Chantell León, for one thing, we don't even know if he's dead! And, no one believes what he did to you was an accident—not you, not me, not the sixty-five tourists on that bus, and surely not the rest of the world."

"Well, things don't feel so cut and dry when someone might be dead," Chantell counters, but she can see that Carol is about to explode again, so she waves her hands in surrender, trying to avoid more chastisement. "I just pray he's not dead." She then says softly, "And I hope it was an accident."

Carol loses it. "Now, listen to me! What if the tabloids get wind of the statement you just made? They would have a field day. I can just see the headline now: 'Chantell Deeply Depressed over Possibly Killing an Innocent Man'! You would be giving that scumbag Gordon Osborn the prize of his life!"

"All right already. I get your point."

"Besides, he probably isn't dead, or they would have found a body at the crash site. He's just hiding somewhere, licking his wounds. Now, it's time to get ready. You've got the meeting at Iconic with your agent and Dwain to go over the song lineup for your next album." Carol drops the paper in the trashcan as she walks back into the house from the patio with Chantell reluctantly following behind.

<hr>

At the meeting, Chantell is seated at a large oval table. Next to her is Dwain Dubray, an intimidating, streetwise black man in his late twenties—both Chantell's boyfriend and an artist in his own right. He's wearing a T-shirt with a picture of himself facing straight on with his head cocked to the left. His right hand is held out with his wrist cocked, holding a switchblade. Below his image is his stage name, "Slash." Though he is holding Chantell's hand, he sits slouching, his body slanted away from Chantell.

On either side of Chantell and Dwain are their agents, Marcus Powley and Drake Stanton. Heading up the meeting is Jeffery Benson, an older black man in his late fifties. Though casually dressed, he exudes an air of confidence that commands respect. On his right is Blake Jackson, a young, handsome mixed-race man, who's trying to gain respect by wearing an Armani suit and a Rolex

Presidential. On Jeffery Benson's left is Ms. Turner, a prim woman in her forties, and on her right is Orrin Machen, looking very much like the lawyer he is. Between the two groups is a secretary, a male assistant, and a very young intern.

Jeffery Benson speaks first. "Thank you for coming, Miss León. I know you have had a very frightening experience, and we are all impressed with your attendance here today. I want to thank Dwain for sticking around after our meeting with him. He has been gracious enough to offer another artist's perspective during the first round of selections for your next album.

"Now, next to me is Ms. Turner, head of our department of sales and demographics, which basically means she's in charge of tracking sales statistics—what age group buys what records and how many each group buys. So, Ms. Turner, please give us your findings relating to Chantell's past album sales."

"Good morning, Miss León, and accept my condolences for what you have been through. I can only imagine the horror you must have felt when attacked."

"Thank you, Ms. Turner. It was rather graphic."

"Anyway, down to business. Miss León, your debut album, *All of Me*, sold over ten million copies, the most ever sold by any female artist. As of last week, your *Uptown Hot* album had sold six million. However, with recent developments involving you and Mr. Milton—and the worldwide publicity that's coming from it—sales of that album have jumped to seven million, which means you sold over a million albums in less than three days. All of this came after we had concluded that sales had run their course and started slacking off."

Marcus Powley, sitting next to Chantell, asks, "Are you suggesting, Ms. Turner, that my client should send Mr. Milton a thank you note for helping your company sell her album?"

"Call it what you may, but the truth is, if this anomaly can last for three more weeks, we predict *Uptown Hot* will outsell *All of Me* by a half-million copies."

Jeffery Benson interjects, "Chantell, this is unheard of, even with us giving in to two God-positive songs per unit! No one can hold a candle to you. You are doing something no one will be able to repeat for decades—if ever! Unfortunately, history has shown that after this kind of success with the first two, the third album drops completely off the charts due to boredom. So, without a major change in the music, lyrics, or general style, your next album could very well be your last. In most cases, the third album is the hardest to produce, so it is vital that we get the mix right. Let me be frank, Miss León, you are poised to explode or fizzle out. Ms. Turner will give you the reasons for my assessment."

"Miss León, you have a huge fan base; however, demographics play a major part in accounting for your current success. We need to keep these demographics in mind when predicting future success. Let me explain. For your first album, 70 percent of buyers were sixteen years old and younger, mostly white, with the other 30 percent of buyers equally mixed among races, from seventeen to forty-two. Your second album scored a more diverse following as the average age of the buyer was twenty-two. I know it is only a six-year difference from the majority who bought your first album, but it makes a huge difference in regards to your longevity as an artist."

Jeffery speaks up again. "This is why the type of record selections for your next album are so important, so I am going to let Mr. Jackson be the heavy. He will explain what is required to keep up the momentum so you don't fizzle out."

"Good morning, Miss León. It's nice to see you again. I hope you have forgotten our little spat from the last time we met."

"It was a little more than a spat, but I'm good with it. Business is business."

"I am very glad to hear it. The real reason we are all here, Miss León, is to keep this empire of yours from collapsing."

"I didn't know it was in danger. I would think that seven times platinum is far from rock bottom," Chantell sneers.

"Let me say it this way: As Ms. Turner explained, your first album had an average demographic of sixteen, which means half of that age bracket was fifteen or below. It also means your music caters more to kids than adults. Your videos are played on Disney and Nickelodeon more than MTV. Is that the age group you are looking to reach?"

Chantell shakes her head no.

"I didn't think so. Kids will keep buying no matter what. Adults will get bored very quickly, as your second album sales suggest. In other words, you need to cater to them and sing adult songs to adults, with adult themes."

"I sing love songs, Mr. Jackson. Isn't that adult enough? I don't hear anyone complaining about it."

"Adults don't complain, Miss León. They simply stop buying. May I be honest?"

Chantell affirms his request by the lifting of her hand.

"You sing about wanting true love and being in love, but you never touch on what love really costs—or of the heartache it takes to get it. Or what about the whole betrayal thing, or what it feels like when love dies? You did get a good uptick in sales from sympathy for your run-in with Mr. Milton, but that's a fluke. The only reason you got above three hundred million was due to the person sitting next to you."

This comment causes Dwain to hold up Chantell's hand, and she gives him a smile.

"Together, your duet stayed at number one for three weeks. Yet, even 'Forbidden Love' only talks about what would happen if you had an affair—nothing about actually having one. To be blunt, Miss León, your most sexually explicit songs still sound like you're dreaming about Prince Charming, not getting down and dirty with him. Frankly, Miss León, you sing like you are still a—"

Chantell asserts herself by standing up and yelling, "A *what*?"

Blake Jackson thinks a moment and continues, "Like someone in need of experience."

"Mr. Jackson!" Marcus, Chantell's agent, shouts. "Is this what you had Chantell come down here for? To have her virtue dragged through the mud as if it is a crime to be sweet and innocent—especially after what she has just been through in the public arena? I would suggest, Mr. Benson, that you please explain to your young protégé here what it means to treat your most valuable recording artist with some respect, or I will have Miss León's attorney speak to your attorney, Orrin Machen!"

"Calm down, Marcus," Mr. Benson says before turning to look at Blake. "I promise you, I will be taking Mr. Jackson to the woodshed for berating my best contract artist in front of all of these people. However, though I am extremely incensed on how he said it, I don't disagree with what Mr. Jackson said. The truth is, Chantell, what my young upstart is trying to suggest is that you need to ramp up your game. Again, my apologies for the way my associate has spoken to you, especially with what you have been through, but the truth of his comments remains. I will have my secretary, Miss Pence, schedule a follow-up meeting in three weeks."

Blake raises his hand to say, "If you please, Mr. Benson, I would like to apologize to Miss León in private."

"If that is okay with you, Chantell."

Chantell nods.

"Please keep it civil, Mr. Jackson, I am already paying Orrin too much already. Okay, remember our meeting three weeks from today, people. Good day."

The door closes, leaving Blake and Chantell alone. "Okay, Blake, you have my ear. But before we go on, I would like to ask you a question. When you decided to run my panties up a flagpole just now in regards to my sexual experience, how much of that was the business of selling records and how much of that was because I spurned you?"

Blake walks over to face her directly before he responds, "Every last word was pure business, and I will swear that on the precious Bible you are forever clinging to. Now, I have a question for you. What's with you and Dwain? I can't think of a more mismatched couple on the planet than you two."

"I'm not sure. I know I'm attracted to his confidence and his persona. Maybe I'm tired of being placed so high on some stupid pedestal that guys won't even touch me. Dwain may speak his mind, but he treats me with respect."

"You ever listened to his lyrics?"

"Not every man is what he sings about."

"Are you what you sing about?"

Chantell remains silent.

"Take my word for it; he is exactly what he sings about."

"I thought this was just about selling records," Chantell says in protest.

"That is exactly what it is. Can you imagine the catastrophe I would have on my hands if that guy finally nails you and then dumps you? You would be sitting in a padded room right next to Samuel Milton. Mr. Milton only took off your top. Dwain Dubray is looking to take something far more personal. I can guarantee you, after he's taken it, you won't last two weeks with him. Come on,

Chantell, you can't be this naïve! His most famous recording is 'I'm Gonna Pop Her—' "

Blake doesn't finish saying the title before Chantell throws up her hands, yelling, "I get it! I get it!"

"Do you even know what the term means?"

"It is a crass street term for taking a woman's virginity." Blake raises his eyebrows, to which Chantell answers with, "I have three brothers, remember, and we all went to public school."

"Nevertheless, it's obvious you haven't succumbed, or he wouldn't be within ten miles of you. I think the only reason you hang with him is because you've discovered that purity isn't very exciting. You're attracted to him because he's dangerous."

Chantell looks away, causing Blake to relent. "Chantell, I really don't like being mean or callous, but let me ask you again, do you want your songs on the Disney Channel or MTV?"

Chantell is looking at the floor as she answers softly, "I want them on MTV."

"Then write and record songs that belong on MTV. Every great recording artist has had to make sacrifices. You're no exception. Just think about it."

9

The Setup

━━━━

A rusty old '56 Ford pickup is parked in the elegant Larson driveway. A bruised and battered Sam is walking with a limp up to the truck, carrying a skill saw and a drill. He stops to look for a place to put them in the overloaded truck bed. His laborer walks up behind him, carrying more tools, and Sam comments, "I think that's all from the garage, Pasqual. Is there anything left in the house?"

"No, Mr. Sam. I think we got everything," Pasqual says in broken English. "Do you need anything more?"

"No, I guess that's all of it." Sam looks for a place to put the last of the tools. He gives up and throws them in the cab of the truck. He turns around and shakes Pasqual's hand. "Thank you for all of your help."

"No problem, sir. We will see you real soon again. You will see, sir."

"You're an eternal optimist, Pasqual." His friend gives him a look of confusion, to which Sam responds with, "Op-ti-mist . . . ¿Comprende? . . . Never mind."

They shake hands again, and as Sam turns toward the truck, he sees Johnny Carson coming through the gate.

"Well, well, the dead walks."

"Hi, Mr. Carson, how are you doing?"

"The dead speaks?"

"No, not really. I'm just a figment of your imagination," Sam says, reaching out for Johnny's hand.

"Quite a solid figment. And it's Johnny, not Mr. Carson! How many times do I have to tell you that?"

"Sorry for the formality. It just feels like I am two inches tall and looking up at everybody right now."

"Some of the papers have you listed as dead from an apparent suicide. Others have you hiding in a mental institution in the Valley. But, my favorite report indicates you've been seen having lunch with Elvis in a small diner in Duluth."

"Well, that just proves they never get it right. We were having breakfast." They both laugh. Sam then says, "I bet the tabloids are having a field day with all of this."

"Only if you call the *Daily News* and the *Times* tabloids. So, where have you been, and what are your plans?"

"Since I have been kicked out of my house, I've been staying at a friend's ranch in the hills off of Decker Canyon; he's in Alaska panning for gold. As for my clients—the Langstons are taking Miss León's side. However, they did say they would keep quiet about my leaving. So, I guess it all works out."

"So, what happens now?" inquires Johnny.

"Well, according to my lawyer, the world-renowned G. W. Osborn—" Sam says facetiously.

Johnny interrupts, "Gordon Osborn? How did you meet up with the likes of him?"

"It's a long story; believe me. Anyway, according to Osborn, 'Her lawyers are going to put me in a hole so deep that I'll never get out.' I expect that to be true, so I will finish up a few things here and start over up north somewhere."

"It doesn't sound to me like they are going to put you in a hole. It sounds to me like you are going to crawl in on your own volition."

Sam shrugs and responds, "What can I say? I don't like fighting. I'm not very good at it."

"What's this all about anyway? You don't seem to be the type to assault someone famous in broad daylight. In the dark, maybe, but not in broad daylight," Johnny says with a chuckle. "Besides, I have heard everyone else's opinion on the subject, but I don't think anyone has heard yours."

"Well, don't get any ideas. I've had all the publicity I can handle for one lifetime, thank you."

"No, no, I'm sure you have. Besides, I kind of let *Geraldo* and *Donahue* have that slice of programming. However, since I had a part in all of this, I think that the least I can do is hear it firsthand from you. And who knows? We might come up with a better way for you to fight than in the headlines. I do have a few connections in this town, you know. I've got the time if you do."

"It looks like I've got all the time in the world, and it probably would do me some good to talk about it. When and where?" Sam asks.

"How about my house when you're finished here, say ten minutes?"

"Sounds good to me. See you in ten."

Sam, hunched over and nursing a famous green bottle of sparking water, sits in a vast contemporary living room lit by a late afternoon sun. He is on the edge of a long white couch, underneath a massive skylight. Seated across from him is Johnny, holding a glass of red wine.

Sam tells Johnny his side of the story. "That's when the door burst open, and I got hit upside the head. I remember falling backward and trying to catch my balance. I tried to grab the edge of the door and missed. The rest, as they say, is history."

"Well, one thing is for sure: You know how to make a lasting impression on someone."

Sam laughs and looks down at his beer. "Yeah, that seems to definitely be a part of my personality."

"Couldn't this have been taken care of with a simple explanation and an apology?" Johnny inquires.

"It all happened so fast that I never had a chance to say anything. By the time I had the chance, some investigative reporter had dug up my past and found something else that, let's just say, until explained, assassinated my character."

"Is that the bit about you and some fifteen-year-old girl? Can you explain that? The news media never gave any details."

"I'm not surprised. Unfortunately, due to who the girl's father is, the news media will never be privy to those details, which means I can't give out any information about it either. However, what I can do is . . ." Sam reaches into his wallet and pulls out an old, tattered business card with the symbol of the State Department on the front and a faded handwritten phone number on the back. "If you call that number, they should explain everything."

"The State Department? Sounds intriguing."

"Not really, but they should explain why I was arrested but never charged. That information will also tell you why I am never to talk about it."

The room is taking on a more golden glow as the sun shifts positions. Johnny looks at the card one more time while saying, "I'll get this card back to you, but it's getting late, and I need to make a phone call."

"I'm so sorry," Sam quickly responds. "I never intended to make you late. You have a show to do."

"It's all covered. So, how did you get involved with Osborn?" As Johnny hands him another Perrier, he also asks, "Are you sure you don't want a beer?"

Sam responds, "No, thank you. Beer got me into trouble once. I notice you only drink wine."

"Ed handles the beer, while I drink wine. But, I indulge every once in a while."

"Anyway, Osborn calls me out of the blue saying he's got a tape that will solve all of my problems. He said someone on the tour bus got off to get a better angle of a celebrity sighting and ended up filming the incident from a position that will prove my story. Somehow, things like this just fall into his lap."

"How well I know," Johnny says wryly, taking another sip of wine.

"Oh, that's right; you and he mixed it up in your last divorce."

"It was my third divorce, but who's counting? He can play rough. You had better watch out for him—even if he is on your side. He would actually be a very competent attorney if he wasn't such an ass!"

Sam frowns. "Well, he put up a lot of money for that tape, so if I don't go ahead with the suit, he will be suing me."

"More than likely, but don't worry about him. I would like to get a piece of his hide, so if it should come to it, I'll take care of him myself. You can bet on that!" Johnny states unequivocally.

"Why should you get mixed up with him again? It's not even your problem."

"For three reasons: The first two are that I hate him and I like you. The third one is I'm in this mess as much as anyone. Don't forget Osborn mentioned *The Tonight Show* in your lawsuit. Because we didn't get the audio cut off in time, Osborn will say that my show supplied Chantell with the noose to hang herself."

Johnny can see that the sun is now shining directly into Sam's eyes, so he pushes a button on a remote and the shade comes down on the west end of the house. "So, what happened with the drunk in the bar when he demanded an answer? Didn't he recognize you?"

"I was scared spitless, so I yelled, 'Let's hang him!'"

"So, what did he do then?"

"The drunk looked directly into my face—for what seemed an eternity—then slapped me on the back and yelled, 'Yeah, that's what we'll do!' "

Johnny laughs.

Sam continues, "And, while I was wiping beer spit off my face, he turned to the others and yelled, 'And we should string up that jackass lawyer of his, too,' and then I slipped out."

Johnny is laughing so hard he has to wipe tears from his eyes. It takes him a few minutes before he can say, "I think that is the best thing I ever heard."

Sam nods with a big smile.

Still choking a little, Johnny adds, "When this all gets resolved, you and I are going to try this skit on the Mighty Carson Art Players."

Both laugh again.

Still laughing, Sam says, "I never realized until now how funny that night was. At the time, I was just scared and panicked! Thank you. I needed that."

"Don't mention it. But now I have to ask, what happened to your car? You didn't try to . . ." Johnny finishes the question with a hand motion, reluctant to ask why Sam drove his car into an underpass.

"I almost did something really stupid, but at the last second, I changed my mind. I think the accident was God's way of making sure I never do that again, and it worked!"

"Is that all of it?"

Sam nods.

Johnny asks, "So, what happens now?"

"As I said earlier, I finish up some furniture for a client and then head north."

"Can you stick around for a little while longer? I have an idea, and I want to make a few phone calls and check it out. It might take some time to make it all work."

"What do you have in mind?" Sam responds immediately, a spark of hope flashing through his consciousness. Then, he thinks better of it and counters with, "Hey, I don't want you to get any more involved in this. You don't need the negative publicity any more than I do."

"Don't worry about the publicity. What I have in mind should avoid any further publicity all together. It's a long shot, so I don't want to get your hopes up quite yet." Johnny looks at his watch. "Well, my ride is almost here."

"I hope I didn't screw things up for you. It's almost four, and if I remember correctly, you have to be in Burbank in an hour."

"Don't worry about it. I have been in this predicament many times. I have it covered."

Out in the driveway, they shake hands and Sam climbs into the old truck. "Don't worry about a thing," Johnny says, smiling. "We'll get this sorted out."

"At this point, I'd settle for bus fare out of LA."

Sam puts the truck in gear and backs up, revealing a large puddle of oil. Utterly embarrassed, he stops and looks at Johnny, who answers his look with, "Sure you don't work for Exxon?"

Johnny waves him off just as the wind kicks up and a familiar noise gets louder. Sam looks over to see a helicopter landing on the tennis courts. He looks back at Johnny and hears him say, "It pays to know who you know."

———

The late morning sun is casting short shadows on a small ranch, consisting of a barn, chicken shed, and a large, unfinished house that looks to stay that way for the foreseeable future. Next to it is a beat-up, old mobile home with dents added from the treacherous drive up the Malibu hills. Behind the battered mobile home is a smaller trailer with a view of those hills, with Boney Ridge to one side and a fleeting glimpse of the Pacific Ocean to the other.

The sound of woodworking machinery can be heard coming from the barn. The sound subsides with the ringing of a telephone. Sam comes out wearing a leather apron. Brushing the dust off himself, he heads to the mobile home.

"Hello."

"Mr. Milton?"

"Yes?"

"Mr. Milton, please hold for Mr. Carson."

"Hello, Sam. I'm sorry for not getting back to you sooner. Scheduling these things takes a bit longer than I thought."

"No problem. This last job I mentioned to you is also taking longer than I thought."

"Does this mean you're going to stay around for a while?" Johnny inquires.

"I don't know. It seems the proverbial fecal matter has hit the fan. I've been thrown out of my house in town, my business license has been revoked, and I've heard several people are trying to serve me subpoenas. At least they and the reporters haven't found me yet. So, I'm staying right here for the time being."

"Well, I hear *Donahue* is looking for you."

"Really?"

"But if I were you, I would wait for *20/20* or *60 Minutes*. They don't pay as well, but you would get more positive publicity than with *Donahue*."

"Just what I need: more publicity. No, thank you. When I'm done with these loose ends, this boy is history!"

"Well, I have an idea that may change your mind. Can you be at my house this Saturday, say around eleven o' clock? There will be someone here I want you to talk to."

"Okay, but it's not a reporter, is it?"

"No, no, there will be nothing in the press of any kind," Johnny states emphatically. "Just the only person that can get through to Chantell León."

"I doubt it. I don't think she'll listen to anybody as mad as she is."

"She'll listen to this lady; you can count on that. She will be here at exactly eleven. Now, before Saturday, I need to tell you my plan. It will take much too long now, but I will give you a call after tonight's show. Is that okay with you?"

"You got a deal."

When Saturday arrives, Sam drives his old truck through the gate at the Carson estate and up to the curved concrete wall, well away from the main house. He gets out and places a large piece of cardboard under his truck to catch the dripping oil. He walks the rest of the way up the driveway; noticing the security cameras for the first time, he realizes he's being watched. He walks past where he parked last time and sees the oil spot has been cleaned but isn't gone completely. Sam mumbles to himself, "Great. That's just great. Now Johnny's probably mad at me."

He walks the rest of the way up to the house. When he gets close, the door is opened by Johnny himself. "Sam, right on time. Come in." Johnny steps aside to let Sam walk past.

Sam comes face-to-face with an elegant black woman who looks familiar to him, though he can't place her. "Sam, this is Angelica Martin. Angelica, this is Samuel Milton," Johnny says as he makes the introduction.

"Good morning, Mr. Milton," Angelica offers. She has a familiar voice, and her elegant appearance makes Sam feel as if he should know her. "We have heard so much about you," she says with an unforgiving smile.

"Yes, and we hope to change that perception," Johnny interrupts while taking Angelica's arm. "Let's go over to the sitting area where we can talk freely, and hopefully we'll get this all worked out." They walk over to the same couches Sam occupied before with Johnny, with Angelica sitting on one and Sam sitting opposite.

"Excuse me," Johnny says, reaching for the telephone. He presses the intercom to say, "Jenny, will you hold any calls and please bring in the tea and coffee? Thank you." He then presses two other buttons and sits back up. "Now, Sam, Mrs. Martin has direct contact with Chantell León, so just tell her what you told me."

Sam nervously rubs his hair back and says, "Um, I'm not too sure about all of this, and haven't I seen you before?"

"I don't think we have ever met, and I can assure you, Mr. Milton, that what you say won't leave this house."

Sam says, "May I ask what your relationship is with Miss León?"

"Let's just say, for now, that I give her lots of advice, and I also know her better than anyone else, including her late father. So, if you can convince me, then I can convince her. But quite frankly, Mr. Milton, as of now, we still believe you have some sort of perverse fixation toward Chantell. Also, it seems this Gordon Osborn character you hired is milking this incident to get whatever he can out of Miss León and her associates." Mrs. Martin then picks up a cup of tea that has just been delivered, takes a sip, looks Sam directly in the eye, and says, "So, where does that put us now, Mr. Milton?"

Sam pours a cup of coffee and nervously takes a sip. This causes Angelica to give Johnny a confident smile, which Johnny returns by cocking his head and using his eyes to express confidence in Sam. Angelica continues the unspoken conversation by looking at Sam with severe skepticism. She gives a quick glance back at Johnny, who smiles and leans back as one would when enjoying a good boxing match. The unspoken conversation ends with Angelica giving a slight exhale that could be characterized as giving a snort. "Shall we start at the beginning, Mr. Milton?" Angelica prompts him again.

Johnny interrupts her with, "Would you like to use the hot lights and waterboarding on him now or later?"

"I know the man is a friend of yours, Mr. Carson, but I think it is only fair to Miss León that we let Mr. Milton here stand on his own two feet. Are you ready, Mr. Milton, or shall we come back another day?"

Sam takes a breath and begins, "I'm sorry for my nervousness, but quite frankly, I feel more comfortable talking to the police. At least they would not be starting out so biased."

He sees her glare back at him and senses she is about to say something, so he speaks first. "As for the car accident, I was on my way to the hardware store on Heather Cliff. I was distracted for a moment, and by the time I saw Miss León's car approach, it was too late."

"What were you distracted by, Mr. Milton?"

Sam sits up straight, looks over at Johnny, and then stares Angelica in the eyes before answering, "A girl, Mrs. Martin. A very pretty girl."

"Thank you, Mr. Milton. You may continue."

Sounding annoyed, Sam chides, "You don't happen to work for the district attorney, do you? You would make a damn good one!"

Johnny cracks a smile but doesn't say anything. He looks away when he feels the same glare Sam got. "If you don't mind, let's refrain from profanity, Mr. Milton."

Sam's nostrils flair. "Yes, I do mind. You wanted me to be honest, so that means there will be no editing!"

Mrs. Martin bows slightly and says, "Please continue."

"Well, after the accident, I ran over to her, but when I saw who she was, I froze."

"Why, Mr. Milton?"

Sam looks at her with complete surprise and answers, "Because it was Chantell! You know, she's every man's dream come true, and all I could do was just stand there. I couldn't say or do anything. I couldn't even look at her, for God's sake! I felt like a complete dork, and it showed. I must have turned thirty shades of red. I had this same problem back in high school. Then, if I saw a pretty girl, my whole body would freeze up until I turned to look the other way. But, I thought I was out of that. I've been fine with girls. I've even dated someone for years. Then wham! I'm back in high school standing in front of Miss León!"

"I see," says Angelica. "Do you still have a fixation with Miss León?"

"No, Mrs. Martin, I don't. It seems when you get your butt chewed off on national TV by someone you admire, the fixation wanes a bit. You can understand that, can't you?"

"More than you could possibly know."

Johnny gives a short laugh at her comment, causing Sam to wonder if his host knows something he doesn't. Sam gives a quick shake of his head and continues, "As I was saying, all I could do was stand there like an idiot while someone else helped her find a phone. The next day, I stopped by where she was filming, and I asked the guard if I could apologize to Miss León. His name was Joe, and he sent me to a soundstage at Universal—and ultimately got fired for it. That's right. He got fired for helping me try to apologize to Miss León. That goes to show you that others have been hurt by this mess, too! He also told me that she liked yellow roses, and thank God I had those roses."

"Why 'thank God,' Sam?" she asks.

Sam is taken aback slightly as he realizes Angelica is calling him Sam—not Mr. Milton—for the first time. A sense of confidence engulfs him. "The roses were the only thing that convinced the police that I might be innocent. They found the remains of the dozen yellow roses I bought before I went to the soundstage. I walked up the stairs to deliver the flowers and apologize, but when I reached for the doorknob, everything went black. All I can remember is falling backward. I instinctively reached for something to grab on to, to avoid going over the handrail, a good six-foot drop. The next thing I knew, security was holding my left arm behind my back with such force it felt broken. I still can't extend it all the way out. I glanced up to see Chantell hunched over, with someone covering her with a jacket. I didn't even know I had torn off her blouse. I didn't find that out until I was at the police station. The rest you can catch on the evening news. What you may not know is that they brought in Joe to verify my story. That's when I found out the whole situation had screwed him over good! It kills me to know I got a nice man fired, Mrs. Martin."

"Why didn't the police tell us about Joe, the guard?"

Johnny breaks in. "We tried to that night on the show as we were verifying Chantell's statements about the police releasing Sam. But by this time, she was becoming so hysterical that she wasn't listening to any explanations. Before I knew it, she was practically using my show as a platform to start a riot!"

Sam adds softly, "I must have scared her badly to cause her say all of that stuff."

Angelica counters, "I appreciate all of this sincerity, Sam, but if you just wanted to apologize, then why the fifty-million-dollar lawsuit with some high-society lawyer like Gordon Osborn?"

"First of all, Mrs. Martin, I didn't go to Osborn; he came to me. The only reason I talked to him was because he said he had a videotape showing what really happened. And I need to tell you, Mrs. Martin, I never gave him permission to go public with anything. He did that on his own, even when I specifically told him not to do anything without my permission. Well, as we all know, he went public anyway. I also need to tell you, the only reason I agreed for him to be my lawyer was to keep her record and film company lawyers from climbing down my throat."

"I see," is the only comment she offers.

Johnny cuts in. "Tell her what happened the night Osborn aired the message about the tape."

"I stopped to have a drink in a bar, which seemed to be the thing to do when you are sad your fiancée has broken up with you."

"May I ask why she broke up with you?"

"No, but don't worry. It would have happened sooner or later. I just didn't need to have it happen that day. It made a bad day horrible, and it was about to get much worse. Anyway, several people in the bar heard my beloved lawyer make the announcement on TV. As you might guess, everyone sided with Miss León. I guess I should thank the Lord that the biggest, loudest guy was also the most drunk—so much so, he didn't recognize me, even though he was staring me in the face. Needless to say, with the tension building exponentially, I was barely able to get out in time."

"And then?"

Sam answers bluntly, "And then I headed home."

"What about your car?"

"What about the car?" Sam answers, with building resentment.

"Sam, I'm not here just to collect facts. I'm here to see if I believe you. So, if you're going to hold back now, then let's just forget the whole thing and let lawyers handle it. It's your choice."

"All right, so you want the details?" Sam asks, clearly annoyed. He stands up and walks over to Angelica. "I will tell you the details," he says, bringing his face close to hers. "In one forty-eight-hour period, I wrecked the car I spent years restoring and looked like a moron in front of one of the most beautiful women in entertainment. And, oh yeah, I tried to apologize to her, but instead I ripped the clothes off of her in public. Then, half the world got mad at me. Then, my lawyer sued her, getting the other half of the world mad at me! Because of the chaos and confusion surrounding the case, I hear on the radio that an angry mob started throwing rocks at my house, killing my cat. Now, with everything in my life getting flushed down the toilet, I find myself angry and desperate, going one hundred sixty-five miles per hour down the freeway, headed for a bridge abutment."

He gets a questioning look form Angelica, which he answers with, "I don't know! The recklessness seemed like a good idea at the time, maybe even an answer to my problems. But in the last second, I changed my mind."

"What changed your mind?" she queries.

With fury in his voice, he yells, "That's none of your god—" Sam stops and takes a breath to calm down, finally replying, "That's none of your business!" He then turns his eyes away from both of them. Looking down, he sees Johnny's phone, which has a small green light flashing. He looks more closely and sees the light indicates the intercom is on.

In an all-out rage, he yells, "Who's been listening to this conversation? I bet you're taping this, aren't you?"

Mrs. Martin looks to Johnny for help, but all Johnny does is shrug as he sighs in helplessness.

"That's just great! That's just . . ." Sam lets his voice trail off as he glares at them both with a look that, if audible, would bury them in profanity. "Now, I suppose the whole world knows about what I've said—or soon will?"

Sam walks to the other side of the couch, slaps the back of it in frustration, and then points to her. "Now, I know who you are! You're that gossip columnist who shows up on all of those talk shows: A. Martin or something or other. Well, that's just perfect! Thanks a lot, Johnny! Just what I needed—more publicity!" Sam throws his hands in the air and leans on the back edge of the couch, facing away from them.

The silence is broken with a different voice coming from the other side of the room. "Her name is Angelica León Martin, otherwise known by the name on her syndicated column, A. L. Martin. She is also known as my mother."

Sam freezes a moment, then slowly turns around to see it is Chantell herself standing there.

10

Six Yellow Roses

═══════

Sam stands frozen, looking at her across the room, not moving or saying anything. Chantell, slowly and shyly, walks toward Sam with her head bowed, wiping a tear from her cheek. As she gets close to Sam, he instinctively turns aside in shyness but checks himself. He forces himself to look straight at her while taking a nervous breath. She stops short, sensing his discomfort.

"I guess I owe you an apology," she says with her head still down, hands clasped in front of her. "If I could have seen things more clearly, I would never have said what I did or caused you so much harm." She slowly looks up at his face, hoping for a positive response.

"Um, I am afraid I do not know what to say . . ." Sam replies hesitantly, struggling not to turn away again. He adds, "Except that I can now apologize to you for running into your car. I should also apologize for standing there like a . . . I don't know, like a starstruck pubescent boy. I am also sorry I don't now have the yellow roses I originally intended to give you."

"It's okay. At least I was able to keep my clothes on this time," Chantell teases, pleased when she hears Sam return a small but genuine laugh.

Angelica now comes up behind Chantell, placing her arm around her daughter and presenting her other hand to Sam. He accepts. She begins, "If I may also get into the apologies, I would like to say I'm sorry for being so rough on you, Sam. I felt it was necessary to make sure we got an accurate account of what actually happened, without getting the misconstrued story from lawyers, both yours and ours—if it were to go that far. "

At this, Sam stiffens and says, "Mrs. A. L. Martin, you are the coldest, most calculating, and heartless woman I have ever met. I received better treatment from the police interrogator, which leaves me with only one question . . ."

All three stand, with shock written across their faces, including Johnny, waiting for him to finish his statement. Sensing their discomfort, Sam steps forward, retakes her hand, smiles, and asks, "Mrs. A. L. Martin, will you be my lawyer?"

The shock is replaced with laughter. Angelica playfully replies, "In that case, Sam, please refrain from calling me Mrs. A. L. Martin, and please call me Angelica."

Sam gives her a slight bow of acknowledgment.

She then adds, "I would like to claim all of the brutally kind compliments that you gave me, but I must point out that it was Johnny's idea to get us together in private."

Johnny then comes over to say, "I must also say that I am sorry."

"For what?" Sam asks.

"For not getting this on videotape. The ratings from this would keep Letterman behind me for years to come."

With smiles all around, Chantell announces, "I'm just glad we finally got all of this straightened out." The relief in her voice is apparent.

"Yes, Sam," Angelica adds, "if we can do anything to make up for the inconveniences, please let us know."

Sam is about to say something, but Johnny cuts him off. "I asked for lunch to be made, and I believe it is ready, so if you ladies would like to walk into the other room."

As the women start to walk toward lunch, Johnny grabs Sam's arm. "Can I see you alone for a moment?"

"Sure, what's up?"

"Look, I don't want to tell you how to run your affairs, but if you let them off the hook, they will leave you with nothing. Trust me, I have been through a divorce or two, and I know a little bit about compensation. And you don't need *some* compensation, you need a massive amount of it!"

"I can't take any money from these people; it was all just an accident."

"Compensation can be more than just money. Look, Sam," he says, placing his hand on Sam's shoulder, "do you know who is in the other room? That is Chantell León in there. I'm talking *Chantell*. You have a unique situation here—one that any other man would die for. Now, I'm not saying take physical advantage of her, but do take advantage of the situation. Do you remember our conversation on the phone?"

"You mean using this to my advantage without looking like a jerk?"

"Good. Did you come up with anything?"

"Um, yeah," he says nervously.

"Well, now is the time to bring it up. If you wait much longer, it will get more awkward by the minute, and eventually the opportunity will dissolve all together. Just think about it, but don't take long." With that, Johnny disappears into the other room, leaving Sam to look both puzzled and nervous.

Casual conversation mixes with the sounds of teacups and silverware as Sam enters the room. "Sam, have a sandwich," Johnny says, pointing to the tray. "On the counter are three kinds of soup: mild, hot, and blow your head off."

"Thank you." Sam takes a quick look and chooses a tuna sandwich.

"Johnny was about to tell us how you two met," Chantell says, pouring his coffee.

"Sam has a much better take on it, so I will let him give you the play-by-play."

"Well, um, my friend Craig and I love playing tennis. We make it a point to play on as many famous celebrity courts as possible—usually without an invitation. It's more exciting that way. Here is an interesting fact: Most celebrities have security all over their estates, but seldom do they have any on the tennis courts. So, most courts were easy pickings. We had all of them under our belts, except the most famous court of all—the one right out there in the center of the cul-de-sac. Do you know those courts are accessed by a tunnel going underneath the road? Anyway, we knew security would be driving around, so we decided to play by moonlight. We waited for the security guard to drive by and then hopped the fence and began playing. It was the perfect night—a full moon and no clouds.

"We were really getting into it when all of the lights came on. We were so busted! All we could do was stand there and wait for the police to show up. We turned toward the tunnel entrance to see Johnny standing there in a white bathrobe."

"So, what happened?" Chantell asks, caught up in the story.

"He said, and I quote, 'I have been sitting here for the past fifteen minutes watching you two play badminton with tennis rackets. I'm hoping that it's just you trying to play in the moonlight that's making it so hard, because you two stink. I'm tired, so I'm going back to bed. Turn the lights off when you leave.' He turned and left without saying another word. Was that cool or what?"

Chantell beams. "Wow, I am impressed, Mr. Carson; that was really cool of you."

"I don't get this. I do something impressive, and it's 'Mr. Carson.' But if I screw up, like I did with you on my show the other night, it's 'Johnny.' I'm starting to get a complex."

"I'm sorry, Johnny, but I am also impressed with Sam here. It's not often I get to have lunch with a man who can play badminton with a tennis racket."

The statement makes Sam choke on his coffee, but then he quickly smiles at the comment as he cleans himself up. He laughs and then says, "You're quick, Chantell."

"Yeah, Sam," Johnny adds. "I think you have some competition."

"I'll make a note of that," Sam says. "Anyway, I was so impressed myself that I stopped by the next day to say thank you. We got to talking and ended up being friends."

Johnny smiles. "We've had a standing tennis date every Friday morning since."

"You forgot to tell them what time it is every Friday. It's five thirty!" Sam says wryly. "Sometimes, we're playing before sunrise. But I also need to add, Johnny has helped me get back on my feet after some rough times."

"It seems he's still doing it," Angelica adds, nodding approvingly toward Johnny.

"Yes, he is," Sam answers. "And so, I need to thank him again."

"How did Johnny help you the first time?" Chantell asks.

"I encountered a tragedy, and I kind of fell apart. When I tried to start over, Johnny gave me my first commission. This very table we're sitting at was my first project, as well as the rest of the cabinets in this room."

"Really?" Angelica remarks. "Most impressive."

"Excuse me, everyone," Johnny interrupts, "but you two kids still have some unfinished business to take care of."

Chantell looks over at Sam and says silently, "Kids?"

"Now, if I'm not mistaken, the world still sees Sam as some sort of racist pervert who should be strung up by his . . . well, you know what I mean. And they see Chantell as this great black heroine liberator, who plans to do just that— liberate.

"Then, consider the things lost on both sides. Sam has lost most everything he has: reputation, career, friends, home, car—even his 'putty cat.' How does he get compensated? As for Chantell, she's not just an individual, but she is also a huge corporation. Beyond movies and record albums, there is her clothing line and perfume franchise, which adds hundreds of people who depend on her for their livelihoods. They depend on her looks, her voice, her movies, and her endorsements. A little ripple in her life can cause tidal waves in others. If this apology is not handled correctly, countless more will also want to be compensated."

"Let's not forget the lawyers," Angelica interjects. "They're going to want their pound of flesh, too."

"You bet they will," Johnny continues. "The last thing they want to see is you two kiss and make up. It will kill their meal ticket, and that goes for both sides."

"Yes, but the opposite is also true," Angelica interjects. "You're on contract, Chantell, with both Iconic Records and Universal. I guarantee the last thing they want to see is this dragged out in court."

"Thank you, Angelica," Johnny states. "I didn't think of that. So, as we can all see, we have a big mess here still, so someone needs to start talking."

After a long pause, Chantell speaks. "Well, I think, first of all, there should be a public apology made by both parties, and Sam should receive some monetary compensation for what he has lost. What do you think of that, Sam?"

"First of all, I'm not interested in getting a public apology, at least not right now."

"Why not?" Chantell asks.

"Because the press went on a feeding frenzy with this thing, and some got quite fat and boated. I don't want to feed them anymore. One thing is for sure: The next time I deal with the press, I'm going to be controlling them. They're not going to be controlling me.

"As for the money, I don't want any of that either. The only positive item I can see is that my savings account is the one thing that hasn't diminished, as of yet. Besides, if money was what I was looking for, I would just continue with the lawsuit and collect the fifty million."

"So, what are you looking for?" Chantell asks.

"I want my life back. I want to replace what I lost, and that's all. Look, as I see it, you didn't lose anything. In fact, you got more publicity from this whole thing than all of the ad campaigns in the world could give you, and it's all positive. The whole world is on your side. I know because I saw it. They bless you and curse me."

Chantell nods as she stares down at the table.

Sam continues to vent. "I was even the first one to try to apologize, and that's how this whole mess got started."

"Just what exactly do you want my daughter to replace?"

"What I want replaced is exactly what Johnny pointed out, something pertaining to my social life, home life, my friends, my business, and my reputation. It's after that that we can get to the public apologies, but somewhere that is tightly controlled."

"Okay, so how do you expect her to do it?" Angelica asks while Chantell continues staring off in the distance.

Sam explains, "I will ask her to do six simple things; each item will be related to one of those areas. Each request must be done where, when, and how I want it done. When completed, you will get a yellow rose. Each yellow rose will be worth ten million."

Chantell turns to him in anger. "What? Are you nuts? This sounds like some goofy game shows where you put stars through stupid stunts just to embarrass the hell out of them. I'm Chantell León, not some circus animal you can train to jump through hoops. I'm not having any part in this!"

Sam looks down at the table, as if defeated, and says, "I'm sorry, Miss León."

Johnny is about to come to Sam's defense, but Sam cuts him off and continues to speak. "I forgot who you are. My apologies to you."

Chantell feels vindicated, but the sensation is short-lived. Sam continues, "I forgot you are the sweet, charming, and innocent Chantell. It seems I was mistaking you for some no-name, simple carpenter who was totally humiliated and whose life was destroyed on national TV." His voice gets louder as his anger escalates. "One should never criticize someone so sweet, even if she called for a vigilante mob to take care of you! However, you didn't need to bother doing that because I came way too close to doing it for you, and in the process, I destroyed a car I spent years restoring!" He is now screaming. "I hear you have a cat, Miss León, one you love very much. I know because it has been on four magazine covers with you. I had just gotten a cat too, Miss León! Now, I don't have one. It's dead, killed by the vigilantes you set out after me! So, Miss León, if you feel you can't lower yourself to the standards of a simple carpenter, then you can start writing a check with the number five, followed by several zeros!"

"That's blackmail!"

Sam slams his fist down on the table, startling even Johnny. "Stop right there! The price is no longer fifty million. The price has just gone up to seventy-five million!"

"What?" screams Chantell.

Sam leans over the table and gets into her face; she has to lean back. He warns, "If you say one more word, mademoiselle, the price goes up to one hundred million! Furthermore, you just might want to know that to avoid me looking like the jerk you think I am, I am going to take every dime of that money and put it into a fund that helps little kids with critical diseases. And would you like to know what the name of it will be? Of course you would! It will be called the Little Paws Foundation. That was the name of my cat!"

Trying to de-escalate the conversation, Angelica transitions it with, "Funny, you don't seem to be very shy or timid now, Mr. Milton. Why didn't you display this side of yourself when this all happened?"

"For three very good reasons: First of all, this is a very private conversation. Second, I have all of my facts in front of me. And third, I'm in control. Back then, I wasn't. Back then it was my fault, and I don't do well when I am to blame. The wife of my business partner made sure that will always be the case. But, I am not to blame for this."

"What is the first item on your list of reparations, Mr. Milton? You said you have six items," Angelica says.

"Mother, you can't be serious."

"Well, what is it, Sam?" Angelica asks, waving off her daughter.

"With all due respect, Mrs. Martin, this is between Chantell and me, and I would like to discuss this in private."

Sam then turns to Chantell and finishes with, "Say, over dinner?"

"Oh, so you think you are going to get alone with me? Fat chance of that!"

"Fine, start writing lots of zeros!"

"Good God, who the hell do you think you are?"

"He's someone who is cutting you down to size, Miss León," Johnny says.

"Hear! Hear!" joins Angelica.

Sam puts his hands up. "Miss León, this whole mess started when you did not trust me at the accident site. Not to mention, you're not being even slightly understanding about my lack of social skills and are degrading me over my shyness. Well, I'm not shy now, Miss León! And a side note to this little game is to force you to trust me. So, is it dinner or zeros?"

"Oh sure. Like someone with my face can walk into any restaurant. I can't even walk into a McDonald's without starting a riot!" Chantell says sarcastically.

"Johnny could find some place we can have a nice, quiet dinner—although the two of us being quiet might be a tad more difficult to achieve."

"I'm sure I can find something," Johnny quips.

"Great! That's just great!" Chantell responds.

"Can you give us a few minutes, Sam?" Angelica asks while Chantell sits fuming.

"Sure, Mrs. Martin. Take all the time you need. I'm thinking of going for a swim to cool off."

"Feel free to use the pool, Sam," Johnny says, "but I don't think this is going to take all that long."

As Sam returns, he sees Chantell sitting on one side of the couch, looking out the window. She does not turn to acknowledge Sam when he walks in. He decides to engage her. "Well, what is it going to be?"

Still looking away, she responds, "Since you leave me no choice, I will agree to your first demand. Mr. Carson has vouched for your character, but I warn you, Mr. Milton, you can't own me even for fifty million dollars."

"Actually, as you recall, it's been upped to seventy-five million. I was going to keep it at fifty, but then I doubt you would take me seriously."

Still looking away, Chantell's first response is to exhale in exasperation and throw one hand up in the air. She then answers, "Even at seventy-five million, you will not own me."

"But I have no intention of owning you, so let's say I'm asking for six short-term leases."

"You won't like it, Mr. Milton."

Sam walks around the couch and puts his face up to hers and says, "But I already do."

Chantell retaliates, "One thing you should know about me, Mr. Milton. My teeth are sharp, and if you ever put your face this close to mine again, I will bite that nose off your face. Got it?"

Sam pulls back and smiles. "I guess that leaves kissing out. Is necking still within bounds?"

Chantell snarls, "I will let my three brothers give you that answer."

"Duly noted. Now, if you will all excuse me, I need to go out and rent a car for tonight."

"Rent a car?" Johnny asks.

"You don't expect me to drive Chantell to a fancy restaurant in an old pickup truck, do you?"

Johnny reaches into his pocket and pulls out a set of keys and tosses them to Sam, saying, "You put one scratch on my 'Vette, and I will own you!"

Number One

After passing through the guarded entry gate, then the pedestrian gate, and finally the three intimidating black gentlemen just beyond, Sam stands at Chantell's door. The ring of the doorbell is a pleasant chime. Sam waits for a few moments before hearing, "You are a half hour early!"

"Did I not say seven o'clock?"

"No, it was seven thirty!"

"My apologies."

Chantell opens the door and stands before him in a royal-blue, shimmering metallic knee-length dress with a matching bolero jacket, her line defined by large shoulder pads. The jet-black ringlets of her hair add to her dramatic look. Sam's instant response is, "Whoa! I didn't expect you in something so . . . Wow!"

Chantell gives Sam's suit a squinting once-over. "And I wasn't expecting Kmart."

"It's not Kmart; it's Montgomery Ward."

"Exactly."

"Would you like me to wait outside?"

"That would be lovely. You can keep my three brothers company." Chantell watches Sam turn away, then relents. "Actually, come on in. I'm afraid of what my brothers might do to you. There's a chair here in the foyer. I will be just a minute."

Minutes later, once inside the white Corvette, the two engage in little conversation. No radio, just defining silence. Sam glances over at her every so often. Chantell continues to stare straight ahead. Under her breath, she is saying, "Please don't let him hurt me, Lord, and don't let me agree to anything I know I shouldn't."

"Did you say something?" Sam asks while leaning her way.

Chantell glances at him with a polite but nervous smile and goes back to staring without saying anything.

Sam keeps having flashbacks to his first date ever and its painful similarities to the present situation. He thinks of using the memory to break through the wall of ice. "What was your worst dating nightmare—besides me?"

No answer.

Knowing the idea could be a bad one, he continues anyway. "The worst date for me was in my junior year in high school. It felt similar to this one."

"We're not on a date, Mr. Milton."

"And that's exactly what my first date felt like."

"How did it end?"

"With me not dating again for two years."

"I'm surprised you dated at all."

Sam sits in morbid silence for an excruciatingly long minute before Chantell thinks better of her comment and adds, "Because of your shyness, I mean."

Now, Sam answers softly while looking away, "It's a shame how little people take shyness seriously. It can be completely debilitating. I once went out on a date with one of the most beautiful women I've ever seen, but she was very shy. In fact, she was such a mess that if I asked anything personal, she just sat and quivered."

"Maybe she just didn't like yo—"

"Don't!" Though he does not speak loudly, his unexpected rebuff causes Chantell to jump. Noticing it, he tones it down, but it quickly builds again. "Miss León, I can say unequivocally that I am the nicest man you will ever meet, as Mr. Carson has probably told you. If you choose not to experience that, it is your choice and your loss. Not mine. You are living up to most people's stereotype of someone of your status and profession."

"That's not fair!"

"Then prove me wrong!" The silence grows intense. Sam lets it go for a few more minutes, then states, "Miss León . . . Chantell, you have done nothing but lie to me ever since I rang your doorbell."

"What the hell do you mean by that?"

"You have been the consummate little rich brat. But, I know that's not you. It's not even close to you. Do you fear me that much?"

She doesn't answer.

"I bet you are afraid I'm going to hurt you . . . maybe not physically but emotionally, socially, and maybe even spiritually. Well, Miss León, that's what this is all about. I'm going to make you change your perceptions by forcing you to trust me."

"Do you know how moronic that sounds? *Force* someone to trust?"

"It does sound a little antonymic."

"Antonymic?"

"Okay, so it may not be exactly the right word, but regardless, I am going to force you to trust me, and you are about to see how, because we're here."

Upon entering the restaurant, they are seated in a reserved booth with their own waiter. The ambiance is warm and inviting; fresh flowers are on the table, and a string quartet provides music. The French cuisine is delicate yet flavorful and is beautifully presented. However, the silence between the two is deafening, with no words spoken throughout the entire first course.

The awkwardness intensifies as every time Chantell looks up from her plate, she finds Sam looking intently at her face. Having enough of it, she puts down her fork and sets her chin on her laced fingers and overtly stares back. She is surprised to find Sam isn't the least bit bothered by the reverse psychology. She looks intently into his eyes, only to find he isn't looking back at her eyes. Instead, his eyes are slowly moving around her face as if studying an ancient manuscript or a map of the LA Freeway.

She picks up her fork and asks, "Can I help you find something?"

He is undaunted.

She sees him looking slightly to her side, so she turns her head slightly. She points to her right ear and says, "The Dead Sea Scrolls are on the tip of my earlobe, and if you look at the tiny mole on my left cheek, Pasadena and Glendale are just above and to the right."

"Oh, I'm sorry. I was just noticing how your right eye is more open than the left, which gives corresponding balance to your nose curving slightly to the left. I also love how your cheekbones could poke an eye out."

"Anything else?"

"I love how you are not at all racially ambiguous—you're perfectly black."

"You don't get out much, do you?" Chantell asks. She then picks up her fork and says, "Let me know when you're finished."

The first two courses are completed and picked up before the iceberg finally breaks into manageable pieces.

"So, you asked about my worst dating experience. I have one that can top your quivering, shy date," Chantell says.

"What do you mean?" Sam asks, unsure of what she is referring to.

"Once, I had a date who sat too close to me at dinner for comfort. I was so unnerved by his intentions, my bottom lip did not quiver. Instead, it was my legs, knees, and stomach—all of me! He was the typical guy who thinks that if he's paying for dinner, he should get a lot for dessert."

Sam takes another sip of red wine and asks, "How did you get out of it?"

"The waitress came over and spilled a drink in his lap. After the screaming was done, he left for the bathroom. That's when she told me one of my next-door neighbors was sitting behind me and had tipped her to spill the drink. She also told me they were waiting in the parking lot to take me home."

"Did you go?"

"Yep."

"Good for you. Do you mind if I ask you what your aspirations are?"

"I would like to finish this movie and then run away to some horse ranch in Wyoming where no one can find me for the next fifty years."

"Are you a cowgirl at heart?"

"Not a bit. I just love my privacy, and when you're in my profession, you don't get any. So, I figure no one would look for a young black singer in the back hills of Wyoming."

Sam laughs and concedes, "I suppose not."

The waiter comes to take the plates and says, "Miss, you barely touched your dinner. Is it not satisfactory? May I get you something else?"

"No, everything is lovely. Thank you. I just have a lot on my mind. That's all."

"May I bring the dessert tray?"

Sam looks at Chantell before answering, "No, thank you. Maybe later. But please bring a caramel latte for her and a cappuccino for me."

"Yes, monsieur, right away."

"That's a good guess. I'm impressed."

"Don't be. Your mother gave me a few suggestions for melting glaciers. How is it going?"

"I will let you know. However, do you mind if we take care of business? This waiting game is driving me out of my mind."

"Sure. I suppose for you the night is still young, and you have better things to do than spend time with a frustrated—"

"Don't."

Sam looks apologetic. "We seem to say 'don't' a lot, don't we?"

She smirks at the word play and says, "I think I shall remember *don't* as our byword for this game."

"Anyway, as I said earlier today, I want you to replace six things in my life that I lost."

"So, what is the first one?" she asks, picking up her glass of wine.

Sam smiles, touches his glass to hers, and says, "You're doing it."

"Excuse me?"

"You're having dinner with me, and that is worth 12.5 million dollars."

"How can this be worth 12.5 million? I know I am considered one hot chick, but 12.5? You are certifiably nuts."

"Think of it this way: Here I am having dinner in one of the most elegant restaurants in Beverly Hills, with one of the most famous and beautiful women in the world. If that doesn't spruce up one's social calendar, I don't know what will."

"And dinner with me is worth 12.5 million dollars to you? I thought this whole game was to deflate my ego, not to make it swell."

"Oh no. You're not worth nearly that much. In fact, you're not worth anything to me at all . . . monetarily speaking."

"Thank you for clearing that up," Chantell says, taking a sip of wine.

"If I were to actually pay you 12.5 to go out with me, I would be certifiable. But I'm not paying anything at all. I am simply subtracting the amount from the money you owe me—money I never expect or want to get. Though this date doesn't have a price tag for me, it is, however, still worth the full 12.5 million to you."

"And this takes care of the social condition, one sixth of your request. Will all the other items on your list be like this one?"

"Oh no. From now on, each one will get increasingly more demanding and costly, though not in a monetary sense—that is, until the last one. I am going to make sure it's the most demanding." He then pauses as if collecting a new thought. He looks down at the table as he adds, "And the last one could be by far the most costly."

"But not financially?"

"Not financially."

Sam takes note of the two big black men sitting near the dance floor. He turns to Chantell and asks, "Care to dance?"

"Is it part of the required agreement?"

"Does it need to be?"

"Yes."

"Then it is."

They head to the dance floor. Sam collects Chantell, and they dance to one of her slower numbers. "Kind of ironic, isn't it, to be dancing to one of my songs just after our conversation?"

"Yes, it is. But unfortunately, it's not the one I remember dancing to with you."

"Excuse me?"

"Never mind; it was just a daydream I was having the day before we bumped into each other."

Sam again notices the two men and leads Chantell in front of them. As he passes by their table, one of them makes a fist and slugs his other palm. Sam responds to the intimidating gesture by blowing him a kiss. The man stands, but undaunted, Sam gently swings Chantell around and lets her deal with him. Though he can't hear what she says, he can tell Chantell sent a blunt message. Sam swings around again to see the man is sitting again. Sam gives him a half smile, knowing he is only fanning the flames.

The music ends, and Chantell leads Sam back to the table. He asks, "What, only one dance?"

"What do you expect for a mere 12.5 million?"

They sit back down, and Chantell wastes no time in asking, "What do you expect to get out of this? Are you expecting me to fall in love with you so we can get married and I can bear your children?"

"Ooh, I like that! But no."

"Am I just a tutor to get over your shyness?"

"Another good one, but no."

"Mr. Milton, suddenly I have this very strong feeling that something more is going on than you just having sport with me."

"I'll admit that I was simply planning to take advantage of the situation and hoping you would have some mutual fun with me. However, something's come up that has made this endeavor far more important and much more serious."

"And what is that?"

"Um . . . I can't tell you—at least not now. If I did, you would think I was psycho, and it might scare you to the point that you would run out of here."

"Well, you don't have to worry about possibly scaring me—because you just did. I will tell you this: If you don't become more forthcoming, I will simply pay the remaining imaginary sum of the theoretical money I owe and leave. Thus, this will be the last event we have. So, start talking."

"Um . . . okay. After Johnny suggested that I needed to do something to get back what I lost—"

"So, this was all Mr. Carson's idea?"

"What? No! It's just during one of the phone conversations we had prior to the two of us meeting, Johnny pointed out that, after going through several divorces, he knew about compensation. He said it didn't always have to be monetary compensation. He said to make a list of what I lost and figure out a way to get each item back. So, please don't blame him for any of this. I'm just glad he reminded me of it when you and I first met, or we wouldn't be having this conversation."

She motions for him to continue.

"Well, the night I was writing this list, I had a dream about you."

"So, you had a dream about me? What's the big deal? I'm sure thousands of pubescent boys have dreams about me all the time. It's just part of being a celebrity. In fact, I have received many letters from fans telling me about their dreams. Most, I must say, are more flattering to the fan than to me. Some are so raunchy they would make a hooker from the Bronx blush."

"I am sorry to hear that, but I guess you're right about it being an unfortunate side effect of fame."

"What makes yours so special?"

"This dream was very . . . ugly."

Chantell's cocky smile fades quickly. "I take it I'm not going to like this."

"No, you're not," he agrees.

Chantell motions with her hand for him to continue.

"I had a vision of you thirty years in the future. You did not look good. You should have been in your early fifties, but you looked to be in your late seventies. It was like your body had been ravaged by alcohol or hard-core drugs. You also looked very angry and bitter as one might look in the grips of a severe addiction."

Chantell sits in silence, taking it in.

Sam continues, "You were walking up this trail in the mountains. I could see a hand behind you, pushing you up the hill. The hand was odd looking. It was male, but not as ragged as yours. It had on a wedding band identical to yours, though I'm not sure it meant that you were actually married to the man. And though the hand was pushing you, it wasn't like it was forcing you to go; it was more like the hand was guiding you. Though it was obvious you were not excited about going, you still went freely.

"Eventually, however, you stopped. I then saw a wider image of you standing on the edge of a very high cliff. I watched in horror as the hand gave you one more gentle push. You could have easily resisted the nudge, but you didn't. You fell to your death."

Chantell isn't saying anything. Her head is slightly down, as if staring at the end of the table. "Chantell, I woke up in a cold sweat, screaming, 'Oh God! Don't let her do this! Please, please, God, don't let her die this way!'"

"Is there any more to this dream?" she asks.

"Yes. It took me hours to fall back to sleep."

Chantell interrupts with, "What color was the hand?"

"Color?"

"Was it white, black, light black, olive, red, or maybe Asian? You know, what ethnicity was he?"

"Um, I don't think the color of the hand had anything to do with—"

"I want to know what color the hand was!"

"Chantell . . ." Sam can see that she is not going to let this go, so he capitulates. "The hand was white."

"So, it will be you?"

"Chantell, I don't think color has anything to do with this. As for the hand being white, in my world, I see mostly white people, so I saw a white hand. You might have seen the hand as black."

"It figures you would say something like that."

"This is silly. Why would I tell someone I just met that thirty years from now I would push her off a cliff? Doesn't that seem a little—"

"Antonymic?"

Sam gives an exaggerated nod.

Chantell cocks her head and waves one finger. "No, no, I'm not letting this go. The way I see it—"

"Chantell!"

Sam speaks loudly enough to be a disturbance to the other diners, so Chantell pauses to let him speak.

"You can't see anything yet because I am not finished! You asked me if there was any more to the dream, and I said there was. So, before you judge me as a racist or a murderer, let me finish."

Chantell now gives him an exaggerated nod.

"Part two explains part one in a way you might not be expecting. Okay?"

Chantell nods again but with less flamboyance.

"Miss León, I have never had a dream like this, and it scared the hell out of me. I was up for hours trying to calm down. A shower and a glass of milk finally did the trick, but when I fell asleep, another dream picked up right where the other had left off. I saw you fall, but my view pulled back and I could see you hanging upside down with your left leg caught on some tree roots that were sticking out of the cliff. The tragic thing was, I saw you kicking the roots, like you were angry they were holding you up. You kept kicking, even though freeing yourself would mean you would fall to your death. And you didn't care!"

Sam can see the vison is making Chantell upset again, so he adds, "Before you say anything, I have still more to say, and it changes everything."

He feels more confident when he sees her expression ease, and he continues, "There came a moment when you stopped kicking. You just hung there, looking straight down. Then suddenly, it was like you finally realized where you were. Then a very strange thing happened. Your appearance changed. Instead of the old, worn-out, and bitter Chantell, you slowly changed into the young, vivacious Chantell you are today. You bent your legs so that you could grab the roots with your hands. You got your leg free and climbed up the roots to safety. Once on top, you sat down on the edge of the cliff and started singing gospel hymns, as if nothing ever happened."

Sam sits back and watches Chantell in deep contemplation. He waits a few moments before suggesting, "I think the interpretation is fairly evident, don't you?"

Chantell looks up, shakes her head, and asks, "Um, what?"

"The interpretation of the dream."

Still slightly out of it, she says, "I'm sorry. I guess I'm scared or something, and it's hard for me to think. What's your interpretation?"

"I think you meet someone. It may start out wonderful. Or maybe you are into dating bad boys like Janet Jackson's song 'Nasty'—number one on the charts right now."

"It's only at number three."

"That's right. I misspoke. You kept it out of number one with 'Uptown Hot.' "

Chantell nods a thank you.

"So, are you? Are you into bad boys?"

"I like my men confident."

"Then I guess it's about how you define confidence. Confidence can be very sexy, but it can also quickly become abusive. I know this is going to sound nauseatingly churchy, but someone in this dream causes you to lose your way. It could be anyone: a record producer, movie exec, or a close friend. Perhaps this is even a great person, able to support and encourage someone else, but with you, the chemistry becomes toxic. As for the roots? Quite simply, you need to cling to your roots, your core values and formative experiences, and not walk away from them."

Sam watches Chantell change from bewildered to skeptical and eventually to angry. She retorts, "You seem to know so much about me, so let me ask you— what are you claiming to be? A prophet or a seer maybe? Possibly a shaman? You don't look like you're Muslim or Jewish. Hey, maybe you are one of those Pentecostal holy rollers. Do you babble in tongues? I guess I should ask if you even believe in God. What exactly are you, Mr. Sam Milton?"

"I thought it was obvious. I'm your guardian angel."

Chantell leans back in dramatic flair. "What's the matter, Mr. Milton? Are there no black angels in heaven, so God's gotta send me your white ass?"

Sam looks shocked and yells a whisper, "Chantell León, if you say one more thing like that, I'm going to drag your butt over to your two brothers sitting behind you. I will tell them what you said and watch as one of them takes you over his knee and paddles your butt. I'm the white guy who doesn't know much about racism. You have no excuse."

She hesitates a moment before shaking her head and standing to leave. Her words are harsh. "How dare you preach to me. How dare you analyze me without knowing anything about me. It sounds like you're using the tabloids as your resource. Thank you very much for the 12.5-million-dollar reduction in my debt, but I am going now."

"Suit yourself, but I know for a fact that you won't step out that door."

"Oh no? Watch me!" She turns and quickly heads for the door. At the same time, the two black gentlemen stand.

Sam, feeling as if he just lost the biggest poker game of his life, manages to say, "Oh, one thing you should know before you step out that door: Not only am I your guardian angel, but unfortunately, you are also mine."

Chantell stops. She pauses for a moment and finally makes a hand motion that causes the two men to sit back down. Chantell herself turns around and comes back to the table. Before sitting down, she states bluntly, "Don't pride yourself, Mr. Milton. I just don't want to give my brothers the satisfaction of rubbing my nose in it about coming here tonight. And I am curious. Why did you say I was your guardian angel?"

Sam looks surprised. "Oh, in that case, maybe I should be asking why it's so important for you to know."

Chantell's response doesn't come easily. "The answer is kind of freaky, so I'm not answering that question until I get more information."

"Okay, but now you're freaking *me* out."

Chantell keeps standing, waiting for an answer. Sam just shrugs as if not knowing the answer. He can see this is really getting to her, so he asks, "You want more information about the dream or about being my guardian angel?"

"The angel."

"The angel? I just told you my scariest dream ever, and you're asking how I know you are my guardian angel?" He sees she is getting more agitated by the second, so he answers her with, "It's just a thought that came to my head, but for whatever reason, I know it's true."

Chantell asks, "Did this ever happen to you before?"

"Just once."

"Are you religious?"

Sam shrugs again in confusion.

"Answer the question!"

"I grew up with no religion at all, but in college, I got involved with the Calvary Chapel crowd."

Chantell finally sits but still looks anxious. She responds, "I know of them. They're that Bible study church, the one into that Pentecostal stuff."

Sam nods and answers, "They're more subdued about it, but yes."

"Are you still going? To church, I mean."

"I haven't been to church in over ten years."

"Why is that? Don't you still believe in God?"

"Oh yes, most definitely. It's just that we're not talking right now, and I don't care if we ever talk again."

"Why is that?"

"I am extremely incensed with him!"

"It doesn't sound like he's stopped talking to you."

"If he wants to use me to talk to someone else, that's fine by me. To put it bluntly, I'm incredibly bitter. I just don't want anything to do with him myself."

"What caused the little tiff between you two?"

"That, Miss León, we will save for another time. Now, back to the topic at hand. What were you referring to when I asked about your fascination with being my angel?"

"Because of this situation we're in, I'm not sure I should tell you."

"Where have I heard that before? And why is that?" When Chantell doesn't answer, Sam becomes confrontational. "You forced me to tell you my dream, so out with it. Why is seeing yourself as my guardian angel so difficult?"

"Because I've known that from the first moment we met in the parking lot when you ran into me," she responds, forcing the words out quickly, as if she has to speak them now or never.

Sam absorbs her statement and then begins to ask a question, but Chantell cuts him off. "It wasn't a voice, just a very loud thought: *You're going to be his guardian angel.* I just figured the pathetic stance you were taking with me prompted the thought. I didn't want any part of it, so I looked at my watch. When I saw the time, I decided to use the filming schedule as my excuse. I thought, *Screw this. I'm out of here.*"

She sees Sam give her his Cheshire cat grin, so she asks, "What's that about?"

"It's just nice to know black angels do exist after all."

Chantell hangs her head. "I'm sorry. I made an ugly statement earlier, didn't I?"

"Kind of sort of. Can I ask, has this ever happened to you before?"

"No, that's why it's so freaky, especially with how it happened. So, it was really too much when you told me your dream and told me you had the same sense that you were to be my guardian angel."

"Does this mean you are warming up to my little game?"

"No, Mr. Milton. Just the opposite. You having that horrible dream about me, especially after hearing how mad you are at God, doesn't make me feel comfortable at all. And, you have been institutionalized, which makes me think you could still be psychotic. The only reason I'm still sitting here is that I'm afraid what my brothers might do to you if I run out of here."

"Is that really the only reason you're still here?"

Chantell looks down. "Yes, but also, I stayed because you called me your guardian angel."

"So, are you now thinking God is in this?"

Chantell sits staring, not answering for a long time. She looks off in the distance, and Sam can see her lips just barely moving but nothing is said. She eventually turns back toward him and says, "I have been praying for an answer."

"Really? Have you gotten anything?"

"No."

"Maybe you should try the Pentecostal method."

"What, start babbling in tongues?"

"No, that would freak out the whole restaurant. I mean you should listen to that still, small voice. Next time you pray, speak your peace and then relax. Say the first word that comes to your mind, then the next one, and then the next one. Eventually, you will realize someone is talking to you. It could even end up a two-way conversation."

"And how do you know it's not just a demon giving you false doctrine?"

Sam laughs. "I have yet to hear the voice say, 'It's now the Father, Son, Holy Spirit, and Bernice.' "

That causes Chantell to chuckle.

"That still, small voice is hard to hear at first, but when you get it, you'll find it's simple yet profound and will always have your best interest at heart. It's fatherly advice."

Chantell gives Sam a smirk. "I see, this is great spiritual advice coming from a man who's mad at God." Sam smiles, and Chantell quickly states, "I know, I know, another antonymic phrase. I will make sure I use your technique the next time I get a conference call with God Almighty."

"Well, until you hear from God . . ." Sam says as he reaches into the bouquet of flowers and pulls out a long yellow rose with a little vial attached. "Since you came here with me tonight, I owe you this. After all, you did complete the first item on the list: I just had dinner with Chantell León. I would say that kind of bumped up my social life, wouldn't you? "

Chantell brings the rose up to her nose. "Wasn't that expensive, a single rose delivered in Beverly Hills on such short notice?"

"Yes, very costly, to the tune of $12,500,057.26."

"I see you got the after-Valentine's-Day discount."

"Yes, all $2.15. So . . .?"

Chantell exhales loudly and announces, "Mr. Milton, with great reservation and trepidation, I will continue with your little game—only because I just got an answer to my prayer."

"Really? What?"

"I asked him, 'If he was really sincere about this, then why didn't he give me the yellow roses he promised?' "

"Wow, I'm at a loss for words." Sam thinks a moment and gives an exaggerated nod, saying, "And there you have it: a divine exclamation point. It seems there are a large variety of roses. I hope I picked one to your liking."

She smiles and says, "This one will do quite nicely. So, what is next on the list?"

"Let's just say it will be a little less formal, but still intimate. It's to replace what most people take for granted, but under the circumstances, it's something I'm sure not going to get for a very long time."

"You used the word *intimate*. I thought you said there would not be anything physical."

"I'm sorry. When I said something *intimate*, I was thinking more of a place than an activity. But hey, if you have another suggestion for intimacy, I'm all in."

Chantell leans back, gives an overtly negative grimace, and replies, "I just bet you would."

Sam leans in and clarifies, "Yes, this a game to replace what I lost; but it is also a game of trust. You will have to learn to trust me, but it is also set up to where I will have to trust you, because that is the only way trust works. However, I'm not going to make it easy. As I said, each item will be increasingly difficult; the last will be, by far, the most difficult. However, you can count on one thing, Miss León. Even though this whole thing is for my benefit, I will always have your best interest in mind, even above my own. As for what is next? Let me ask you, what is your favorite home-cooked meal? It can be as simple as pancakes or as complicated as oysters Rockefeller."

"Oh, I see," Chantell says, thinking she has to endure an intimate, home-cooked meal at his place. "You mean regardless of the effort it takes?"

"I'm game for anything, Miss León. I happen to be a pretty good cook."

"In that case, beef Wellington."

"Really, beef Wellington?"

Chantell nods confidently.

"Wow, that's going to be tough, but okay. I think I can handle that. And for a side dish?"

Chantell smiles. "Fried okra?"

"With beef Wellington?"

Chantell gives Sam a cocky nod.

"Okay, then I'm looking forward to tasting your beef Wellington and fried okra."

"What? I can't cook beef Wellington! I thought you were offering to be the cook."

"No problem. You have two weeks to learn."

Chantell shakes her head hard. "I can't learn to cook beef Wellington in two weeks! Not with my schedule!"

Sam smiles, putting his fingers together as he leans his elbows on the table. "Then, Miss León, I suggest we revisit this *trust me* thing. When I ask you what your favorite home-cooked meal is, I suggest you tell me what your favorite home-cooked meal really is. And something is telling me it isn't beef Wellington.

However, I will be making the dessert, so I will send you a list of the ingredients I'll need."

"You thinking you're making dessert in my kitchen?"

"It's that intimacy thing. Of course, we could do your more physical suggestion instead."

Chantell snorts, "Just give me the list!"

"Ah, ah, ah," Sam says as he stands to his feet. "God has been very kind and talkative to us tonight. Let's not piss him off."

He stands and sticks out his hand for her to take. Instead, she stands by herself and walks to the door in front of him. She pushes through it before he can help her. While waiting for the valet to bring the car, Sam steps to the street side of the sidewalk, as manners dictate. Chantell looks perturbed at his chivalry and asks, "What are you doing?"

"I have been well trained, Miss León."

"What kind of BS is that? These are the '80s, Milton. You know: women's lib, women of power."

"Miss León, I'm going to treat you like a gentleman should treat a lady, whether you like it or not—even if I have to make it a requirement of the game. So, you are just going to have to endure it."

"Fine!"

Soon, they are in the car. The drive home is as uncomfortably quiet as the drive to the restaurant. When he pulls up to her door, she quickly disconnects her seatbelt. When she sees him doing the same, she asks, "What do you think you're doing?"

"I am a gentleman. I'm going to walk you to the door."

"This is not a date, Milton. And don't you dare think it's going that way!"

"Okay, fine. Good night, Miss León."

Chantell closes the car door. It's not a slam, but it's still hard enough to get the point across. She turns and walks toward the door. When she realizes he's not leaving, she turns to ask, "What are you waiting for?"

Sam touches the button, and the passenger window goes down. "I'll leave when you are safely inside."

She throws her hands in the air and mouths, *What?*

Sam responds, "It's called etiquette, Miss León." She turns, opens the front door, steps inside, and closes it without looking back.

Inside, Chantell tosses her jacket over the back of the sofa and hears, "How was your date?"

She shoots back, "Mother! Don't you dare ever call any of these items on his checklist dates! I am not doing this willingly. I'm being forced!"

"Then how was your event? You're home later than I expected, so you must have talked a little. How is Mr. Milton?"

"Mother, he's weird! All through dinner, he kept staring at me like he was trying to see how he was going to carve up my face. Then he commented on how my right eye was more open than the left, which gave corresponding balance to my nose curving slightly to the left. He also loved that my cheekbones could poke an eye out. So, what am I—a Picasso?"

Chantell gets frustrated when her mother starts laughing. "Yeah, go ahead and laugh, Momma. After telling me about all of my lopsided facial features, he then tells me I am not at all racially ambiguous. He says I'm perfectly black." Chantell throws her hands up. "What's that supposed to mean?"

"It sounds to me like he's an artist trying to give you compliments."

"Mother! Whose side are you on anyway?"

"The right side. And that doesn't sound like yours at the moment. Did he talk about anything else besides body parts?"

"Oh yeah! This is the best one yet! He had a dream about me."

"A dream? Was it really sexy like the one you showed me the other day?"

"Mother, that was blatantly pornographic and you know it!"

"I don't know. I liked it. If he were my age, he would have been a keeper."

"Mother, Sam dreamed of me as an old hag. Oh, and the best part? Though he didn't exactly say it, he made it sound like we were married! And then he pushes me off a cliff!"

"I don't know. If I were married to an old hag, I would push her off a cliff, too."

"Mother!"

"Did he show any other signs of violence?"

"He said he wanted to take me over his knee and paddle my butt!"

Angelica looks skeptical. "Why am I positive you are leaving something out of this? What's behind the story?"

"Okay. I may have made a racist statement, so he was going to drag me over to my brothers and have one of them spank me. But he was still going to watch!"

Angelica laughs hard enough that tears are running down her cheeks. This infuriates her daughter. "I'm sorry, Chantell, but I'm really starting to like this guy. How did he treat you? Not like the guys you date who walk all over you, I hope."

"Are you gonna start badmouthing Dwain again?"

"It's pronounced *going to*! And no daughter of mine is going to marry a guy who can't sing a note yet sells millions of records with swear words in the title like 'I'm Going to _____ that Girl!' What is that? And when are you going to realize guys like that are going to treat you just like they treat the girls in their lyrics?"

"Momma, I like Dwain, and I like his music!"

"Music, my fat butt! I hope this Sam Milton guy does take you over his knee and paddle you, because you need it, girl! So, how did Sam Milton treat you anyway?"

"Like a wuss, Momma! He was always running around trying to do things for me."

"What kind of things?"

"Well, he ran to open doors for me and insisted on walking on the street side of the sidewalk, stuff like that."

"Really? You are upset because he acted like a gentleman?"

"Momma, I was so mean to him. I insulted him every way I could. I embarrassed him. I even made fun of his suit. And he took it, Momma. Even when I was screaming at him, he barely raised his voice, and he never even said a swear word. No guy I know would have taken any of that. I would never have any man who doesn't respect himself."

"Girl, you have no idea what respect is! You would rather have him insult you like Dwain does on his records, calling women bitches and sluts. I suppose you would let him hit you upside the head like I let your daddy do to me! Girl, when are you going to figure out that what you admire in the guys you date is fake? It's all talk; they're bragging and strutting down the street like peacocks, wearing gold draped around their necks and on their fingers. They wear gold earrings, and some even have diamonds in their teeth. And all of that just to hide the fact that they are a peacock without any tail feathers. Strip them down, and you won't find even a speck of integrity. Not a speck of it!"

"Mother, I'm going to bed. Malcom said he would drive you home."

"Chantell León, don't make me write a column about you!"

"You already have five times, Momma."

"Well, this time I will add your name to it."

"Good night, Mother."

12

Number Two

===

Walking out from the makeup trailer, Carol asks Chantell, "Hey, have you heard from your pervert lately?"

"No, and it's been over two weeks."

"Maybe the sicko forgot about you. Say, are you ever going to tell me how the meeting went with you, your mom, and him?"

Chantell quickly turns around. "Shush! Nobody's supposed to know about that. You didn't tell anybody, did you?"

"No, and it's the most difficult job you have ever given me."

"Wait here. I need to get something out of my trailer." Chantell steps inside and then quickly sticks her head back out. "Carol, come in here, quick."

Carol steps inside the small dressing room and sees Chantell standing frozen in place. Over her shoulder, Carol can see two yellow roses with a card attached. "What? Ah! Well, it looks like you just heard from the pervert . . . Well, go on, open it."

"I'm afraid to."

"You want me to open it?"

"No! No, I'll do it." Chantell opens it up, quickly reads the note, and hands it to Carol.

The card reads, "#2 Home life. Dinner, your house, two weeks, no beef Wellington, no brothers. Pick a time and day. Call me back and leave a message. List of ingredients: brownie mix, cocoa, powdered sugar, real vanilla extract, real vanilla ice cream, real whipped cream—spray can okay."

110

"What the hell does this all mean? Doesn't this guy know how to talk in a sentence?" queries Carol.

"Evidently not."

"Does he know you're going to be in Miami for a month?"

"No, so I will have to fly him out. After all, this whole mess is all my fault."

"That sounds so troublesome. You *are* going to have your brothers there, right?"

"Yes. Momma is going to make sure of that."

Carol reads the note again. "It sounds like someone versed in writing ransom notes. I'm going to dig into this guy some more."

Chantell glances back at Carol and says, "Make sure it's before next Tuesday. It's the only day I have free."

"Wasn't that the day you were going to Dwain's concert?"

"I guess I'm not going now."

"He isn't going to like that. I hope this Milton guy knows what he's in for."

"Oh, I can guarantee you he doesn't."

"Ooh, does this mean you're going to be mean to him again?"

Chantell only answers with a wicked grin.

"Ooh, you go girl! I'm going to love hearing about this."

———

"He wants what?"

"I said he wants a home-cooked meal."

"That's all?"

"That's all, Momma, and he wants me to cook it."

"Uh-oh."

"What do you mean by 'Uh-oh'?"

"Well, dear, you are a wonderful daughter, a great singer, and even a good actress, but you can't cook—not a lick."

"Boy, I can testify to that!" one of Chantell's brothers chimes in from the other room.

"Lawrence, you stay out of this," Chantell yells back.

"Hey, no way, man. The last time I had your spaghetti, I was on the toilet for three days."

"I told you I accidentally used expired mushrooms!"

"Knowing you, they were toadstools. Hey, that's a great idea! Let him eat some of your cooking. That will get rid of him for sure. That is, if it doesn't kill him."

Angelica intervenes. "You're not being fair to your sister, Lawrence."

"What do you mean, 'not being fair'? Mom, she is the only person in the entire state of California who is required to post 9-1-1 on her refrigerator."

Angelica squints. "You got that from last night's *The Tonight Show*, didn't you?"

"Well, it fits. Oh yeah, do you remember the time she had all of us over for her meatloaf, and Uncle Lucius brought all of those warning labels off old paint cans? When we passed the food around, each plate had a warning label that said, 'WARNING: DO NOT TAKE INTERNALLY!' "

"Oh yes," Angelica says, slapping herself on the knee and laughing hysterically. "And another said, 'IF TAKEN INTERNALLY, DO NOT INDUCE VOMITING AND CALL PHYSICIAN IMMEDIATELY!' I thought everyone was going to die laughing."

"Mother!"

"I'm sorry, dear." Still laughing, Angelica asks, "What does he expect you to cook?"

"He said nothing special. Just whatever I would fix for myself—"

"Oh, I can't wait to see this," Lawrence interrupts. "He's going to travel clear across the country to sit down for a nice, traditional home-cooked TV dinner."

"Will you both take this seriously? I've got 12.5 million dollars riding on this."

Lawrence and Angelica stop to look at each other before breaking out in the most hysterical laugh yet.

Chantell gets up from the table to leave, but her mother takes her hand and motions her to sit down again. "I'm sorry, dear. We'll stop giving you a hard time," she says, wiping tears from her eyes. "When does he expect you to have this dinner?"

"I'm flying him out in about two weeks, when our schedules coordinate."

"You're flying him out?" Lawrence asks. He then sees his sister's scowl and rethinks his statement. "Oh yeah—you made him lose everything he owns."

"Thanks for the reminder, Lawrence!"

"Don't worry, dear," Angelica says, comforting her daughter. "Two weeks should be enough to get something together—even for you. Hey, what about that blackened chicken recipe your sister made?"

"Hey, sis, that's perfect. He could never tell you burned it!"

"Out, both of you! Out now!" Chantell explodes.

"I'll get the recipe for you, dear."

"Out!"

The door opens, and Chantell walks in with a large sack of groceries. She places them on the counter and says to her mother, "Okay. I've got everything: the chicken, spices, potatoes, and okra. Oh, and a tiny jar of . . . well, never mind. Thanks, Mom. It's really nice of you and Lawrence to come over and help me get things started for tonight."

"Don't mention it. You're lucky it's your sister's birthday next week, and her little Zinnia's a week later."

"And, of course, it wouldn't have anything to do with your birthday being two days after Zinnia's?"

"I'm only here to give you support."

"Yeah right. And my brothers?"

"Okay, so I like birthdays. Just remember, we're all just down the hall in case you need us."

"I guess there's an advantage to us having condos in the same building."

The phone rings, and Angelica goes over to answer it while Lawrence sits at the counter eating a brownie.

"Hey, those are for tonight, by special request!" Chantell admonishes.

"Sorry, sis."

"Hello? Yes, Mr. Hastings, we've been waiting for your call. What do you have for us?" Angelica takes the phone in the other room while her two kids continue to bicker.

A few minutes later, Lawrence teases, "Hey, sis, you're not going to fall for this guy, are you?"

"Please! Have a little more respect for me than that! I don't like him any more than you do. It's just the situation, and that's all."

"Yeah, right."

Chantell is about to lay into her brother but stops when she sees the concerned look on her mother's face. "What's up, Mom?"

"Honey, maybe we had better rethink this dinner tonight."

"Why?"

"That was Bob Hastings from the detective agency Carol hired to look into Sam's background. We know Mr. Milton spent time in a mental institution. He insinuated it was for depression after a personal tragedy of some type. Bob Hastings found out that when he was in the mental hospital, he was transferred from ward B to ward D."

"What does that mean in English, Momma?"

"Ward B is for people with severe depression, and ward D is for those with sexual disorders."

Lawrence interjects, "So, Carol was right. He's a pervert."

Alarmed, Chantell asks, "Why didn't it show up on the police report?"

"It was a self-admittance, so there was no need for the police to be informed."

"So, are you saying this whole thing of ripping my clothes off may not have been an accident after all?"

"We don't know that, but you might think of canceling your plans for tonight."

"Momma, it's not like he's coming from across town. He's flying in from LA. Besides, we don't know why he changed wards, so how can we—" Chantell stops when she sees her mother holding up her hand.

"Unfortunately, there's more, and it may shed some light on why he was admitted into the sexual disorders ward. Hastings also found what's called a nonbinding assessment from an orderly in ward D. It's mainly for inner hospital attendants as it discusses special needs or troublesome patients. It states, 'Sam Milton can be exceedingly difficult to manage. This patient has an acute obsession with certain foods, namely he has an unnatural obsession for chocolate sauce and whipped cream. He has become violent when served chow mein noodles, to the point that physical restraints were required.'

Lawrence asks, "Didn't that thing with this Milton guy and the fifteen-year-old girl involve whipped cream?"

Angelica reacts with her eyes before saying, "That's right, it did. And he wants to make chocolate sauce tonight."

"Momma, Malcom will down an entire can of whipped cream at one time. And you, Lawrence, will put an entire jar of chocolate sauce on one bowl of ice cream! And neither of you has been in a mental institution, though you should be! Good Lord, can this get any more complicated?"

"We're just trying to keep you safe, honey."

"I know, Momma. I don't like it either, but Johnny did vouch for this guy. Hey, I just remembered—my neighbor Tember and her husband are out of town visiting her parents. I will call and see if the boys could use their condo for a few hours. Mine backs up to hers, so I could call or bang on the wall."

"It's okay by me, sis. I'll check with Malcom and Eddie."

Angelica takes a deep breath. "Well, that should work. And who knows? There could be a simple explanation for the whole thing."

"I hope not," Lawrence spouts. "I would like to bust his head."

"Great, Lawrence. While I lie dying of a stab wound, you make sure to bust his head."

Sometime later, Sam rings the doorbell dressed in the same suit as their dinner date, with a different shirt and tie. Chantell opens the door dressed in sweats. She looks him up and down.

"I hope you were not expecting candlelight," she offers.

"I didn't know what to expect."

She looks him up and down again before saying, "Obviously."

Sam holds up a bottle of wine and a decorative wine bag. Changing the subject, he says, "It needs to breathe, so can I open it and set it here?"

Chantell nods. "That's fine," she says as she looks back at the kitchen. "Um, something came up, so dinner is going to be about a half hour late."

"That's okay with me. Would you like me to wait outside again?"

"That would be lov—"

"Hi, what's your name?" The little voice comes from behind Chantell.

Sam looks down to see a little seven-year-old girl with a bright smile, cornrows, and two missing teeth. He hunches down to her four-foot level and engages with her. "My name is Sam Milton. What's yours?"

The meek voice answers, "Zinnia."

"Sam, this is my niece, Zinnia. I'm watching her until my sister comes home."

Sam feels a little tug on his pant leg. He sees little Zinnia looking at him. "Can you teach me how to ride my bike?"

"I'm sorry, Zinnia, Mr. Milton and I will be eating in a half an hour," Chantell replies.

Sam, however, says with enthusiasm, "Well, that's plenty of time to teach you to ride a bike!"

Zinnia gives Sam a big smile, displaying her two missing teeth. "Really?"

Chantell looks shocked. "Sam, what are you doing?"

Not paying attention, Sam continues with Zinnia. "Well, sweetie, that depends on whether you have three things."

"What things?"

"First, do you have a bike?"

Zinnia nods.

"Good. Do you have any tennis courts on these palace grounds?"

"Yes," Chantell answers for her, "and stop calling it a palace."

"Now, for the biggest question: Do you have a hoodie, Zinnia?"

She nods quickly.

"Very good. Go get your hoodie, your bicycle, and we'll all go to the tennis courts in five minutes."

As Zinnia runs off, Chantell all but yells at her unwanted guest, "What do you think you're doing?"

"Weren't you about to tell me to wait outside? Well, that's what I'm going to do—and teach your niece to ride a bicycle while I wait."

"What makes you think you can get her to ride it in thirty minutes?"

"I have no intention of teaching her to ride in thirty minutes."

"What? You just lied to a seven-year-old girl?"

"No, I didn't. I will have her riding her bike in less than fifteen minutes."

"What? Fifteen minutes? All three of my brothers plus my sister and I have been trying to teach this kid for two weeks now, and she hasn't gotten it yet."

"Has anyone helped her while she was wearing a hoodie?"

"What has a hoodie got to do with anything?"

Sam smiles. "That's how I will do it—and in less than fifteen minutes. It could be less than ten if everything she learned from you guys kicks in."

"What kind of bull are you giving me? Fifteen minutes, my . . . hiney."

───

Soon, Chantell and Sam are standing on the tennis courts, with Zinnia on her bike. "Okay, Mr. Milton, the pressure's on. You have exactly thirty minutes until I have to go and pull dinner out of the oven."

Sam begins, "Are you ready, Zinnia?" She nods excitedly. "All righty then. I will hold you up by your handlebars to start. Then, I'm going to hold you up by just your hoodie. Okay?"

She nods, and they are off. As soon as they get up a little speed, Sam grabs the top of her hood and holds her up with it. Zinnia wobbles, trying to keep the bike straight. By the time they get past the net, Sam can feel she is steady enough on her own, but he holds on anyway until they get to the end of the court. They turn around and start again. When Sam feels she is again balancing on her own, he lets go, and she is off. Sam runs along beside her, giving encouragement so she doesn't think he has let go. When they get even with the net, Sam stops, and little Zinnia is riding on her own.

Chantell applauds and jumps up and down like a schoolgirl. "Oh, my blessed Lord! She's doing it!"

"Yes!" Sam answers. "And in less than four and a half minutes—a new world record."

Chantell's sister comes on to the tennis court and starts jumping up and down. Two of her brothers stand back, but Lawrence comes and stands next to his sisters and cheers.

A very impressed Chantell asks, "How did you know you could do it so fast?"

"I taught all ten kids in my neighborhood this way; all were wearing hoodies, and all learned in under fifteen minutes."

"Wow," Chantell's sister says. "You should write a book."

After they say good night to Zinnia and Chantell's siblings, they make it back to her condo. Chantell tells Sam, "Dinner will be ready in just a few minutes, and I need to prepare a few things. You can wait in the living room, if you like. I have something in there you might be interested in."

"Is it your 'weird hobby' that the tabloids keep trying to guess at?"

"Maybe. Just take a look and tell me what you think."

Chantell is reaching into the oven to pull out a side dish when she hears Sam yell, "Oh, this is soooo cool!" Chantell stops and smiles.

Sam's mouth drops completely open as he stares at a six-foot-long hunter-green model train with the name Southern Crescent printed on the side. It is only comprised of the engine, tender, and one passenger car, but it takes up the entire mantel of the fireplace and extends several inches beyond on each side.

Sam's excitement increases as he looks at it closely. "Wait, this isn't store bought; this is hand built! It's incredible! Who built it?"

"I did."

Sam turns around to see Chantell leaning against the doorjamb. "No way! Really? The whole thing?"

"Every square inch. It took four full years. I started it my first year of high school and finished it just before graduation. My brothers showed me how to put it together, but I wouldn't let them touch even one part of it. The reason it took so long is that I had to practice building and painting two other engines before they would let me touch this one."

"Where are the other two engines?"

"My brothers blew one up and then wrecked the other one reenacting *The Bridge over the River Kwai*."

"Boy, I bet you were pissed. But, *Bridge over the River Kwai*?"

"That's not what you would think little black boys would be playing, is it?"

Sam looks a little sheepish.

Chantell holds him there until she adds, "Since my mother started out as a singer, then becoming a Hollywood gossip columnist, she was on TV a lot, so we grew up in Hollywood, in a mostly white neighborhood. It also helped that our next-door neighbor's grandfather was into studio special effects and worked on the movie. So, I was more honored than pissed that they had used my engine. We made a video of both if you would like to see it later."

"I would be honored to see it. Thank you. Say, why the Southern Crescent?"

"It has to do with my great-grandfather. I need to put dinner together, so why don't you come into the dining room while I give you the explanation?"

As Sam follows Chantell into the dining room, he thinks to himself, *Wow, it seems the iceberg has finally melted.* Out loud, he asks, "Say, would you like some help?"

Chantell stops and puts one hand on her hip as she looks back to say, "I haven't forgotten why we're doing this. I may be forced to cook dinner for you, but I will not let your white butt step foot in my kitchen!"

"Ouch! Say, where's your thermostat? It suddenly became very cold in here."

"Have a seat, Mr. Milton. As for my great-grandfather and the Southern Crescent? He was the conductor."

"Wow! That's fantastic!"

"It was quite an honor. Most black men at the time were porters, not conductors. Did you know that it isn't the engineer who's the boss on the train, it's the conductor?"

"No, I didn't know that. I wish I could have met him. I bet he had stories!"

"Oh, yes he did. Did you ever have any model trains, Mr. Milton?"

"I had HOs as a kid, but I always wanted to get into G scale. Yours is O scale, isn't it?"

Chantell has to speak over clanging pots and pans. "Yes, halfway between the two. If it were G scale, just the engine would be over three feet long. I think O scale looks better. G looks fake to me."

Sam looks over the nicely set table. The plates have a contemporary style. The silverware is sleek, with real walnut handles. "I like your place setting and dining room furniture—all very sleek and modern."

"I call it early-'60s modern. Everyone else is going to that rounded, oil-rubbed oak. I want my things to stay in style more than a week and a half."

"Good point. So, what's for dinner? It sure smells good."

"Well, I was going to make meatloaf, but I changed my mind."

"But I love meatloaf. When I go to the Cheesecake Factory, that's what I always get."

Speaking from the kitchen, Chantell says, "And that's why I didn't make it. There's no way I can compete with theirs. And so, I made Louisiana blackened chicken."

Coming out of the kitchen with two plates, she sets one down for each of them. "Are you familiar with Cajun cuisine, Mr. Milton?"

Sam looks at the dark roasted chicken pieces on the platter. "Oh, I've had it a couple of times. As I recall, it can get a little warm."

Chantell gives Sam a mischievous smile. "Yes, it can get a trifle hot."

"What are the side dishes?"

"Everything is Cajun, from the salad dressing to the fried okra. Only the mashed potatoes are not. They're still Southern, but not hot. You shouldn't have any troubles with those. But, please, try the chicken; it's my favorite. Let me go and get the wine."

As she leaves, Sam tries a small bite of the chicken. Instantly, his face turns beet red. He goes for his water, but it only makes it worse. Chantell comes back with two glasses of white wine. "How is it?"

Struggling to speak, Sam asks in a hoarse, whispery voice, "Can I get a glass of milk, please?"

Chantell's smile increases tenfold. "I'll be right back. Say, would you like me to make you a peanut butter and jelly sandwich?"

"Yes, please," he says as loud as he can, but it is barely a whisper.

She turns and comes back to the table. "Here, take my plate," she says, handing it over to him.

He throws his hands up and says, "No, thank you. I may need to go to the hospital."

She smiles at him before asking, "You don't know the first thing about Cajun food, do you, Mr. Milton?"

"Evidently not," he says with tears streaming down his face.

"I know you don't because what you have been trying to eat isn't the least bit Cajun."

"What is it?" he asks, now coughing.

"I'm not sure. The grocer told me it's an Asian pepper—the hottest pepper on the planet, in fact. So, for your sake, please try mine."

Still unable to see, he pokes around her plate until he locates the potatoes and gravy. He takes a small spoonful. He smacks his lips. "Hey, this is mild."

She smiles as he takes a bigger bite.

"I don't taste anything. Does this have any Cajun spices in it?"

Chantell sits back in her chair, smiles, and announces, "Nope! I can't stand the stuff."

Wiping the tears from his eyes, he sighs, "Miss León, you are the meanest woman I've ever met!"

"Meaner than my mother?"

"By far!"

Chantell leans over the table, places her hands together in prayer fashion, then rests her chin on her two thumbs. "Yes, Mr. Milton, I can be extremely mean. So, if I were you, I would watch out for me and consider carefully what you ask me to do."

"Can we call a truce through the rest of dinner?" Sam asks, still panting.

"If you like."

"I would like," Sam says, still trying to get the burn out of his mouth.

"Are you going to stare at me like you did last time?"

"Probably."

"Why do you do that? It's kind of creepy."

"Miss León, do you know how beautiful you are?"

Chantell gives a sideways nod, indicating *sort of.*

"No, you don't, and that is a wonderful part of your personality."

"I would ask if you are the kind of guy who undresses a woman with his eyes, but I have never seen your eyes get past my face."

"I see a woman as a beautiful sculpture or a painting. However, I prefer them clothed, though depending on the situation, it could be as little clothes as possible."

"Good, I was beginning to worry about you."

He further explains, "I design and build furniture. With furniture, it's all in the details, along with balance and proportion, and your face has it all, as perfect as one could get."

"So, you think I would make a beautiful desk?"

Sam drops his head, laughs, and tosses up his hands in surrender.

Chantell changes course. "I'm curious. Why did you ask for red wine when we're having chicken? You do know it's supposed to be white wine with chicken?"

Sam notes the dig, but chooses to ignore it and say, "To be brutally honest, I hate red wine. It all tastes like hydraulic fluid to me. But, I must say, it doesn't taste so bad once you've had your taste buds burned away."

Chantell gives him a quizzical look.

He answers with, "When I got my first car, I went and showed it off at a friend's house. He gave me a beer. Just one beer! Forty-five minutes later, I was heading home when I hit a small child."

"Oh my! That's horrible! You didn't kill—"

"No. I was driving slowly because I saw a bunch of kids run up to the curb. They all stopped, so I kept going. One child in the back didn't stop and ran right in front of me. I saw him go up on my hood and then fall down. I thought I was stopped on top of him. Fortunately, I saw him get up and run. I was afraid he was hurt, so I pulled him down and held him there until help arrived. There was one man who really let into me verbally. I thought he was going to hit me. Well, the police showed up, took notes, let the boy run home, and let me go. They never suspected or checked my blood alcohol."

Chantell smiles mischievously, forcing Sam to ask, "What?"

"I can tell you don't drink, Mr. Milton. One beer in forty-five minutes? No one would suspect alcohol caused that accident. Was the boy okay?"

"His mother called me the next day and said he didn't even have a bruise. She then gave me an apology."

"She apologized? Why?"

"It seems the man screaming at me about driving too fast was the boy's father. He was so mad that he never knew it was his son who got hit."

"Wow! I'm glad you and the child got out of there without bruises."

"So, how did you do in high school?" Sam asks as he takes another bite. "I bet you were the most popular girl in school."

"Just the opposite. I went through what my grandmother calls a 'severe molting stage'—

you know, like the ugly swan. I didn't even get asked out at my junior prom."

"Really? I would have never guessed that."

"How were you in high school? Did your shyness give you problems?"

"Yes, that, and I dressed like a geek. Because of it, I was known as the school's punching bag. I kid you not. Within one week—one week, mind you—I got beat up three times. The first was when I was sitting in the quad. I happened to be sitting next to the only black guy in the school. For some unknown reason, he hauls off and lands one across my jaw. Maybe someone said something; I don't know. Anyway, two days later, seven Hispanics jumped me. Those guys were little, so I did a little better, but I still got beat. Then, just to prove the school was not biased or prejudiced in any way, shape, or form, two white guys kicked my butt. All in one week!"

"Oh, that is bad. Glad to see the school was well-rounded."

They both laugh.

Sam then accentuates with hand gestures. "But that's not the best one."

Chantell sits wide-eyed.

"This little redheaded kid comes up and picks a fight. I mean this kid was little. My big Dutch friend said, 'Go for it, Sam. You deserve to pound one.' The kid kept asking for it, so I was just about to lay into him when God spoke to me for the first time."

"God?"

"God himself! Something bothered me about how the kid was standing; he was way too calm. That's when a loud voice in my head said, 'Ask him what his father does for a living.' So, I did. I asked him, 'What does your dad do for a living?' He gets this disappointed look on his face and says, 'He teaches karate at the Navy base.' "

Chantell laughs so hard that wine comes out of her nose. Wiping it up, she says, "Yep, that was God all right."

She takes another bite before asking, "You mentioned you read a lot. What do you like reading the most?"

Sam pauses before answering, "Um, no comment."

"No comment? You have me curious. Is it porn?"

"I don't think anybody actually *reads* porn."

"Oh yeah, I suppose that's very true. But romance novels can get pretty erotic."

"Yes, that I do know."

After another long pause, Sam notices Chantell isn't saying anything; rather, she is looking at him intently. "What?"

"How do you know?" she finally asks him.

"How do I know what?"

Chantell puts her chin on her laced fingers and continues, "How do you know romance novels can get very erotic?"

"Well, I a—"

"You're starting to blush, Mr. Milton. I'm onto something, aren't I? Are you an avid reader of romance novels, or do you just read the erotic ones?" Chantell sits back and enjoys the show. She watches him squirm, the discomfort noticeable. She finally breaks the silence. "That is the one cool thing about white people: They all have this built-in lie detector when their skin turns red."

"That's a little racist, isn't it?"

"Maybe, but you're not proving me wrong. Man, look at you go. So, Mr. Sam Milton reads gushily erotic romance novels. Or, should I call them erotically gushy?"

"I'm not into gushy."

"Oh, so they're just erotic?"

Sam just keeps looking away, trying to find any distraction.

Chantell keeps going. "Maybe I should get you together with my girlfriends so we all can share."

Sam now puts his head between his hands, causing Chantell to gloat. "Ooh baby, I just nailed your butt!"

The bantering goes back and forth, with Sam losing most of the time. He's relieved when he hears Chantell say, "Well, now that dinner is finished, would you care to look at some photo albums?"

"Do you have any of you building the train?"

"Only about four."

"Pictures?"

"No, albums."

"Lead on."

An hour later, Sam closes the last album. "I'm so impressed! And you did it all by yourself, huh? Where did you find the time?"

"You have plenty of time when you're going through a molting stage. Well, Mr. Milton, this is your night. What would you like to do now?"

Sam gets a mischievous look on his face. He turns to Chantell and asks, "Do you really want to know?"

Chantell leans back and gives him a nervous, "Yes."

Sam gets uncomfortably close. He drops his head inches from her lap, then brings his head up slowly, looking past her belly button, up to her chest, and continuing past her neck to her face. He then says, in a deep, sensuous voice, "Miss León, I want to give you a hot-fudge climax!"

Chantell's eyes get huge.

Sam gives her a mischievous smile. Then he asks, in the same sensuous voice, "Do you mind if I use your kitchen? I need to heat up an item."

Chantell is so stunned that all she can do is nod.

So, Sam disappears into the kitchen, leaving Chantell alone with a huge but silent profane word on her lips. She picks up the phone and starts pounding on the numbers. Busy! She does it again. Still busy! A third time. Busy!

She can hear Sam banging around in the kitchen. He yells, "Where are your knives? I need to cut something open."

Without thinking, she answers, "In the drawer next to the stove." She then slaps her forehead as another profanity forms on her lips. She dials again. Still busy! She thinks and then pounds again. "Thank God! Hello, Momma? Carol was right! I think he's going to do something bad!"

"What do you mean? What?"

"He looked at me all wickedlike and said he is about to give me a hot-fudge climax!"

Angelica screams, "What?"

Chantell continues, "I tried calling the boys at Tember's. The phone is busy! I tried four times, Momma! . . . What? Oh my God! I forgot to pound on the wall."

"Do you have any whipped cream?" Sam asks from the kitchen.

"It's in the refrigerator," Chantell yells back. Then, she speaks into the phone, "What? I know I shouldn't have told him that! Just get over here fast!" She puts down the phone and runs into her bedroom, closing the door behind her. She pounds three times on the wall as hard as she can. She hears loud music, and profanity again leaves her lips.

"Hey, where did you go?" Sam asks from the kitchen.

Chantell looks up to say a prayer, "Oh God, oh God, oh God, oh God. Protect me, please." She walks to her bedroom door, takes a breath, and opens it slowly. She steps out and sees Sam standing there with two large bowls of ice cream.

"What's . . .? That's an ice cream sundae!" she exclaims.

"Well, technically, it's a brownie sundae. You look kind of surprised."

"Ah, well."

Suddenly, they hear a door slam down the hall and people running up to Chantell's door. "Oh dear God! Get in the kitchen, Sam!"

"What's going on?"

"Get into the kitchen now!"

Sam steps through the kitchen door just as Chantell's brothers burst through the front door. They move with such force that the door hits the back wall, causing a painting to fall to the floor. Sam can hear Chantell yell, "It's a mistake!"

"Where is he?" the largest brother yells.

Chantell stands in front of the kitchen door, holding Malcom back. "I made a mistake! I made a horrible mistake!"

"Is he in the kitchen?" Malcom responds, trying to push his sister out of the way.

Lawrence pulls him back. "Hey, dude. She said it's a mistake! Calm down!"

"I'm not calming down until I see that guy standing in front of me. Now!"

Sam steps out of the kitchen, still holding the dessert and looking terrified. "Ah . . . what's going on?" he asks timidly.

"You just about got your head broken!" Malcom yells, standing five full inches above Sam.

Angelica runs into the room and stops abruptly when she sees what Sam is holding. "What? That's a sundae. I thought he was going to do something to you with . . ."

Chantell shakes her head.

Angelica asks, "So, then what is a hot-fudge climax?"

Chantell cuts her off, "It's a sundae, Mother! Just a simple ice cream sundae."

"Well, technically, it's a hot-fudge brownie sundae," Sam says, his voice breaking with fear.

"Is that a hot-fudge climax?" Eddie asks. Everyone is surprised by the question. Sam quickly nods.

"What did you call it?" Chantell and her mother speak in unison.

"Oh, those are the greatest things in the world! I always get one when we go to that Trancas restaurant in Malibu. They have the best hot-fudge sauce ever."

"That's it?" Lawrence yells. "This is all about a stupid bowl of ice cream?"

"Well, it's tech—" Sam begins.

"Oh, shut up!" several yell.

"Okay, everybody," Angelica says. "Show's over; everybody go home." She starts pushing the boys out the door.

"Hey, I want one!" Eddie demands.

"I have plenty of sauce," Sam says. "I will send one over."

"Hey, thanks, man."

Malcom points his big finger in Sam's face. "I catch you outside this door, and you are going to be wearing your hot-fudge climax!"

"Out, all of you. Now!" Chantell yells. "Not you, Mother. You have some apologizing to do, along with me."

Chantell closes the door and points first to Sam and her mother, then to the couch. "Both of you, sit. Now!"

"Gee, what did I do?" Sam asks, sitting down while still holding the two sundaes. He leans over to Angelica and comments, "Boy, your family is rough."

Angelica turns to him to say, "You're telling me? Child, you better run out that door fast! This one is the worst of them."

"Mother!"

"See?"

Chantell closes the door and walks over to Sam. When there, she starts slapping, hitting, and kicking him, screaming, "Why the hell did you do that to me? You scared me to death! Are you completely out of your mind?"

Most of her anger is discharged verbally, so the blows aren't strong enough to hurt Sam physically. However, Sam sits in frozen devastation.

"Chantell León!" Angelica yells.

She turns to Angelica. "Mother, this whole thing was caused by Mr. Milton trying to make a joke. He acted all naughty and secretive about the sundae. What was I supposed to think?"

Chantell starts hitting him again and continues, "What the hell did you expect me to do? You gave me half information. Why not tell me the climax was strictly from chocolate?"

Sam sits mortified. He stares at the floor, not moving or saying anything. His emotional state goes unnoticed by Chantell, who is flailing her hands while screaming at him. However, it doesn't go unnoticed by her mother, so Angelica stands and forcefully grabs her daughter's arms, bringing them down to her side. She then shushes Chantell until she becomes quiet. Angelica then points toward Sam, who sits stunned, as if in a coma.

Chantell, finally noticing Sam's reaction, says in exasperation, "What? Again? This is the same crap he pulled on me after the accident!"

Angelica slaps her daughter across the face to shock her back to reality.

Chantell stops, looks at her mom, and turns her attention to Sam. She takes a deep breath and whispers to her mother, "I guess this explains the hospital stay."

Chantell then sits down in front of Sam and tries to take his hand, but Sam just sits rubbing his legs with his open palms.

She offers an apology. "I'm sorry, Mr. Milton. I had no right to unload on you like that. You were just trying to be humorous, and I missed it completely. I'm very sorry."

Sam glances up at Chantell, then quickly looks back down before saying, "You have every right to unload. I didn't just hurt you. I hurt everyone in your family." He stands to his feet. "I'll be leaving now. Please accept my apology, and it's not necessary for you to pay for my flight home. I should be paying for both anyway."

Before Sam gets to the door, Chantell asks politely, "With what money, Mr. Milton? I took it all away from you."

Sam pauses to think and says, "I still have a credit card."

"And I'm quite certain the flight back will max it out. Then what?"

"That's my problem, Miss León."

"Mr. Milton, you are such a putz."

Sam pauses again, then reaches for the door.

Chantell bluntly states, "Your job isn't finished yet—and neither is mine."

"I said I never wanted the money. If you would like, I will send you an itemized list; that should square us up."

"That's not what I meant when I said our jobs weren't yet finished, and finishing is far more important to me than the seventy-five million."

Sam stands in silence.

Chantell continues, "God will spank my butt hard if I let you walk out that door without completing my mission. And don't forget, you're my angel, too. Or is feeling sorry for yourself more important?"

Still staring at the door, Sam exhales loudly. "Miss León, you are just like your mother. You are by far the meanest woman I've ever met." Turning around, he adds, "And unfortunately, you're even more articulate."

Chantell pats the couch. "Please come sit next to me. I think it's only right for you to explain a few things. Besides, we haven't had our dessert yet. I would really like to try this hot fudge sauce that caused everyone so much grief."

"Everyone except Eddie," Angelica says, also patting the couch.

Chantell smiles. "Yes, that's right, and I believe you promised my brother one of your desserts. He can get a little testy if he doesn't get his sugar fix. It's bad enough having one of my brothers mad at you. It would not be healthy to make two mad. Besides, I haven't gotten my yellow rose yet. And you ain't leaving without me getting it. I earned it!"

Sam shyly goes over to the table and retrieves the decorative wine bag. He brings it over to Chantell and says, "Your flower, Miss León."

Chantell looks into the sack and smiles. She reaches in and pulls out a crystal bud vase with two yellow roses. She looks relieved and then waves to Sam, saying, "Okay, Mr. Milton, now you can go."

Sam is looking confused, so Angelica assures him by saying, "She's kidding, Sam. Come sit."

He sits and is about to speak but gets interrupted by Chantell and Angelica. "Whatever you want to say, Mr. Milton, will have to wait. We have dessert to eat."

Sam looks into the two bowls. "I think I should remake them. The hot fudge sauce is cold, and the ice cream is warm."

"No, Mr. Milton, this one is just fine; and I will share it with my mother. Please take the other. If you would like, you can make one later and give it to my brother on your way out."

Sam takes a spoonful of what ice cream is left. "I feel the need to apologize again for my chronic shyness. I was shy in school, but it was never this bad."

Chantell digs in deep and takes a big spoonful while still attempting to speak. "What happened to you?" Before Sam can answer, Chantell exclaims, "Say, this is really good!"

"I'm telling ya," Angelica says, licking the spoon.

Sam gives his first big smile of the night, then slowly explains, "I have this problem. I don't remember anyone who embarrassed me or hurt me, but I never forget any time I have hurt someone else, and I still grimace every time I remember it. That can happen several times a day, and I'm afraid I will remember this night for a very long time."

Angelica asks, "Then how can you be so shy and timid, then suddenly be strong, assertive, and even funny?"

"I know it's weird, but I've been told I have a quick wit, and if I'm properly introduced, I can hold my own with anyone, no matter how big or important, hence Johnny Carson. Yet, I will stand in line at the DMV for an hour and a half and not be able to speak to a single soul unless they speak to me first. If I'm caught off guard, and the person is as beautiful as your daughter, I crawl into myself and become . . ."

"Sam Milton?" Angelica asks.

Sam looks at the floor and says softly, "Yeah, and to the nth degree."

"You are really one very screwed-up guy, Mr. Milton," Angelica says, then adds, "but still cute." Sam doesn't know how to react to her comment, so he keeps looking down to hide his embarrassment. Seeing it, Angelica lets up the heat and quizzes, "But shyness doesn't explain what we saw just a few minutes ago. You were totally traumatized. Where did that come from?"

"Oh, that," Sam says, lifting his head. He is forced to explain while trying not to notice the big dollop of whipped cream on the end of Chantell's nose.

"My, my psychologist calls it post-traumatic stress disorder, like those coming back from Vietnam."

Chantell beats her mother to the question. "Where did this PTSD come from?"

To keep from being distracted by Chantell's whipped-cream-covered nose, he looks back to the floor. "I guess I should start by telling you about my partner dying on one of our construction projects. It was my fault. I took a brace off of the scaffolding we were working on to unload a truck, and I forgot to put it back on. The first time I met his wife after the accident, she started hitting and screaming at me, the same way you did. It was ten years ago, but I still remember every word: 'You killed my husband! You screwed up, and now my husband is dead! That should have been *you* that died! Why wasn't it you? Why aren't you dead? You're the one who left that cross brace off, yet you jumped off the scaffolding before my husband, and now he's dead and you're not. Explain that to me, Sam, and then go explain it to my son!' "

"Is that true? You jumped off, letting your partner fall to his death?" Angelica asks with shock in her voice.

"As the scaffolding pulled away from the house, he was behind me, so I had to jump off first to clear the way. When I swung around to grab him, he was already beyond my grasp, and his hands slipped through mine. Anyway, when she unloaded on me, I sat there traumatized. I couldn't move or say anything, and just like you, it made her even angrier!"

As Sam stares at the floor while he talks, he doesn't see Chantell's tears. He continues, "They eventually had to take me to a hospital. I never moved or said anything for several days."

Anjelica puts her hand on Sam's back and asks, "Is that why you checked yourself into the sanitarium?"

"No, that came later. You see, Mrs. Martin, Ben's son had leukemia, and at the time, he was beating it. That is, until his father died. His wife committed suicide two weeks after her son's funeral."

Chantell gets up and quickly leaves the room. Angelica taps Sam's hand and says, "She'll be back in a minute. Something tells me this wasn't your intention tonight, was it?"

"I don't want your daughter feeling sorry for me. I do a great job of that all by myself. My whole intent was to show her I was a nice, normal guy. I succeeded in showing her I am the exact opposite. I bet she's afraid I could snap at any time."

"I don't think she thinks that at all. Here she comes, so let's ask her."

Chantell walks up to Sam, and he can see that her eyes are red. "Mr. Milton, I owe you another apology. You just explained the absolute hell you went through, and because of my actions a few weeks ago—and just now—I put you right back into it."

Sam looks up to think a moment. "Yes, but thanks to your blunt and assertive personality, you managed to do in thirty minutes what ten years of therapy hasn't."

"While you have a quick wit, my daughter has a quick temper." Angelica smiles at Chantell standing next to her. "She's still worth knowing though."

Sam now pats the couch for Chantell to sit. "The only way I'm going to get beyond what happened is to force myself to face my fears, triggers, and insecurities. So, you said you had more questions for me."

Chantell sits and faces Sam. "Sure you're okay?"

Sam exhales and then smiles. "This may sound chauvinist, but it's lucky that when girls get really mad, they don't hit hard."

"Well, then, I will just have to work on that."

"Please don't. With all that emotion behind you, even Muhammad Ali wouldn't stand a chance."

Angelica laughs so hard, she has whipped cream coming from her nose.

Chantell gives Sam a gloating smile before asking, "First, explain how you went from ward B, which housed patients with depression and anxiety, to ward D, which housed, among others, sexual predators."

"How did you find out about that?" Sam looks into Chantell's and Angelica's faces, understanding they want an answer, not a counterquestion. So, he explains the change in wards. "I found out the facility had a cabinet shop as part of their inpatient therapy program. Unfortunately, they weren't going to let anyone with clinical depression handle power tools and carving knives, so my doctor had my paperwork changed. It was supposed to be relabeled ward C, which is substance abuse. However, it was switched to ward D, which dealt with sexual predators. The paperwork was eventually corrected, so how your people found that error, I have no idea. Obviously, you had someone digging deep."

Angelica then asks, "Now, please explain the chow mein noodles incident, and why you needed to be restrained."

"That would be Hector."

"Hector?"

"To explain Hector, I need to explain my chocolate sauce obsession. Like your brother Eddie, I discovered hot-fudge climax at Trancas restaurant. I spent months getting my recipe to taste just like theirs. In the hospital, I shared the recipe with the cook, who shared it with everyone. After that, everyone loved me but hated Hector.

"Hector was an abusive orderly who had it in for me. He found out I hated chow mein noodles, so he had chow mein noodles put on everything served to me: eggs, pancakes, soups, and sandwiches. When I kept removing them, he went so far as to slice a slot in the side of a hamburger and insert them so I couldn't see they were there. These things were really making me sick, so when I found them in my tomato soup, I lost it. I threw the soup in his face. The soup was kind of hot. He pulled the alarm, and I was rushed upon and restrained. Fortunately, I had a hundred witnesses, including the cooking staff, testifying for me. I was released from solitary confinement, and Hector was let go."

Chantell and her mother look relieved.

Sam asks, "Anything else?"

Angelica asks, "What about the fifteen-year-old girl and the whipped cream?"

"Didn't you call the number on the card I gave to Johnny?"

"Yes, we did. That section of the State Department was closed down soon after your incident. The name on the card was Bryan Stanton, but he doesn't work there now, and no one could reach him."

"Yes, he was retiring because that entire wing was shutting down. Bryan knew it could get ugly if anyone checked into this, so he was kind enough to put his personal number on the back of the card. You did call the number on the back of the card?"

"Back of the card?" Angelica asks, confused.

"Mother?" Chantell asks intensely.

Angelica sits speechless, so Sam explains, "The name and number were in pencil, so both might have faded, but the police officer who first questioned me was still able to read it."

"I will check with Carol; she was the one checking into it."

"I'll save you the call. The senator's daughter had a seductive reputation. Is there anything else you want to know?" Sam asks.

After a long moment of silence, Angelica stands up. "I'm satisfied, Mr. Milton, and I'm sorry things got so messed up."

Sam stands and takes her hand. "Ten years of therapy in thirty minutes? I'm good with it."

"I look forward to what comes next, Mr. Milton. Until then, I will let you two finish up here."

"Goodbye, Mrs. Martin."

"It's Angelica, Sam."

"Goodbye, Angelica."

"Goodbye, Mother."

Chantell closes the door. "So, what would you like to do now, Mr. Milton? I hope it's not another hot-fudge climax."

"I do owe your brother one, though, don't I?"

"Can you leave the recipe?"

"It's already written down in the kitchen."

"Then I'm sure he'll be thrilled. He's actually a very good cook. Is there anything else?"

"No, I believe you have your roses, yes?"

"Speaking of that, what am I to expect next?"

"Our next engagement, Miss León, will be the toughest one yet. As for what it will require of you, I think you will enjoy it very much, but getting there will require you to trust me. Just remember, nothing will be as it seems."

"It sounds intriguing. I'm sorry you came all the way out here just for my dinner. I can arrange for a hotel if you would like."

"Actually, my sister lives an hour from here. I'll probably spend the night at her house." Sam stands a moment, assessing the distance between the two of them. Sensing it, Chantell takes a half step backward. Reading her cue, Sam smiles and shyly turns toward the door but then stops and quickly turns around and walks toward her.

Becoming scared, Chantell holds out her hand to push him away. Continuing to press forward, Sam takes Chantell's hand in his. She tries pulling it away, but he hangs on to it long enough to kiss the top of her fingers. "What are you doing?"

"I'm kissing a dignitary's hand," he replies. When she meets his comment with an angry expression, he adds, "If I were meeting the Queen of England, you would expect me to kiss her hand, would you not? And I would also kiss the Pope's ring, and he's a guy. So, why wouldn't I kiss the hand of an American dignitary?"

"I'm no dignitary."

"I most humbly disagree, mademoiselle. When you visited the Queen's palace, did not Prince Charles kiss your hand?"

"Well, you ain't no Prince Charles!"

"No, but like it or not, you are an American dignitary, whom I respect very much. Good night, Miss León."

Chantell closes the door without saying goodbye.

Sam stands facing the closed door and hears it lock. He takes a deep breath, turns, and starts walking down the hall. He speaks softly to himself, "You are right, Miss León. A six-hour flight is a lot to endure to have dinner with someone who doesn't like you."

When the taxi driver asks him where he wants to go, Sam takes his sister's address from his wallet, but instead of telling it to the driver, he asks, "When is the red-eye flight back to LA?"

"Flights leave every two hours. With a little luck, you should make the next one."

"Then let's do that." Sam leans back and stares out the window while looking at nothing.

13

Number Three

===

Sam picks up the phone. "Hello."

"Sam, this is Gordon Osborn."

"Mr. Osborn, how may I help you?"

"Why have you been avoiding me?"

"Probably because I have no use for you."

Sam hears a loud inhale and figures he is about to encounter what Gordon Osborn is famous for. True to Sam's prediction, Gordon launches into a full-on attack. "Mr. Milton! I have invested fifty thousand dollars in you, and I don't intend to lose a dime of that investment. In fact, I expect to gain substantially from it."

"Mr. Osborn, let me correct you. You didn't invest fifty thousand dollars in me. You invested fifty thousand dollars in twenty percent of the fifty million you expect to get from my case."

"My fee is 40 percent, and I do not plan to lose 40 percent of anything."

"I'm glad to hear you suggest that you will take 40 percent of anything, because you need to get up to date, Mr. Osborn. The price of the resolution has gone up substantially. It was as high as seventy-five million."

"That is very good news, but what do you mean by '*was* up to seventy-five million'?"

"Miss León pissed me off, and I raised the amount to seventy-five million. She has since atoned for some of her bad behavior, and the price has been reduced back to fifty million."

"I'm curious, Mr. Milton—how did Miss León atone for her bad behavior to earn back twenty-five million dollars?"

"I'm sorry, Mr. Osborn, but I cannot tell you. Chantell and I have a silent clause as part of our negotiations. She has kept that part of the contract, so I intend to keep mine."

"You have entered negotiations with the León party without the input of your lawyer?"

"Mr. Osborn, I never asked you to be my attorney, and I have no written agreement with you for such services. The only thing I received from you is information about a video clip that had come onto the market. I never agreed to have you purchase it, and I never suggested that you take such action."

"Mr. Milton, do you know what legal intent is?"

"No, not really, and I really don't—"

Gordon pushes forward. "Let me articulate the legal ramifications in a way you can understand. The very fact that we discussed details about the case, and even exchanged evidence as to a resolution, will be seen by a jury as a substantiated verbal contract between us. You should also know that all of our conversations have been recorded, including our first phone conversation. Therefore, Mr. Milton, I would strongly suggest that I be invited to any and all further conversations or negotiations you have with the León party. Otherwise, you may find yourself on the wrong side of a contract dispute between us."

"Mr. Osborn, I will tell you what I have told the news media: I have nothing worth taking, and after this is finally resolved, I expect to have nothing worth taking still. So, good luck to you, Mr. Osborn."

"I see. It may interest you to know that any resolution you obtain from the León party, no matter how insignificant, is directly connected to our negotiations. Therefore, it is all subjected to a fee. This fee is based on the percent of outcome we initially discussed: fifty million dollars. Since the León party is attached to this suit, they will be subjected to the fees if you are unable to supply payment yourself. You should also know, I will not be seeking my fees to be paid by all parties involved. Excluded will be Mr. Carson, *The Tonight Show*, and the NBC local affiliate. It will be required to come from Chantell León herself. Those fees could easily bankrupt Miss León. Please keep that in mind, Mr. Milton. To keep this from happening, any contact you have with Miss León will go through me. Have a good evening, Sam Milton."

========

Sam and Johnny come off the tennis court and grab a Gatorade. Sam drinks his down while Johnny takes his time. "So, what's the latest with you and Chantell?"

"Two down, four to go."

"I know about event one, what about two? That was the home-cooked meal, wasn't it?"

"Yeah, that is one wicked lady. She almost killed me! She said she cooked Cajun blackened chicken, which probably would have been too much for this northern white boy to eat anyway. What she didn't tell me was that she covered it with a sauce made from the hottest Asian peppers on earth."

Johnny laughs.

"My mouth burned for three days!"

"Was hers just as hot?"

"No! Hers wasn't even Cajun. She can't stand the stuff."

"Oh, I think I love this girl!" Johnny says, laughing. "Anything else?"

"Well, I thought things were going really well until I told her I wanted to give her a hot-fudge climax."

"A what?! A hot-fudge climax? Oh, wait a minute. You mean like the one at Trancas?"

"See, you know about it."

"You mean she thought you were going to . . . you know?"

"The whole family thought I was going to . . . you know. And her brothers were about to take me out."

"How did you escape?"

"I had to dump all of my mental baggage in front of her and Angelica—all of the Channel Islands Mental Hospital stuff. So, Mrs. A. L. Martin has enough to hang me ten times over."

"Don't worry; she isn't going to do anything with it," Johnny says, smiling as he puts his racket in its cover. "She called me yesterday. I'm not supposed to say this, but she's quite taken with you."

"Well, her daughter sure isn't. She can be warm and sweet and then instantly turn into a frozen mackerel. Good luck to anybody trying to woo her!"

"Is that what this is all about?"

"I will admit I'm slowly gaining back the admiration I once had for her, but this was never about that, though I knew there would be a risk of me developing feelings for her. But then, who wouldn't? I'm just glad I don't have to worry about her having feelings for me. Could you imagine someone as private as me getting involved in that media hype?"

"You mean as shy as you are? I don't know if all of that media hype would be such a problem. I'm very private, yet I'm as big as they get. Anyway, enough about that. Have you heard anything from our Gordon Osborn friend?"

"Just yesterday, and you called it. If I don't include him in everything, he's going after me. Also, he must know something is going on between Chantell and me because he said if he doesn't get his fees from me, he's going after her exclusively."

"I told you he was dangerous; but don't worry too much about him. His type doesn't win in court. He slams the media and gets you to capitulate before it goes to court. Stand your ground; however, it will get ugly. So, what about number three? Isn't it the big one requiring absolute trust?"

"Yep. And this is where your production company comes in. However, I'm getting nervous. The way she kicked and hit me when I scared her with the hot-fudge climax, I'm afraid she will take a baseball bat to me with this one."

"Well, it's all set up. So if you're going to cancel, I need to know pretty soon."

"I can't back out now." Sam looks at his watch. "She should be getting her yellow rose any minute now."

"If we're in 5A and 5B," Chantell asks her mother, "where are the boys?"

"I have them sitting in the business section. I know you don't want to hear them playing their video games for hours on end."

Chantell gives her mother a hearty, "Thank you." She goes to store her handbag when she freezes. "Oh, Mother? Have you been talking to Mr. Milton behind my back?"

"Why do you ask that, dear?"

"You know very well why!"

"Oh, lookie there. Three yellow roses? I wonder where they came from."

"Mother!"

"Why do you only call me 'Mother' when you're mad at me?" Angelica takes in her daughter's burning glare and answers it with, "Watch it, dear. The look you're giving me will burn a hole through this airplane."

"Not if it goes through you first! How could you?"

"I like the guy. He's a little timid, but I like him."

"A little timid?"

"Okay, so he's a big wuss. I still like him."

"I kind of like the wuss too, but I'm with Dwaine. Remember? And yes, I know about his Slash side, and I don't want Sam to get hurt. So, if you have any compassion for this . . . this guy, let it go. Just stay out of it!"

"So, you don't think he's interested in you?"

"Maybe a little. But what difference would it make?"

"Girl, I can't believe I raised such a fool for a daughter."

"What?"

"Look, Chantell. If all goes as Mr. Milton plans, what do you think he's looking to get out of this?"

"I don't know—an apology maybe, along with a couple of autographed albums?"

"And nothing else?"

"Well, if he thinks he's going to get *me*, he's the fool, not me."

"So, you are really going to let Slash hurt him?"

"Momma, Slash isn't going to hurt him; but he's going to hurt himself. And there ain't a thing I can do about it."

"After all he's been through?" Angelica asks.

"Mother! Mr. Samuel Milton is a thirty-seven-year-old baby. He wouldn't know a real relationship if it bit him on the butt! I pity the woman who marries him. She's going to have to keep wiping slobber off his chin for the rest of her life."

"So, you are going to keep being mean to him?"

"Momma!"

"Come on, girl! Decide what it's going to be: Momma or Mother!"

"Okay, *Mom*! I'm going politely to him and nothing more. If he keeps pushing, then I will have to get mean. I'm not going to spend my life being his babysitter. End of story."

"Oh, sit down and read the stupid note on the flowers! You're blocking everybody's way."

Ungracefully ripping the envelope open, she reads, "Number three, replace my social life. You're going to entertain my friends at Red Light Bar, Vermont Street, Los Angeles, at exactly nine o'clock Thursday night. Wear something flashy!"

"It sounds like a ransom note."

"That's what Carol said the first time he wrote a note. Oh, there's something else written here: 'This will be by far the hardest item. Nothing will be as it seems. More to follow.' "

"Wow, that doesn't sound too fun. I wonder what he means by 'nothing will be as it seems'? I guess we will find out."

"So, Mother, are you going to hand deliver this 'more to come' stuff for him? Or, are you just going to give Mr. Milton my phone number?"

"That would be far more convenient."

"Mother!"

"See, you're mad at me again."

———————

Later in the week, Chantell asks her mother, "So, why aren't the boys coming over for dinner?" Chantell picks up a piece of garlic bread to go with her lasagna. "They would never pass up lasagna."

"Someone gave them tickets to the Lakers game. So, I thought it would be fun with just you and me."

The two continue to chitchat through dinner.

"Would you like some more, Chantell?"

"No, I'm good and thank you. It was fantastic."

"Why, I only cook the very best frozen lasagna for my kids."

"Well, you've got plenty left for the boys."

The phone rings.

"Can you get that, Chantell? My hands are a mess."

"Sure, Mom. Hello. Martin residence." Chantell pauses to listen to the speaker. "Yes, this is Chantell. Why, Mr. Milton, it's interesting you should call here, right now, right when I am here for dinner. Excuse me a moment."

Chantell places her hand over the receiver and yells to Angelica, who is cleaning up dinner. "Mother! How dare you give him my phone number."

"I didn't give him your phone number. I gave him mine. Can I help it if my hands were dirty at exactly six forty-five p.m. on Tuesday night? I mean, really. What are the odds?"

Chantell takes her hand off the receiver just when Angelica adds, "Besides, maybe he isn't calling you. He and I have been having an illicit affair for the past two weeks."

"Momma, you've been with me in Miami for the past two weeks."

"No wonder I'm so tired."

"What is that, Mr. Milton?" Chantell returns to the phone and then yells to Angelica, "Okay. Sam says he's on for Saturday night. He says same room, same hotel."

"Ask him if he wants the pink or the red lace nighty."

"He says you wear the pink; he's going to wear the red."

"Ooh, I like him!"

"Can I ask: Are you two about done?" Chantell exhales loudly before saying, "He wants to know if you want him in the four-inch or the five-inch pumps."

Angelica yells from the kitchen, "Five inch!"

"Okay, now you two are making me sick. So, what is this about, Milton? Wait, let me put this on speaker so my mother can get every detail." Click. "You're on, Milton."

"Hi, Sam."

"Hi, Angelica. Um, Miss León, I have some things to tell you about Thursday night. First, for reasons I can't go into, you will be dropped off two blocks down from the Red Light Bar. But don't worry, you will have a security escort the entire way. Come alone. No brothers. If we see you're being followed, simply write a check for the remaining fifty million and leave it on the bar by the cash register. The whole evening should last about two hours, maybe three."

"Three hours? What am I supposed to be doing for three hours?"

"Miss León, this mess you created cost me all of my friends but a few. Even they are not sure they can trust me any more than you do."

"So, how am I supposed to resolve that?"

"By singing for them Miss León."

"You want me to sing for your drunken buddies!"

"I can assure you, none of them drink. A few may be slightly drugged up, but not drunk. Oh, and I would like you to give each of my friends a kiss before the night is over."

"You want me to give your slightly drugged-up construction worker friends a kiss? What kind of a woman do you think I am?"

"I'm simply requiring you to give each a kiss, Miss León. Anything more you want to offer is solely up to you."

Chantell looks away from the phone in disgust. "This is unbelievable!" she mutters.

"Mr. Milton," Angelica says, "I am acquainted with that establishment. I performed there thirty years ago. It was kind of low rent back then. I can only imagine what it must be like now."

"Mrs. Martin, I can assure you, without a doubt, that this neighborhood is just as bad as you imagine it to be, but I have a reason for choosing this location. Your daughter's little tirade on *The Tonight Show* took away all of my personal security. It still isn't safe to walk down my own street. Chantell is going to get a little taste of what that feels like.

"And another thing, through no fault of my own, this city, no, this 'world,' does not trust me—all because your daughter didn't trust me. She didn't trust me when we first met. She didn't trust me at our first dinner. She didn't even trust me in her own living room. And by the sound of her voice, she doesn't trust me now. The way I see it, the only way I will ever be able to lift my head up in this world is to regain their trust. Well, that needs to start with your daughter, and by the time this event is over, she will have no doubt she can put all her trust in me.

"But, I am not going to make it easy. True trust only comes when it is tested. It will be definitely tested. That is why, Miss León, I insist that you take along that note I tied to the rose I sent you on the plane. Every time you think this is going too far, I want you to pull that note out and read the line, 'Nothing will be as it seems.' Do you have any questions or comments?"

"Yes, Mr. Milton, I do. What's going to happen if I get hurt?"

"Miss León, I promise you, in front of your mother, that if you get hurt in any way, I will stand in a vacant lot in front of your brothers, and they can do to me anything they want. I could not live with myself if I caused you harm—as my psychiatric medical records will testify. So, do we have a deal?"

"Only if I can watch my brothers have their fun."

"As you wish. Anything else?"

"Mr. Milton, you do know that my security team is tracing this call as we speak."

"I would, of course, assume that, Miss León. That's why I'm calling from the phone in the lobby of your condo. I look forward to seeing you on Thursday night. And good evening to you, Angelica. Oh, one more thing. Do you want me to wear the plain red pumps or the one with the cute little bows?"

Angelica plays along. "Bows always go with lace, Sam. You should know that by now."

"Ah, yes, I forgot. Good night then."

Chantell puts the phone down and looks at her mother. "You two should take your act to Vegas."

"That's why I like him. And I will say this, girl: If you don't take him, I will."

"He's all yours, Momma. He is all yours."

"Just remember you said that."

On Thursday evening, a limousine turns the corner and stops midway up the block on the narrow and almost deserted street. The window lowers, and the two women look out at the surrounding buildings that hold only a resemblance to its marginally famous past.

"I can just make out the same old red light above the door," Angelica says as she looks up the street. "Does it *ever* bring back memories, with most of them being bad!"

"I can't believe I've been talked into doing this, and I can't believe you are going along with it, Mother!"

"What are you worried about? He said he would have two security guards walking you the two blocks to the bar."

"Why am I worried? Take a look around, Mother. Notice the bars on the windows of these places—more than Alcatraz—and only a handful of them are still in business. I don't need two security guards. I need a Sherman tank! And why do I have to walk two blocks? Why can't we just drive up to the place?"

"I don't know. Maybe it's a construction site? Anyway, here we are at Tenth and Vermont. It should be two blocks up."

A knock on the glass startles both women. Chantell looks out to see two policemen. She rolls down the window. "Excuse us, ma'am. We're here to escort you up the street."

"See, Chantell, two of LA's finest, and they're not bad looking either," Angelica says, looking at them instead of her daughter.

"Are you saying that because you're interested or because you think I should be?"

"Just send them back here when you're done with them."

Chantell takes a deep breath. "I can't believe this SOB is making me do this! Where are my brothers when I need them?"

"Oh, they're around."

"Mother, he said they can't be anywhere on this street."

"They're not on the street, but they're around. They weren't about to let you do this all alone, and I don't blame them. Just look at this slum!"

"Mother! For God's sake, make up your mind. Are you supporting me in doing this, or do you want me to bail?"

"I was just making a comment on the atmosphere. You have two fine specimens looking out after you, and they are getting impatient, so get going."

"Where are you going to be, Momma?"

"Oh, me? I'm going six blocks over to the Hilton, where it's safe."

"Mother, I swear—I'm going to put you in the dumpiest old folks home I can find. And I believe we passed one a block back."

"Good, maybe I can get my singing career back at the Red Light Bar. I hope it doesn't look as bad on the inside as this neighborhood does on the outside."

Chantell just rolls her eyes as she takes one of the officer's hands and steps out of the limo. Her shimmering silver gown sparkles under the street lights. "Right this way, ma'am," an officer directs her.

They walk to the left side of the street corner. Two Hispanic men standing at the bus stop say something in Spanish. One of the officers turns and speaks something in Spanish in reply. The two men start walking in the opposite direction. Chantell can see the glow of a red light two blocks up. "I take it it's up there?

"Yes, ma'am."

"Can you please say anything but 'ma'am'? I'm twenty-five, not ninety-five."

"Yes, miss."

"Thank you."

Halfway up the first block, two black men come out of a door and almost run into them. Both look at Chantell, with one saying, "Whoa! Would you look at this? My, my, do you look fine! What're you walking the street for?"

The three keep walking, not acknowledging the two men.

"She must think she's so hot, needing a police escort."

The other looks at his friend and comments, "You've got that right; she needs an escort!" Both men give each other a knuckle bump and keep walking.

Chantell and the officers come up to the next corner, wait for the light, and then cross. They step up on the other side of the street when all three hear police dispatch on the officer's radios: "We have a 211 in progress at 4520 Tenth Street. Suspect is armed, Adam 30 and 42 responding. ETA ten minutes."

"That's one block back! I'll go around the block and enter from the opposite side. You go down and to the left."

The taller officer presses the mic on his shoulder. "Officer Janson and Morales on foot patrol. ETA three minutes, from the east."

"Roger that. All units, be aware: Officers Janson and Morales are on foot."

"Hey!" Chantell yells. "What about me? You sure as hell aren't going to leave me on the street!"

Officer Morales turns and points up the street. "Miss León, ma'am, the Red Light Bar is one half block up. I'll call the security guard there and have him come to you. You can stay here, but it would be safer if you start heading to the bar now. Don't worry. There will be more squad cars than people in a few minutes."

Both officers run off, leaving Chantell on the street corner. She turns toward the bar and whispers, "Dear God, please keep me safe until I get there. And keep me from killing Mr. Sam Milton! Better yet, don't!"

She starts walking cautiously, looking at the bar to see if anyone is coming. "Well, one thing is for sure, Chantell," she says to herself, "you definitely can't hide in the shadows wearing this getup."

She doesn't get twenty feet before she sees three men standing next to a street sign. They notice her and quickly turn in her direction. In a slightly shrill voice, one asks, "Well, hello. What's a nice uptown sister doing so far downtown? Did those mean policemen abandon you? Too busy doing police work to walk you home? Or are you going somewhere else?"

"I'm fine. I'm just going up here."

"To that nasty old place? You might get hurt walking around here all by yourself."

One man says to the other two, "Don't you think, gentlemen, we should escort this fine-looking sister?"

He tries to put his arm around Chantell, forcing her to step back and into a self-defense stance. The guy takes a look at her, and all three laugh. "Hey, would you look at this? I think momma here knows *ka-ra-te*."

Another says, "No need to get all bothered now. We just want to treat you nice. *Real nice.*"

One of the other two hits the guy on the shoulder and points to a police cruiser turning up the street. His tone changes as he says, "You take care now, sister."

All thee turn and start walking down the street.

Chantell exhales and walks faster toward the bar. She steps over an underground vault register, which causes her gown to lift and flutter. She tries to step forward but realizes her heel is caught in the grille. This catches the attention of the officer in the patrol car. He shines his spotlight on her. The intense light reflects off the silver sequins of her gown, sending rays of glittering light in all directions, giving her an angelic glow. The officer driving hits the other and points toward the strange anomaly. "Whoa! What is that?"

"You got me."

"Drive forward, but keep the light on whatever it is."

As the patrol car slowly pulls forward, the light only intensifies. Chantell, still struggling with her shoe, grumbles, "Somehow I doubt Marilyn Monroe had this much trouble."

She finally reaches down to take off her shoes. This causes her to lean over a homeless drunk lying between her and the street. He wakes up to see this dramatic vision. It terrifies him, and he yells out, "Oh God, an angel. I mussst beee dead! Dear God, no, please don't let me beee dead."

This startles Chantell, causing her to jump backward and out of the light. To the drunk, she completely disappears, so he sits up, petrified!

Chantell, needing her shoes, has to lean back into the light; one is still stuck. She yanks hard, pulling her shoe free. It is then that Chantell sees her shoe's heel is broken. This causes her to look up, throw her arms out, and scream, "Dear God in heaven, how much more do I have to take from this guy?"

She is screaming about Sam, but the drunk thinks she's screaming at him. Chantell takes her shoes and clutch, turns, and stomps barefoot out of the light and toward the bar, leaving the drunk mumbling, "That'sss it thisss time. I'mmmm goonning too stoppp drinking and goo bbbackkk homemmm."

The officers in the car sit enjoying the show. The one driving finally asks, "Do you need some assistance, ma'am?"

She looks at them and yells, "No! I'm just trying to get to that bar. And why does everyone keep calling me 'ma'am'?"

"Well, we'll keep the light on you until you get safely inside."

She yells a quick thanks and continues to strut barefoot up two more doors to the bar, desperately trying to regain any dignity she can. She gets to the door just as the guard steps out. She glares at him, saying, "Really? Now you come out?"

Chantell pushes through him and steps into the entrance. A partition is blocking her view, so she listens to the muffled conversations, trying to gauge what to expect. She pulls herself together, checking to see everything is in place but her shoes. Then, with an aristocratic air, she turns the corner. All conversation stops as everyone looks up to get a view of the breathtaking sight. She scans the bar and sees six booths going along the windows. A small stage is set up between the booths and the old wooden bar, with another set of booths placed in front of the bar.

At the bar sits a Caucasian couple, and a mixed couple sits in the first booth. She also recognizes her three brothers sitting four booths back; Lawrence is facing away. Anger shows on her face as she mouths, *What in hell do you think you're doing?*

Malcom glares back at her while Eddie just holds his hands up in surrender. Chantell shakes her head and steps up to the bar to ask, "Is Sam Milton around?"

"He's in the back. Have a seat, and I will get him," the bartender responds.

Chantell turns to glare at her brothers again before turning to the booths in front of the bar. She finds one less torn than the others and plops down ungracefully, facing away from her brothers.

It only takes a minute for Sam to walk up and sit across from her. His mouth drops as he says, "Wow, you look beautiful! And you're perfectly on time. How are you this evening?"

Chantell sits unmoving, glaring at Sam.

"You don't look to be your cheerful self. Did you have a rough time getting here?"

Chantell, without taking her eyes off Sam, reaches over, picks up her shoes, and drops them in front of him.

"Oh, I see. I'm so sorry. Here, let me see if I can take care of this."

Sam gets up, walks over to the bar, and calls out, "Hey, Elliot, you wouldn't have any Super Glue back there by any chance?"

"I'll take a look." He pushes aside a vase with three yellow roses and rifles through a drawer for a few moments before coming up with a small tube. "You're in luck. Hope enough is left for you." He then nods his head toward the flowers.

Sam sees him nod at the roses. He glances back at Chantell, who is still fuming. He turns back to Elliot and gives him a smile before saying, "Perfect." Sam takes the glue and works a minute on Chantell's shoe and then sets it aside with the other. "It should be fine in five minutes. At least, that's what the commercials say."

"I seriously doubt that, Mr. Milton. I paid over three hundred dollars for those shoes."

Sam looks right at her. He cocks his head slightly only a few seconds but long enough to get his point across.

Chantell looks down and whispers, "I'm sorry; that was very rude of me."

Sam lets it sit for a minute before changing the subject. "I must say, I know I asked you to wear something nice, but this goes above and beyond."

"Mr. Milton, you did not ask me to wear something nice; you demanded that I dress flashy."

"Ah, yes. Well, you look incredible."

"Just trying to live up to your requirements," Chantell returns. After looking around a few moments more, she comments, "Such an interesting place. Are you into shabby chic?"

Sam smiles and gives a sideways nod.

Chantell hears some whooping noise, along with a few swear words, prompting her to ask, "Are those your friends in the back room?"

"They're the guys I work with."

"Shouldn't we be getting back there? I would hate to be entertaining them when the beer runs out."

"I'll take you to my buddies in a few minutes. I'm waiting for someone to show up. Would you like a drink?"

"Water—in a bottle, please. I'm afraid of what would be growing in the glass."

Sam returns with two famous green bottles of sparkling water. Nothing is said for a few minutes, so he reverts to studying Chantell's face. She answers his stare with, "Your stare is still creepy, Mr. Milton!"

"Sorry. I can't help myself. I love to study your face."

Chantell looks outside and sees two big black men walking up to the door. She quickly taps Sam on the wrist and exclaims, "Hey, I just think I saw Kareem Abdul-Jabbar!"

"Really?"

Both men step in, with Kareem giving a polite nod to Sam. Sam responds with an upward nod. This odd movement makes Chantell curious. "Do you know him?"

"We've met once, but I don't know him."

Sam watches the two men head toward Chantell's brothers. The two facing toward the bar look up in shock. Eddie taps Lawrence on the hand and motions him to turn around. Kareem nods and holds out two fingers toward the brothers as he passes by. Malcom responds in like manner, letting the two men's fingers touch with a flick. Kareem sits in the last booth and faces the bar. It's not long before the boys invite themselves over to his table. When all three brothers are facing away, Sam leans in to Chantell and says, "Okay, let's go meet my buddies."

Sam stands and holds out his hand. She refuses to take it, preferring to stand by herself. As she grabs her shoes, another couple come from the back and sit down in their booth. Chantell looks back and is very curious to see the couple look very much like the two of them, with the woman wearing the same hairstyle. She attempts to mention it to Sam, but he seems very intent on getting her into the back room as quickly as possible.

Once in the hall, Sam quickly looks back to see if anyone noticed their leaving. He smiles when he sees all three brothers enthralled with Kareem.

"What was that all about?" Chantell asks as Sam moves back in front of her.

"What do you mean?"

"You know exactly what I mean! That couple looks just like us."

"We'll talk about that later," he stalls as he opens the door to the billiards room and escorts Chantell inside. It is a rough-looking bunch of twelve men—all with a week's worth of facial hair and their shirts untucked. The air smells of beer and body odor.

The most overweight and tattooed of them yells out, "Hey, what do you know? Milton wasn't BSing; he really does know Chantell León!"

Chantell tries in vain to be cordial. "Where would you like me to stand, Mr. Milton?"

"Stand for what? Oh no, these aren't the friends you're going to entertain. They're next door." Sam reaches up over the fire exit and flips a switch so he can open the door without the alarm sounding. "Right this way, Miss León."

Chantell looks shocked. "You certainly don't expect me to go out into the alley of a place like this."

"Take a peek outside, Miss León."

She sticks her head out for a second, gives Sam a frustrated look, and says, "It figures. Come on, Mr. Milton."

As Sam is about to step out, he looks back to his coworkers. "Now, remember, any minute, three big black guys will be running in here looking for us. Point them this way, and whatever you do, don't make trouble. Remember, there are three of them and only twelve of you."

"What the hell do you mean by that?" the big guy snorts.

"You will see soon enough. Oh, flip the fire exit switch back on when the door closes. And thanks; I owe you guys."

Sam sees Chantell leaning on the handrail of the loading ramp. Her gown is reflecting the yellow caution light of a police car. Sam tries to take Chantell by the arm, but she pushes him away. He responds by saying, "We just need to move quickly, my dear."

They walk quickly across the alley and up the stairs of a very large industrial building. At the top of the steps, Sam quickly keys in some numbers. A green light comes on, and he opens the door. He escorts Chantell inside, where she finds an overly sanitized hallway. They quickly walk upstairs and meet Sam's ex-fiancée wearing her residency scrubs.

Sam makes the introductions. "Chantell, this is Linda McCall; Linda, this is Chantell León."

Linda gives Sam the shush sign. "It is way past visiting hours, so no one is supposed to know we are here. Follow me, please."

<hr>

Back in the alley behind the bar, the back door of the bar bursts open, setting off the alarm. The three brothers run out onto the loading ramp and hear the words, "Freeze!" A spotlight lights up the alley. "Up against the wall and spread them!"

"Hey," Malcom yells, "what did we do?"

The officer comes up and frisks Eddie, answering, "I don't know. Maybe I'm just curious why three gentlemen like yourselves burst through the fire door of a bar setting off an alarm. Are you running to or from something? Which is it?"

"Someone kidnapped our sister!"

"Was she with some white guy?"

"Yeah, where did the white puke go with my sister?"

"The two of them are safe and sound. I would expect you three are the León boys."

Eddie answers, "Those two are. I'm their half-brother, Eddie Martin."

"Either way, you three are not supposed to be here, so why don't you be good little boys and go home and let your sister finish her business with Mr. Milton?"

"You know about this?"

"Just enough to send you packing. Now, run along before I book you for trespassing."

The three start walking down the alley. When far enough away, Malcom says, "Follow me. If this is a setup, I bet they'll be coming back the same way."

<hr>

Back inside, Linda leads Sam and Chantell down several hallways, passing a nurses' station where staff is conspicuously absent. They turn the corner and walk down another short hall to a large door. Linda opens it and escorts them into a dark room.

When the door is closed, the light comes on, and Chantell is surprised to see thirty kids staring back at her. Most are in beds, but some are sitting in wheelchairs with their IV stands next to them. Their ages range from three to sixteen, with parents of the younger ones standing next to their kids. All the kids cheer loudly, so Doctor Linda tries to quiet them down.

Sam smiles broadly. "Kids, this is the world-famous Chantell León. Chantell León, meet my buddies."

Chantell stands speechless until Sam takes her by the hand and leads her to each child, giving each a personal introduction. Some have no hair; others are without limbs. Still others have all kinds of sophisticated machines with lots of lights, making beeps. Chantell is amazed that Sam not only knows each one's name, but also has a personal relationship with each. Some of the kids have tears of joy to see her. Others are quivering with giddiness. The older ones speak to Chantell very politely. Chantell hugs the ones she can and holds hands with the others. She also takes special care to hug the parents of the younger ones.

Eventually, Sam introduces Chantell to a very sick little boy. "Miss León, this is my special friend Gabriel. He has leukemia and so did his brother. Gabriel was doing very well until his twin brother died a few weeks ago. When I found out his favorite singer, I had to get her to come here."

Chantell asks, "So, who is your favorite singer, Gabriel?"

Without any hesitation, he proudly says, "Janet Jackson!"

Chantell yells, "Janet Jackson?"

She then sees Gabriel give her a big smile, so she asks him, "Did Mr. Milton put you up to this?"

He gives her a big nod.

She smiles back and asks again, "So, who really is your favorite singer? At least your favorite one in this room?"

He smiles and says, "Chantell León." She gives him a hug. "Now, promise me you are going to try very hard to get better. Okay?"

He nods quickly.

"I'm going to hold you to it, which means I'm going to sneak in here and check up on you. Okay?" He nods again. She gives him a hug before moving on.

It takes almost an hour to get around the room because Chantell tries to spend as much time as she can with each child. She is thrilled to be there because they are thrilled about her.

As she finishes her rounds, the last child is a shy little red-haired girl. Linda comes up and introduces Chantell and Sam to her. "This is Rebecca. She is six, and it is her first day. She was having a rough time up until now. Do you have anything you would like to ask, Miss León?"

She nods quickly.

"What would you like to know about me, Rebecca?"

In a soft voice, she asks, "Are you and Mr. Milton getting married?"

Sam and Chantell look wide-eyed at each other.

Chantell leans in to say, "I'm sorry, sweetie, but no, we're not getting married."

Without batting an eye, she asks, "Why not?"

Sam leans in to answer, "Well, honey, Chantell is seeing someone else right now, and I would never want to interfere. Besides, Miss León is so beautiful and very famous. Don't you think she needs a handsome prince?"

Little Rebecca nods.

"See? So, maybe someday we will all see her marry her prince. Would you like to see that, Rebecca?"

She nods again.

Chantell is taken aback by Sam's comments. She at first seems radiant, but then looks perturbed, as if angry with something. She has to be tapped on the hand by Sam to come back on line. She recoups by saying, "We love you, Rebecca. I'm going over here to sing some songs."

Everyone cheers.

Chantell takes Sam's hand and leads him aside, but still within earshot of Linda. Sounding almost angry, she states, "Mr. Milton, you are the type of guy who would find a diamond in the dirt and then spend the rest of your life trying to find the person who deserves it more than you."

Sam holds up his hands as if saying, "Yes, so what's the point?"

Chantell shakes her head in disbelief. "Did you ever think that just maybe you should be the one to keep the diamond and that the world would be a better place if you did?"

"What would I do with a diamond?"

Chantell rears up, "Ooh, you are hopeless!" She walks past him, saying, "I'm going to sing some songs now."

Linda comes up to a very confused Sam. He turns to her and asks, "What did I miss?"

She answers cynically, "You're such an idiot. I can't believe I almost married you."

"What?"

"Who do you think she was referring to as the diamond?"

He still looks confused, so she gently pats his cheek and says, "No guy in the world has to worry about you stealing his girl. Come on; it's time to announce your guest."

Sam speaks up. "Miss Chantell has agreed to sing a few of her songs."

Everyone cheers, so Chantell bows as Sam pulls out an acoustic guitar and a really cheap electric piano. He hands the guitar to Chantell, and he places the piano on his lap.

"Do you play, Mr. Milton?"

"I play your songs."

"Do you play well, even on that?"

"I think I sound pretty good."

Chantell can see several kids shaking their heads no, so she smiles and says, "Let me try it solo for a bit."

"Suit yourself, but you don't know what you're missing."

"Yes, we do," several of the kids say.

Sam throws his hands up, but then gives a big smile.

"Okay, which song should I start with?"

Sam suggests, "How about starting with your newest and then go backward?"

He turns to the kids and asks, "So, which one is first?"

All the kids answer with a resounding, " 'Uptown Hot'!"

"Really? That's perfect. I was afraid you were going to ask for 'Forbidden Love,' a duet with Slash, who isn't here. So, okay, for you parents, this will be 'Uptown Hot,' from my album by the same name. Let's see if I can play forties-style music on an acoustic guitar." She starts in and soon has everyone in a wonderful trance.

She sings song after song, and is about to start one more when she is interrupted by a hospital volunteer bringing in pudding and Jell-O. Sam jumps in and starts passing the snacks out. He takes his time and helps one little boy who can't feed himself.

Chantell takes the snack break as an opportunity to pull Linda aside. "Can I talk to you a moment?"

Linda puts her work down, joins Chantell out of earshot of Sam, and says, "Thank you so much for doing this, Miss León. This is a treat for the kids."

"I'm just embarrassed by the fact that I had to be forced into doing it by Sam. But that brings up a question: What happened between you and Sam, if you don't mind my asking?"

Linda smiles. "Sam and I have been best friends for ten years, and a year ago, we finally tried to see if there was something more, mostly out of desperation. That's because I'm overworked, and Sam is, well, Sam."

"Speaking of that, how often does Sam act as if . . . I don't know . . ."

Linda finishes her sentence with, "A soggy bowl of Rice Krispies where Snap, Crackle, and Pop have all drowned?"

Chantell laughs. "I haven't seen him look that bad, except when he's been traumatized, and you nailed him."

Linda continues, "No, that was Sam just about every day before you came along."

"Really, every day?"

"Unfortunately, yes. But he never used to be that way. You see, Sam and I first met when his partner's son was ill with leukemia, but I had known about his reputation years before. That man over there was the most dynamic man you could ever meet. Nothing could stop him. Do you know he had a horrible fear of heights?"

Chantell raises her eyebrows.

"And to cure it, he went skydiving!"

"Really?"

"He only did it twice. The second time was to prove he could do it without peeing his pants. He ran triathlons and headed up search and rescue. He doesn't have a mean bone in his body, yet he wouldn't take lip from anybody." Linda stops, exhales, and says, "Now, he cowers if someone says boo."

"So, how do we fix him?" Chantell asks.

Linda has to hide her elation at Chantell's use of the word *we*. She answers with, "I don't know. I have tried everything, including sitting with him through counseling and group therapy. I even hauled off and slapped him once, just to see if it would do any good. It didn't. Now, I want to kick him in his balls just to see if he has any."

Chantell looks over at Sam as she says, "As you and the rest of the world may recall, I just did it to him, twice! If he ever had any, they're long gone now."

"Maybe that's it!"

"What? You actually want me to kick him there?"

Linda waves her hand. "Not kick them—expose them."

"What do you mean?"

"His therapist, Doctor Khadar, had an interesting idea. He found that if Sam really gets mad at a problem he's having, like fear of heights, he'll go to extreme measures to fix it. So, Khadar thinks if we can humiliate him at something he is passionate about to the point he gets mad, he'll fight back."

"Have you not been listening? I humiliated him twice. Not only did it not work, it only made things worse."

Linda waves off Chantell's comment. "That's because he felt he deserved it. It has to be something he knows he doesn't deserve and preferably in front of lots of people, so he can't hide."

"And you think I am the one to do this?"

"If you don't mind me saying it, you seem to have the knack for it, and despite the proverbial bloodbath you have given Samuel Milton, you are the best thing to ever happen to him."

Chantell now looks over at Sam. "I don't know. Maybe it's my temper, combined with the stress of recording albums and making a movie, but running into Sam has really changed me, and not for the better. Before I met him, I had a reputation as the nicest person in the world. Now, I see myself as the meanest thing on two legs. I'm afraid if I slap Sam one more time, the world will see me the same way!"

"Maybe, but I can tell you this—you have already punched a hole in that thick shell of his."

"How do you mean?"

"This game he's playing with you, that's the old Sam. So, do all of us a favor, including Sam. Take a sledgehammer and smash that shell of his so he can't crawl back into it."

Linda's comment leaves Chantell pondering, but she refocuses on the kids when Sam comes up to them to say, "We're starting to lose them, so we had better wind this thing up."

Chantell picks up her guitar, and all of the kids applaud, waking the ones who had fallen asleep. Sam notices applause coming from the back and turns to see half of the hospital staff crammed in behind them.

Linda leans over and gives a big hug to Sam and tells him, "You did good!" Sam turns and points to Chantell.

Chantell smiles and waves her finger back and forth, saying, "No, no, no. This night belongs to Mr. Sam Milton."

Chantell turns back to her audience and says, "Well, it seems I've lost over half of you, so I'm going to make this last song a lullaby. It's from the Masai. Does anyone know who the Masai are?"

"They are a tribe in Africa," a twelve-year-old shouts from the back.

"Where in Africa?"

"Is it Kenya?" another asks.

"Yes, Kenya and Tanzania, but more accurately, the Masai Mara."

A ten-year-old boy from the back asks, "Is it true they live in houses made of cow poop?"

Chantell smiles and answers, "Yes."

Several kids say, "Ooh, yuck!"

So, she answers their concerns with, "I believe they would rather say their homes are made out of dung. And, may I tell you, they are beautiful people who wear beautiful clothes. Anyone know what colors?"

"Red and white."

"Yes, and some other colors, but mostly red. Also, their kids are very well taken care of, very happy and educated. The last time I was there, I saw a huge TV dish next to the chief's hut."

The kids all laugh, so she continues with questions. "Anyone know what other interesting habits they have?"

The same twelve-year-old answers, "They live out in the open with the wild animals."

"Yes, they do. They live in the open and in harmony with the lions and the cheetahs. So, would you like me to sing one of their lullabies?"

Everyone claps, and she starts singing.

One of the Hispanic parents comes up to Sam, crying and speaking in broken English, "Thank you so much for this thing you do for us." Sam accepts a hug.

After Chantell finishes the lullaby, she turns to see that Sam is the only one left in the room besides the kids. "I guess no one cared for my lullaby."

Sam smiles. "Most had to get back to work, with so many sick people around here. The rest, I think, wanted to leave us alone."

Chantell comes over and sits with Sam on a child's bed and notices the little girl has curled up around him. "Okay, Sam. Um, I can call you Sam, can't I?"

"I would be most honored, Miss León, or can I call you Chantell now?"

Chantell looks at him for a few moments before answering, "I think I would prefer Miss León."

Sam gives her a halfhearted nod until she adds, "Because I love the way it sounds when you say it. It's full of respect instead of awe, like most say it. But Chantell is fine, too."

"Well then, Miss León, does this mean you are warming up to me, enough to even like me?"

Chantell takes his hand to say, "This was incredible tonight. I can't believe you set this all up."

"You mean all I had to do is get you to sing to a bunch of kids to get you to believe I was *good people*."

"Though I refused to believe it, I knew you were good people way before this."

"Really. When?"

"It involved another child."

"Oh, teaching a little girl to ride a bike, eh?"

"No, even before that."

"Okay, now you've stumped me."

"It was when Zinnia came up to you to say hello."

"Really? Why?"

"Sam, that little girl is so shy, far more than even you. She still runs from her aunts and uncles. When she came up and tugged on your pant leg, I was in absolute shock. So, explain to me, how did you get to know these kids?"

"It came about through my partner's son. I saw him every day after his father's passing until the little guy passed away, too. I would bring in funny-looking balloons, make puppets out of socks and paper bags—whatever made him smile. I would do funny little dances, but what he liked most were my made-up stories, most improvised right on the spot. I got to be pretty good at it. The other kids started enjoying it all, too."

"I bet! You do have a quick wit."

"As I said earlier, I spent three years in a mental institution after little Jason and his mother died. When I was released, Linda—Nurse McCall back then—insisted that I had to come back the very next day. I just thought she wanted me to keep ministering to the kids—you know, playing with them like some trained circus animal."

"But that wasn't it, was it?"

"She knew I needed the kids to help me, too. Anyway, I made a lot of lifetime friends here. Unfortunately, a lot of those friendships were short-lived. Anyway, it was the best thing for my PTSD and shyness."

"I bet. So, the hospital is where you met Linda?"

"Yep, and the rest, as they say, is history. Well, it's late, and you need to get home. Can I have the privilege of taking you home?"

"That would be nice except for two reasons: One, I don't think my brothers would let you. And two, we can't be seen together, and I have the paparazzi on me like flies to dog poop."

"I figured that might be the case. It was another reason for having you walk two blocks so we could intercept them."

"And did you?"

"As of yet, I don't know if we did or not, but you bring up some good points. I can at least walk you back to your brothers. It's dark and scary out there, you know."

"Would you two like to leave by the front door this time?" Linda asks, startling Chantell.

Sam speaks. "Oh, hi, Linda. I think we need to go back through the alley. I have to send a lot of people home."

Linda escorts them out of the room and down the hall. Sam is pleasantly surprised when Chantell takes his arm. It doesn't go unnoticed by Linda, who smiles as she watches them walk away. She speaks out. "You know, Sam, things look a lot different from the last time you left here."

Sam stops and looks back with a smile. "Yes, they are, just like you said they would be."

"It's only because I know you very well."

"Good night, Linda."

Chantell asks, "So, who do you need to send home and why?"

Sam opens the rear hospital door, and as Chantell steps out, Sam answers her, "I need to send home all of the actors."

Chantell exclaims, "You mean everyone at the bar was acting?"

Sam nods confidently.

"So, that explains the couple who looked like us."

"I needed to keep your brothers thinking we hadn't left, at least until we got safely across the alley and into the hospital."

"So, everyone was acting, including the police escorting me to the bar?"

"Yep. They were the same ones in the police car and here in the alley later."

As they step back into the bar, Chantell sees the billiards room is empty. As Sam latches and resets the alarm on the door, she asks, "So, where did you get so many actors?"

"Johnny used his production company. But, most were free. They are all from acting schools and can use this type of thing for acting credits. They will do anything for a credit that has the Carson Productions label on it."

"Even playing a drunk sleeping on a curb?"

"We didn't have any drunks in the script."

"Well, I sure scared the hell out of somebody."

They turn the corner and walk up to the bartender. Chantell catches her breath when she finally sees the vase with three yellow roses. She takes a full breath of their aroma before turning back to Sam. "I thought you forgot."

"They've been sitting here all night."

"What? No way! Even when I came."

"It's amazing how much one can miss when they're angry." Sam smiles to himself when he sees Chantell take them out of the vase and hold them to her chest. He sees the bartender and speaks loudly, "Okay, Elliot, that's a wrap."

Sam turns to Chantell and comments, "I always wanted to say that."

Chantell and Elliot chuckle. Elliot picks up a radio and says the same thing to the rest of the crew.

"Thanks, Elliot, and be sure to tell everyone thank you. It went perfectly."

"Okay, what about Kareem?" Chantell questions emphatically.

"I was told he was doing Johnny a favor, and when we explained what was happening, he loved the idea."

"So, Kareem knows about our agreement?"

"He knows we're trying to work it out, but not much more."

"So, you knew my brothers were going to be here?"

"I was pretty sure they would show up somewhere. I wouldn't have nearly the respect for them if they didn't. Oh, that reminds me, I meant to ask you, which one of your brothers owns the '62 Cadillac?"

"Malcom, why?" Chantell asks as she holds out her arms to let Sam put on her jacket.

"When we were driving Johnny's 'Vette to the restaurant, I saw in the rearview mirror the right headlight was burned out."

She picks up her clutch, and they head for the door.

"They can be hard to find, so I picked one up." Sam pushes the door open for Chantell.

As she walks out, Chantell turns back to Sam and touches his cheek as she remarks, "That's so sweet."

Sam smiles at the touch and says, "It's in my car across—"

Sam hears Chantell scream, "Malcom, don't!"

Suddenly, Sam sees a flash of bright, fractured light as Malcom's fist lands squarely on his jaw. He is hit so hard that his head slams into the edge of the bar's brick entrance. His head leaves a blood stain on its corner. Then, Malcom's left fist plows into Sam's stomach, doubling him over. It's followed quickly by a knee to his ribcage. Sam can hear Chantell screaming as Malcom picks him up by his collar and slams his head into the brick again. "This will teach you to mess with my sister!"

Everyone is pulling Malcom off of Sam, including Chantell, who's screaming, "Malcom! What have you done?"

She watches helplessly as Sam crumples and slides down the brick wall. His head lands hard on the concrete. Chantell runs over to him. She sees pink fluid pouring onto the sidewalk from his head. She kneels down and instinctively places her hand over Sam's cracked skull and applies just enough pressure to stop the loss of fluid. She can see that he is still conscious. Crying, she tells him, "I'm so sorry, Sam! I am so sorry! Here, let's try and sit you up."

Sam says in a slurred voice, his jaw dislocated, "No, phere's poo mamy prings boken. Chanpell, you nee po gep oup of here!"

"Sam, I'm here, and I'm not leaving you. Dear God, has anyone called 9-1-1?"

"Here," Elliot says. "I'm an EMT when I'm not acting. Let me take over." Chantell slides her hand out from under Sam's head as Elliot slides his hand under.

Again, Sam pleads, "Chanpell, you nee po gep oup of here pe for poice so up."

Chantell pulls away, still crying, "I'm so, so sorry, Sam."

Sam calls her back. "Rmemper, you are spill my garpiam angel."

"Your guardian angel? How can you say that after this?"

"I'm nexp poor a hospipal. Am I'm pill your garpian angel, poo. No, peases ko."

Sam watches Chantell's brothers pull her away as everything fades to black. Just before Chantell turns to leave, she sees Sam's whole body thrash violently. Elliot yells for someone to help keep him still. Chantell wants to go back, but Eddie and Lawrence pull her back. "Come on, Chantell. We gotta go. You don't need to be seen mixed up in this."

With sirens and flashing lights, the paramedics round the corner. Chantell and her brothers pull away just as the police show up. With tears still streaming down her face, she looks back to see the colors of all the flashing lights.

14

Aftermath

"This is a special *Channel 7 Eyewitness News* break. Hello, everyone. I'm Monica Sanford. We have breaking news in the ongoing battle with Chantell León and her alleged attacker, Samuel Milton. We go straight to Donna Dean, who is standing in front of Children's Hospital Los Angeles. Donna?"

"Monica, Sam Milton is close to death tonight. Almost right behind this hospital, within the past hour, he was brutally attacked, supposedly by a vigilante in support of Chantell. His doctors say it is a miracle that the attack took place so close to a hospital or Mr. Milton would not have made it this long. He is suffering from extreme head trauma. Along with the concussion, he has a broken jaw and cracked ribs, which resulted in a punctured lung.

"He has just come out of surgery, but reports are grim. He's been placed in an induced coma to let his body heal. Despite several witnesses, police have little to go on. The assailant is described as a large black man in his late twenties or early thirties, dressed in jeans and a white T-shirt. It has been rumored that the eyewitnesses have been tight-lipped, seeing this vigilante as some sort of neighborhood hero. That is it from Children's Hospital Los Angeles. Back to you, Monica."

"Thank you, Donna Dean. A United Press report has just issued a statement from Chantell León, and I quote, 'Chantell feels heartfelt regret that this has happened and is grateful for all of her devoted fans. However, no one deserves this, so Chantell pleads with all fans to exercise restraint.'

"Well, ladies and gentlemen, this story is just not going away, and it just keeps getting uglier. This is Monica Sanford. Now, back to our regularly scheduled program."

Day Two

"Doctor McCall, this is Angelica Martin."

"Yes, Mrs. Martin, how is your daughter?"

"As you might expect, she is terribly distraught. We are calling for an update on Mr. Milton's condition."

"He's still in a coma, but he's stabilized and out of intensive care. The procedure for putting an opening in his skull to relieve the swelling of his brain was successful. Thank God he was right next door."

"Please let us know when he is able to be transported. We want to place him in—"

"A better facility, Mrs. Martin?"

"I was thinking a quieter place, with fewer distractions."

"And less paparazzi?"

Before Angelica can respond to the dig, Linda says without reserve, "Mrs. Martin, I would strongly suggest that you leave his treatment plan up to the doctors. As for myself, I believe Sam is going to need the support of the very kids he has been supporting. He has had nothing but hate coming his way from Chantell's fans, and now many are rejoicing that he almost died! And all thanks to your daughter."

Thinking better of her statement, Linda quickly adds, "I'm sorry, Mrs. Martin. I know Chantell never wanted this to happen. It looked like they were even starting to be friends. But I still strongly suggest that you ask the doctors where Sam should be treated. And also consider the kids' love for their friend."

"You have a point, Doctor McCall. Will you please inform us when Sam regains consciousness?"

"Yes, Mrs. Martin, I would love to."

"This is Monica Sanford, *Eyewitness News*. Gordon Osborn has hired the private investigation firm of Stewart Braswell to investigate the attack on Samuel Milton. Quoting Gordon Osborn: 'Due to the overwhelming favorable biases of the Los Angeles Police Department toward Chantell León, we have decided to hire a private firm to look into who attacked Samuel Milton. We have reasons to believe that Chantell herself may have contracted for his attack. I can promise that no stone shall be left unturned, and we will prosecute any and all persons found to be involved with this attack, even if the attack has ties to Chantell León herself.'"

Day Three

"Good evening. I'm Monica Sanford, and this is *News Break*. And yet again, we have another bizarre twist in the León/Milton Story. We have just discovered that Chantell is paying all of Samuel Milton's medical bills. Primitive, a production company and an offshoot of Universal, which is primarily owned by Chantell León, has been secretly paying for all costs related to the care of Samuel Milton. This just adds to the speculation that someone close to Miss León may have had something to do with the recent attack on Samuel Milton.

"In a related story, letters of support in regards to Sam Milton have been pouring into Children's Hospital Los Angeles. All are written by close relatives of children who are currently treated or who were treated at the hospital in the past. All claim that Mr. Milton is the most kind and generous man they have ever met, with a personal relationship to their child. We have an investigative reporter looking into any relationship Samuel Milton has with the hospital. Samuel Milton remains in a coma. Updates to follow."

Day Six

"This is Connie Chung. *NBC Nightly News* has been following up on the twist in the León/Milton case. We have now learned that Samuel Milton has been receiving his own letters of support, most from parents of patients treated at Children's Hospital Los Angeles. In fact, Mr. Milton has a ten-year history with the hospital. Doctor Linda McCall can verify firsthand that Samuel Milton has been coming to see all of the kids from one to three times a week for the past ten years, ever since his partner's son lost his fight with leukemia. Sam has dedicated his time to children fighting the battle with cancer. It is believed his long-standing commitment to these children is the reason he remains at Children's Hospital."

At the same time NBC is on the air:

"Good evening. I am Donna Dean, *Channel 7 Eyewitness News*, in for Monica Sanford. We have just been informed that the Los Angeles Police Department is close to making an arrest in the Sam Milton case. It is believed the suspect is a direct relative of Chantell's. We will bring you more details as they develop."

Day Seven

"This is Donna Dean for *News Break*. We have just learned that the Los Angeles Police Department has placed Malcom Philip León under arrest on attempted murder charges. Malcom León is the older brother of Chantell León. Mr. León turned himself in and confessed to the attack on Samuel Milton. He faces arraignment tomorrow. His family, including Chantell, could not be contacted for comment. This investigation is now looking into any personal involvement Miss León may have had in Mr. Milton's attack."

Donna looks into the camera and adds, "How fast things can turn around. Things are not looking good for Chantell. One week ago, she was the angel in this story and Samuel Milton was the evil one. Now, it's looking like Samuel is the angel and Chantell is the devil.

"Related to this story, Samuel's attorney, Gordon Osborn, has stated that the evidence used to arrest Malcom León was brought to light by his investigation. He now suggests that the lawsuit brought about by Samuel Milton could reach into the hundreds of millions. I am sure there will be more twists to this saga in the coming days."

―――――――――

"Hello, Ms. Angelica Martin?"

"Yes, this is Angelica."

"Angelica, this is Linda McCall, and I have good news. Sam has come out of the coma!"

"That's wonderful."

"The first thing he asked for was to see Chantell. Is she available to come by tomorrow? I'm asking because Sam does not want us to release this information to the press until he has met with Chantell."

"I will make sure she is there. Let's say eleven?"

"Perfect. The paparazzi are all over the place, so I have an idea I want to discuss with you on how to get Chantell and Sam together. It might be a little tricky."

Chantell's mother answers, "I can assure you we're all in!"

―――――――

"I never knew you could actually rent an ambulance."

"Well, you are doing it, Miss León," the EMT says as he is prepping Chantell for her entrance. "Now, we are almost there, so let me get these bandages on your face."

"I wish I could go in with you, Chantell."

"I know, Momma. But your face is as famous as mine, so they would be looking for you, too."

"Too bad. I would like to lay hands on that man and pray for him. He needs it."

"Speaking of that, Momma, do you know of any tech schools for guardian angels? I suck at it!"

"There's nothing like on-the-job training. You'll do a better job next time. Do you know what you're going to tell him?"

"Not really. I expect to be a bawling, blubbering mess by the time I finish apologizing. I just hope he accepts it."

"Well, do you have your checkbook, just in case he doesn't?"

"It's right here with me."

"Okay, Miss León," the attendant says. "We're two blocks away, so it's time to clear some traffic out of the way."

Chantell nods, and the siren starts blaring.

───────

Sam has a young girl without any hair on his bed giving him a hug. "I'm glad to meet you, Mr. Milton."

"Come on, Lupe, we're best friends now, so call me Sam."

"Okay, Mr. Sam."

With a knock at the door, Doctor Linda walks in. "I have a little surprise for you, Sam. She is a special friend of yours."

"Really?"

"Okay, you may come in now."

Chantell hobbles in on crutches, with a brace over her left leg and bandages around her head and face. She stops at the door and tries to hold back the tears.

"Who is that, Mr. Sam?" young Lupe asks.

"It's hard to tell, but I think it's my guardian angel."

Lupe looks first at Sam, then at Chantell, then back to Sam before getting close to Sam and whispering a little too loudly, "I don't think she is very good at being an angel. She looks as bad as you do."

"We're working on it. Trust me, she's going to do great next time."

"You promise, Mr. Sam?"

"Cross my heart and hope to . . . get much better very soon."

"Okay." Lupe gives Sam another hug before Linda carefully lifts her off the bed.

"I'll see her back to her room," Linda says. "You two need to be alone."

"Thank you, Linda," Chantell says as she unwraps the bandages from her eyes, now overflowing with tears. "Sam, I'm so very sorry, so very, very sorry!"

Sam motions her to come give him a hug.

She does so, being very careful not to hurt him. "Just look at you," she says. "You look like the aftermath of a mouse that got into a fight with a cat."

"I feel like it, too."

"It looks like your jaw is wired shut. How can you talk?"

"I discovered that if you have lips and a tongue, you don't need a jaw. Unfortunately, you do need a jaw to eat, so everything I get comes through a straw. Still, I'm feeling a lot better than the night it happened. Now, how is Malcom?"

"As best as he can be. The police are holding him without bond. I hate to say this, but he says the inmates all see him as a hero for beating the crap out of you—and I cleaned up that language a lot. In his defense, he keeps insisting he's no hero but an idiot who deserves what he gets."

"I am so sorry. I tried everything I could to keep this from happening to him. What led the police to him?"

"A private investigator found one of the three yellow roses you gave me trampled on the ground, and I guess he put two and two together."

Sam tries to put the best spin on it. "I guess holding my brains in and hanging on to a rose can be a little difficult, huh?"

"A little difficult? You try it."

Sam now puts his hands up in surrender.

"Anyway," Chantell continues, "we always knew his temper was going to get him into trouble. As my grandma use to say, 'That'll learn him.' "

"Well, I'm not pressing charges or anything."

"Thank you, but I'm afraid it goes beyond you this time."

"What are the charges?"

"Well, since you are awake, it's no longer murder or manslaughter. At best, it will be aggravated assault with the intent to do bodily harm."

"I am very sorry. I guess this is a bad time to give this to him, but can you bring me that package on the tray over in the corner? It's the headlight for his '62 Cadillac. I was walking you out to the car to get it that night at the bar."

"Do you still want to give it to him after what he did to you?"

"Originally, it was to be cheap insurance. I figured that if he got the headlight first, I wouldn't have gotten this beating. The way I see it, I am more to blame for this than he is."

"Okay, now only a crazy person would say that."

"Hey, I never said I was sane! But to be blatantly honest, I was enjoying antagonizing your brothers. There's no reason I couldn't have told them to meet us at Children's Hospital. I could've let them in on the plan. Anyway, please tell Malcom this is to apologize for baiting him into this mess."

Chantell shakes her head. "I still think you're nuts, but I will tell him. So, does this mean you're my brother's guardian angel, too?"

"No, just yours. He's going to need far more of a real angel than me."

Chantell snickers. "I don't think even Gabriel would take the job."

Sam chuckles, then says, "Oh, by the way, I should thank you for holding my brains in. I hope my cerebral spinal fluid didn't stain your evening gown."

"Seeing all of that pink fluid spilling out of your head was kind of gross, but I'm proud that I held most of it in."

"Pink? The doctor said it's supposed to be clear."

"It was definitely pink, and I have a stained dress to prove it."

"Pink, huh? I wonder if that makes me a Klingon."

"Since I had to hold your brains in, it's obvious you don't have the cranial bone structure to be a Klingon."

"Thank you, I think."

The bantering continues for several more minutes before turning into pleasant conversation, and it continues until Chantell asks, "So, Mr. Milton, where do we go from here?"

"I thought it was going to be Sam now."

Chantell holds her hands up in surrender.

Sam smiles and continues, "This does put a hitch in the get along. With my jaw wired shut, the French kissing thing I had planned is definitely postponed."

"No, it's definitely *out!*"

"Gee, and I thought you were warming up to me."

"Warming up to you, Mr. Milton, is a universe away from getting hot for you."

"I'll make a note of that. Um, all of this means we are both going to have to bounce a bit, being this is going to delay things a month or two."

Chantell adds, "Or ten."

Sam rebuts, "No, no. I need it to happen as soon as I can stand on my feet."

"Yeah right. Anyway, this should at least help our problem with the press. We will be old news by then. Anyway, I have a mountain of promos to do and an album to put together."

"I guess it will give you time to reconnect with Slash."

"Don't worry, Dwaine is on tour for the next six months, so I will keep coming around." Sam is about to give a broad smile until she adds, "After all, someone has to take your place with the kids."

He gives her the exact look she was hoping for as he mutters, "Oh yes, the kids."

Figuring her comment may backfire, she picks him back up with, "And can I help it if you are just down the hall." She sees him smile and says as she turns to leave, "That's better."

She stops when she hears Sam say, "I'm glad my guardian angel is back on the job."

She turns back to him, her eyes filling with tears. "Sam, I would strongly suggest you hire yourself another guardian angel, one that knows his business far better than I do."

"Miss León, I didn't have a choice, and I wouldn't change it if I could, simply because it is going exactly as planned."

"So, you have this beating you took all planned out, do you?"

"Nope. Haven't a clue. Though for some reason, I feel very confident of some plan behind all of this, and it may even be divine."

Chantell's skepticism registers on her face, so he adds, "Think of where we were a few weeks ago. I was your worst nightmare, as I was my own, meaning I was an extremely shell-shocked and timid, pubescent thirty-seven-year-old whose only friends were sick kids. Now, I am no longer your nightmare, and I have Chantell herself sneaking in to see me. That's worth more than a few bruises to me."

Chantell stares at him a moment, smiles, and asks, "Do you mind if I sneak in again? It would seem I have a lot to learn about this guardian angel thing."

"I would be extremely honored, Miss León, however, my soon-to-be ex-lawyer is coming any minute."

"You're firing Osborn?"

"No, I never actually hired him, and to get that point across, I am going to introduce him to a lawyer I did hire."

"Ooh, can I watch?"

"I think him seeing us together would be rather counterproductive."

"Well, then let me get back into my Halloween costume so no one will see me leaving." Chantell puts her head bandages back on and wraps gauze around her face. She then picks up her crutches and hobbles to the door.

Chantell isn't out the door for two minutes before Gordon Osborn walks in. "Good morning, Mr. Milton. Did I just see . . .? No, it couldn't have been. I hope you are going to be okay."

"I will survive."

"Well, we want you to do more than just survive, Mr. Milton. I think the punitives just increased substantially, don't you? I would say to the point of one hundred and fifty million dollars."

"And your cut would be?"

"With this amount, I don't want to seem overly greedy, so I will reduce my fee from 40 percent to, let's say, 35 percent."

"Wow. I can barely contain my elation."

"I'm glad to hear it. Now, if you would be so kind as to sign our little agreement."

"I am so glad you brought that up, Mr. Osborn. I would like you to meet my official attorney, Stan Carlen."

A tall, thin man in his late sixties steps into the room and goes over to shake Gordon's hand. "Gordon, it's been a long time. How are you doing these days?"

"What is the meaning of this, Mr. Milton?"

"The meaning is very simple, Gordon. I don't like your personality, reputation, or your ethics. So, I found someone much more to my liking."

"We have a contract, Mr. Milton."

"Maybe, maybe not, Gordon, and as you so graciously pointed out, I never read it or signed it."

"We still have an agreement—verbal it may be, but it is still binding."

"Gordon," Stan says bluntly, "are you going to try and use the classic 'Gordon Osborn's legal intent' again? That is all bull, and you know it. I will have that blown out of court before the court takes its first potty break."

"Mr. Milton, I have more valuable things to do with my time than spar with a has-been attorney like Stanly C.! I will see you in court, Mr. Milton."

"Oh, that felt so good!" Stan says, turning back to Sam.

"Are you sure you can handle someone like him?" Sam asks.

"Nope, not a prayer."

"Excuse me?"

"If I was the only one going up against him, he would have me for lunch. But, Mr. Milton, I will not be alone. Do you have any idea of how many attorneys have been wanting to get a piece of him? I already have five corporate attorneys lined up to bury him in subpoenas, and they are all related to this case."

Looking nervous, Sam asks, "Do you mind me asking what your fee will be?"

"That is privileged information. However, your benefactor is getting a healthy discount based on the amount of enjoyment I plan to have."

"He wouldn't have the first name of Johnny, would he?"

"Again, that is privileged information, Mr. Milton, but I will tell you this: It's not just one benefactor, but five, and I expect more to join in as this case develops."

"Gordon Osborn is hated that much?"

"More than you know, Mr. Milton."

Two Months Later

The door opens with a squeak, causing Sam to spin around to see Chantell walk into the room. "Hey, you're back."

"Yeah, and look at you. You're up and walking around." Sam gives her a big bow.

"Do you know how long it took me to find you? What is this place, a bomb shelter from the '60s?"

"Good guess. I had them remove the sign before I would accept the room."

"Then why didn't you have them remove the janitor sign as well?"

"Didn't you know? That's my middle name. Samuel Janitor Milton at your service. So, how was your twenty-city talk show tour?"

"Exhausting. Moviemaking is much harder than being a pop star."

"I bet. I have to say, you looked good on *Donahue*. That was a nice touch to have Slash surprise you with an unexpected appearance."

"Yes, wasn't he sweet?"

Sam gives her an unenthusiastic nod.

There is an awkward silence until Sam states, "Well, now that you're back, I can get out of here."

"Whoa. They said you needed to recoup for three to four months. It's barely been two and a half."

"I heal fast. Besides, this whole mess caused me to shift gears. So, number four on our list—you are going to help reestablish my business."

"How am I going to do that?"

"By helping me finish a project I need to get out. So, plan on four to five days, and it has to happen in the next two weeks."

"Five days! Do you have any idea what my schedule is like for the next two months? Why don't I write a check for 12.5 million and just go on to the next one?"

Sam looks at Chantell for an excruciatingly long time before asking, "And that is going to benefit your moral character how?"

Chantell looks back at him, continuing the standoff before giving a snort. "Fine, I'll give you three to four days, and I suggest it be three. But I happen to know they're not going out of unless you have someone to take care . . ." She stops when she sees his grin. "No way José, not me. I'm not going to be your nursemaid!"

"Oh yes you are. But just for five days."

"I said it would be three to four tops."

"Good, I'm glad we agree."

"What? Ooh, you make me so mad!"

"Good. We're back to that love/hate relationship we've been working. But, please don't bring Dwaine. I don't have the room."

It takes a few minutes for things to calm down before Sam gets back to business. "So, this takes care of number four. Now, what I had planned for number five is going to be impossible now that I am physically limited. So, I came up with a replacement, and it is so good that I think it will be the best one yet."

Sam pauses, forcing Chantell to ask, "Well, what is it?" Sam gives her a huge smile, which she answers with, "I don't like the looks of that smile. I'm going to hate this one, aren't I?"

Sam continues the smile just long enough to make her completely tense before answering her, "You're not the one who has to worry about liking it. I will."

"Now what is that supposed to mean?"

"I am not the one who will be coming up with it. You are."

"What? How do you figure that? That doesn't make any sense."

"It makes perfect sense. Let's just say it is part of the relationship thing I lost. In any relationship, each should benefit from the other, and each should have a say in where the relationship goes."

"Oh, but Mr. Milton."

"It's *Sam!*"

"Not when you're thinking we have a relationship!"

"Oh, but we do. I'm mad at you; you're mad at me. I'm forcing you to grow up. And you keep insinuating that I need to grow up. So, find something you think I need to grow in. And before you panic, I don't believe it takes physical intimacy, or even a solid friendship, to make our kind of relationship go in a beneficial direction, do you?"

"No, I suppose not. So, I get to choose number five? And it can be anything I want?"

"Yep. Your choice. Just as long as it benefits me in a positive way."

She mumbles a choice word before adding, "You would have to add a positive spin."

Sam picks up on it. "Now, now, guardian angels need to keep their language clean."

Chantell snorts, "I only swear when I get angry, and that is something you bring out in me."

Sam squints, causing her to answer with, "Okay, I'm sorry. But, the apology isn't to you. It's to my mother, because if she doesn't slap me for foul language, my personal assistant, Carol, would."

"Good, remind me to send Carol some roses."

"Ooh! Do you have any idea how much I hate you?"

"Does this make it a love/hate relationship?"

"Don't push, Milton!"

Sam smiles. "I would love to continue batting expletives around all day with you, but I have to get number four worked out in just two weeks. And don't forget, yours is two weeks after that."

Chantell quickly calculates. "Wait a minute. That would be the week of the fourteenth."

"Yes, I believe so. Why?"

"That's my only free weekend! Why is it that you always have to pick my free weekends?" Sam just lifts his hands. "You do know that it's this kind of thing that makes my temper boil?"

"Ooh, does this mean our relationship is heating up?" Before she can comment, he adds, "It's just the kind of relationship I love best—hot and steamy."

Chantell turns and says, "You are so lucky you can't read my lips right now."

"Is that any way for a guardian angel to act?"

Chantell has to bite her tongue and then asks, "Whatever happened to this mild-mannered, socially traumatized Samuel Milton that Linda was talking about?"

"I don't know. Do you want me to go back to that guy you first met?"

Chantell takes a moment to study Sam before answering with, "Never."

15

Number Four

Chantell opens the door to her small dressing room, followed by Carol, who closes the door with a marked abruptness. "All right. What's the problem?" Carol demands as her anger builds.

"Nothing."

"Bull! You've been preoccupied for two weeks now. But for the last several days, you've been a real mess. Now, I know you could walk through one of these rehearsals in an afternoon, but it's taken three days. Now, what's the deal?"

"I guess I'm a little tired. That's all," Chantell says while desperately looking through her mail. "Say, you don't know if anything came for me today, do you?"

"So, that's what it is. *Him again!* That guy has you really screwed up!"

"I don't know what you're talking about."

"You know exactly what I'm talking about. I can tell by that look on your face. How many times did you see him in the hospital?"

"Many, but before you say anything, remember he almost died, Carol! Twice! And because of me."

"Yes, yes I know. But, for God's sake, Chantell! You know how dangerous this is. The man is nothing but bad press, and if the media gets a hold of any of this, you're going to go from the top to the 'Where Are They Now' section of *Reader's Digest*. Do yourself a favor and take this long weekend to forget about the roses and shake this guy off."

"Roses? What roses?"

Carol curses herself. "They're in the other room. They came yesterday."

"Why didn't you tell me?" Chantell chastises, retrieving the vase of four yellow roses.

"You haven't heard a word I've said, have you? The guy is messing with your head!"

Chantell reads the note that came with the flowers.

"And you're still not hearing me, are you?"

Chantell looks up from the note, gives Carol a huge smile, and tells her, "Let's go rehearse," as she prances out the door.

Carol pauses a moment, letting out a big sigh and shaking her head. She says to herself, "I feel a major headache coming on," as she follows Chantell out the door.

———

An older yellow Corvette slowly negotiates the dips and ruts in the road leading up to the old ranch. It stops in front of the mobile home. The driver guns the healthy V8 and turns it off. The door opens, and Chantell climbs up and out. She stands and straightens her back as if glad to finally be out of the car. She looks around. Hearing the sound of a saw coming from the barn, she heads in that direction.

Inside, she finds Sam, still with his head bandaged, working with a large radial arm saw. She walks up behind him and taps him on the shoulder, saying, "Hi."

Sam is startled by the unexpected touch, and without looking back, he shuts the saw off and turns around to face her. With a glare, he says, "Rule number one: Don't ever do that when someone is working with one of these saws! It's a great way to make him lose his disposition, as well as some fingers."

"Sorry," she says, still smiling. "Well, here I am."

"You're late."

"Say what? I dropped everything and drove all the way up here, as commanded, and all I get is, 'You're late'?"

Sam relents, "I'm sorry. This is kind of a make-or-break deal for me. The owner has scheduled a party, so I'm under a lot of pressure to get this done."

"Apology accepted. So, what would you like me to do? Sing for a busload of nuns? Make dinner for your high school glee club? Donate a kidney?"

Sam walks over to a closet and pulls out a pair of overalls and hands them to her. "Here. Put these on. I have a lot of living room and dining room furniture to make and a short time to make it."

"You are going to risk dying from a head wound that hasn't finished healing yet, plus spend one of your 12.5-million-dollar events having me help you make furniture?"

"Yep."

"Expensive stuff."

"Only if the quality isn't any good. So, these are your choices: You can cut and assemble or sand and finish. Which do you prefer?"

"I expect that you don't want the cabinets stained blood red, so maybe I should stay away from the saws."

Changing his tone, he tells her, "I love the detailing you did on your Southern Crescent train engine, so how about you sand and finish?"

"Where do I put my stuff?"

They walk outside, and Sam points to the mobile home. "You have a choice. You can stay in the bedroom on the left or stay in the guest house suite in the back."

Chantell looks around before asking, "Guest house suite?"

Sam points to a tiny, old beat-up travel trailer behind the mobile home. "I just cleaned it out yesterday. I think most of the fleas are gone. Watch out for Eight Legs. My friend keeps his tarantula in a fish tank, but he gets out every so often."

"Why don't I stay in your bedroom and you stay with Eight Legs?"

Sam smiles. "You would be far more comfortable with Eight Legs than staying in my room."

"Okay then. Does the spare bedroom have a lock on the door?"

"Yep, it has a lock, but it doesn't work. You can put a chair under the door handle if you want, but the door swings out. Even so, it still might make you feel better."

"I will take the spare bedroom."

Sam picks up Chantell's bag and starts walking toward the mobile home when he hears Chantell add, "I'll need a long kitchen knife. And I have my mace!"

"And I have a gas mask, so that makes us even."

"Not when I have the knife."

"Good *point*. Pun intended."

Soon, Sam and Chantell are working intently. He explains in detail what he needs and is impressed by how quickly she gets it.

A few hours later, Sam brings out sandwiches and drinks. It gives Chantell a chance to break from what she is working on and stand to stretch her back. Sam clears off a pile of sawdust so they can sit and eat. He wipes sawdust from her cheek, and she, in turn, points to his hair. He shakes out his hair with his hands, creating a big cloud of dust that she tries to keep off the food by waving her hands.

After lunch, Sam is so engrossed with what he is working on, he doesn't see Chantell come up behind and dump a bucket of sawdust over his head. He takes a handful and throws it at her, and the sawdust fight commences.

Later, Sam makes a quick dinner that they eat in the small kitchen of the old mobile home. To Chantell, it is like camping out. After resting for a short time, they both head back to the barn but stop to look at the evening view. They see a little of Malibu and all of Santa Monica, clear to the Palos Verdes Peninsula. They watch planes taking off over the ocean from LAX. In the distance, they hear waves breaking on a sandy beach. Chantell inhales and says, "You have surely been blessed to see this every night."

"Don't you have a view from your condos in Santa Monica or Miami?"

"Fantastic views, but neither are the least bit peaceful."

The two finally leave the view and continue on to the barn.

After a few hours, Sam looks up from what he is working on to see Chantell sound asleep over her project. He looks at the clock on the wall that reads twelve thirty-two a.m. He scoops her up and takes her into the mobile home. Fifteen minutes later, he returns to work.

The next morning, the sun is just filtering through the barn door when the light is broken by Chantell's silhouette. She stands leaning against the door, watching Sam work. "Do you ever sleep?" she asks.

"I got plenty of sleep."

"How much?"

"I went to bed at two and slept in until six thirty."

"Slept in, huh? Do you mind telling me how I fell asleep wearing shorts and a tank top, yet woke up in just your T-shirt?"

Sam smiles mischievously. "The clothes were the easy part. You should be asking me how I was able to get all of that sawdust off of you without waking you up."

"And?"

Sam smiles. "Fear not, little one. I did all of it without seeing anything you wouldn't want me to."

"And just how did you manage that?"

"No, no. It's a trade secret. Next time, you will just have to stay awake."

Giving up, she turns and starts walking away until she hears, "Nice tush, though."

She looks back quickly to see his big grin. She shakes her head and says, "I have breakfast ready."

"Hey, that's great! I will be in in just a minute. I'm right in the middle of something."

"Don't let it get cold."

About ten minutes later, she sits in front of a table spread with bacon, eggs, hash browns, and fruit. Also on the table is a vase with fresh wild flowers and a stalk of papyrus she picked from the hill out back. She looks at her watch. A few minutes pass, and she checks her watch again. She sighs in exasperation and continues to wait.

Five minutes later, Sam arrives. After several bites, he takes another big bite out of his burrito. "It's amazing what can go into a burrito: bacon, eggs, cheese, and hash browns."

"Even wild flowers," she adds.

"What's that?"

"Oh, nothing."

Sam swallows the last of his burrito, wipes his hands on his pants, and puts his tool belt back on. "That was fantastic. Breakfast burritos were a perfect idea."

"It didn't start out that way."

Sam looks down at the tray and sees the flowers. "I'm sorry for not coming in, but I was gluing something together, and I couldn't get away. But, I promise. I will make it up to you with dinner." He then takes the tray out of her hand and sets it aside, taking her hand and saying, "Hey, I have something to show you."

He leads her toward the rear of the barn, directly behind the table saw. There she sees a big object covered over by a blanket. "I finished the first piece for the client. Would you like to see it?" Chantell nods, and Sam pulls the blanket off to reveal a traditional buffet accented with a modern craftsman flair. It has two large sets of drawers on the bottom with a beveled glass mirror on the back. The mirror is flanked by corner shelves and tied together with a layered wood cornice across the top. It's built out of solid, dark-stained oak.

Chantell just stands stunned.

"Well, what do you think of it?" Sam asks impatiently.

"Oh, Sam!"

"I finished it last night after you went to bed. I wanted to surprise you with it. I think it's the best work I've ever done."

"It's the most beautiful thing I have ever seen,"

"Well, one down and three to go."

Chantell keeps staring at it.

Finally, Sam says, "Well, back to work."

"Don't you want to cover it back up?"

Sam looks at it and says, "It should be safe way back here. Besides, I like to look at it for inspiration."

Chantell picks up the breakfast tray and heads out the door but then stops and turns back toward Sam to ask, "Are you always this intense when you're working on a project?"

"I suppose so" is all she gets.

"You know, it's okay to stop every so often and smell the roses."

Sam looks up at her and then over to the buffet before replying, "The buffet is my rose."

Chantell looks back at Sam and shakes her head, muttering, "Never mind!" as she walks out the door.

Chantell is sanding the top of the coffee table when Sam walks up behind her and places a wooden rose on top of it. The intricate flower is made of large redwood shavings for petals, thin slices of maple for leaves, and a sliver of ebony for the stem. It is all woven together with a green thread of wool. Chantell swoons when she sees it.

"I'm sorry for taking your breakfast so lightly, and I want to make it up to you with dinner."

Caught completely off guard by his sentimental gift, she fumbles for something to say, but she can only manage a quick little nod. Sam pauses to note her reaction and gives her a quiet smile before returning to his project. Holding the rose close as if smelling a real flower, Chantell leans back to watch him work. She cocks her head slightly, enjoying the pleasant distraction.

It's late morning, with no breeze, and the barn is hot with tiny gnats buzzing in both Chantell's and Sam's ears. Chantell shuts off her sander, stands, and announces, "I need to cool off."

Sam finishes clamping a table leg together and joins her at the garden hose. He pulls his T-shirt off and uses it to slap the sawdust off his back, arms, and face as Chantell splashes cool water over her face and neck. When she hands him the hose, she looks at his bare chest and tells him, "I wish I could do that."

"Don't let me stop you."

She gives him a look that he answers with, "It's hot!" He then puts the hose to the top of his head and lets it run down his body.

"Oh man. Get me my sunglasses!" she screams in mock horror at his blinding complexion. He's not paying any attention to her. "Dude, there's white and then there's *white*! But you be *way* white! Boy, you gotta get some sun! Hey, wait a minute." She starts walking up to him. "What is this I see? Why, you have a six-pack!"

Sam looks back and forth and then back at her saying, "Okay?"

"How could someone who dresses as frumpy as you have a six-pack? This is a crime of the greatest proportions. You need a keeper."

"Are you applying for the job?"

"Not me. I don't want to work that hard."

Sam squirts her with the hose before turning away and pouring it over himself again. Suddenly, he stops and drops the hose. "What's that?"

"What do you mean, 'What's that?' "

"What is that '70 Stingray LT-1 doing here?"

"Funny, I thought it was a Corvette. How could you have just noticed it? I drove in with it yesterday. My Mercedes is still in the body shop, so I drove my uncle's car."

"That's one of my dream cars."

"I thought you were into Barracudas."

"I like Mustangs, too, but nothing compares to a Corvette Stingray. Is it fast?"

"Not really. I mean, it is definitely fast, but not nearly what I was expecting. Something must be wrong with it. I couldn't get it into third and fourth gears."

"What? That doesn't make any sense. Show me what it's doing."

"Now? We're both soaked."

"It has vinyl seats. Come on. I want to see what you're doing wrong."

"Hey, what makes you think *I* am doing something wrong?"

"We're about to find out."

They make their way out to Decker Canyon Road. Sam tells Chantell, "Turn left, go up to the stop sign, and turn right. Good. Now, go up four hundred feet and make the first left. Perfect, now you are on Mulholland. It's pretty straight, so punch it, and let's see what this has got."

Chantell floors it. As the car takes off, its force pushes them back into their seats. "See? It's fast, but is that all? And look, I can't get it into third or fourth. What's the deal?"

"That's odd. Stop, and do it again."

Chantell stops and does the exact same thing, with the same results. "See? I'm doing everything right."

"Yes, you are—except for one thing."

"What's that?"

Sam smiles. "You've never really driven a muscle car, have you?"

"Ah, well . . ."

"It's quite obvious the answer is no. Chantell, my dear, you are an incredible singer and actress. And you are by far the prettiest idiot I have ever seen!"

Chantell is about to fire back but stops when she sees his soft smile. Instead, she just says, "What?"

He starts laughing before he finally tells her, "The reason you can't get it into third and fourth is because you are already in third and fourth. You have yet to be in first or second!"

"What? Nooo!"

"Oh yes. Stop the car."

When the car comes to rest, Sam reaches over and shifts the car into first. "Now, try it. Give it some gas, and go!"

The two are thrown back into their seats. Burning tire marks and smoke are all that is left behind. "Let it get up to six thousand and . . . now, hit second. Let it get up to six and hit third. Good, very good!"

Chantell has a big grin, but it soon turns to a look of horror. She yells, "Sam!"

A sharp curve is coming up fast. "Downshift to second!" he commands.

"How do I do that?"

"Then hit the brakes!"

The car is not stopping.

"The brakes, Chantell!"

"I'm trying, but these are weird power brakes! I can't get—"

Sam grabs the wheel with his left hand and turns hard to the left. Using his right hand, he pulls up the emergency brake, all as Chantell stomps hard on the power brakes.

This throws the car into a spin, and they slide sideways toward the edge of a cliff. The car hits a low embankment and stops, but it tips up on two wheels toward the cliff. It hangs there for a second before dropping back onto all four wheels.

Both sit stunned.

Finally, Chantell pulls out the keys and drops them into Sam's lap. "I am never driving this car again!"

"Ah, Chantell. I'm afraid you have to."

"Hell, no! I am never, ever driving this car again!"

"Um, yes, dear, you are," he says, looking out his window and down. "We are on the edge of a drop-off, and I can't get out of the car. Furthermore, the back tire is halfway off the edge. So, please start the car and put it into third gear."

"Third? Why not first?"

Sam loses it. "Just trust me!"

She starts the car and puts it into third.

"Good, now ease it forward slowly. But, I may tell you to floor it. Okay?"

Chantell nods nervously and pulls forward slowly.

Sam watches as the rear tire is about to drop off and commands, "Punch it!"

Chantell does just that as the wheel drops off. The forward momentum pushes the wheel back up and on. The car lurches forward and squeals to a stop. The car is still in gear, which causes it to jerk forward and stall.

"Now, will you take the key?"

"Gladly."

They switch places, and Sam drives the car more slowly than normal, figuring Chantell has had all the excitement she can handle. Eventually, they head up a foggy Pacific Coast Highway. "Are you getting hungry?"

Chantell looks over and exclaims, "What? After that? What's wrong with you?"

"I'm hungry."

They pull into Neptune's Net, a quaint seafood restaurant. Chantell tells him, "I can't go in there. I will start a riot!"

"No, you won't. Lots of famous people eat here, and besides, it's a foggy Friday. No one comes here in the fog."

Convinced, Chantell agrees, and they have a nice, quiet lunch, with fish and chips and clam chowder. Sam sees someone pick up a payphone and look back in his direction nervously. Sam excuses himself and goes to talk to the person holding the phone. "Hi, Harold, who are you calling?"

The guy jumps when he turns to see Sam.

Sam presses down the receiver, cutting off the call. "I asked, who are you calling?"

"Sss . . . sorry, Sa-Sam, bu . . . but that's Chan . . . Chantell!"

"Yes, it is Harold, and she doesn't want anyone to know she's here, and she especially doesn't want anyone to know who she is sitting with. Got it?"

"But, Sam! I just want to tell my wife, Denise."

"I'll tell you what, Harold. Do you see what I look like?" Harold looks at him nervously and nods. "This is what I got from her brother when he was protecting her. I almost died. Now, your wife wouldn't want to see you looking like me, would she?"

"I suppose not."

"Is there anything wrong, Sam?" Chantell asks, coming up from behind.

"No, Miss León. My friend Harold here was just asking for your autograph. I told him that I would get him one in exactly one month. And he was thrilled. Weren't you, Harold?"

"Yes . . . uh . . . Miss León."

"Okay, Harold. It was nice to meet you, but I'm sorry. Mr. Milton and I have to finish our police reports on what one of my brothers did to him. However, I promise to get you an autographed album in one month. Does that work for you?"

Harold nods quickly.

"Okay then. Let's go, Mr. Milton."

Sam and Chantell start walking out the door but look back to see Harold hanging up the phone and sliding down the wall in shock.

"Do you think your friend will tell anyone?"

"Not a word, but remind me to send a thank you note and a rose to Malcom."

"I'm sure he would love that . . . not!"

"I'm impressed with your line about the police reports," he tells her. "You're quick."

"Around you, I have to be."

———————

The fog has risen up the canyon and has cooled everything off. They go back to work refreshed.

After an hour, Chantell tells Sam, "I'm going to the bathroom. You want me to bring you back anything?"

"Water would be nice, but not from the bathroom."

Chantell rolls her eyes and heads inside. She is about to head back out the door when she stops and looks over at the master bedroom. She can hear a saw running from the barn, so she walks over to the door and slowly opens it as if walking into a foreboding place. Inside, she finds a typical bed, perfectly made, and a dresser with a few knickknacks on it. On the walls are sketches and watercolors of all kinds of cabinets and furniture. They include technical drawings and blueprints. In front of the window is a drafting table with piles of drawings. Next to it is an easel covered over with a small bedsheet.

Curiosity gets the best of her, so she lifts the sheet and is startled. "Oh my! So, that explains it." On the easel is a large, beautiful painting of her with a yellow rose put up to her nose. Most every feature of her is there, except her right ear isn't finished yet. The hand holding the rose is still a sketch, as is the rose. She is amazed at how accurate and lifelike the painting is. She looks around for pictures or photos of her, but can't find any, no magazines featuring her either. She mouths, *No way! This is all done from memory?* She stands staring at it. She is so transfixed, she doesn't hear the saw turn off.

She shakes her head out of a trance and starts looking around again. Heading over to the dresser, she looks to see that she is alone as she slides the top drawer open and pokes around Sam's T-shirts. She then opens the next one down and finds what she is looking for. She looks around again before reaching in. She lifts something up, and her eyes get big. She smiles as she sorts through pair after pair of Sam's briefs. She stops to examine one more closely and nods approvingly. "Well, well, Mr. Samuel Milton, you aren't nearly as dull as you look."

She quickly puts everything back in order and closes the drawer. She looks at the things on the dresser and finds a picture frame facedown. She lifts it to see it is Linda in her nurse's uniform, holding one of the kids. Sam is in the background.

She puts it facedown again and freezes when she hears, "Find what you were looking for?"

Thinking quickly, she turns and says, "I'm looking for my car keys."

Sam reaches into his pocket, pulls out the set of keys, and tosses them to Chantell. "Let me know when you're done. I need your help in the barn." He turns and goes back outside.

Chantell leans against the dresser and mumbles to herself, "Chantell, you are so stupid!"

Back in the barn, the two work until it starts getting dark. "Didn't you promise me dinner?" Chantell asks, wiping sawdust off her face.

"That's right. I did. Let's see. We have most everything done, so tomorrow we just stain and finish. Let's go. I know the perfect place."

"Are you sure? Have you forgotten what happened at lunch?"

"All kinds of famous people go to the place I have in mind, and nobody is going to care who you are."

"How dressed up do I need to get? I didn't bring much."

"Just wear something clean. Nobody's going to care. Besides, the rougher you look, the more inconspicuous you look."

"Great, so I need to look like a biker chick?"

"Ooh, that works for me. Do you have the leather to go with it?"

Chantell rolls her eyes again. "You fantasize a lot, don't you?"

"I'm a guy; it's hardwired. I'll get cleaned up."

Heading for dinner, Sam is driving the 'Vette, and they are on the road for some time when he asks, "Did you find anything in my underwear drawer that scared you?"

Chantell looks down in embarrassment before saying, "I have a friend that says you can find out a lot about a man by looking at his underwear. It's nutty, I know, but I couldn't resist."

"You didn't answer my question."

"Ah, no, nothing that scared me; in fact, I was intrigued. I'm glad you have the physique to wear something like that."

Sam looks over at her for a second but then looks away again so she can't see him smile. "I bet you found some interesting stuff in Dwain's underwear drawer."

"That's getting a little personal, isn't it?"

Sam shakes his head before saying, "Is it, now?"

Chantell, knowing she's busted, remarks, "Surprisingly, his is quite boring. And no, I have never seen any of it on him."

Sam gives her a funny look.

She drops her head. "That sounded bad, didn't it?"

Sam just smiles.

"No, I didn't see him with or without it."

Sam pulls up and stops the car. "Well, this is it."

"This is what? Where is the restaurant?"

Sam points straight ahead.

Chantell looks again and asks, "That? That's nothing but an abandoned shack."

"An abandoned shack with a lit-up Budweiser sign."

Chantell looks and sees the sign.

"It's The Old Place. I hope you like steak or clams, because they don't offer much else. Oh, if anyone recognizes who you are and makes a fuss, go with my lead."

"We're really going in there?"

"Yep. Come on. You will love it and want to bring everyone here. I promise."

They open the squeaky door and step inside. Chantell is amazed. It is a very small place that looks like it belongs in the Old West. On the right is an old wooden bar that takes up half of the building. Small private booths line the left side. Near the door is an old upright piano.

"Well, what do you think?" Sam asks.

"Are there gambling tables in the back, with the showgirls and barmaids?"

"No gambling and no showgirls, but the food is good, and the comradery is the best!"

They seat themselves in one of the semiprivate booths.

A bearded man in his forties comes up. "Hey, Sam, it's been awhile." He looks over at Chantell. "Whoa, what's the story here?"

"Jeff, this is Chantell. Chantell, Jeff. We're trying to work things out, and I picked neutral ground."

"I see nothing and I hear nothing, but just remember the rules: If it gets ugly, take the fight outside. Nice to meet you, Miss León."

"Likewise."

After Jeff takes their orders, he turns and walks away.

Chantell remarks, "Wow, I'm impressed, but what if someone else sees us?"

"Jeff will tell them what's going on, and they will all respect your space. Privacy is an unspoken rule."

When their dinner comes, they both enjoy steak and steamed clams. Sam has iced tea and Chantell has a glass of red wine. When they finish, Chantell asks, "So, does anyone come in and play the piano?"

"No one is paid to play, but usually someone will come in and start playing. They may even get accompanied by a guitar. Bob Dylan has played on that piano."

"Well, it looks like we have been stood up. Do you think anyone will mind if I play it?"

"Go for it. That's what this place is all about."

Chantell goes over and plays something not her own. A young man in his twenties comes in and asks, "Do you know anything by Chantell?"

Chantell looks at Sam, then back at him. "I think so," she says. She starts in softly, playing one of her old hits. Four songs later, the same man says, "Thank you. Say, you're pretty good." Then he starts walking out of the restaurant.

When the man is outside, everyone in the place busts out laughing. Sam speaks up. "He will never know he had a personal concert by Chantell herself." Everyone starts clapping. Sam comes over and sits next to her. They play together, and he sings a duet from her first album. Before the night is over, two other celebrities join in.

More than an hour later, outside, Chantell takes Sam's arm. "Thank you! That was the most fun I've had in a long time. Do you think they would mind if I came back?"

"Oh, it's required. That wasn't an autograph you signed; it was a ten-year contract to play here every week."

She leans her head on his shoulder and says, "If it is anything like tonight, I'm good with it."

———————

They drive back to the ranch. "Okay, give me one hour, and we will call it a night."

"What? You've got to be kidding! I'm tired. I want to go to bed, and I don't want to fall asleep in the barn again only to wake up with one of your T-shirts over me, not knowing how it got there."

"Okay, just give me fifteen minutes. Please."

"Fine, but am I going to get sawdust all over me?"

"No, you will be on the opposite side of the table saw. You just need to take the end when it comes out of the saw and walk backward with it. All you have to do is keep it against the fence on top of the table saw so it doesn't bind the blade. This is a three-horsepower table saw, so if it binds, it will kick back on me so fast that it will go right through me. So, we will take the first few really slowly."

Sam turns on the table saw and runs the twelve-foot-long board through the saw. When it comes out the other side, Chantell takes it and guides it back. The first try goes perfectly, then the second, and third. "Okay, only four more to go."

Chantell yawns before taking the end as it comes toward her. It also gets cut perfectly. She takes the next one and gets it halfway through when she trips and the board binds in the saw. Sam tries to hold it, but it gets away from him. It shoots back so fast that it grazes Sam on his side, tearing his shirt.

Before either can react, both hear a crash and the sound of breaking glass. They turn to see the cut board has pierced clean through the buffet, shattering the mirror and leaving jagged shards of mirror sticking into the countertop. As if in slow motion, the cut board ricochets off the back wall and again hits the back side of the buffet, causing it to tip forward. Sam desperately tries to catch it, but it crashes to the floor, breaking the rest of the mirror and the lower glass doors.

Both stand in shock. Sam drops his head into his hands and stands motionless. Chantell goes over and tries to console him, but it has the opposite effect. He pushes her hand away and jumps up. He starts screaming and cursing. "That's it! I can't take this anymore! I am done!" He looks up and continues, "Are you done with me yet? I am done with you! Strike me dead right now! Go ahead. I dare you!"

"Sam, please don't say that."

"Say what? The inevitable? My life the past ten years has been some insane joke, and I'm the punch line! Well, I am done!"

Chantell again tries to calm him. "Sam, I am so sorry!"

"What are you sorry about? You told me I should cover up the buffet to protect it, but did I listen to you? Hell, no! You told me we shouldn't do this tonight, but I pushed it anyway. It's not your fault. None of it was ever your fault. I'm the one who screwed up and tore your top off, not you! I'm the one who tried to make some game out of this, only to get beat up by your brother. And don't apologize for him! He was just trying to protect his sister from me. In fact, I wouldn't have any respect for him if he didn't! So, I am now declaring that we are done! You are free to go. You did everything I asked, so you are free and clear."

"Sam, I don't think we should—"

Sam cuts her off by screaming, "I said go home! We are through with this! Get the fu . . . You just ought to go home and leave me alone!"

"But . . ."

He comes toward her, towers over her, and screams, "I said we are done! Now get off this ranch! Now!"

She quivers and cries. He looks at her, tempted to console, but then stops. Instead, Sam turns and stomps out of the barn with a final, "Miss León, get in your car and go home!"

Minutes later, back in the trailer, he opens the refrigerator, finds a beer, and chugs it down. He then throws the empty bottle against the refrigerator door, where it shatters. He goes into his bedroom and throws himself onto the bed.

Later, a car door slamming wakes Sam out of a sound sleep. He hears a car start and looks out the window to see a Mercedes driving out the gate. He checks the clock. It reads three forty-seven a.m. "What the?"

He gets up and goes outside. He sees the Corvette still parked where they left it. Now, even more confused, he yells, "Chantell! Hey, Chantell, where are you?"

His question is answered with only the sound of crickets.

The light is still on in the barn. He walks in. He scans the inside but doesn't see Chantell anywhere. He turns to walk out, but stops when he notices something. He turns to his right and sees the coffee table completely finished, both stained and varnished.

He speaks out loud, expecting Chantell to still be there. "Wow, it looks fantastic, Chantell! Chantell?" He notices a note propped up next to the coffee table. It reads:

Dear Sam,

I had someone come and pick me up. The Stingray is yours. I owe you a replacement. I couldn't find a Barracuda, and you said it's one of your dream cars. I hope it is okay. I meant to surprise you with it before I left but, well, things happen.

I am so sorry about the buffet! You are an amazing man, Samuel Milton. I hoped we could be lifelong friends. Yes, you turned my world upside down with your apology gone wrong. But I am a much better person for it. I would like to come back and spend time with your little buddies, if that is okay with you and Linda.

One last thing. If you're curious about why I stayed to complete the coffee table, it is because I always finish what I start. The four years it took to finish the Southern Crescent proves that to be true of me. Mr. Milton—I mean Sam—I think you need to complete what you have started.

With the greatest respect,

Chantell León
Your bumbling guardian angel

"So how was Zurich?" Angelica asks Chantell as she watches her daughter and Lawrence struggle to get the luggage through the front door.

"It was gorgeous. You could stick a camera out the car window, randomly shoot pictures, and every one of them would be a keeper. You are coming with me next time. Just tell your editor to stick it! Say, did anything come for me today? It's been two weeks, and that's usually when he starts the next adventure."

"Is that what you're calling them now?"

"So, did I get any roses?"

"Ugh . . ."

"What?"

Angelica exhales before saying, "You got a letter from Sam but no roses, I'm afraid."

Angelica can see the devastation on her daughter's face. She answers it with, "I am so sorry, honey!"

Chantell stays quiet for a long time before putting on a positive face. "Well, at least I get an official letter ending it. My record label will be very happy."

"You don't know that's what it is. Have faith in the man."

"Momma, you didn't see him the way I did. I guess I should be thankful I got the letter. It means he didn't commit *you know what*. Oh God, I hope it isn't a suicide note!"

Chantell runs into the other room to get the letter, leaving her mother saying, "Sam would never do that to you or his kids, and you know it."

Chantell holds the letter up to her chest. "I can't believe a weird guy like Sam Milton would get *me*, Chantell León, to act like this."

Her mother smiles. "I can, and it's about time. Go ahead. Open it!"

She looks up, pleading, "Please don't let it be a suicide note." She opens it and reads. It only takes seconds before she drops her hands to her side. Her mother braces for the worst.

Chantell sits down on the couch and holds up the letter to read. Angelica can see her daughter's arms quiver slightly. She can see she's nervous, but can't decide if it is out of remorse or elation.

Chantell reads the note aloud, noticing it lacks a signature:

Dear Miss León,

Per our previous discussion, number five is to be selected by you. So, please let me know when, where, and how it is to be done. Oh, since you are setting this one up, I expect to get five roses.

Within a split second, both women squeal.

"See, Chantell? You gotta have faith in the man," Angelica playfully chastises her daughter. "So, what do you have planned for Mr. Milton?"

"Momma, I got the perfect setup. He is so going to hate it! But, I guarantee it is what he needs most, and oh, is he going to get it!"

━━━━━

Sam finishes tying off the cabinets in the back of his truck. He needs to deliver them to a client but is suddenly aware of how hungry he is. He looks at his watch, looks down the street to a Denny's, and decides to get lunch. He is just about finished eating when Dwain sits down in the booth across from him, with two of his friends sliding into a booth across the aisle.

A little unnerved, Sam asks, "Can I help you with something?"

Dwain looks at the dessert menu and speaks with the intimidating confidence a gang member standing on his own turf might have. "Do you know who I am?"

Sam thinks a moment and chooses his words. "You're Slash, the rapper who's dating Chantell León."

He continues to look at the menu, not at Sam, as he replies, "That is a nice, white way to put it. I prefer to say that she is my woman."

"Can I ask how you found me?"

"I have eyes, Mr. Milton, lots of them, and I don't like what my eyes are seeing. I know you are not from the 'hood, so I'm going to explain things to you in a nonconfrontational way—this time—if you get what I'm saying."

Sam nods.

"Good. So, Mr. Milton, why are you messing with my woman?"

"I'm simply trying to resolve our issues and keep them out of the public eye, so that—" Sam stops speaking when he sees Dwain wave his hand.

"That was not a question, Mr. Milton. It was a warning. I don't like someone messing with my woman. It makes me . . . fu . . . messed up in the head." Dwaine shakes his head. "Do you see the positive influence 'my woman' has on me? So, Mr. Milton, you are going to end it now."

Sam tries to say something, but Dwain cuts him off.

"I'm trying to say this in a way you can understand. You're not liked in the 'hood. You're not liked anywhere in this town. You realize you have a great big bull's-eye on your forehead, right? Many want to see you gone, including my two . . . associates here. So, Mr. Milton, if you end it, I can probably convince my . . . brothers not to, let's say, vent their anger. If you continue, I can't guarantee your safety nor that of anyone who might be asked to guard you. Now, I would hate to see any of Chantell's brothers get hit by a stray bullet. Though I would not mind comforting Chantell at your funeral, I would, however, feel bad to have to comfort Chantell at her brothers' funerals. Have a safe day, Mr. Milton."

A minute later, Sam goes out to his truck to find it covered in blue spray paint. The cabinets in the back are also covered in the same paint.

16

Church!

Sam comes out of the barn wiping his hands. He sees a white van with flowers painted on the sides and the back as it goes out the gate. He walks to the front door and sees five yellow roses sitting on the stoop. He looks up to wave thank you, but the van is long gone. Opening up the letter, he reads:

Mr. Milton,

You asked me to pick something that either you need or would benefit you. I came up with a good plan as it is definitely something you need. As you have proclaimed me to be your guardian angel, I have every right to require this from you. Mr. Samuel Milton, you are going to church!

This is not just any church; this is the AME Church of Los Angeles, short for African Methodist Episcopal. It's a church everyone is proud to attend. Everyone dresses to the nines, including the men, so you will be required to dress in the best suit possible.

Arrive thirty minutes early and enter from the west side. I will have my mother meet you at the door.

Chantell

The next Sunday, Sam pulls up to the church. Because the first service hasn't let out, he is forced to park the Corvette on a side street. Before getting out of the car, he looks around and feels moved to pray. "Lord, I know we haven't talked much lately, but I hope you have a spare guardian angel hanging around, besides Chantell. Lord, I am not well liked by most and even hated by many around here."

He takes a deep breath, gets out of the car, and adds, "And Lord, if you don't, please make them a good shot so no one else gets hurt."

Sam then quickly walks a short block to the church, feeling at any second a bullet might enter his body. He walks around the church to the west side. The church is large compared to most, with a seating capacity of fifteen hundred. The building is understated but nicely kept, more pleasant than the surrounding neighborhood. The closer he gets to the door, the more self-conscious he gets. He is not sure if it is because most of the parishioners are black or if it's because he's afraid of being recognized. Turning the corner and starting up the stairs, he paces himself with the others entering. He pauses for a moment and notices two openings in the stucco that resemble something like bullet holes. His stomach ties in knots.

When he enters though the doors, Angelica is there to meet him. "How are you this fine Sunday morning, Sam?"

He answers, "I am alive and well," but as he is speaking, he notices Angelica scrutinizing his appearance. "I'm sorry. Am I overdressed? Chantell told me to wear a suit."

"Despite wearing a suit, Mr. Milton, you are severely *underdressed*. Please, come with me."

They go through a side door and down a hall.

Sam mentions to Angelica, "I'm a little afraid that people may recognize me. Is that going to be a problem?"

They turn a corner and stop in front of a door. She answers, "They're not looking at you, Mr. Milton. They're looking at your suit. How old is that thing?"

"Four, maybe five years?"

"Exactly." She opens the door, and they step into a small conference room. On the edge of a bathroom door is a suit sealed in plastic. "There you go. I will wait here for you."

Through the bathroom door, Angelica hears, "Isn't this way over the top?"

She answers, "If you are going to marry my daughter, you will need to look perfect."

"What?" The conversation through the door intensifies tenfold. "Is that why your daughter had me come here today?!"

She answers, "That is what this is ultimately about, isn't it? You marrying my daughter?"

After a split-second pause, Angelica hears, "Ugh . . . Now, wait one minute!"

"No need, Mr. Milton, you just told me everything I needed to know."

Angelica can hear Sam fumbling with his tie and thinks she hears a swear word. He answers her out loud, "I never said anything!"

"You said plenty, Sam."

The door opens, and Sam steps out in a finely tailored Versace suit, yelling as if he were still behind the door. "I never said I was marrying anybody! And I sure am not getting married today!"

Angelica reaches up and adjusts Sam's tie and then puts on a finely crafted tie clip. "No, Sam, Chantell isn't marrying you today, but you look stunning. How does it feel?"

"Hey, I've got to say, this is very nice! Really nice! But, what did you mean when you said Chantell isn't planning on marrying me *today*, like it is a definite thing, but just not today?"

Angelica ignores his last question and answers his first. "The suit looks very nice on you, and it should; it's the best available." She reaches into her oversized purse and pulls out a plastic bag and hands him a pair of wingtips. "Here, put these on."

As Sam scurries around, looking for a place to sit and put his shoes on, she finally answers his second question. "Chantell doesn't know anything about this discussion. It's just between you and me."

"What's between you and me?"

"Come on, Mr. Milton, service is about to start. Just leave your old clothes here. The janitor will see they get to a homeless person . . . maybe in Albuquerque. Even the chronically homeless wouldn't be caught dead in them around here."

They walk in at the back of the sanctuary, where she hands him off to an usher. "Good morning, Mel. Please be so kind as to seat Mr. Milton in row three, on the inside left."

"Excuse me, Mrs. Martin. Couldn't I sit somewhere closer to the back? Don't you think my notoriety might cause a distraction to the other parishioners?"

"But that's just the point. My daughter is planning to make you a spectacle," she says as she turns back to the usher. "Please make sure he's seated in three on the inside left."

Turning back to Sam, she reassures him, "Don't look so nervous, Sam. I will be joining you in a few minutes. I wouldn't miss this for the world."

Sam's self-consciousness escalates, along with his apprehension, the farther down the aisle he gets. The church is already more than half full, and the parishioners' ethnicity isn't completely one sided as he had assumed it would be; both of these facts give him some comfort. However, he soon finds himself sitting alone, up front, with all rows empty around him. He can't help but feel a huge spotlight is shining right on him. He can hear the murmuring increase. He checks his watch and sees it is an excruciating seven minutes before reinforcements are due to arrive in the form of Chantell's three brothers.

Finally, Lawrence slides in, forcing Sam farther in. He sees Eddie coming in from the other side. Considering they are the only ones in the pew, Lawrence and Eddie are sitting well within Sam's comfort zone. Though he feels scrunched, he knows not to argue.

Sam looks over his shoulder and sees Dwain sitting one pew back on the right side. He also notices that Dwain is looking at him continually, with an expression that's not in keeping with such a sacred occasion. One minute before the service begins, Angelica slides in behind Sam, along with Malcom, who is sporting a new ankle monitor.

Sam looks around and sees the church is filling up quickly. The choir comes in and takes their seats. Sam looks but can't see Chantell anywhere. Without warning, far to the right side of the church, Chantell's voice pierces the air:

"Heeeeeeee . . ." She holds the note long after she should be out of breath, and then she cries out, "Cannnnnn." Again, she holds the word before finishing the line "He can work it out!" She then appears on the right as the choir joins in behind her. It's Chantell's version of the Dottie Peoples hit. She has everyone standing, swaying, and clapping, including Sam.

No one sees it, but Chantell slips away from view, which lets her do it all again from the back-left corner of the church. She's getting everyone fired up in the Spirit as she again rejoins the choir. She does this two more times, each from a different corner. Each time, the worship gets more intense. Chantell glances over and sees that Sam's eyes are closed and he is wearing a big smile. Seeing him this way gets her even more into the Spirit, and she closes the number out with a long and powerful "Amen." She leads two more songs before turning it over to the choir director, but she stays up front and blends into the choir.

When the music ends, Sam is hoping Chantell will sit with him, but he sees her walking to one of two chairs on the platform for the guest singers. When there, she first acknowledges her boyfriend, Dwain, with a nod and smile. She then turns to Sam and does the same thing. A young man sitting with Dwain slaps him on the shoulder as if saying, "Are you going to take that from this guy?" Dwain moves his hand in front of his friend to signify he's got it covered. His friend rolls his eyes but then sits quietly.

After announcements, Reverend Bernard comes up to a small podium in front of the choir and yells out, "Is there anyone here mad at God?" He lets the stunned congregation reflect on that a moment before repeating, "I said, is there anyone here really—I mean *really*—mad at God?" This gets Sam's attention, and he also notices the congregation is murmuring at a low volume. The minister repeats his question again, only louder.

"Did you hear me? I asked, is there anyone here mad at God?" The murmuring intensifies. "Are you mad at him because he did not do what you expected him to do? Did he not heal your child, free up your bank account, or keep you from losing your home? Did he not keep your child off drugs or keep your husband from losing his job? Is that why you're mad at him?"

Sam is thinking, *Where can he possibly be going with this?*

The reverend continues to dig in deeper. "Let's take the worst of it. If you blame God for not healing your sick child, spouse, friend, or other relatives, that, my friend, is the stupidest thing you could ever be mad at him for. Why? Well, if they were not healed and have passed from this earth, then they are hugging on Jesus as we speak!"

Cheering and applause erupts in the congregation.

"It's a parallel to the old adage, 'Christ is dead and in the grave, but Sunday's a coming!' So, it is like that. We grieve our lost, but Sunday's a coming!"

The cheering intensifies with several saying, "You tell it, preacher. You tell it!"

He continues, "So, instead of looking at what you're mad at God for, look for the miracle that's coming from it! Yes, you heard me right. I said a *miracle* either has come or is coming! Now, I know, it may not have come as you expected, and that is my guess as to why you are mad at him. But, look at it again and find his miracle. I assure you; a miracle is behind whatever you are mad about. Who has your tragedy brought to you? Or has it brought you to your knees? Yell to me, 'Hallelujah!' if it has brought you to your knees."

"Hallelujah!" the congregation answers.

"Through tragedy, one of two things is going to happen. Through it, we are either going to get better or we are going to get bitter. If we let adverse circumstances make us bitter, we die ugly! If we let it make us better, we die glorious! Can I hear an amen?"

From the congregation comes a resounding, "Amen!"

"Do you want to die ugly?"

The congregation yells, "No!"

"Do you want to die glorious?"

"Yes!"

"Moses was born to free his people. He was raised to free his people. Then, Moses killed the Egyptian, and he had to run. The man ran out on his people for forty years. I said, for forty *long* years, he felt he was the biggest screwup in biblical history, and he was! No doubt about it! But old, dear, sweet Moses let it be known to you that Sunday's a coming. I have news for you! The burning bush appeared to Moses on a Sunday!"

The whole congregation is now screaming, shouting, and dancing!

"God is the King of Multitasking. He can do so much through so many circumstances, and all at one time. He can turn our tragedies into our triumphs! He can turn our biggest mistakes, our most hopeless, helpless situations, into our greatest blessings—if we let him! I have just one thing to say: Let him!"

The whole congregation is in a Spirit-filled frenzy, including Sam. Chantell can see tears running down his cheeks, which, in turn, moves her to cry. No tears come from Dwain.

"So, I tell you, instead of screaming at him in anger, yell out to him, 'Show me what I am not seeing, Lord! Show me what I am missing! For I know a miracle is in this! I said, a miracle is in this! Let me see it!' "

The applause becomes thunderous.

His sermon continues as he quotes several Bible passages, which Sam writes down. When the reverend finishes, he turns to the congregation. "Now, I want to thank our guest Chantell León—or, as she is known to us, 'Chanty'—for getting us fired up for Jesus today. It makes my preaching so much easier."

Everyone applauds.

"Now, Miss León would like to speak a few words. It is mainly to one person in this room, but it pertains to all of us." He turns to Chantell and says with excitement, "Okay, Chanty, let him have it!"

Sam sits wide-eyed as Chantell picks up the microphone. She first turns to Reverend Bernard. "I want to thank you for asking me to come back. By that, I mean coming back to my roots. It is vitally important to me that I came back, and the fact that I did is all thanks to one man."

Then, turning to face everyone, she continues, "What I am about to say may cost me seventy-five million dollars."

A hostility comes over the church. Though not overt, it still can be heard and felt by Sam. He can feel fifteen hundred people staring at him and is thankful he has Chantell's brothers surrounding him.

Chantell speaks above the murmuring. "But I think it will be worth seventy-five million to say it. I asked someone to come here today, which you may have already guessed. His name is Samuel Milton."

The hostility becomes so apparent that Chantell must wait to speak. Tears flow down her cheeks, and it brings a silence to the entire church. "Your outcry of hatred toward this man is wrong. It is just as wrong as what I did to him on *The Tonight Show*. What happened to me coming out of that soundstage door was an accident! It has been proven to me with photos and video that have come to light since my tirade on national TV. His innocence has also been proven to me by the character I have observed in this man since then. What I did and said on *The Tonight Show* cost this man everything he has. It almost cost him his life, twice, and for that, Sam, I am horribly sorry."

Chantell looks over to the right side and sees that Dwain has left. She continues speaking to the congregation anyway. "Mr. Milton and I are trying to work this all out, and we are about there."

Turning to Sam, she asks, "What, about another week or two will finish it?"

Sam nods.

She can now see tears forming in his eyes, but she presses on. "So, I am asking everyone in this building and everyone outside this church to let this man be. I don't know what Mr. Milton has planned in the next couple of weeks, so I may not get the chance to say what I am about to say if I don't say it now. Mr. Milton has no idea any of this was coming, which may get me into more trouble, but I feel the risk is worth it.

"Mr. Milton has a few quirks—as we all do. It was those quirks that made me think wrongly about him. Despite his flaws, this man hears from God. Just as Joseph in the Bible interpreted King Nebuchadnezzar's dream, Mr. Milton did the same for me. He informed me that if I kept going in the direction I was going, I would die early, and as Reverend Bernard said, I was going to 'die ugly'! Sam told me the only way to keep it from happening was by clinging to my roots. I believe Mr. Milton thought my roots were family, but I now know it's something else."

Chantell holds up her hands and makes a big encompassing circle around the congregation as she says, "These are my roots."

She sees Sam nodding, with more tears streaming down his cheeks.

She adds, "So, I am changing course."

A soft applause can be heard.

"I am still going to sing the songs I love to sing, but now I am also going to sing the songs I cherish, the songs we sang today!"

The applause gets louder. "Everyone can thank God Almighty for speaking to me through Mr. Samuel Milton. Mr. Milton has shown me things within me I have not seen or was too stubborn to acknowledge. However, today I am privileged to have shown him things within himself he has not seen for a very long time."

Chantell glances over and sees Dwain is back. She pauses for half a second before finishing with, "I do not know how this will all get worked out, but I hope the least I will get from this is a really good friend."

The congregation is dismissed and everyone gets up to leave, except Sam and Chantell's brothers. Not only do her brothers stay seated, but all three of them also continue to look so intimidating that no one comes up to talk to them. Sam watches Chantell run over to Dwain and give him a kiss.

"Thank you for staying, Dwain; it means a lot to me. Come with me. I need to say goodbye to Sam." She pulls on his hand, but he doesn't move, so she motions for the four to come to her.

As they stand, Dwain leans into Chantell and says, "You said your apologies, and that's enough. Let's go."

"Well, I need to at least say goodbye to the minister." She then pulls a scowling Dwain toward the back door.

Meanwhile, as the brothers escort Sam out, he says to Lawrence, "I would like to talk to the minister." They head in that direction.

When the line finally lets Chantell and Dwain get to the minister and his wife, Chantell takes his hand excitedly and says, "Thank you, Reverend Bernard. Things couldn't have gone better."

He leans in to kiss Chantell on the cheek. "So, are you really going to sing gospel again?"

She nods enthusiastically.

"Then, this Sam fellow has really had a powerful effect on you."

She gives a hesitant nod.

"Say, will the two of you please stand next to my wife, Veronica, a moment? I would like to talk to you and Mr. Milton. He's coming through the line now."

"It's so good to see you in church again, Dwain," the minister's wife tells him.

He doesn't respond.

Veronica can feel the tension between the two of them, so she takes Chantell's free hand and pulls her close, persuading her to stand next to her until Sam makes his way through. Veronica can feel Dwain pull on Chantell's other hand to go, but Veronica keeps a firm grip. The standoff between the three occurs in seconds, but it feels like an eternity to Chantell. She pulls Dwain to her side as he puts up stiff but polite resistance. However, he finally capitulates and stands next to her. The look on his face keeps all but the most devoted of Chantell's fans from coming up and asking for her autograph. Only a few dare to ask for his.

When Sam finally comes up, Lawrence steps back to let Sam speak to the minister. "Thank you for your words today, Reverend Bernard. You spoke directly to me. Did Miss León ask you to say those things?"

The minister smiles. "Mr. Milton, I only listen to two people: my wife and the Holy Spirit—in that order."

This gets a chuckle from everyone standing around.

"So, if the Spirit hit you between the eyes, you will have to stand in line with the other two hundred and fifty who came before you today. And I must admit, I needed to hear it myself."

"You, sir?"

"We all stumble, Mr. Milton, as Veronica here can testify."

Another chuckle is heard.

"So, Mr. Milton, does this mean you will be going to church more often?"

"Yes, sir, especially this one—if Chantell's brothers can be my bodyguards."

Reverend Bernard laughs. "Well, hopefully this all blows over so that won't be necessary. We have only lynched two people in church so far this year."

Sam stands wide-eyed until he hears everyone laugh, including the minister.

"You're too easy, Mr. Milton. We will have to let Chantell here break you in a little more."

"Oh, don't worry, reverend. Her mother has been doing plenty of that."

Sam feels a slap on his shoulder and instantly knows Angelica is standing right behind him.

"Thank you for coming, Sam," Chantell says, leaning in to give him a kiss on the cheek.

Sam smiles and tells her, "It's exactly what I needed."

Chantell smiles. "Yes, I could see that. I am so excited for you and for me; we both needed it."

"I guess we're both getting a lot better about this guardian angel thing."

"Yes, Mr. Milton, it seems we are."

Sam turns to Dwain and holds out his hand, but it's not accepted. "You have quite a girlfriend here, a real keeper," Sam offers.

"I will be doing just that."

All of Chantell's brothers escort Sam to his car. He says thank you and gets into the red 'Vette.

Sam drives down the street, misses seeing the freeway sign, and gets lost. The unfamiliar neighborhoods are making him nervous, so he doesn't notice the yellow Toyota following behind him or the car following farther back.

Block after block, Sam looks for a freeway bridge in the distance. He pulls up and stops at another stop sign. Looking right, he doesn't see the yellow Toyota slowly pull up on his left. When he finally looks left, he sees the Toyota with its window rolled down and a gun aimed at him.

The young passenger informs Sam, "Mr. Slash says it's time to say goodbye."

Before Sam can react, he hears a loud crash as the yellow Toyota is hit from behind by a much larger car with such force, the impact causes the gun to fire, tearing the lobe of Sam's left ear. The crash also sends both cars careening across a four-lane intersection. Sam instantly recognizes the back of the '62 Cadillac.

Malcom yells to Lawrence, "Take the Toyota. I'm going back for Sam."

When he gets to Sam, he gives a big sigh of relief. Except for a little blood running down his cheek, he's all right. Malcom says, "Just lean back and hold this hankie to your ear. And whatever you do, don't get any blood on that new suit, or my sister will kill you herself." He then looks at the blown-out rear window of the 'Vette and the two other destroyed cars down the street. He slaps

Sam hard on the arm. "What's with you and cars, man? You have killed or broken four cars since I've known you!"

Sam smiles. "I guess I'm having a bad month."

"You got that right! You almost died three times in five months. Take it easy, bro. It's hard work keeping you alive."

Lawrence approaches the two of them and says, "They're not going anywhere. It's going to take the fire department an hour to get them out of that mess. You all right, Sam?"

Sam nods.

"Well, don't get any blood on that suit if you know what's good for ya."

"So, I have been warned."

As the sound of sirens draws closer, Sam says, "Sorry about your car, Malcom."

"Don't worry about it. It had a rattle in the door anyway. But now you need to get me two headlights."

"And a front bumper, hood, and fenders," Eddie adds as he walks up.

Just then, a black BMW pulls up and stops with a screech. "Hey, it's Chantell and Dwain."

As Chantell is getting out of the car, Dwain, surveying the situation, floors it, jerking the car door out of Chantell's hand and knocking her to the ground. Chantell gets up swearing as all see Dwain cut off by the police not more than half a block away.

Chantell is still yelling profanities at Dwain as she runs up to Sam, who is just getting out of the car. She gives him a bear hug. "Oh dear God. I am so sorry, Sam."

Sam holds out his arms, trying not to get blood on her or his suit.

"Are you okay?"

Sam gives her a hearty smile.

"Other than feeling a little like van Gogh, I'm okay."

"Did Dwain have anything to do with this?"

Sam gives a slight nod.

She then looks up and gives him a quick kiss, which is captured on film by the paparazzi. "Busted!" Lawrence says as he looks around at the arriving police, news vans, and helicopters.

"Well, Miss León, what do we do now?"

"We finish this. We only have the last one left, right?"

Sam confirms with a nod.

She asks, "How long will it take you to plan and get everything together?"

"About two weeks," Sam answers.

"Can you make it one week?"

Sam pauses. "It might be tough, but I think so."

Chantell smiles then frowns. "Then we don't say anything to the press until then. Agreed?"

"Agreed," Sam answers, "and we stay away from each other until then."

Chantell now gives him a hug and a smile. "As long as you don't end up in the hospital again."

"I keep trying not to, but I'm not having much luck with that."

<hr />

"I'm Monica Sanford, *Channel 7 Eyewitness News.* We have yet another development in the Chantell León/Samuel Milton case, which now should be called a dramatic miniseries. My colleague Donna Dean continues her play-by-play commentary. Donna, please bring us up to date on this saga."

"Yes, Monica. Well, this has been another eventful day. It started with Chantell forcing—yes, I said *forcing*—Samuel Milton to go to First AME Church in Los Angeles. While there, she gave a very touching apology to Mr. Milton and disclosed they had been secretly meeting as part of an arrangement to resolve their differences without lawyers."

Monica Sanford says, "Thank you for the update, Donna, but now this melodrama has just taken a dramatic change. Can you fill us in on that?"

"Yes, Monica. I am now standing near the corner of Hobart and Seventieth. Within thirty minutes of the services letting out, two men in a yellow Toyota tried to gun down Samuel Milton. A shot was fired, but that bullet missed Mr. Milton by a fraction of an inch, grazing only his left earlobe.

"And get this—none other than Malcom León interrupted the gunshot. He foiled the gunman's attempt by ramming his 1962 Cadillac into the backend of the Toyota, saving the very man he almost killed just three months ago. Within minutes, police arrested the boyfriend of Chantell León, the notorious rapper Slash, for organizing the would-be murder of Samuel Milton.

"To add a final twist to this story—the best one yet—we report that shortly after the incident, our camera crew at the scene captured this picture of Miss León kissing Samuel Milton, generating speculations of romance. Back to you, Monica."

"Thank you, Donna. Well, what do you say that in a week we get all of our viewers together with popcorn to watch the climax of this melodrama?"

17

Number Six

"Come in, Miss León. Mr. Benson and Mr. Jackson will see you now."

Chantell, along with her agent, Marcus Powley, and her attorney, walk through the doors of her record label's office. Chantell instantly feels a heaviness.

Blake starts the introductions. "Chantell, I am so glad you could come on such short notice. You remember Jeffery Benson and our staff legal consultant, Orrin Machen, and our secretary, Lora."

Feeling like someone about to get chastised and wanting it over with, she responds tersely, "Yes, I remember everyone. This is Mr. Jacob Tannenbaum, my attorney. So, Blake, what is the reason for this meeting that requires our lawyers to attend?"

Familiar with her volatility, and knowing what is coming, he first glances at his boss, Mr. Benson, then goes straight into it. "I have a couple of matters to discuss with you, starting with your potential breach of contract."

Jacob speaks for Chantell. "I nor my client are aware of any potential contract discrepancies. What are the issues?"

"Miss León, did you not make a public statement this past Sunday that you are, and I quote, 'changing course'? You also mentioned that you will be coming out with your own gospel album. We do not have a gospel division or subsidiary with that form of music."

Chantell answers before her lawyer. "Then I will use another label for my gospel music. What's the problem?"

Orin takes over. "Miss León, you signed an exclusive contract with our label. You cannot sign with any other label without our consent."

Jacob answers with, "And just what problem do you have with my client signing with another label since you don't deal in the Christian music genre?"

Marcus, her agent, adds, "It's not like a lot of money is at stake, compared to what you are bringing in with Miss León on the secular end."

Blake speaks up again. "Chantell, just a few months ago we all sat in this room discussing this very topic. We said then that you have to make a decision about where you want your career to go. To try and do both secular and gospel music will split up the sales between two groups, hurting both. We decided that you would continue on the course set—more adult-topic music with no more than two 'God-positive' cuts per album. Even with that concession, we feel sales will drop considerably."

Chantell stays quiet for a long time before noticing and remarking, "Mr. Jackson, I just realized that your hands are very white."

Blake is offended by the comment and shoots back, "That seems like a very racist statement."

"And you're right. That's exactly what I thought when I first heard it."

"Well, what the hell does the color of my hands have to do with anything?"

"It just verifies the accuracy of a dream a very good friend of mine had."

"And just what does this dream have to do with the color of my hands?"

"I just realized it is your guidance that is sending me over a cliff."

Completely caught off guard, Blake is unsure of how to respond.

Not waiting, Jeffery Benson speaks first. "I don't know where you're going with that comment, and I don't much care." He nods to his secretary, who displays a photo of Chantell and Sam kissing. "May I ask what the meaning of this is? I thought this Milton character was some perverted mental case. So, why are you kissing him?"

"He came within an inch from having his head blown off. I wouldn't wish that on anyone, even if he was a perverted mental case."

Blake takes back the conversation. "Is there any particular reason why you invited him to your church on Sunday?"

"I believe even a perverted mental case needs salvation."

"And did Mr. Milton get this salvation?"

"Yes, I believe he did."

"Well, isn't that nice?" Blake says sarcastically. "Does this, along with your kiss, mean Mr. Milton is forgoing the fifty million?"

"We're still working that out."

Blake leans over to Jeffery. "Well, what do you know? It looks like Miss León's virginity is worth fifty million dollars."

Both Chantell and Marcus hear the comment, but it's her lawyer, Jacob Tannenbaum, who retaliates first. "Mr. Jackson! That mouth of yours is about to cost your boss, Jeffery Benson, one hell of a lot of grief!"

"Calm down, Jacob," Mr. Benson says in an authoritative tone. "We are all adults here."

Chantell pats her lawyer's hand and turns to look at Blake while speaking to his boss. "I believe, Mr. Benson, your colleague here has just proved your statement wrong."

"My apologies, Miss León. It looks like I will be taking my colleague back to the woodshed once again. However, though you and God may have acquired a warm and fuzzy feeling about Mr. Milton, I haven't. All I know is that this perverted mental case has cost this record label far more than your fifty-million-dollar problem. Our third biggest artist is headed to prison because of your Mr. Milton. You, yourself, have been a basket case, causing Universal to delay filming four times—and all because of him. And let's not forget *The Tonight Show* ratings are still in the toilet because of this guy. He is destroying you, Chantell! He is totally destroying you. The instant the media sent that kiss over the wires, you lost all credibility with your peers. I have fifteen people who want to speak to you about what this arrangement has cost them personally. Only three of them are executives; the rest are common churchgoing people. Lora, please bring the first three in."

The onslaught continues for two more hours. Even Chantell's own staff is advising her to cut ties with Sam Milton.

Two days later, Sam sees a strange car pull onto the ranch. A blonde gets out and introduces herself. "Mr. Milton, I am Carol Schawk, Chantell León's personal assistant. It's nice to finally meet you."

Sam shakes her hand but then asks, "I'm curious, Miss Schawk. This ranch can be tricky to locate. How did you find me?"

"I was the one who picked up Chantell at four in the morning awhile back."

"I see, and you are here because . . .?"

"Can I be frank, Mr. Milton?"

"If you feel you need to be."

"Chantell doesn't know I'm here. She would probably fire me if she found out. Anyway, we're just now finding out that you have the reputation for being a very kind and thoughtful man. So, I thought you should know what this relationship, whatever it may be, is costing Chantell."

"What is it costing her?"

"Everything, Mr. Milton. As much as she has taken away from you, you are now taking away from her. A few hours ago, we finished a meeting with everyone Chantell is connected with: her record label, studio, clothing line, and perfume company. All are taking massive hits. She is also depressed about Dwain, who, like it or not, can be considered another casualty of your relationship with Chantell."

Sam's calm demeanor changes instantly. "The man tried to murder me! So, how could you possibly think he is the casualty?"

"It's not what I think; it's what Chantell thinks. Why do you think she was attracted to him, Mr. Milton?"

"I haven't a clue!"

"His strength. Most women want to feel secure, so we are attracted to strength. It doesn't even need to actually exist; it only needs to be perceived. Take away Dwain's posse, and what is he? But even with the events of the past few days, Chantell still isn't seeing it that way. Did you know, just yesterday, she had a two-and-a-half-hour conversation with Dwain?"

"No, I was not aware of it. I must admit, it doesn't make sense to me."

"That's because you tend to think more with logic than emotion. So, let's look at a relationship with Chantell logically. If your intentions with Chantell are as I think, I must warn you that you will be dealing with a woman within a culture where the men are not the least bit inhibited. Chantell gets hit on five times a day. Most are light flirtations, but a lot are overt and obnoxious. I know one reason she dates Dwain is it puts an end to these invasions of privacy. Few would ever think of taking on Slash. It's the same reason the famous date the famous, I guess. It gives them peace on the streets.

"Since you're not famous or aggressive, the men around her will read your personality and demeanor instantly; and I can guarantee they will not have any respect for you. None! They will hit on her right in front of you. It's not a matter of if; it is when. And what will you do? How can you gain a position of power when they're confident you will do nothing? Mark my words, you will be challenged—and you will lose."

Her speech makes Sam visibly nervous, which is the response Carol is looking for.

"Mr. Milton, the picture I just painted may seem extremely negative; however, the positives of a relationship with Chantell may not be much better. By becoming involved with her, you would be entering a social climate far above your expectations or abilities. Again, knowing your personality, you would not be comfortable; thus, you would deflect your discomfort onto Chantell, making her and those around her feel ill at ease."

Sam holds up his hand to stop her. He first looks down at the ground to collect his thoughts then back to her face once his resolve is set. "I see where this is going. You're suggesting that I finish this and simply fade away so that everyone involved can get on with their lives."

"Not at all, Mr. Milton. You're very good for her."

Shock registers on Sam's face.

Perceiving it, Carol smiles, but controls her arrogance so she can finish the job she came to do. "She considers you a confidant, and she desperately needs that in this profession. However, you should just keep it a friendship, or you may get hit by one of her most notorious defense mechanisms."

"And what would that be?"

"Do you remember in the movie *Moonstruck*? Do you remember the scene in which Cher's young suitor tells her he's in love with her? She then slaps him in the face and yells, 'Snap out of it!' If you do what I expect you will, and if she is as smart as I think she is, she will haul off and slap you. Not physically, mind you, but, oh, will it feel like it! It's not to hurt you. It's to wake you up to reality and to make sure you never do it again. Then, she will turn into the best friend you've ever had. She has done this more than once. She is so good at it that some have nicknamed this move 'The Chanty.' You have already seen what she is capable of on *The Tonight Show*, though that was extreme."

"And you think that's where she'll take it?"

"I do. Look, I'm sorry for pummeling you, Mr. Milton, but no one is going to tell you this side of things—and that includes Chantell, especially if she is in love with you."

"Oh, and you feel that is possible?"

"Yes, it is possible. But, if that is what she chooses, it will destroy both of you. I think she is too smart for that, and I think she likes you too much to let that happen." Carol pauses to observe his reaction. Liking what she sees, she keeps the same confident composure in concluding, "You are both very good people. I would hate to see you two get hurt. If you keep it a friendship, you won't."

Sam runs his hand through his hair one last time. "I will take all of this under advisement, and I guess we will all see how this all turns out. Thank you for coming all the way up here."

"You two are worth it. So, I guess we will see you in a few days?"

Sam nods.

She also nods and tells him, "Goodbye, Mr. Milton."

As Carol drives off, Sam looks out over the view and speaks out loud. "Lord, again I have to say, we haven't talked in years, and I want to thank you for speaking to me again on Sunday. Oh, and for saving my life . . . a little detail I shouldn't leave out. Anyway, I sure could use your advice about now. I have no idea what I should—" The phone rings. "Hold that thought."

"Hello?'

"Hi, Sam, it's Linda, and I have two of Chantell's three choices wrapped up and ready to go. What will be the third choice? As if I didn't know. I'm getting all excited."

"You know, you have perfect timing. I will meet you at your place in an hour."

222 | An APOLOGY *Gone Horribly Wrong*

"Okay, one hour, but come clean! No sawdust this time!"

"Yes, dear." Sam hangs up the phone and heads for the shower but then stops and looks up to say, "Woah! You work fast!"

An hour later, Sam steps in the door, and Linda greets him with a quick kiss. "Come on in; I can't wait for you to see this." She pulls him to the kitchen table. On the table, Sam sees three boxes, all bright red with white bows. The first is a two-by-two-foot cube, while the other two are one-by-one-foot cubes. The third is still open. "What do you think?"

"First, I want to thank you for helping me with these. I can't believe you're able to do this with your schedule."

"Are you kidding? Sam Milton and Chantell León! I wouldn't miss this for the world!"

"Well, thank you anyway. Setting up this sixth event for Chantell is very stressful for me."

"I bet it is!" Linda agrees, having a hard time not acting like a giddy schoolgirl. "This is so exciting!"

"So, do you think Chantell will like them?"

"Of course she will; they're perfect."

"Okay, the clothes are in the first, and the record contract is in the second. What goes in the third? As if I didn't know. So, come on, let me see it."

"See what?"

"The third item."

Sam suddenly looks melancholy as he pulls out an envelope and hands it to Linda. She looks concerned and responds to it with, "What's this?"

"You know. It's what we talked about, the long-term commitment. If she chooses it, she will be required to spend two days a month with the kids in the hospital for five years."

"What kind of BS is this Sam? That isn't what you were planning, and you know it!"

"I know. It's just I don't think we would be a good fit. She's 'Chantell' and I'm just . . . I'm just Sam Milton."

Linda explodes. "I want to contact every girl you ever dated so we can all line up and slap you!" Her eyes burn into his. "So, who got to you?"

"No one got to me. I just received insight as to some of the negatives we could expect—several things I never thought about before. Quite frankly, they scared the hell out of me!"

"What things?"

"You wouldn't understand. Just guy things."

"Guy things?"

Sam gives a loud, frustrated exhale before saying, "I don't think I can protect her."

"You're afraid someone is going to steal your girl? Or is it you don't think you're man enough for her?"

"Something like that."

"You do know that's why people like Chantell have security guards and go to exclusive resorts—just so they don't have to deal with this stuff, right?"

"That isn't me."

"Do you think it's Chantell?"

Sam clasps his hands and says hesitantly, "Yes, I guess."

"She only goes there because she has to, and so would you. Have you ever asked yourself, 'What does Chantell think?' "

"Only every minute of every day."

"I will tell you this: If she isn't already in love with you, she is well on her way."

Sam gives her first a look of shock that is quickly replaced with reserved elation.

Linda explains, "When you two were spending time with those kids, I wasn't looking at them or you. I was only looking at Chantell. Did you know she was looking at you almost as much as she was looking at those kids? And do you know what she saw? She finally saw a man worth her time, someone she could be proud of—and for all the right reasons. Money isn't important to someone like her. She has all she could ever use. She is looking for a man with integrity and compassion, two things that are very rare in her line of work."

Linda picks up on Sam's building excitement, so she tempers it with, "Look, I will admit you two would make the oddest of odd couples, and she may say no, but give her the chance. I know she is expecting you to ask, and she will be heartbroken if you don't—even if she was planning to say no."

"Okay, you lost me?"

"It's more of a girl thing, but trust me, it will be important to her to hear you ask."

Trying to bring himself back to reality, he tells her, "You do know she has a reputation for being volatile, meaning she tends to blow guys off when they get too close to her. And she's not known for doing it in a nice way."

"I'm sure she does, and it's necessary for someone like her, but she does it to guys she's not into. Look, even if she completely blows up on you, it couldn't be any worse than what she already has done to you. I know you have had a hard time handling emotional things, and this has got to be extremely difficult for you. I'm also sure a future with her will come with some difficulty, but look how much she has changed you! Who you've become over these past five events is not the same Sam I knew just weeks ago.

"Anyway, I got to get to work. So, decide what you are going to put into the third box, and I will wrap it up for you when I get home. I promise I won't look in the box."

Sam looks at her. "Thank you so much for doing this for me. It's hard to believe we were engaged just a few months ago."

"Yeah, and we both know it was more out of friendship than love. And what did I tell you about finding someone else?" She goes up to him and gives him a kiss. "You do know that I will always love you. Oh, and I'm hoping to get to be a godmother from this, so you know what my vote will be."

Chantell walks into the office trailer used on location and speaks to her secretary. "Good afternoon, Lorraine. Did anything come for me today?"

"Yes, Miss León." Chantell lights up but then frowns when she hears, "A letter form Blake's office, a large UPS package with a bunch of demo tapes and the usual fan mail."

"Nothing from . . .?"

"No flowers yet, Miss León."

"I was expecting them today. Where is Carol?"

The secretary looks caught off guard; she haltingly confesses, "Um . . . she went to Malibu."

"Malibu? Did she say why?"

"Yes . . . Um, she went to talk to somebody."

Chantell is becoming agitated. "Did she say who?"

"No, Miss León. She got a call from Blake and had to run off to Malibu."

"Was anyone's name mentioned in that conversation?"

Lorraine looks away before saying, "I did hear Mr. Milton's name mentioned, along with some profanity."

"I bet there was, but not nearly the amount she's going to hear from me. Call my lawyer, Jacob Tannenbaum, and have a termination letter written up."

"Should I tell him who it is for?"

"You know who it's for."

"Will it be effective immediately?"

"No, have Jacob leave that blank for now, but I want it faxed and on my desk before Carol gets back. Oh, and page her. If she calls in, let me know. I think she would prefer to hear this conversation over the phone. I will be in my office, looking over the script changes."

"Yes, ma'am."

As Chantell leaves, Lorraine exhales loudly.

Carol walks in a half hour later. "Is Chantell here yet?"

"Oh yeah, and she is pissed!"

"She found out I talked to her pervert?"

"She knows you went to Malibu, so I think she put it all together."

"Has she called Jacob yet?"

"Yes, indeed. The letter was just faxed two minutes ago. It's on her desk."

"Well, Lorraine, this proves the turnover rate in this business is still very high."

As Carol softly knocks on Chantell's door, she turns back to Lorraine to say, "It's been nice working with you."

Inside, Carol hears Chantell going through her lines. She also notices a letter addressed to her sitting on the counter.

Chantell turns and says to her, "Good, I'm glad you're here. I need to have someone be Devin." She hands Carol a script. "Page eighty-five, scene one thirty."

"I thought you were planning to fire me?"

"Oh, that's coming, but I need to get these lines down first."

"What? Come on. Let me have it if that's what you're planning."

As Chantell tosses the script on the couch, her anger flares. "Fine! So, what were you doing in Malibu?"

"What you yourself hired me to do."

"Really? And what is that?"

"Did you not ask me to keep you from making critical mistakes?"

"Such as?"

"This 'game' with this Samuel guy."

Trying to keep her voice down, she strains to say, "This 'game' with Mr. Milton has nothing to do with you. We're doing this to keep all of you out of this. You know, no publicity and no lawyers."

"And that would be fine if it stayed just some silly game that ends in three days, but the way you are cooing all over him, this could turn into something critical."

"Critical, in what way?"

"Sam is a very lonely guy who now has the most sought-after woman in the world over a barrel. So, you know exactly what he's going for."

"Well, you can't blame the guy for trying. So, exactly what were you talking about?"

"I told him what an intimate relationship with a celebrity would be like. I warned him that if a relationship is what he has in mind, he had better take a look at the drawbacks to the lifestyle he would be getting into."

Chantell fires back, "Like what?"

Carol returns the heat with flames of her own. "All the stuff you're not telling him: the lack of privacy, the lack of time together, screaming fans at every turn, the paparazzi looking for any dirt or embarrassing tidbit they can get their hands on—and what it's like to be owned by a record label or a production company."

"He's a big boy; he would grow into it."

Shock comes over Carol's face. "Oh, come on! You're not actually thinking of saying yes, are you? Your lifestyle would destroy him, and you know it! Every single reason you like him, whatever about him attracts you, would be stripped from him, leaving you with what? He's too nice for this!"

It's an unexpected statement, one that makes Chantell pause and turn aside.

Before she can respond, Carol continues, "Don't believe me, just test him. Let him know how many wedding guests would be invited. Could he handle it? And ask yourself how many would be sitting on his side compared to yours."

Chantell remains quiet. This isn't the argument she was rehearsing for.

Carol keeps pouring it on. "You know what you went through. How many anxiety and antidepression medications did you have to go through before you were able to cope? He's a lot worse than you! You will be sending him right back to the mental ward—or worse! Have you forgotten he tried to commit suicide?"

Carol finally sees what this is doing to her friend, so she changes course. "Chantell, when I finished telling him all of this, he asked me a question. He asked, 'So, you're saying I should just fade away?' I told him, 'No, you're good for Chantell, and she needs a close friend.' And you do. But even being a close friend to someone in this business is going to be taxing, but I think he's up for that part of it."

Chantell nods a thank you, so Carol asks, "So, am I still getting a pink slip?"

Chantell tears the envelope up. "Just tell me what you're doing next time. Okay?"

"Would you have let me go out there if I had? No, you wouldn't." After a pause, Carol adds, "So, what are you going to do?"

Chantell turns her palms up. "I don't know. I guess I'm going to take a long walk on the beach while having a conference call with God. Anyway, it's all over in four days—if I ever get my six roses."

"Don't worry. No matter how much I hope you don't, you will."

Linda walks into her small office and drops a stack of folders on her desk. She rubs her neck and is startled that someone else is in the room. She turns to see Chantell sitting behind her.

"I'm sorry for startling you. Since everyone around here knows me now, it was suggested I wait for you in your office."

Linda looks around. "I'm sorry it's so small. I'm in my final year of residency. Next year, I get a bigger one with a window—if I survive. What brings you by? Are you here to see the kids?"

"No, but I'm scheduled next week for that."

"Will you be coming with Sam?"

"Um, no. I'm not sure how this is all going to turn out, but I want to make sure I stay committed to the kids either way. However, speaking of Sam, this last event is just two days away, but I have not heard anything from him about it. I have yet to receive any roses or the usual weird ransom-note-like message. Have you talked to him at all?"

"I know he's really into this and was working very hard on it. Maybe he's just playing with you. He tends to do that when he gets comfortable with someone. If so, consider it a major compliment." Linda sees Chantell's face brighten slightly, so she asks, "Is that what you came here to find out?"

"Not exactly. Do you remember us talking about Sam when we were singing to the kids?" Linda nods, so she continues, "Well, tomorrow brings finality to this whole thing, and depending on what he has planned for tomorrow night, I'm afraid I may never see Sam again and . . ." Chantell struggles to get her words out. She sniffs and quickly rubs her left cheek before continuing, "I'm afraid I may leave him more broken than he was before we met, and that would be tragic." She wipes away another tear. "Anyway, you and I had talked about how we might fix Sam, you know, break him out of his shell. You mention a Doctor . . ."

"Doctor Khadar?"

"Yes, that's his name. He told you about an odd therapy. What exactly does he think Sam needs?"

"He doesn't think long-term therapy will do any good. To break Sam out of his shell, he thinks Sam has to be shocked out of it. He needs to go through an experience similar to the time his partner's wife verbally accosted him. Sam took it because he felt he deserved it, so this time that treatment must be undeserved. It needs to be so extreme that it makes him angry and forces him to stick up for himself."

"Something like what I did to him on *The Tonight Show*."

"Exactly, only he would need to be in the audience this time and called out so he can't hide. And, he can't have anyone come to his defense either, or it will be like someone cutting a butterfly out of his cocoon. The butterfly needs the stress on its wings to get the circulation going; if you help it, you kill it. It's the same with Sam. He needs to muster his own strength to break out of his shell. However, it has to hit him hard. The more brutal the better."

"And you think I am the one to do it?"

"History has shown you know how to put him in his place. So, you know the old adage, 'If the shoe fits . . .'"

Chantell waves her off. "I know I deserve that. But even if I could come up with something, what happens if it doesn't work? He already tried to commit suicide once. This could give him enough incentive to succeed the second time."

Suddenly, Linda looks very nervous. "Chantell, I need to be honest with you. The incident in the car wasn't his first attempt, nor his second, and not even his third. So, understand that if he tries it again, even right after your event, you did not cause it, and it would have happened anyway."

Chantell can feel the tension in her body increase. "But the world will blame me just the same."

"Yes, I expect they will, and it will be ugly. But let me ask you, is Sam worth the risk? I'm not you, and I don't have nearly as much at stake, but I believe he is worth every bit of it."

"It has to be brutal, does it?"

"This is one huge boil he's been carrying on his backside, and the only way to lance it is with a sharp knife." Linda sees the anguish on Chantell's face. "You really care about him, don't you?"

"He opened my eyes to truly seeing myself. He kept me from allowing my record label to push me off a cliff. And though I was mean and unfair to him, he never took revenge; he never insulted me back; and he's been so damned polite about the whole thing!"

Linda gives Chantell a hug and tells her, "If you don't get a delivery by the time you get home, you might want to give him a call. But you'll get the roses; I'm sure."

———————

"It's tomorrow night, Momma, and I still haven't received any roses. This isn't like him."

"Oh, suddenly you're the expert on this guy? You haven't seen him more than what, seven times? And for most of those encounters, you two were not, let's just say, holding each other in positive regard."

"Actually, it's been fifteen times. Five were in the hospital when he was recovering from a brotherly encounter."

"I thought you just went that first time; you didn't tell me you went four more."

"Well, two visits were while he was still in a coma, so I guess they don't count."

"Did you talk to him when he was in a coma?"

"Yes, and I also prayed for him."

"Then those visits count. It's probably kept him alive. But, how did you manage getting by the media and paparazzi?"

"Even they don't want to get up at three a.m. Fortunately for me, his friend Linda kept getting stuck on the graveyard shift. She let me in the same door Sam used. So not only do I know him, I know him enough to justify my killing him for not getting my roses days ago! Doesn't he realize this is a huge deal to me? This event is the last event, and it is tomorrow, for God's sake. I still don't know where it's going to be or even what time! He can't do this to a girl!" Chantell screams. "Where are my roses?"

"I don't know, but it's already nine thirty, so it's safe to say nothing is coming tonight. I'm going home."

"Fine, go ahead, abandon me!" She pauses for a moment to calm down. "I'm sorry for unloading on you. Good night, Momma."

Angelica kisses her daughter and opens the door saying, "And I am positive you will be getting your roses first thing tomorrow morning." She steps out, stops, and looks down. "Or, maybe not," she adds.

"What? Why not?"

"Because you already received them," Angelica says, motioning Chantell to come to the door. Both women look down to see a bouquet of six yellow roses and a letter.

Chantell picks up the flowers, takes one look, and says, "He made this arrangement himself."

"It's beautiful, but what makes you think he did it?"

"Because he used papyrus instead of baby's breath."

"I must say, it is unique. I've never seen it used before."

"I saw papyrus on the north side of the ranch house, and these beautiful rosebuds are not store bought like the others were."

"Well, in that case, I have to go."

"Why? Don't you want me to read his letter?"

"Forget the letter. If that guy can make flower arrangements like this and isn't gay, I'm going to propose to him before you do! I sure hope he likes kinky old ladies, and I wasn't kidding about wearing those red five-inch pumps with the bows."

Chantell pulls her mother back inside. "Momma, even if he were into kink, I doubt he's into old ladies."

"So, he was just leading me on?"

"God I hope so!"

"Then explain to me how you know what's in his underwear drawer? Never mind. I'm just glad you aren't as squeaky clean as I thought you were."

"I'm reading, Mother." Chantell opens the envelope marked only with the number six. She quickly scans it and tells her mother, "This is different from his other ones. This one is a full letter."

Dear Chantell/Miss León,

Before we get to the sixth event, I would like to tell you how much this experience has meant to me. I am not sure how you feel about it, but my running into you in the parking lot was the best thing that ever happened to me. I wouldn't trade this experience for anything, even with all the bumps and bruises and near-death experiences.

Did anyone ever tell you that you are hard to get to know? The greatest part of this was getting to know Chantell León. Not Chantell, the famous singer and actress that the public thinks they know, but the real Chantell León only her friends and family know.

Also, I want to thank you for getting me back to church. I got the biggest hug of my life the Sunday before last. So, despite the numerous character flaws, you are by far the best guardian angel I've ever had.

Now that I am talking about God and going to church and all, I have to confess something. I had planned for you to get your six roses days ago, but some big event took every yellow rose in LA County. I was pulling my hair out trying to get them to you. So, though I did not steal the first rose I gave you—as you accused me of—I did steal these. I took them from the ranch down the road. So, right now, you are handling hot merchandise.

As for number six, believe it or not, we will be meeting at the Hollywood Bowl Saturday night at eight. Someone from the rock group Styx called me. Someone told him I was looking for a venue to host an event. Three members of the band, along with the roadies, came down with food poisoning, and they had to cancel *their concert at the last minute. The venue has all been paid for and is being held for us.*

Now, once we are all there, we will explain to the audience what happened from the time of the car accident to the night of this event. For an added twist, we each will be explaining it from the other person's perspective. I'm still anxious about speaking in public. So, to help me get through this, I have enlisted a public speaking coach. If I can keep from passing out or peeing my pants, I should do okay.

Then comes the apology we will each give to the other. After that, you will have to choose from three ways to apologize. The first choice is something very embarrassing you will be required to wear continually for one year. The second option will be something you make, and it may require the help of many people. And the third is something you will do. It's far less embarrassing, but as such, it will require considerably more time than the others.

And with that, Miss León, this whole mess will be finished, and you will not be writing a check for any part of the seventy-five million. If you have any questions, concerns, or comments, please call me.

Signed,

Your guardian angel "in training"
Samuel Bartholomew Milton

Chantell finishes the letter without saying anything. Eager to know her thoughts, Angelica asks, "So, what do you think?"

Chantell sits down, still staring at the letter. She glances up at her mother then back to the letter. Sounding concerned, she says softly, "Um, I don't know what to think."

"You sound disappointed."

Chantell nods.

"Were you expecting something more?"

Her daughter nods again.

"You were expecting him to propose to you tomorrow, weren't you?"

She nods yet again.

"Would you have said yes if he did?"

"I don't know. I was hoping to at least have the option."

"He sure got to you, didn't he?"

"Yes, Momma, he did. But I guess Carol made sure that a proposal isn't going to happen."

"The third option did sound like it might be a proposal."

Chantell gives a reluctant nod, but adds, "I would feel better if he said number three would involve much more of a commitment than time."

Angelica sits and holds hands with her daughter. "Chanty, honey, I will admit, it doesn't look like a proposal is coming, but I have far more years of intuition than you do. In fact, I've made a living at it. So, it is my professional opinion that you should spend some time alone and decide how you will answer him when he does propose."

"You really think he will, Momma?"

"Honey, that man thinks the world of you, but he's scared. To propose to anyone at any time is nerve racking to most men, but to someone like Sam, doing it in front of thousands is an absolute terror—not to mention how it went with Linda."

Chantell nods.

"So, what are you planning to do between now and then?"

Chantell looks into her mother's face and tells her, "I'm going to put it in the hands of the one I always do and pray Sam does the same."

"Well, after what I saw on that Sunday, I know that is what Sam will be doing as well. Good night, honey."

"Good night, Momma, and thank you."

Her mother kisses her and steps out the door. When the door is closed, Chantell leans against it and looks up to ask, "What do you say we go for a walk?"

Later, in Malibu, Sam is propped up in his borrowed bed at the ranch reading. The electronic ring of the phone startles him. He puts down his book and glances at the alarm clock on his nightstand. It's two fourteen a.m.

Expecting it to be Linda, he says, "Hey, Linda, what's up?"

After a long pause, as Sam is about to say hello again, he hears, "Sam?" The voice isn't Linda's.

"Yes, this is Sam." Sam suddenly recognizes who it is. "Chantell?"

After another pause, he hears, "Hi, Sam. Um, did I wake you?"

"No, I couldn't sleep, so I'm reading."

"What are you reading?"

"*Centennial.*"

"Wow, and you can't sleep reading that?"

Sam smiles. "Now that you mention it, it is kind of slow. What about you? What's keeping Chantell León up until two fourteen a.m.?"

"Um, I couldn't sleep either."

"I hope it's not about tomorrow."

"A little." After another uncomfortable silence, he hears, "Sam . . . I need . . . I need to ask you something."

"Sure, what is it?"

After another nervous pause, she finally says, "I don't know what you have planned for tomorrow, but I know that people have been talking to you about what you should do. My assistant, Carol, for one, and probably your Linda."

"This is true. They both seem to be far surer of what I'm planning than I am."

"Can I ask, did either make you change your mind?"

Sam is unsure of what to say, but he eventually answers, "Both had good advice, and I must say, both seemed to want what is best for both of us."

More silence ensues, which is making Sam nervous.

Chantell finally speaks. "Sam . . . if they made you change your mind about anything, I would like you to change it back."

Sam is about to speak but stops when Chantell continues, "Whatever you're planning, I want it to be from you, with no influence from anyone—including me."

"I'm sorry, Chantell, but I can't change it. I have this thing where I have to go with my first choice. Any time I have changed my mind and abandoned my initial plan, it has been a horrible mistake. So, I wrapped up the boxes and sent them away so I couldn't change anything."

"Oh, I see."

"You don't have to worry. I'm aware that I don't know you that well, but I varied the choices, so I'm sure there will be something to suit you."

Chantell takes a long time to speak again. "Um, I guess it will all work out." Longer silence. "Um, Sam?"

"Yes?"

"I want to say something else, and it's even more important than what we just talked about."

"Oh?"

"When I couldn't sleep, I took a walk on the beach."

"I hope you had someone with you."

"No, but it is a guarded beach, so security was watching out for me. Anyway, I tried your Pentecostal method of listening for the still, small voice."

Sam chuckles. "I'm not sure it is just for Pentecostals. I know a Baptist or two who like it. So, did you hear from God?"

Sam has to endure another painful delay before hearing, "I think so, but it wasn't what I was expecting."

"Oh?"

"Um, I was thinking about this guardian angel thing, and I asked if there was any more to it. I suddenly thought of you and started to cry. Sam, I have never cried like that before, ever! I couldn't stop, and it kept getting worse. I was even convulsing. I was sure security was going to call the paramedics."

Chantell pauses, expecting Sam to say something, but he keeps quiet, so she continues, "Sam, I cried hard for two hours. The odd thing was, I knew I wasn't crying about you. I was crying *for* you."

Another long, silent moment passes, but Sam still isn't saying anything, so she again continues, "Sam, I suddenly knew what your problem is. It's not anger or the bitterness you feel about God. It is anguish, horrible anguish about your partner's death and the death of his family. Can I ask you if you ever cried when your partner was killed?"

It takes Sam a long time to answer as tears run down his cheeks. "Um, no, I never did, at least not like with tears and outward emotion. I guess I kept my feelings internal."

"You need to cry, Sam. It's important to let those feelings flow through you. I don't know why I'm saying this, but you know how we can't see clearly when we are mad or depressed? That's because, in reality, we don't want to calm down. We want to wallow in the feeling; we think it would be wrong to let it go. So, we get even angrier or more depressed.

"Sam, I know with absolute certainty that if you would cry—I mean really have a hard, cleansing cry—it will get a lot of hurt out of your system. When that happens, I know you will see what you have been missing. You're not mad at God for not preventing your partner's death. You're in anguish because you don't know why God didn't prevent it. I know what the answer is, Sam. It is a single word, very bizarre, and nothing like I would expect. However, I can't tell you what it is. You need to find it out for yourself."

Silence fills the phone for so long that Chantell has to ask, "Sam, are you still there?"

After more silence, Chantell is about to hang up. Finally, Sam answers, "I'm sorry. I'm still here. I was just contemplating what you said. You have a good reason for not being able to sleep. That is a heavy spiritual weight you have been carrying. I want to say thank you for being my guardian angel. You started out kind of rough, but boy, have you grown in to it!

"As for crying about my partner, it seems I am doing it now, and because of it, I don't think I will be getting much sleep tonight. However, you, on the other hand, should be able to sleep very well now. You don't have to worry about what is in the boxes tomorrow because you just confirmed something for me tonight. When you open the last box, remember that it was sealed up before we had this conversation."

Another long pause comes to a close as Chantell says, "Sam? I don't want to freak you out, but I need to say something else. I have lots of friends. In fact, I have more friends than I can count, but for whatever reason, I can't say I ever had a true best friend. I guess I was always too busy. I know we have only just met. We've seen each other for, what, fifteen times now? So, it is odd for me to say this, but thank you for being that kind of friend. If nothing more comes out of this, I trust I will always have that."

Chantell can hear Sam's smile, especially when he tells her, "You have just made my life very sweet. Good night, Miss León."

"Good night, Mr. Milton."

═══════════

Chantell is in the hallway of her old high school talking to friends when the fire alarm sounds. She, along with everyone else, starts looking around. She realizes the fire alarm has the same tone as her phone. She opens her eyes and reaches for it. She notices it's four thirty-two a.m.

She shakes the sleep out of her head and says, "Hello?"

"Hi, Chantell. Was the word you got *autopsy*?"

"Uh, what? Who is this?"

"It's Sam, and I'm asking if the word you received when you were on the beach tonight was *autopsy*."

"The word I got is *compassion*, so, I guess we didn't actually hear the same thing. I'm sorry, Sam. I really thought I was giving you something from God."

"But you were. *Autopsy* and *compassion* fit perfectly together."

"Maybe it's due to lack of sleep, but you totally lost me."

"With any accidental death, an official inquiry is conducted to determine the exact cause. For my partner, Ben, I had to read countless reports about anything that could even remotely be related to the cause of death, other than blunt force trauma from the fall. I remember seeing something odd, but it didn't mean anything at the time."

"What was it?"

"Ben had AIDS."

"AIDS? Is that what caused him to fall?"

"No. It had not metastasized beyond the initial infection. He had a blood transfusion a year before his son was born, and the doctors assume the blood was tainted. This was long before blood was routinely tested for AIDS. So, if Ben had it, he more than likely gave it to his wife, who passed it on to their son. Unfortunately, here we are in the end of the '80s, and we still have no cure for AIDS."

Chantell remains silent, desperately trying to understand.

Sam picks up on it and asks, "Chantell, what would be more compassionate: to prevent Ben's accident and have all three family members survive, only to suffer and eventually die from AIDS—with all the agony and stigma that comes with it—or to allow the accident and let all three die quickly within weeks of each other?"

"That's a hard one to pick," Chantell answers.

"Yeah, it's not easy being God."

"Does this give you any solace?" she asks.

Sam exhales. "It's not the answer I was hoping for, but how can I stay mad at someone I feel sorry for?"

Chantell considers Sam's answer and asks, "You're feeling sorry for God?"

"Sure. He's faced with those decisions all of the time. I wouldn't want to make them. So, I feel compassion for God. But I'm also feeling compassion for myself. I see that I didn't actually cause anyone's death. God's plan was that Ben and his family all die together. It was a compassionate plan, allowing them to avoid a painful, drawn-out death. I can forgive myself because I was only playing a part in some greater plan."

"I see your point and am so glad God is giving you insight. Can you sleep now?"

"I think so." Another awkward silence ensues before Sam ventures, "Chantell?"

"Yeah, Sam?"

"Thank you for tonight. Your words really helped me. I am looking forward to seeing you again tomorrow."

"Me too, Sam. Good night."

18

D-Day

The small table holding three decorative boxes looks completely out of scale under the big expanse of the Hollywood Bowl. Sitting to the left of the table, some distance back, is an overly excited Linda and a petrified Sam.

"Can you believe all of these people?" Linda declares with exuberance, clutching Sam's arm as she looks out over the crowd.

"You're not helping me, Linda. Saying that to me is like talking about waterfalls to someone who has to pee!"

"I'm sorry, but this is so unbelievable. The rows are filled as far back as sections D and E. I thought this was private, by invitation only."

"Well, obviously someone didn't get the memo."

"Where did all these people come from?"

Sam responds nervously as he rubs his arms and legs. "I simply asked to have a public apology where I could control the press; but I guess if it's got Chantell's name attached to it, then this is what you get. And don't forget Johnny Carson himself is moderating. Now I know why I was offered the Hollywood Bowl—somebody knew something. I bet Johnny had more than a bit part in all of this. Anyway, I can't believe I have to stand up and speak in front of all of these people! I'm going to pee my pants, even without talking about waterfalls. I know my leg is going to start twitching as soon as I start talking."

"What's that from?"

Sam shakes his head. "I don't know. In college, when I had to stand in front of the class to have them critique my project, I'd be so nervous, my leg would twitch."

"Did anyone notice?"

"That's how I got the nickname Twitch'n Sam."

"Ooh, that's bad!"

"Tell me about it, and that was only twenty or maybe sixty people. How many are here so far, two thousand?"

"That times ten!"

Sam looks at his watch and asks, "Where is Chantell? It's getting late."

"Uh-oh," Linda says. She whispers to Sam, "Here comes that Carol woman, Chantell's assistant."

"Good evening, Mr. Milton," Carol says with a smirk.

"Good evening, Carol. This is my close friend Linda McCall. Linda, Carol Schawk. Do you know where Chantell is?"

"Oh, haven't you heard? Slash, I mean Dwain, had a Jesus experience and got saved last night." Sam initially is pleased until reality sinks in. Carol watches Sam's countenance change from excitement to mild anxiety and then to all-out dread. She smiles at his discomfort and piles it on. "Isn't that great news, Sam?"

Sam, caught off guard, is fumbling for something to say. Linda, knowing what he's feeling, comes to his rescue. "That is wonderful news, however, I know we just met and I apologize if I am wrong, but I don't take you as . . . . I don't know . . . a God-fearing woman, Carol. So why are you so excited about it?"

"Oh, I'm not at all. I just love being right, and it looks like I'm going to be extremely right. Aren't I, Sam?" Sam is still frozen. "In fact, Chantell is all giddy about Dwain's conversion. She's even spent the last four hours at Los Angeles County Jail talking to him about this very thing. It seems he's got quite a story to tell.

"Anyway, she called to let me know she's running a little late. Oh, and she has a big announcement to make. But don't worry, Sam. She is very conscientious. I'm sure she will wait with her big announcement until your little thing with her is finished. Oh yeah, don't forget about her bite, Mr. Milton. But remember, it was always intended to be the best for everyone involved. Well, I suppose

I should tell Johnny and the Bowl staff that there will be a delay. Enjoy the evening, you two."

As Carol walks off, Linda rubs Sam's shoulder. "Why does someone as nice as Chantell León hire a demon like that?"

"Someone as nice as Chantell needs to be protected. You wouldn't want to see her protected by someone milk-toast like . . . never mind."

"I am so sorry, Sam. I am so, so sorry!"

Sam sits rubbing his hair. He looks up to eye the third box sitting on the table. He looks down and says something to himself. Linda leans in. "Did you say something, Sam?"

Sam looks up and changes the wording slightly. "I think I made one really big . . . I think I made a huge mistake."

"You don't know that for sure. Besides, remember what we talked about. She will be expecting it, and she will be disappointed if you don't try, even if the answer is no."

Sam relents. "Well, I hope for Dwain's sake his commitment is real—and for Chantell's sake too, for that matter."

"You're really hoping for that?"

Still rubbing his hair nervously, he says, "If this changes his eternal destination, how can I stand in the way?"

Linda returns Sam's answer with a smirk. "If it's even legit, though, right? He could be saying something like that just to keep her hanging on the line."

"Maybe, but having those two together would make a fantastic testimony, much better than Chantell's and mine."

Linda gives Sam a searching look. "Well, your mouth may be saying it, but your face isn't agreeing with it. Come on, Sam. Get over this pathetic, self-denigrating, and self-effacing crap!"

Sam just sits staring down, rubbing his hands.

Frustrated, Linda looks up and yells, "Lord, if you're disagreeing with what Sam's spewing, as I know you are, please smack him!"

Linda moves one chair over, leaving Sam to wonder what she's up to.

She responds to his questioning look with, "I'm just getting a better view to see what He does. I hope he leaves bruises."

"Okay, I get your point." Sam glances up at the third box again. "I don't mind being embarrassed; I just don't want to be humiliated."

"She loves you, and if it turns out that she doesn't want to marry you, she would never humiliate you."

"That's not what I've been hearing."

"You've been listening to Carol, the wicked witch from the Hamptons."

Sam answers it with, "She's just looking out for Chantell's best interest."

"Yeah, and she would rather see Chantell with Dwain?" Linda looks up and yells, "Lord, if you don't smack him, I'm going to!"

"Hey, what's with all the yelling?" Johnny Carson asks, walking up to Sam and Linda. "Are you making a habit of getting every woman in California to scream at you, Sam? It sounds like you two have been married for years."

"We might as well be," Linda groans. "He listens to me so little, it's as if we're married!"

Sam jumps to his feet. "Oh, Johnny, this is Linda McCall. Linda, Johnny Carson."

"It's a pleasure to meet you, Mr. Carson."

"It's Johnny, and, Sam, you look just like I did after my second divorce, and you haven't even proposed yet—or have you?"

Sam loses it. "Why does everyone insist they know more about what is going on than I do?"

"It's right here in tonight's itinerary: Eight forty-two p.m., Chantell León marries Sam Milton to avoid doing embarrassing antics in public. Reception to follow."

"What?!"

Linda reprimands, "He's kidding, Sam. Calm down already; your yelling has the news media thinking something is going on, and now they're all coming over to get an interview."

Sam starts freaking out. "I can't handle this."

Linda pats Sam on the back of his hand. "Don't worry, Sam. I got this." Just as reporters and cameras start scrambling to see who goes first, Linda covers her ear with her hand and turns away, saying, "What's that? Chantell just arrived? Where? The east entrance? Great, don't let anyone know."

Within seconds, every reporter is heading to the east gate, leaving the three of them alone.

Johnny looks wide-eyed at Linda. "Wow! I'm impressed, Doctor McCall. Come see me about a job on Monday."

"Is Chantell really here?" Sam asks.

Johnny and Linda turn to Sam. "Really, Sam?" they both say in unison.

Sam responds, "Okay, so I'm freaking out a little!"

Linda and Johnny look at each other and smile. Johnny looks at Sam and says, "Define *a little*." They laugh; Sam doesn't.

Sam and Johnny start going over the itinerary, but Sam keeps looking at his watch, noting Chantell is now a half hour late. Johnny goes up to the mic every ten minutes and gives a humorous excuse for why she is late. Finally, after forty-five minutes, a big commotion occurs at the VIP dropoff. Sam and Linda walk toward the commotion but can't even get close as the reporters and hundreds of fans swarm a black limo. Except for the sweatpants and oversized T-shirt she wears, Chantell exits the car with all the flair expected of a movie star.

Figuring they will be passed by, Sam takes Linda's hand and has to shout, "This is nuts. Let's go back up to the dais and wait for her there."

Linda nods and they turn, but they stop when they hear Chantell calling, "Sam!" Security clears a path for her. Sam notes Chantell is acting way too excited, even for the evening they have planned. She runs up to Sam and gives him a hug. Cameras click to capture the moment.

As the extended hug continues, Chantell tells Sam, "I have some fantastic news. Can we talk a little later? I would like to make an announcement after this is over."

Sam reluctantly nods his approval.

"Great! I'm going to go change. I will be out in just a few minutes."

Sam nods again, and Chantell gives him a quick peck on the cheek. She runs off, leaving Sam handling the photographers alone. Reporters are hounding him for an interview. He answers with a stern, "We said there would be no interviews until after the event. Please honor that request, or I will have security escort you out." Sam then takes Linda's hand and starts pushing his way through the crowd back to the stage.

Sam exclaims, "This is insane! Where did all these people come from?"

Linda answers, "Welcome to the life of Chantell. Sure you want to live a life like this?"

Sam stops and turns to Linda. "Suddenly, the humiliation of rejection I have been fearing is starting to look pretty good to me."

"It ain't going to happen, Sam. You had better get used to this."

"Are you kidding? What have you been smoking? She's already made her choice. Come on. I just want to get this thing over with."

Sam checks his watch again. "Where is she? She said just a few minutes. It's been twenty-five already."

Linda scoffs, "Why are you worried about the time? It's not like you have a pressing *engagement* afterward. Oh, did I say that out loud?"

Sam looks at her. "You are so cold! I thought you loved me once."

"Nope, never. That's why you're marrying Chantell, remember?"

"You know, you're making me feel like a tennis ball slammed back and forth by Connors and Borg."

"I'm just toughening you up. After all, the world has already seen Chantell tear you apart."

Sam shakes his head. "Remind me not to send you a Christmas card next year." He looks up to see Chantell. A look of relief spreads across his face. "Finally."

Chantell comes out wearing an elegant, green party dress, fully made up. She comes up to Sam, who is all agog. Her hands actually shake as she tries to speak. Sam interrupts her attempts. "Wow, you look incredible!"

Speaking with the same eagerness, she answers his comments, "Oh, thank you, and you look good, too. That's the suit from church, isn't it?" Sam gives her a gloating smile until she adds, "My mother dresses you gooood!"

Linda laughs as Sam rolls his eyes. Chantell continues trying to speak as her excitement escalates. Waving her hands, she exclaims, "Anyway, Sam . . . Sam, oh, Sam, I have the best news to tell you!"

Sam holds up his hands and physically coaxes her to spill it.

"Are you ready? Dwain got saved!"

Sam knows Chantell is looking at him with great expectation, so he calls upon what little energy for the subject he has and gives her a big smile. "Wow, that's fantastic!"

"Isn't it though? I just came from seeing him. He's asking so many questions; he's just like a kid in a candy store."

Sam hears Linda say softly, "Or like a con artist sizing up his mark."

Sam reaches back and slaps her thigh.

Linda ignores the reprimand and asks more loudly, "Um, not to be a pessimist, Miss León, but he is in prison. Are you sure he's not just posturing himself for the upcoming trial?"

Sam winces, fearing the comment will be taken as an insult, but it doesn't faze Chantell at all. Instead, she gives Linda a big smile. "Oh no, you don't have to worry about that. I know for a fact that this is as real as it gets, because he asked me to . . ."

Suddenly, Chantell becomes very self-conscious. This causes Linda to mumble, "Oh, she's gone. She's completely gone!"

Sam slaps her again.

Chantell then speaks directly to Sam. "I'm so sorry, Sam. I'm forgetting our thing."

Sam waves off her apprehension. "No, please finish what you were about to say. It sounds very exciting."

Chantell, looking embarrassed, shakes her head and recants, "No, it needs to wait. Come on. Let's finish this first. It's very important to me."

Sam musters the last bit of a smile he has left. As he tries desperately not to throw up, he says, "Okay then. Let's begin. Take your seat, and I will let Johnny know he can start."

19

Good Lord,
How Do I Get Out of This?

Johnny approaches the microphone. "Good evening, ladies and gentlemen. I'm Johnny Carson." He gets thunderous applause before continuing, "And welcome to *This Is Your Life, Sam Milton.*"

Sam mumbles something to Johnny, making Johnny look at his note cards and then back to Sam. "What? I got it wrong? It's not your entire life? Oh, just five months of it?" Laughter rises quickly. "Okay then, welcome to *Five Months in the Life of Samuel Milton.*" Johnny looks back and asks, "Better? Good! Boy, I'm sure glad of that! We were headed for one long, boring night." Everyone laughs, even Sam, but especially Linda.

"I'm here to reveal shocking revelations about Mr. Sam Milton, now sitting behind me." The mention of Sam's name gets a few boos and hisses from the audience, so Johnny motions for the crowd to calm down. "The first shocking revelation is that Sam Milton is a personal friend of mine, and I have known him for over ten years, after I caught him sneaking on to my tennis courts at three in the morning. The second shocking revelation is, he does not have a perverted bone in his body. Well, the bones in his big toes turn out, making him look like an alien, but he's not a *perverted* alien.

"The third revelation is the fact that Sam Milton is, well, how can I say this? Boring!" Johnny is now using his high nerdy voice. "And just how boring is Sam Milton, you ask? Sam Milton makes Tommy Newsom seem exciting!"

He pauses for the laughter and then continues, "That is, Sam leads a boring life except for these past two months. And, oh, how Sam Milton's life has changed! For one, Sam has developed quite a thing for cars. He likes to wreck them. He has killed four cars in five months, and only one was his. This strange car fixation all started back when Sam was an extremely shy pubescent boy—which was about five months ago. He was just driving along, minding the rear end of a pretty girl walking across the parking lot, when out of the blue, something much better showed up and interrupted his daydream. It was Chantell, his favorite singer and the crush of his life. Finding it difficult to talk to a pretty woman, he tried an innovative approach for introducing himself: He ran into her car.

"However, this ploy had some drawbacks. When he saw it was really Chantell he had run into, his extreme shyness instantly kicked in, rendering him unable to speak or even look at Miss León. He was acting like Tommy Newsom trying to do Shakespeare. Chantell, on the other hand, doesn't see Sam Milton; she sees Pee-wee Herman, a weird man standing like someone just out of a mental institution. Not wanting to have anything to do with this mental case, she gets back into her car and drives off, with his driver's license, insurance card, and the front bumper of his car.

"Feeling remorseful for his less-than-impressive introduction, Sam tries to apologize by tracking Chantell down."

Johnny turns to Sam and says, "Big mistake! Huge mistake!"

Turning back to the audience, he continues, "Mr. Milton finds out that Chantell is filming at Universal, so he takes a dozen yellow roses and heads to soundstage thirty-four. He then proceeds to run up the flight of stairs. As fate would have it, however, Chantell is leaving the soundstage just as he approaches. She swings the door open, hitting him in the head and knocking him backward. To keep from falling, he reintroduces himself to Chantell with a far more intimate introduction . . . by way of her breasts!" The audience laughs loud and long. Chantell, Linda, and Sam all have tears in their eyes from laughing so hard.

"Now, let's look at this introduction from Chantell's side. Chantell, who is having a typical day, with dozens of reporters, cameras, and members of her security team pushing her around, sees Sam's intimate introduction and apology from a slightly different perspective; she perceives his intentions to be anything but kind and apologetic. When she opens the door, she doesn't see a nice, fair-looking but shy guy—she sees Norman Bates form *Psycho*! He reaches in and rips her top off, running down the stairs with it as some sort of souvenir."

Johnny turns to Sam. "The least you could have done is go back and ask her to autograph it for you. And no, Sam, you can't do it now!"

Returning to the story line, Johnny continues, "Now, I suppose this one event could get one's emotions all knotted up, but in the words of Flip Wilson, 'You ain't seen nothing yet, honey!' A tornado is about to hit Samuel Milton, and unfortunately, it didn't take him to the Land of Oz—though I bet he would have happily settled for Kansas.

"Now, as luck would have it, Chantell was scheduled to appear on my show that very night. It probably would have benefited everyone if Miss León was privy to some background information about Sam Milton prior to arriving at *The Tonight Show*. However, about two minutes before she comes on my show, she finds out about Sam's prior visit to the Channel Islands Mental Hospital. She also finds out the police had just released Sam so he could get Chantell to autograph his special souvenir. With no time to process this information, Chantell walks on stage, and the world gets to see a whole other side to Chantell!"

From behind Johnny, everyone can hear Lawrence yell out, "Oh yeah! Try living with her for eighteen years. You'll see it!"

Chantell responds, "Shut your mouth, Lawrence!"

Lawrence responds, "See, I told you. She's like that at home."

It takes several minutes for Johnny to get the laughter to die down. He then laughs himself and says, "See, everyone, just your typical American family. Remind me to talk to you guys about doing a sitcom together. Anyway, after Chantell's little chat with America about Mr. Milton, things did not go well for the man. His house was destroyed, his pet killed, and his car totaled. He also suffered bodily harm and came close to death three times."

Johnny turns to Chantell and tells her, "Even Arnold Schwarzenegger would ask for a police escort while dating you. Oh, and the worst part, he had to sit face-to-face with Gordon Osborn for forty-five minutes!"

After another delay for laughter, Johnny says, "Now, because he is the world's nicest guy, he did not want Gordon Osborn, or any other lawyer, making things worse than they already were. He wanted to do that himself. So, I helped him by arranging a meeting between Sam and Chantell. As a result of that meeting, he came up with a unique plan for having Chantell replace what he had lost. So, at this point, I would like to bring up both Chantell León and Sam Milton."

Enjoying thunderous applause, Chantell stands to her feet. The room is far more subdued when Sam stands to his feet. This causes Johnny to turn toward Sam and say, "Don't worry, Sam. We had all of the tomatoes and rotten fruit collected at the entry gates: four bushels full. We're making a stew with them later. If this all goes well, there's a good chance you won't be in the pot with the vegetables."

Sam's nervousness is evident as he walks up to the mic. It takes several tries before he and the Bowl's sound engineer get his cracking voice in sync. He still sounds nervous as he tells everyone, "I don't know about putting me in the pot with the vegetables. Knowing my luck lately, I would give everybody heartburn, and you all would *still* be mad at me." This gets a subdued laugh from the audience, which makes Sam even more nervous, but he forces himself to continue. "It is true, Mr. Carson and I have been friends for over ten years, and I am honored that he considers me a friend. But that is the kind of guy he is. He can dine with kings and queens yet have a burger and beer with the guy down the street. I also would like to say he has been a huge help in resolving this predicament."

Sam speaks slowly and deliberately, sounding equal parts articulate and nervous. "I first would like to apologize to you, Miss León." He turns and faces Chantell. "I never meant to scare you, and I am still mortified that I did. As for the rest of it, I would like to tell everyone that this giant mess was one innocent accident stacked on top of another, which continued to compound until it turned into an all-out nightmare.

"Most everyone knows the story leading up to the moment I accidentally pulled Miss León's top off." This still gets a few boos from the crowd. "As for her outburst on *The Tonight Show*, can anyone blame her? I can't. She was a very scared young woman who thought the police were not protecting her.

"As for what followed, it was very unnerving for me, but even then, I did not want to involve any lawyers. The only reason I met with Gordon Osborn was because he contacted me, letting me know he had a video proving my side of the story. I just met with him once, and no contracts were signed. The fifty-million-dollar lawsuit was his idea. I told him to sit on it until he heard back from me, but he announced the lawsuit without my knowledge or permission. I have now been informed he is also suing me, along with everyone else." This gets far more boos, which Sam views as positive.

His confidence builds as he tells the next part of his story. "It was my intention to leave town and let this all fade away, but then Mr. Carson reminded me of how much I lost and how little chance I had of getting any of it back. I didn't want any monetary compensation, so I came up with this little game idea, a way for Chantell to pay back some of the intangibles that were taken from me after her *The Tonight Show* appearance. However, when I proposed my plan to Chantell, she bluntly told me she didn't want anything to do with my list of reparations. I told her that rebuff caused the price of a potential lawsuit to go to seventy-five million. Suddenly, she had a change of heart." This gets an outcry of boos. Sam waves his hands and tells everyone, "It was still seventy-five million I had no intention of collecting, and I still don't hope to ever see a dime.

"The rules for the game were simple. I would ask her to replace six nonmonetary items I lost. Item one was my personal life; number two, my home life; number three, my social life, including friends; number four, my business; number five, my spiritual life; six, an apology from Chantell for what she had taken."

This last remark gets many more boos, so Sam ad libs, "Now, before you retrieve eggs and tomatoes from the pot of stew, let me say that all of the previous five items have been interesting and even fun. It is my intention that this last one, the apology, will likewise be enjoyable for all. However, though each of the five was simple in nature, each required Chantell to place more and more trust and faith in me.

"From this point on, I would like Chantell to explain each event in her own words. I have not heard her responses, so Miss León, if you so choose, this is the time to get me back if you feel any of the past events were inappropriate." Sam then points with both hands to Chantell and says, "I give you Miss Chantell."

Cheers radiate up from every section of the Bowl as Chantell walks over to the microphone. Sam starts to sit back down, but Chantell grabs his hand and pulls him back to her side. She takes a deep breath and announces, "Ladies and gentlemen, my family, and especially my devoted fans, and you, Mr. Carson, I am here tonight to tell you how embarrassed I am. However, it's not because of anything Mr. Milton is making me do. It's because of why I am required to do it. I have come to realize in the past two months just how mean and ugly I can be. I was so self-righteous with Sam, never thinking there could possibly be any more to the situation than *my* point of view. Though the world may not perceive me as pompous and pious, I see the truth about myself now. This ugly ego of mine is not only responsible for hurting this man, but it is also responsible for the pain and injury of all those rioters in Baton Rouge and Los Angeles. It wasn't Sam's actions that started those riots. It was my comments about him.

"Now, to be honest, even if I hadn't seen any sound evidence proving Mr. Milton's side of the story, it wouldn't have made any difference. That's because I have seen Sam, in every way possible—other than naked." She then says quickly, "But I have seen him with his shirt off, and let me just say, *he is fine!*"

Chantell lets everyone calm down before continuing, "What I have seen in this man in the past five-plus months proves to me, beyond any shadow of a doubt, that whatever he says is the God's truth. I don't know a more honest, compassionate, or kind man in this world today. And to think I almost destroyed a man like this! He came very close—no, he came *extremely* close—to dying three times because of the viciousness I set in motion on *The Tonight Show*. He more than deserves a seventy-five-million-dollar settlement for everything I stripped from him. However, he chose not to involve attorneys, the press, or even his own desires for revenge in his plan to settle up with me. Though I must say, those three boxes on the table are making me nervous."

Chantell turns to Sam and takes his hand. "Mr. Samuel Milton, I am so sorry for what I did to you. You had every right to take out your revenge on me, but instead, you chose to help me see what I refused to see in myself. You also taught me to trust and reawakened in me the experience of grace. So, it will be my honor and pleasure to explain the five things you required, which ultimately humbled me and made me grow up."

Murmuring ripples throughout the audience. Cameras flash, and reporters all speak softly as if covering a golf tournament. Chantell smiles and lets the anticipation build a few more moments. Her smile is giving Sam comfort for the first time tonight, and she knows it.

She turns back to the audience but still holds one of Sam's hands. "Mr. Carson—that is, Johnny—brought me, Sam, and my mother together. This meeting at Johnny's house was the first time I heard his account of our misunderstandings, and I believed him. I was then ready to write a check for the loss I had caused him. I expected our disagreement to be over after we settled on an amount. However, he explained his game to me instead.

"In response, my ego exploded, and I became incensed! I thought, *Who does this guy think he is? I'm Chantell. I should not have to play his games!* However, my mother, who was developing a strong affection for Sam, set me straight in her own calm, polite way—she slapped me! So, I relented, and agreed to his first item: dinner out to repay the harm I'd caused to his personal life.

"I have to tell you, I was mean to him the entire night. In fact, during our meal, he dared to bring God into the picture, and that made me furious! How dare he challenge my faith and what I was doing with my life. But he wasn't trying to hurt me; he meant everything for my good. He told me something that scared me, and I told him something that confirmed what he was saying was true. It was then that we both knew there was far more to this game than either of us had expected. What was said is too personal to share tonight, but it put the fear of God in me.

"Over dinner, he explained the next steps to his game, leaving out details so each event would be a surprise. Unfortunately, because I am a *slightly* volatile person . . ." She pauses to preemptively shout, "Shut up, Lawrence!"

He yells, "See!" over the laughter.

"I was still both angry and scared of this man, for reasons I can't explain. So, I bluntly asked, *When does this game start?* He smiled, reached into a flower arrangement, and handed me a yellow rose, saying, 'You just completed the first item on my list. You had dinner with me, so you can write off 12.5 million dollars.' Now, for those of you who are slow with math, that amount is one sixth of the seventy-five million he teasingly threatened to sue me for.

"I then asked if all of the items would be like this. He told me, 'Each will be just as simple but will require you to trust me more and more.' He wasn't kidding!

"The next item, number two on his list, simply required me to make him dinner. I guess you could say this was also a near-death experience for him because I can't cook."

Lawrence yells out, "You got that right!"

"Lawrence! Don't make me come hurt you!" Chantell snaps back.

She shakes her head and then continues, "I won't bore you with the details of my home-cooked meal—but I will share one detail, which had nothing to do with dinner. Before we sat down to eat, something amazing happened. My niece, little Zinnia, is the shyest girl in the world. She runs away from everybody, including family members. Yet, when I opened the door to let Sam in, this timid little girl ran up to him and grabbed ahold of his leg as if he was her best friend in the whole world. She batted her big eyelashes and asked, 'Can you teach me to ride my bike?' Well, in fifteen minutes, he had her riding her bike—after no one in the family had been able to do it.

"It was like God Himself sent this little cherub to say, 'Chantell, you are missing something important.' But, I tried to kill him anyway. I was so mean to him! I spiked his dinner with the hottest Asian chili peppers on the planet. You should have seen this white boy turn colors! I think he turned three different ethnicities in the few seconds after he took a bite. Even so, he didn't get mad—he got me back. Though he didn't do it intentionally, he got me back but good! It's much too personal to talk about here, so you will have to ask my mother. She would love to tell you everything. She is a gossip columnist, you know!"

Angelica shouts, "You got that right, baby! I got all the dirt."

Chantell continues, "The next item was even worse! He told me I had to sing for his buddies, but he wouldn't give me any details. In fact, he made me meet him at some seedy little bar, in some God-only-knows-what slum, at night, dressed in something flashy. The taxi dropped me off two blocks away. It was so bad that two police officers were there to escort me the rest of the way. On foot! Halfway there, they got some emergency call, and they left me standing alone on a street with all sorts of lewd characters around! I had to fend for myself in the middle of the night."

Sam leans over to the mic and says, "It was eight thirty."

She looks at him and yells, "But it was dark!"

He smiles while everyone else laughs.

She turns back to the audience. "And there were all of these weird street thugs, all offering their services—if you know what I mean."

Sam leans in again. "But remember, all of these people were . . .?"

She turns and glares at him and says with vengeance, "Actors. They were all actors, but I didn't know that at the time!"

"What?" can be heard from several people.

Sam again leans in to the mic and explains, "All of them were actors, including the two policemen—everyone except the drunk she tripped over. We don't know how he got in there."

Everyone is laughing hysterically, except Chantell.

When it calms down, she finishes describing event number three. "I finally made it to the bar to see my brothers sitting there, waiting to watch over me—just as I knew they would be. So, at least I felt safe . . . until Sam sent in a distraction to turn my brothers' attention from me. It was some basketball player."

"Come on! It was Kareem Abdul-Jabbar!" Lawrence yells from the back.

This gets all kinds of oohs and aahs.

Chantell takes back control with, "Okay, so Johnny Carson set Lawrence up with Kareem Abdul-Jabbar!"

"It wasn't me," Johnny says from the back.

This causes Chantell to look at Sam quizzically.

Sam just shrugs.

She proceeds. "Now, while my fearless protectors were going all googly-eyed over this basketball player—"

Lawrence yells back, "I *said* it was Kareem Abdul-Jabbar, man! Cut us some slack."

Chantell yells, "I'll cut you some slack!"

She then shakes it off and continues, "As I was saying, after my brothers were thoroughly distracted, Sam took my hand and led me out the back door into the alley behind this sleazy bar. We crossed the alley and walked up to a steel door. He keyed in a code, the door opened, and we walked into this sterile institution. A doctor met us and took us to a dark room. Just as I was beginning to worry this might be some mental hospital, she flipped on the light, and I saw fifty-plus kids! These sweet children were in hospital beds, with tubes and wires coming out of them." Chantell tears up and pauses. "It was Children's Hospital Los Angeles, and we were in the cancer wing."

She sniffs, wipes her eyes, and says, "It turns out that Sam had been visiting these kids twice a week for most of ten years! Ever since his friend's little boy had cancer and died, he has kept coming back. He has silly hand puppets." She is now all-out crying. "He sings, badly, but mostly he makes up these funny little stories to entertain the kids. I'm not supposed to tell you this, but he also tells them about God."

She is crying so much now that she is having a hard time talking. Sam puts his arm around her as she speaks. "And he tells the . . . terminal . . . ones about how this cool Jesus dude is so excited that he gets to meet them . . . so dying is nothing to be scared of." Everyone on the dais is now crying, as well as most in the audience. The TV cameras are panning, taking it all in.

Still crying, she continues the best she can, "Mr. Milton, or as he is known by them, Sammy, introduced me to each one. I sang songs and talked to every child. We weren't supposed to be there because it was after visiting hours. But when I turned around, the entire hospital staff and other patients were standing behind us and all the way down the hall. It was the most blessed night of my life! We were only supposed to be there for forty-five minutes at the most, but we were there for over three hours."

With her face still toward the floor, she starts speaking very slowly. "What I just told you was the most beautiful thing I have ever seen, but what happens next is the most horrible thing I ever witnessed. As we were heading back, Sam introduced me to some of the actors he had hired for the night, and it was great. However, my brothers didn't know where I was, and they had been running around, frantically looking for me. I guess the basketball player didn't distract them the full three hours, and they got worried.

"When Sam and I stepped out of the bar, he was picked up and slammed against a brick wall. Sam's head hit the edge of a door, and it cracked his skull open. I did as much as I could until help arrived. All the while, he kept telling me, with a broken jaw, that I had to leave. I begged him to let me stay. He started screaming for me to leave so I would stay out of the limelight. When help did arrive, I stepped back. I saw him starting to convulse violently. My brothers pulled me away to keep me out of the press.

"I wanted to see him the very next day, but I found out that he had been placed in a drug-induced coma to help him heal. I did get to talk to his doctor on the phone. He didn't pull any punches when he said, 'Your friend is very lucky. He must have had a guardian angel standing next to him. If there wasn't a hospital next door, he would have died! We were seconds from losing him.' Well, as you can see, Sam survived, though as you can see, his head is now kind of lopsided."

Sam laughs.

Chantell enjoys his laughter and then goes on to describe event number four. "Next, I was to help Sam build furniture to bring back his business. The ranch where I joined him was hot and very dirty, but I had the best time of my life. I snuck off to snoop around. I wanted to see what this man was really like. I poked my nose into everything in his bedroom—and I mean I looked at *everything*. The only thing I can say is, this man isn't quite as dull as he looks."

Chantell's mom yells out, "Yeah, baby. Come on, now!"

Sam puts his head in his hands as he shakes it back and forth.

"Now, now, Momma; he's all mine." This statement causes a flutter of excitement in Sam, until Chantell adds, "You can have him after, but right now, he's all mine."

"I'll be waiting, honey!"

Sam is turning red, and the embarrassment doesn't go unnoticed by Chantell. "Wow, he's changing colors again, Momma. He's just like a chameleon." Everyone is laughing.

Her comment only makes things worse, causing someone from the back of the audience to yell, "You bet he is; we can see it from here! Someone get a fire extinguisher."

Sam leans in, trying to change the subject, but she is having none of it. "Oh no, baby. You had all your fun embarrassing me. Now, it's my turn, and I like it!" She then stops and says, "Unfortunately, I'm afraid if I keep going, I will have to pick up Mr. Milton off the floor with a mop." This gets boos from the crowd.

"As for the next event, Mr. Milton told me I had to come up with the plan myself. The first time we had dinner, I asked him if he was a Christian. He was, but he also admitted that he and God weren't talking. It seems Sam has been extremely angry with God ever since his partner's young son died. Well, a little voice told me that Sam needed to go to church, and I made him. Ladies, you should have seen this all-white boy in a practically all-black church! And surrounded by my brothers, no less! It was glorious! And?" Chantell says to Sam.

Sam leans in and says, "I absolutely loved it! Best church ever!"

Chantell speaks. "And I am very proud to say that he and God are talking again!"

The audience erupts in applause.

Chantell smiles and says, "And then he got shot!" The audience first laughs but then goes silent.

Chantell reassures them, "No, it wasn't in church; it was after. Thank God, the bullet only grazed his earlobe—though it made him look even more lopsided. Fortunately, my brothers were there to help."

Sam interrupts with, "They came at a rather high rate of speed!"

Chantell smiles again. "This time, instead of trying to kill him, they actually saved his as—er, butt!"

The crowd is laughing and cheering. Chantell puts her arm around Sam and pulls him close. "So, you can see why I've changed my mind about this man. And I hope I have convinced you to change your minds about him as well."

Everyone in the Hollywood Bowl erupts in applause.

Chantell gives a slight bow, turns, and walks back to her seat. Sam takes her arm and pulls her back, saying, "I'm sorry, Miss León, but we aren't done yet. You still have to do the last item on my list and in front of all these people."

"Oh, I thought my speech and apology would be enough."

"No, no, Miss León. You just had your fun with me; now I get to take my revenge out on you."

"Can't I just write you a check for the last 12.5 million? I happen to know you could use the money."

Sam turns to the crowd. "Should I let her off the hook by letting her just make a payment?"

The response is loud nos and boos.

"Your fans have spoken, Miss León."

Chantell exaggerates a pouty walk as she makes her way over to the table holding the three boxes.

Sam picks up his mic and explains, "Miss León, you are required to choose one of these three boxes. If you choose the first one, which contains four items, note that one of the four items must be on your body twenty-four hours a day, seven days a week for one full year. The items vary, so you can wear the item that will fit your specific occasion. The more inconspicuous items can only be worn during special engagements, such as filming a movie or photo shoots."

Chantell reaches into box one and pulls out an extra-long T-shirt in bright pink. In bold, black lettering, "I'M SORRY, SAM!" is printed across the front and the back. Chantell looks at it and asks, "Can I get this in florescent orange? Pink is not my color."

"I will make the arrangements. However, this is to be worn at bedtime or when lounging around the house."

The next clothing item is a skimpy bra and panty set. They are still in hot pink and have the same message printed, but in appropriately sized lettering. She looks over at Sam and asks sarcastically, "Planning to see me in these, are you?"

"Only if we have matching rings on our left hands."

"I am afraid most men would disagree with the necessity of doing that."

"I wouldn't be doing it for other men."

His remark gets a loud laugh.

"I'm glad to hear it, I think. You do know this hot pink will show through most of my clothes, don't you?"

"That's the point."

"Of course it is. How did you know my size? Never mind, I don't want to know!" she says, glancing at her mother. Chantell then picks up a small ring with the same wording imprinted on the outside. "Let me guess—this is to be worn during fashion shoots?" She slides it on to her finger and says, "Thank you, Momma, for also giving him my ring size, along with my other vitals."

"You're well . . . oops!"

Chantell picks up the last item in the box and holds up a small toe ring. She turns to Sam and asks, "For?"

Sam shrugs. "You never know; you might get a *Sports Illustrated* cover."

"You're right. You never know."

While moving to the second box, Chantell asks Sam, "How will you know if I'm keeping my end of the bargain?"

"Your mother."

"Yeah, she would rat me out all right."

Hearing her daughter's comment, Angelica shoots back, "You bet I would!" Her retort brings more laughter.

Chantell holds up the second box, which is the size a shirt or top would come in. Sam speaks. "Okay, this one requires you to do something major. So, you will need help with it."

"What kind of help?"

"You will know instantly. Fortunately, it's right up your alley."

Chantell opens the box, removes the tissue, and pulls out an old 45 vinyl record. The label with the record title has been changed to read, "I'M SORRY, SAM."

"If you should choose this one, it will require you to write, produce, and record a song of apology. But, it can't be some quick little ditty. It has to be professionally done and released as a single. It will also need to make it to at least number ten on the Billboard Hot One Hundred."

"You don't mind asking for the world, do you? Do you have any idea how difficult that is? How can I guarantee it will make it to number ten? How about giving me a more practical goal, like somewhere in the top one hundred?"

"I know I'm not in the music business, but it would seem to me, just with the publicity from today, you could hit the charts at number ten."

"I would put my money on it," says a familiar voice from the first row. Chantell looks over to see Jeffery Benson, the president of Iconic Records.

Sam acknowledges the comment with, "Thank you, Mr. Benson. Oh, and all proceeds will go to Children's Hospital Los Angeles."

This gets a standing ovation from everyone in the Hollywood Bowl.

Chantell smirks. "Well, it seems that's the winner so far."

Sam and Chantell can't help but notice that sitting next to Jeffery Benson are several other men in lawyer's attire. Chantell wonders who they are, but dismisses the thought as she steps over to box number three.

Sam tells her, "Miss León, the third item is not as physically obtrusive nor as embarrassing. However, it involves a much longer commitment."

Chantell opens the third box and pulls out a letter. This causes Linda to go up behind Sam and hit him hard on the shoulder. "You copped out and gave up!" Sam grabs her hand before she can hit him again. He gives Linda a stern look and nods in Chantell's direction. Linda relents and lets go.

Chantell reads the letter silently. Tears start flowing down her cheeks again. She turns to Sam and smiles. "Now, I know what you meant last night when you said we weren't finished yet, and I am very thankful for that."

Feeling very relieved, he tells her, "Please look further; the real box is much smaller."

Chantell roots through the paper and finds what she is looking for. No one can see it, but her eyes get huge. With a slight quiver in her voice, she asks, "Is this what I think it is?"

Sam gives her a nervous yes.

"I thought so." She stares at it for a long time, making everyone curious as to what it is. To Sam's chagrin, Chantell looks at Linda before looking back in the box. She shakes her head slightly. The movement grows until it becomes obvious.

Chantell's pleasant expression morphs until it eventually becomes a look of complete disdain—all of which is picked up by the TV cameras. Without looking up, she states bluntly, "How dare you?"

Sam turns white and closes his eyes as he hears her say again, "How dare you do this to me?" Sam is starting to cringe and shrink back in his chair. Everyone else is doing the same.

Chantell's anger continues to escalate. "Do you actually think that this is all I am worth?" Everyone turns aside, as if expecting it to get much worse. It does!

Pointing into the box, she shreds Sam. "You actually believed you could have me wear something like this?" she asks. "Wear it for something like this?" She waves her hand over the entire stage. "Who do you think you are, Mr. Milton?" She turns and stares right at him, wags one finger, and loudly chastises, "No, no, no, Mr. Milton, no! No, you don't, not here and not now! How dare you treat me this way! Treat my emotions this way!"

Sam sits mortified. He sees Carol shake her head and look sideways at him, giving him a loud but silent, "I told you so!"

Linda takes Sam's hand and squeezes it and says, "I am so sorry, Sam. I completely misread her."

Chantell sees Linda's display of sympathy and stomps over to the two of them. "No you don't, lady! This has nothing to do with you. This is between Mr. Milton and me! You're out of this one! And don't get all teary-eyed for him. You are as much to blame. I am doing exactly what you suggested."

Linda sits confused but soon looks as if she has received a revelation. Seeing it, Chantell quickly turns toward her assistant. "And don't you gloat either, Carol! I see you over there. This isn't between you and me either! I won't let what either of you think enter into this. This is only between this man and me!"

Everyone in the audience sits in silence. All of Los Angeles sits in silence. Everyone in the world who is watching this live sits in silence. Linda thinks a moment and then smiles. She quickly puts her face down so no one can see it.

However, Angelica has had enough of her daughter and stands. Without even turning toward her, Chantell yells, "Stay out of this, Mother. This is not your party, and anything you've got to say, I don't want to hear!"

Angelica yells, "Chantell Ray León!"

Chantell screams, "Sit down, Mother! When are you ever going to start trusting your daughter with the men in her life? It's my life, not yours!" Then, glaring at Sam, she states bluntly, "Well, Mr. Milton, what have you got to say for yourself?"

Sam feels so small, as if he's nonexistent. He sees a tiny loop in the carpet sticking up and wants to crawl under it.

"Well? The world is waiting!"

Chantell can hear murmuring punctuated with every profane description imaginable! This only instigates more rage, and her voice volume increases tenfold. "Mr. Milton, are you suggesting that I might feel guilty enough to accept this? Was this whole game of yours just a setup to make me feel so sorry for you? Did you think I'd feel sorry enough to sacrifice everything I am?"

Sam sits with his head down. Even those who despised Sam for what they thought he did to Chantell are now cringing at the brutality of her words.

Sam sits frozen, feeling every verbal slash. He feels unable to lift even a finger to stop the carnage. As Chantell continues her tirade, he sits praying and pleading. He silently prays, *Lord, you're the one who got me into this . . . this mess! I did my part. I said what I was supposed to say. This is both mortifying me and making her look horrible! So, what do I do now? I have no idea what to do.*

Suddenly, a weird confidence comes over Sam. It's not as if he doesn't care, but it is as if he knows her ranting isn't real.

Chantell sees Sam sitting as if engrossed in a distant thought. She screams in rage, "Are you even here with me in this? Or do you even care what I am doing to you?"

Sam repeats the thought out loud, "Her ranting isn't real." He doesn't realize his mic is picking up everything.

Chantell screams, "What are you telling me, Mr. Milton?!"

Sam lifts his microphone to his lips and speaks confidently and with force. "I don't know what your game is, Miss León, but I have had enough! However, you are right in saying we are not done!"

Chantell is taken aback, by finely seeing Sam's assertiveness. She lets him speak.

"Chantell León, you have three choices on that table. You are only required to choose one. I, along with the whole world, know now that you do not care for number three. So, pick one of the other two! And please do it now so we can finish this and all go home!"

She looks intently at Sam for a long time. He looks back at her as if waging war with his eye contact. He finally repeats his command, "Pick one, Miss León!"

For another moment, she holds position. She then looks at the boxes on the table. She takes a deep breath, lifts her head high, and answers, "Since my only choices for my life are on this table, and you are forcing me to choose, then I choose . . . all three."

After a momentary silence, the buzzing of voices builds. Questions like, "What?" "Huh?" and "She said what?" permeate the entire Bowl.

Sam, who is still staring at her, completely perplexed, opens his eyes wide and shakes his head as if to see if something is wrong with his perception. He finally asks, "Um, Miss León, I'm totally lost here. You do know you only have to choose one?"

Not changing the look on her face, she asks, "Do I have the option of choosing all three?"

"Um, I guess so, but I never expected that to happen."

"Then, I choose all three."

Sam looks away in embarrassment as a huge smile forms on his face. He is, at once, confused, elated, and petrified. He wants to believe the best, but he's also afraid this could be a setup to shame him again. So, he slowly asks, "Can I take it that you are also choosing what is in box number three?"

"You are picking up on that, are you?"

Slowly turning toward Chantell, he says with growing confidence, "That would mean that you are willing to . . ." He stops when he sees her smile. It takes everything he's got to keep from becoming a puddle on the floor.

Lawrence leans over to his mother. "I'm confused. What's happening here?"

Angelica leans toward him and whispers, "A miracle."

Sam shows his feelings with tears and a smile. He stands and says, "Then you want to . . ."

Chantell's face turns cold as she points her finger at him. "Oh no you don't, Mr. Milton. Don't you dare get the wrong idea!"

Angelica leans back toward Lawrence and whispers, "Or, maybe not."

One of the reporters turns toward her camera and says bluntly, "Okay, she's now just screwing with all of us!"

Sam looks down, puts his head in his hands, and exclaims, "Miss León, are you deliberately trying to drive me insane?"

"No, Mr. Milton. I am trying to teach you a lesson."

Those words instantly bring back Carol's warning. His elation turns to all-out anger as he lashes out at Chantell. "Oh, so that's what this is all about? Well, thanks a lot! I got the message. So, let's just pick things up and all go home!"

Sam turns, prompting Chantell to ask, "What in hell do you think you're doing? You just sit your butt back down in that chair. Go on. I said sit!"

Sam closes his eyes, turns back to Chantell, and says in a controlled scream, "No, Miss León. You are going to be the one to sit back down, and you are going to tell me and the rest of the world what the hell is going through your mind!"

She doesn't move.

He yells, "I said sit down!"

Instead of sitting, Chantell looks past Sam to Linda, and with a growing smile, asks her, "Well, how did I do?"

Linda raises her fist high in the air and brings it down quickly, yelling, "Yes! You go, girl!"

Sam looks over at Angelica, who is also smiling. Totally confused, Sam looks back and forth at all three women before asking Chantell's mother, "Would any of you like to tell me what I'm missing?"

Angelica cocks her head sideways, smiles, and says, "I'm not exactly sure, Mr. Milton, but I believe my daughter just gave you some brass balls." She cocks her head in the other direction and adds, "And I must say, they look pretty good on you."

Sam stands in shock. He looks around to see everyone laughing. Chantell's three brothers are on the floor with tears in their eyes. He turns to get help from Linda but sees her saying, "Yes! Finally!"

Chantell looks at him lovingly and tells him, "And it's so nice to know you actually have some under there. I'm sorry I had to use such a big jackhammer to find them."

Sam's confusion is turning into anger until he sees Chantell sit down and fold her hands in her lap, acting docile and submissive. Sam slowly gets it. He shows it by bobbing his head sharply. He then smiles and looks at Angelica while pointing to her daughter. "She's got a lot of you in her," he says with a grin.

"Oh, you bet she does, honey, and you had better get used to it!"

Sam beams and holds out his hands, causing the whole crowd to erupt in applause. He turns to Chantell with arms still outstretched to take her in, but she steps back and wiggles her index finger back and forth. "Oh no, Mr. Milton, not yet you don't. We're not finished with this by any means."

Sam looks up. "Good Lord, what now?"

Chantell walks back over to the third box and stands behind it. "There was a very good reason I told you no the first time, and nothing changed in that regard."

Sam shakes his head again, unsure what to think.

Chantell chastises him. "Now, don't go getting all huffy on me. If you want me to wear what's in this box, it can't be tied to any silly game, not even one as important as this. It can't be part of revenge, payback, or even guilt."

She turns to Linda and says, "It can't be because of what someone else suggested."

She now turns to Carol and adds, "Or because you want to prove someone else wrong."

Turning back to Sam, she states, "Do you remember our conversation last night?"

"Yes, very well."

"Good, so you know a proposal has to come directly from you and only you."

Sam nods.

"So, is it coming just from you?"

"It is most definitely coming from me."

"That's good to know. However, Mr. Milton, if you want me to wear this ring, then you will have to ask me properly."

Sam looks at her, pleading with his eyes.

Chantell doesn't give him any slack. "Come on, Mr. Milton. You know what to do."

Sam looks like a deer caught in the headlights. "Um, you mean here? Now?"

"Yes, Mr. Milton. Right here and right now. And you better do it quickly, because I could change my mind at any minute. Then you will be stuck proposing to my mother."

Everyone hears Angelica yell out, "That's fine by me, honey."

Chantell puts one hand on her hip and motions with the other. "So, come on and get that little white butt of yours over here."

Sam nervously walks over to her, scared to death. Chantell points to the box. Sam reaches inside and fiddles with it before pulling out a huge diamond ring. Everyone cheers and whistles. The cameras zero in to let the world get a good look.

He holds the ring to his chest and looks into her eyes as he begins, "Miss Chantell León . . ."

Chantell holds up her hand, saying, "Come on, now. I said *properly*. Get down on your knee."

Sam looks around and then slowly gets down on one knee. This gesture gets more cheers and whistles. Chantell says, "That's better."

He looks again into her eyes and asks, "Miss Chantell León, will you do me the profound honor of becoming my wife?"

Chantell gives Sam a huge smile and says, "No."

"No?"

"No!"

Sam is utterly puzzled. "What do you mean, no?"

Angelica yells, "Yeah! Why *no*?"

Linda cries, "You can't mean *no*!"

Everyone in the Bowl is questioning her no.

Chantell firmly repeats, "No!" Then, she explains, "I'm not going to marry you with that ring."

A confused Sam mumbles, "But I have been told it's four carats."

"That's right, honey, and that's why it's not nearly good enough."

Sam's skin turns to ice. He looks down, shaking his head. "I, I, I don't know what to do . . . I . . . just can't."

Chantell looks down at him. "You're not marrying me with that ring, that's for sure." She then reaches down and pulls his chin up with one finger and looks into his face. "I'm going to tell you why this ring isn't good enough by asking you one question: How does a simple carpenter come up with enough money to buy a four-carat diamond ring?"

Sam just shrugs.

"Which means this ring isn't from you, is it?"

Sam embarrassedly shakes his head no.

"And that's why it isn't good enough. I want a ring from you."

Sam looks around and takes a deep breath. "Okay, I expect to get a few past checks coming in soon. So, if we both go to look at rings I can afford, can we continue?"

"Well, you can try. I think I might say yes."

"Might?"

"Oh, come on now; have faith."

Sam exhales loudly and asks slowly, "Miss Chantell León, if I promise, in the near future, to get you a ring you approve of, will you marry me?"

Chantell smiles and gives an enthusiastic *no*.

"No? What now?"

"I don't like what you said about 'in the near future' you will get me a ring."

Sam holds up his hands in surrender.

She answers with, "Sam, I don't want a ring you will be able to afford in two months or one that you could have afforded two months ago. I want a ring you can afford right now."

"Chantell, the only ring I could get you now would be from Kmart, and it would probably turn your finger green."

"Then that's what I want."

"I'm sorry, but that isn't good enough for me. I don't want my wife, Chantell León . . ."

Chantell cuts him off. "That will be Mrs. Chantell León Milton, thank you very much."

Sam exaggerates a nod and says, "Chantell, why would you, Chantell—soon to be Mrs. Milton—*maybe* accept a ring like that? Why would you want me to give you one like that?"

Sam is still on his knee as Chantell softly strokes his face. She wipes a single tear and says to him, "For two very good reasons. For one, I will look at this ring twenty years from now and marvel at the joy it brings me to know I married you. The second reason is far more important." Her tears are now flowing. "It's for the same reason why you are requiring me to wear the clothing. You want me to wear it to remember what I did to you, right?"

Sam nods.

"I need my engagement ring to be worn for that reason, too. Every time I look at my wedding ring, besides seeing the joy it brings me, it will always remind me of what Chantell, the famous singer, did to you." Chantell's crying turns to convulsing, making it hard for her to speak. "I took everything from you, Sam, which almost included your life, three times. Because of my actions, I decided I don't like Chantell León very much. She is an egotistical maniac who needs someone with enough balls to keep her in her place. But I know I will love being Chantell León Milton—almost as much as I will love Samuel Milton."

Sam can't hold back his own tears as he replies, "I . . . um, I can't believe anyone would love and respect me enough to say what you just did!"

Chantell wipes tears from his eyes and mixes them with hers. "It's all true. You are the most beautiful human being I have ever met. So much so that I don't know why you would want a loudmouth, spewing, maligning, me first, rich b . . ." Chantell stops, takes a deep breath, and finishes with, "woman like me."

Sam gives her a puzzling smile before answering, "Well, I kind of have to." Chantell gives him a quizzical look that he answers with a smile. "God and I have been pissed off at each other for a very long time. I'm beginning to see that he is a lot bigger than me. So, if I screw this up, I had better look for extra-heavy-duty sunscreen, if you know what I mean. And, I don't need that kind of pressure."

"I see. So, you think marrying me will be less pressure? I think you need to visit that mental institution again."

"I know he does!" Angelica yells.

Sam answers, "Only if you go with me."

"Can I take my mother?"

"Only if you promise to leave her there."

"What?" Angelica yells. "I used to like you!"

Sam switches to the other knee. "Okay, Chantell, if I hold you to it, will you . . .?"

"You can try and see."

Sam tilts his head way back and says to himself, "Okay, Sam, one more time, with feeling." Then he says to Chantell, "Miss Chantell León, will you do the profound honor of marrying me?"

Chantell smiles again, causing everyone to cringe except Sam. Once again, tears flow from her eyes as she says, "Sam, I am suddenly having a very difficult time with this." This causes Sam's whole body to slump. Chantell quickly puts her hands on his cheeks and pulls his face up. "No, Sam, you don't understand. I cannot fathom why someone so kind and gentle as you would want to marry someone like me, especially after I was so incredibly mean to—"

Before she can finish, Sam jumps to his feet and grabs her in his arms. He pulls her in and presses his lips hard against hers. She stands frozen for a moment and then slowly melts into him. She moves her hands up high on his shoulder blades and presses him into her. All of the lights in the Bowl come on, flooding it with brilliant white. The applause is so deafening that the vibration can be felt in the floor. The TV reporters remain silent and just let their camera crews take it all in.

Angelica and Linda come up to them, but they are not even slightly distracted. Chantell waves them away, with the kiss continuing.

Finally, they pull slowly apart. Chantell inhales and looks Sam in the eyes to say, "Yes, Mr. Samuel Milton, I will marry you, and it will be my honor to do so."

They kiss once more. After some time, she pulls back once again and comments, "Why, Mr. Milton, I believe that is the first time we've really kissed."

"How did he do?" someone yells from the crowd.

Chantell turns toward the questioner and answers, "Not bad. Not bad at all! In fact, he kisses a whole lot better than he dresses—at least for now." They kiss again. Sam tips her backward, and both really get into it. The applause erupts again. The passionate kiss continues for five minutes. Johnny Carson finally says to them, "Come on, you two. This is getting embarrassing. Either go get a minister, or go get a room!"

Eventually, the kiss is interrupted by someone clearing his throat. Sam and Chantell come up for air to find Gordon Osborn standing next to them. "Congratulations on your engagement. This will make the paperwork much easier." He smiles and hands them an envelope as he says, "Consider yourselves officially served."

Sam gives Gordon an exaggerated smile and tells him, "Mr. Osborn, how convenient. It turns out a few people are here to see you, too. Please turn around and say hi, once again, to my legally hired attorney, Stan Carlen. Stan has been very busy getting my butt out of hot water by successfully explaining the situation to the opposing counsel. So successful was he that several of these law firms are here tonight for an entirely different reason. So, let me introduce Chantell's agent, Marcus Powley, and her attorney, Jacob Tannenbaum. Let's not forget the chief attorney of Iconic Records, Orrin Machen. Did I get that right?"

Orrin nods.

"Good, and notice the four other lawyers standing behind him. I'm sorry, but I don't have the foggiest idea of who they are, but I'm sure you will find out soon enough. Now, if you'll excuse us, Chantell and I didn't get much sleep last night. So—"

Some yells, "Ooh la la!"

Sam turns around and yells, "We weren't even together, so nothing happened. But follow us around, and you might see something get started!"

Chantell looks at him. "Why, Mr. Milton, your shyness has completely disappeared. May I ask why?"

"It seems someone taught me a lesson, and I am a quick learner."

"Oh, I am glad of that! Lead on, Mr. Milton. Lead on."

"Don't you think we should go and talk to your mother first?"

"Oh, don't you dare! I'm not sharing you with anybody. Besides, I can guarantee, you will be seeing plenty of her!" Chantell then jumps up, putting her legs around Sam's waist, her arms around his neck, and her lips on his while cameras click away.

The kissing continues for several minutes until Chantell pulls back and looks at Sam with puzzlement. "You seem to be looking a little nervous. This did go the way you were expecting, didn't it?"

Sam starts looking more nervous and can see it is worrying Chantell, so he explains, "It went the way I was hoping, but nothing like I was expecting."

Chantell relents, "I was kind of hard on you, wasn't I?"

"Kind of? I was in a sheer panic most of the night, even before the proposal." Chantell gives him a quizzical look, and he answers it by asking, "What's with you and Dwain? I was sure he proposed to you, and you had already said yes."

"What? How did you come up with that?"

Sam gives a look of frustration before asking, "Then what was the big announcement going to be about, and how were you so sure about his sincerity because of what he asked you?"

Chantell thinks a moment, and then a huge smile comes over her face. "Oh no! You thought that he . . .?"

Sam gives her an affirming nod.

"Oh, I'm glad you mentioned that. Everyone needs to hear this. Come with me." She takes his hand and pulls him back to the mic stand. "Excuse me, everyone." She waits until she has their attention. "I need to make an announcement about my ex-boyfriend, Dwain Dubray, and to relay a request he made to my nervous fiancé."

In the back, Chantell hears a lady of color yell, "Yeah, why did you dis your man when he needs you most and agree to marry this . . . this white guy? That's cold, lady!" Two other female voices aggressively agree with her.

Sam fears a verbal confrontation but is surprised, along with everyone else, when he hears Chantell say, "Because I didn't break up with him; he broke up with me. Let me explain. I received a call from him early this morning and was he ever pumped! I am so excited to say, Dwain Dubray experienced Jesus last night! I mean, he got a full-blown salvation!"

She waits for both the applause and the negative murmuring to subside. "Now, someone behind me asked how I could be so positive this transformation was true, based on Dwain's recent past involving Sam. I can answer that by retelling his rather blatant confession, starting with him admitting that I was just going to be a conquest: *Slash nails the prom queen and nothing more*. Then three hours into sharing his excitement, he asked a favor of me."

Chantell looks at Sam as she speaks to everyone. "Dwain did not say *if* Sam proposes to you, he said, '*When* Sam Milton proposes to you, say yes because he is a good man, and he'll keep you safe from guys like me.' "

"Did he really say that?" the same lady asks.

"Yes, he did, but that is not all. Though he asked me, it was more of a request to Sam."

Chantell's eyes again fill, and she chokes up as she struggles to continue. "He said, 'I have no right to ask this, but something inside of me says I should ask anyway. So, here it goes: Though it's not likely to go down, but if 'the man' lets me, and your fiancé agrees, can I have the honor of giving you away?' He stipulated, 'This is not some BS stunt to get a reduced sentence. It's because I feel excited about doing it. But let Sam decide.' "

Chantell looks at Sam and then Linda and says, "That is how I know what happened to him is real." She sees Sam nodding and takes his hand. "So, what do you think?"

Sam's answer surprises everyone. "I think we need to celebrate."

Chantell looks shocked and asks, "You mean a party? You?"

"Yes, for us, for Dwain, and for your mother."

"My mother?"

"Who do you think gave me the ring?"

"Mother!" Chantell says, turning toward her. "You and I are going to talk!"

"Well, you can do all the talking you want while we take that ring back."

Johnny comes over and says, "Excuse me, Sam, but I believe your fiancée needs to change into something more appropriate." He holds up the oversized pink T-shirt.

Sam laughs and tells her, "You agreed to it for one year. But now that we are engaged, I don't think it's necessary for you to wear it."

She answers, "Oh no, Mr. Milton. Johnny is right. You started this, so on our wedding night, this is what I will be wearing, along with big, fuzzy pink bunny slippers."

Everyone is laughing, and Sam is looking so forlorn that she relents and whispers in his ear, "But underneath, I will be wearing something else that's in box number one."

Sam smiles.

Epilogue

Jessica smiles. "Now, I know why my producer wanted me to do this story. That was amazing, and you're right. There was far more to the story than just what was caught on film thirty years ago. I can't believe what your wife, Chantell, put you through. It must have been such agony."

Sam picks up Chantell's hand, kisses it, and says to Jessica, "Yes, she did, but we still have four kids and twenty-five years under our belts, so it was worth getting my tail feather singed." He turns to Chantell and adds, "But did you need to use a blowtorch?"

Chantell smiles and shrugs, leaving Jessica to ask, "So, did it work?"

"Excuse me?" Sam asks.

"Did Chantell's ranting break you out of your shell?"

"Too well!" Chantell exclaims. "He's become my ultimate protector! The press is afraid of him. If someone says something malicious about me, you can bet he's going to be showing up at your door!"

"Wow! Is this true, Sam?"

Sam shrugs. "A little, but as we all know, Chantell can be a little fiery herself, so she seldom needs my help."

"Sam, how is it having Angelica Martin as your mother-in-law?"

Sam gives a huge smile before saying, "I love that woman!"

"She keeps you on your toes."

Chantell shakes her head. "Sometimes, I think I should have let my mother marry him. All I know is, when they get together, I don't stand a chance. Do you know that when the TV game shows call, asking us to play for charity, they want my mother to be paired up with Sam?"

When the laughing dies down, Jessica asks, "Speaking of odd relationships, explain yours with Dwain Dubray."

"Well, that is one relationship I am proud of. We have just finished our latest tour together. I sing while he preaches through rap. It's a killer combo."

Jessica leans in. "You do know, many people think you two are really married."

Chantell laughs. "I sure hope his wife, Symone, doesn't find out. You think I have a temper? You never want to get in her crosshairs."

"Wow, Sam, how do you handle such tempestuous women?"

"It explains why Dwain and I are in therapy together. It's to help us deal with the two of them."

"That intense, are they?"

"Oh yeah. So much so, both of our families have been asked to do a reality TV show together."

"Are you?"

Chantell and Sam shake their heads.

"Okay, Chantell, so explain just what this peculiar hobby of yours is, and why did you keep it secret?"

Chantell laughs as Sam starts to squirm. She points to Sam and says, "I think my husband should tell this one."

"Why is that?" Jessica asks.

"Oh, Sam knows why. Go on, honey. You've been rubbing my nose in it all afternoon, so it's payback time."

All of the cameras and mics turn to Sam, who exhales loudly. "I did not find out about this hobby of hers until a few months after we were engaged. I noticed her Corvette was missing. She said her brothers were playing with it. Soon, Chantell herself would be missing—and for days on end. Then, one day, Lawrence shows up at my door saying he's got tickets to the Winter Nationals in Pomona. It's located at the LA fairgrounds. He wanted to know if I would like to go. I said, 'Sure, I'm not about to pass up tickets to the hottest drag racing event in California.' Then he said he got pit passes for the practice runs that very night. The next thing I know, I'm escorted around the track like a VIP and am introduced to everyone as Chantell León's beau. I just figured they were all into her music.

"Anyway, Lawrence comes running up to me and says, 'Hey, how would you like to ride shotgun in a pro-stock? A friend of Chantell's wants to take you along on one of his practice runs. That is, if you're not chicken.'

"Hey, I couldn't pass up a challenge like that, though I should have. The next thing I know, I'm all suited up with a helmet that had my name on it. Go figure. I am escorted out to the line and pointed to the third car back. It's a 'Vette unlike any I have ever seen: built for racing, jacked up in the back, with a parachute, racing slicks, and uncorked headers. I mean, this car was loud!

"I am put in and strapped down. I yell thank you to the driver, and he gives me a thumbs-up. Looking around, I was a little surprised; the inside of the car was pretty much stock. Except for the added gauges, different seats, and all of the safety equipment, you'd think this car was right off the street. Just before the Christmas tree falls, the starting lights, I noticed the wooden rose I made for Chantell taped to the dash. When she sees me looking at it, she yells over the revving engine, 'Welcome to my hobby, Mr. Milton.'

"Chantell has the engine screaming as the tree counts down. The exact instant the green flashes, I'm pinned to the seat. We take off like a rifle shot. I yell out, 'Why do I get the feeling you've been lying to me?' "

When the laughing dies down, Jessica asks, "So, how did you do, Chantell?"

Sam interjects, "She took her division as she always did."

"And nobody knew about this hobby? Why?"

Chantell answers, "Record companies and movie studios tend to frown on activities that could kill their stars."

"So, I take it you knew the car was in first and second all of the time you let Sam give you a driving lesson back at the ranch?"

"Of course! I was starting to like the guy, and since I beat the stuffing out of the man, why not build him up a little? But can you imagine how I had to keep my mouth shut while Sam was trying to teach me how to drive a car?"

When everyone laughs, Sam scoffs, "That doesn't explain how you almost drove us over a cliff."

"Hey, that was a curvy road. I race on a straight track. But, honey, you haven't finished the story. Tell them what you did at the end of the practice run."

Sam hesitates as he squirms in his seat, causing Chantell to add, "Come on, my macho husband, out with it."

He exhales loudly again, looks at the floor, and says, "I peed my pants."

Acknowledgments

First, I would like to thank my family for letting me have the time to write this novel. Working in construction ten hours a day, six days a week, and then hiding up in the loft, writing for four hours a night, seven days a week, is an incredible sacrifice.

I would like to thank Dianne Brock and my wife, Laila, for helping me navigate the sea of red left by Microsoft Word and for correcting all the errors that didn't show up in red. To let you know their true contributions to my writing, to this day, if I am required to generate even three lines of a handwritten note, there will be at least two misspelled words within it.

I especially need to thank Diane English (the creator, writer, and director of sitcom *Murphy Brown*). While building the French ranch for her and her then-husband, Joel Shukovsky, Diane read one of my Christmas letters and suggested I write a book. The rest, as they say, is history.

Thank you to the estate of Johnny Carson for allowing me to keep his name, humor, and incredible personality alive in our hearts.

Renee Freeman, thank you for taking me to the First African Methodist Episcopal Church of Los Angeles. And, yes, Renee picked out a really nice suit for the occasion. I am privileged to have visited twenty-plus denominations over the years, and other than when my wife, Laila, and I were married, this AME church is still the greatest church experience of my life. The preaching was powerful and something you could take home and use that day. The music was just as fantastic as I describe, including the lead singer, starting from all four corners of the sanctuary.

The Old Place is still there on Mulholland Drive near Troutdale in Malibu, California. Other than additional menu items, nothing has changed. It was Bob Dylan who was playing at the piano when a young kid asked him if he knew any

Dylan. He left without ever knowing he'd had a personal concert from the man himself.

Special thanks to John Wieland for the use of his '68 Corvette. Except for the drag strip, everything that Chantell experienced while driving the Corvette happened to me, including being embarrassed by my shifting abilities. To this day, I doubt if John knows how close I came to totaling his 'Vette because of those power brakes!

The idea for Chantell building the Southern Crescent model train came from when I attended my first Bible study at the home of the Folkmans in Redlands, California. Sitting on their coffee table was this beautifully hand-painted G scale "Golden Spike" locomotive. What impressed me most: It was Mrs. Folkman who had restored it.

About the Author

William Hammes currently lives in Thousand Oaks, California, with his wife, Laila, and their daughter, Emma. Before writing, Bill attended San Bernardino Valley College, where his passion for extreme exotic architecture was nurtured. One of his instructors told him, "Bill, you're never going to be an architect until you learn to build what you are designing." He took that to heart, and one of his first construction projects was working on the Bob Hope residence in Palm Springs, designed by  the famed architect John Lautner. After a short stay in John Lautner's office, he continued in the construction field, working on three more homes for Lautner, including John's most famous and wildest, the Allen Levy residence in Malibu. One of Bill's favorite projects was the Los Angeles Museum of the Holocaust, in Pan Pacific Park, a twisting underground concrete structure designed by Hagy Belzberg.

After receiving encouragement from Diane English, Bill has written three novels in the *Last Minute Redemption* series, two children's books, several allegories, and a screenplay—with the novel *An Apology Gone Horribly Wrong* being the first to be published.

Bill is also very involved in his local church, which feeds his second writing passion, contemporary Christian allegories. Bill and Laila's home away from home is any campground along their way, which is Bill's favorite place to write.

You may view Bill's architectural projects and get information on all of his writings on his website www.whhammes.com.

Morgan James makes all of our titles available
through the Library for All Charity Organization.

www.LibraryForAll.org

Printed in the USA
CPSIA information can be obtained
at www.ICGtesting.com
JSHW021956150824
68134JS00055B/1013